PUBLISH AND PERISH/

CORRUPT AND ENSNARE

PUBLISH AND PERISH/

CORRUPT AND ENSNARE

TWO LEGAL MYSTERIES

by

Francis M. Nevins

RAMBLE HOUSE

PUBLISH AND PERISH

ONE

ON THAT WEDNESDAY MORNING in the spring of 1974, eight days after the probate hearing where he had met her once again only to lose her once again, Loren stumbled out of bed at seven as usual. He made the bed, showered, shaved, put a beige turtleneck and slacks on himself and the Janacek *Slavonic Mass* on the record changer, with the sound up on the kitchen speaker so he could listen as he made sausage cakes and a cheese omelet and reheated last night's coffee. With no Wednesday morning classes during the spring semester he hoped to spend a few quiet hours in his office above the old law library, translating documents of Hitler's bureaucracy for use in the legal history of the Third Reich that Loren had been working on for two years. That was what he hoped.

At 8:50 A.M. he swung the VW fastback into the exit lane of the thruway and got off at the Tully Avenue ramp which hung precariously over the Midcontinental Railroad freight yards. At Tully he made a right and put the industrial north side of the city behind him. Two miles ahead the downtown skyline gleamed in the crisp sky. Sunlight glinted from the glass sides of the new skyscrapers. Loren turned left onto University Avenue, made another sharp left into the narrow alley just beyond the faculty club, and two minutes later he snapped off the radio and eased the fastback into the law faculty parking slot stenciled MENSING.

As he topped the low hill between the parking area and the law building, he saw the unusual arrangement of bodies. A line of young men and women stretched like a living conveyor belt from the law school side entrance to a City University panel truck in the deliveries bay. Bulky cartons slid out of the doorway from hand to hand along the line at the end of which a bare-chested young black man tossed them over the tailboard into the back of the truck. Loren remembered that the move to the new law library had been scheduled to begin today. He squeezed past the students blocking the entranceway and exchanged greetings with the ones he knew.

"Loren!" a high-pitched voice squealed overhead.

He peered up the stairwell and saw Gael Irwin halfway up the first flight. "Come help us?" she panted at him.

Loren watched her struggle to catch each descending box and pass it to the student four steps down from her. Perspiration glistened on her perky face under a tangle of short dark curls. She was wearing blue jeans and an olive drab T-shirt that was studded with peace and women's liberation symbols, and Loren liked her very much. In the subdued seventies she was still keeping the faith of the strident sixties. Only a few of the law school's six hundred students would ask a professor to share in coolie labor and call him by his first name rather than his formal title while doing it. After three semesters he found himself thinking of Gael Irwin more and more often with dirty-old-man's thoughts, even though he was well under forty and showered daily.

Since he liked to think of himself as an enemy of elitism, he could hardly refuse her invitation. He tossed his tan sport jacket over a doorknob and the line shifted to make room for him next to her.

"Isn't it great we finally get out of this stupid old building and into two thousand one?" Gael puffed. Two thousand one was her private name for the futuristic building that would house the law library and faculty offices plus several seminar rooms by fall semester. "But, oh, Loren, it's going to take us *weeks* to get all the books packed and moved and unpacked! You teach jurisprudence, tell me why judges can't just decide what's morally *right* instead of putting fifty pages of shit in every opinion?"

"You know what you're asking for?" he grunted as she thrust a lawbook carton into his midsection. "You want me to give you the whole jurisprudence course right here on this staircase."

"And I haven't paid the university any tuition for your course so you won't tell me, right?" Gael swung her hand across her forehead in the moment between boxes. "Capitalistic pig. Not you, Loren, the university. You're just a male chauvinist pig."

"You always used to describe me as a big grizzly bear with glasses. What makes me a pig all of a sudden?"

"Oh, Loren, I can't call you a male chauvinist *bear,* can I?"

It was on these notes of lofty juristic discourse that Loren happened to glance down as he handed on a carton and saw the tall thin man in gray staring up at him from the bottom of the iron staircase as if Loren were a tyrannosaurus skeleton that had suddenly come alive. Loren didn't have to ask who the newcomer was. He had seen that cadaverous face every working day for eighteen months before he'd beaten a strategic retreat to the ivory tower. It was Stanford W. Nalbin, the law partner of Loren's late father.

"Ah, there you are, Loren," Nalbin intoned darkly. "I, ah, hope I'm not disturbing you?"

"Not in the least," Loren panted. "Care to join us? It's a contribution to legal education."

Nalbin's bony frame almost shuddered. "I need to see you at once, Loren. Something most serious has come up."

Loren recognized that tone of voice. It was the one Nalbin reserved for the most pressing problems of the most affluent clients. Loren hadn't heard it since he'd left the firm, but it meant deep trouble. He broke ranks, retrieved his jacket and slung it over his shoulder. "Gael, I think I have an emergency. I'll try to get back later. Let's go to my office," he called down to Nalbin.

As Loren led the way up three flights he made a mental picture of the old litigator's reaction to the jeans-clad box brigade that lined their route: eyes chill, lips tight, patrician nostrils aquiver at the realization that here in all their longhaired unkempt glory labored several dozen future members of the bar. "Still playing the radical democrat, I see," Nalbin muttered as they climbed. "I must say I think you made a wise decision when you left the firm and decided to devote yourself to the education of these young, ah, people."

"Better the kids than the corporate and probate work. Besides, I get three months off every year if I don't want to teach summers. What do you give the junior associates now, three weeks?"

"Enough, Loren. Let's get down to serious business."

Loren unlocked his office door and motioned his guest through a jumble of lawbooks and course materials and miscellaneous paperwork strewn on every flat surface of the room.

Nalbin adjusted himself daintily on the edge of a segment of sectional sofa upholstered in faded gray wool.

"Don't bother looking around for the other half of the couch," Loren advised as he removed a stack of salmon-covered advance sheets from the swivel chair behind his desk and lowered himself. "It doesn't exist. That's why the part you're sitting on cost me only ten bucks. Now, what seems to be the trouble?"

"Those letters in the newspaper were correct," the old man announced mournfully. "Graham Dillaway and Jackson Corby were murdered."

TWO

SOMETIMES IT SEEMED to Loren Mensing that he'd been running into the names Dillaway and Foxworth all his life. Of course, Graham Dillaway's historical novels about America's heroic past and Hope Foxworth's sentimental romances had appeared regularly on best-seller lists and introductory offers from book clubs since Loren's childhood. But through his years of high school and college and law school that was all he knew about the two authors and their work. In the early 1960s he had taken a date to see Charlton Heston and Kirk Douglas in the movie version of one of Dillaway's epic best-sellers but the experience had not inspired him to read that or any other Dillaway title.

When the scandal broke, Loren was six months out of law school and working in his father's firm. Graham Dillaway had obtained a Mexican divorce from his wife after a marriage lasting twenty-two years, and three days later he had married Hope Foxworth in a Mexican civil ceremony. Loren had glanced at the news item in the city papers, heard it on TV, and filed it away in his mind with thousands of other scraps of useless information. Three weeks later the information was no longer useless.

That icy November morning the other junior associates of Mensing & Nalbin were either in court or down with flu. Loren's father was in South Dakota arguing an estate tax appeal and Stanford Nalbin had had to go to the state capital on an emergency, which left Loren the only attorney in the office. He was sitting slumped in his swivel chair, glasses askew on his nose, a red and blue pencil dangling from an ear. The desk, visitor chairs, bookcase tops and several open file drawers were piled high with pages of an overdue appellate brief. Precarious heaps of law report volumes made an obstacle course between his desk and the doorway.

Connie tapped on the open door with her fingertips. "Mr. Mensing," she began in a low hesitant voice.

Loren looked up, his eyes grimed with frustration. "Connie,

please don't bother me, this has to be in the mail today."

The firm's senior secretary made a vague gesture of apology. "I hate to tell you this, Mr. Mensing, but you have two clients and you have to see them right away. They had an eleven o'clock appointment with Mr. Nalbin but they've been on the road driving back from Mexico and we couldn't reach them to cancel when Mr. Nalbin had to go to the capital."

Loren hurled the red and blue pencil into the jungle of papers. "Damn it, Connie, I can *not* do twelve things at once! Give them another appointment."

"I can't, Mr. Mensing. They'll go somewhere else and your father and Mr. Nalbin would boil us alive if we lost this account. It's a matter of drawing up wills."

"And who are these wonderful clients, if I may ask?"

Connie's voice dropped to a tone approaching awe. "Graham Dillaway," she told him, "and Hope Foxworth. Hope Foxworth Dillaway now, of course. You must have read about them in the papers."

Loren plucked scraps from his memory. "Oh yes, the writers, the Mexican divorce and remarriage."

"The attorneys who handled the property settlement on the divorce recommended us as the best firm to do their new estate planning. Mr. and Mrs. Dillaway are both in the outer office right now!"

Constance F. Waller had been the office manager and secretarial supervisor at Mensing & Nalbin for almost as far back as Loren could remember. He had never seen the bony fiftyish spinster so excited, and he did not think it would be difficult for him to name two of her favorite authors, but he still refused to budge. "Connie, the rules of procedure say this brief has to be filed with the court no later than tomorrow. I have to work on it all day today till it's done."

Connie's face became almost maternal behind her forbidding spectacles. "Why don't you let me draw up a motion for another extension of time? I'll do an affidavit for your signature explaining that we just can't get it finished by tomorrow. We can get an extra ten days; Judge Simon was in practice thirty years and knows how things are. You clean yourself up a bit and I'll show the Dillaways into the law library. You'll scare them to death if you talk to them in here."

Loren released a long weary breath. "Okay, Connie, do that. And thanks. Tell them I'll be with them in five minutes."

In the men's room, as he tried to rearrange himself into the semblance of a cool and collected technician, he cursed himself for well over the hundredth time for ever having let his father pressure him into going to law school. Then he refined his dissatisfaction to a more precise form. His three years in law school, the process of learning to play with skill a game infinitely more complex than chess, all the intellectual part had been stimulating fun. But he had come to hate the actual practice of law with a cold fury. The game now was not to let his father or anyone else know how he felt. With his hair combed and glasses straight and white shirt smoothed he turned the knob of the law library door.

The man and the woman were seated at the oval table in the south corner. They were holding hands and looking into each other's eyes so intimately that Loren felt like an eavesdropper. The man appeared to be in his middle forties, medium build, close-cropped hair beginning to gray. There were lines of stern authority in his face but joy and a sense of high adventure in the brightness of his eyes. The woman was tall and regal, with masses of blonde hair piled high, a poised and self-assured and maturely lovely woman whose age Loren guessed as somewhere in the late thirties. They touched hands in a way that made Loren envy them. He kicked the leg of a library stool loudly to let them know they were no longer alone, and they stood up as he crossed the room.

"Mr. Mensing?" the man asked. "I am Graham Dillaway." His voice was low and vibrant; with more power behind it he'd make an excellent public speaker, Loren thought. His handshake was firm but he didn't make a test of manhood out of the act. "And this is my wife, Hope Dillaway." There was a new pride in his tone as he introduced Loren to his wife. The hand she offered was cool and silky. "We have to change our wills," Dillaway went on. "If you read the newspapers you know why."

Loren drew a chair up to the table between them, pulled a fresh yellow legal pad out of the drawer, and began to ask questions as to precisely what they wanted their new wills to accomplish.

"It's quite simple," Hope Foxworth Dillaway explained. Her deep South accent had a lilt that was like music. "This is a second marriage for both of us. My first husband was killed in the Battle of the Bulge when I was nineteen. Graham has one child by his first wife, a son in his twenties. I have a son and a daughter just a few years younger. My children are the chief— is beneficiaries the right word?—in my present will. Graham's will takes care of his son and also, of course, provides very handsomely for Amanda—the former Mrs. Dillaway. That will have to be changed *at once.*"

"And now I presume you each want to leave your estate primarily to the other?"

"Well, we want to take care of each other," Graham Dilla- way said, "and also my son and Hope's kids."

"Graham's son, Will, is a darling," Hope added. "He wants to be an author like his father. And my James and Doreen. . . ."

"Great kids the both of them!" Graham Dillaway boomed. When he was excited about something his voice carried like a revival preacher's. "Jim wants to break into the writing game too; wants to do private-eye stuff, he says. Doreen just started college last year and she's gotten involved in some activist groups that I'm afraid may get her in trouble, but I love her and Jim as if they were my own."

"You see, Mr. Mensing, we are a very loving family," said Hope Foxworth Dillaway. "We don't want to leave our money—and I'm sure you're aware there is quite a bit of money—we don't want anyone in the family to be hurt or dis- appointed by how we dispose of our estate. We want everyone to be treated equally. After all, there is nothing more important than love, is there? The relationships within a family are the foundation stone of. . . ."

Loren suddenly realized that Hope Foxworth Dillaway was treating him to a capsulization of the Deep Thoughts un- derlying her romantic novels and tried desperately to keep a look of intense interest on his face. When he had weathered the storm of her philosophy of life, he pulled the conversation back to testamentary intent.

"In effect then, primarily you want to benefit each other, and secondarily to provide for all three children in equal shares?"

"I think that's an excellent summary, Mr. Mensing," Gra- ham said, and clapped Loren on the shoulder in a gesture of hearty approval.

"One question. Suppose that you and Mrs. Dillaway should decide to—have children of your own? You realize of course that the birth of your own child would involve rethinking your estate plan all over again."

Hope's smile held a shadow of sadness. "I had to have a hysterectomy several years ago. We can have no children."

"Well then," Loren concluded briskly, "I think the answer to your problem is mutual wills. In other words, we can draw a will for you, Mr. Dillaway, leaving everything to Mrs. Dillaway, provided that if she should die before you, your estate on *your* death is to be divided equally among James and Doreen Foxworth and Will Dillaway. And Mrs. Dillaway, we can draw you a will leaving everything to Mr. Dillaway, but provided that if your husband should predecease you, your entire estate on *your* death is split among the three children."

Graham Dillaway's stern features beamed with delight. "That's a *brilliant* idea!" he roared. "You see, Hope? We'll have identical wills, and no one can possibly be hurt by the way the property is left. Mr. Mensing, I'm absolutely delighted with the job you're doing. I can't tell you how happy I am that your firm was recommended to us for this."

The mutual wills device was hardly a ground-breaking innovation but Loren didn't bother to reveal that to his clients. They continued to discuss the details, went out together for a late lunch, and resumed their discussion when they returned to the cool oaken hush of the law library. They were interrupted only once, when Connie brought in the affidavit and motion for further extension of time for Loren's signature.

Shortly after 3 P.M., when the Dillaways were on the point of leaving and Graham had picked up his worn cowhide briefcase and laid it on the oval table, Hope suddenly caught at his arm. "Wait a moment, please, darling." She unzipped the case, took out a book and displayed it before Loren, who surmised from the title *If It Breaks My Heart* that it must be her latest romance. She borrowed Graham's ball-point pen, opened the volume and scrawled something on the title page that, upside down, Loren couldn't make out. When she presented the book to him and he tried to read the inscription he still couldn't make it out. He stared at it as if it were in the dialect of a lost tribe.

Hope smiled graciously on his bewilderment. "You don't have to tell me how atrocious my handwriting is. It drives my secretary to distraction too, and sometimes when she can't make out a line and she brings it to me, I find I can't decipher it either! It says, 'For Loren Mensing who draws a mean will.'

Like it?"

"Love it," Loren lied. Privately he thought that any secretary who could read and transcribe such ink droppings day after day must have the dedication of a kamikaze. Aloud he thanked Hope profusely for the memento. But as soon as the Dillaways had passed through the gold-lettered entrance door of Mensing & Nalbin and were safely ensconced in a down elevator, he tossed the unoffending book neatly into the umbrella stand in the coat closet. Constance F. Waller stood by the water fountain and glared at him.

In due course the notes Loren had taken in the law library were transformed into two wills, virtually identical in their provisions. Loren was in court the morning the Dillaways returned to the office for the signing. He never saw Graham Dillaway again. By the time he walked out of Mensing & Nalbin and into City University Law School he had almost forgotten that he'd ever met or dealt with either of them.

He had no occasion to think of the family again until a late December afternoon a few years later. While on a flight to the annual meeting of the Association of American Law Schools, he happened to pick the current issue of *Time* from the selection offered by the stewardess. Thumbing through the book reviews, he noticed that one of them dealt with *The Presbyterians: An American Success Story,* by Will Dillaway. Following the review was a brief account of the careers of what the writer called "the most successful literary family now in business." Loren learned a few facts about the Dillaways that he had either never known or long forgotten. He discovered that Graham Dillaway had been an ensign in the Navy during World War II, that his first book had been published in 1948, that three percent of the movie version of his novel *The Eagles* belonged to him, that he had been an ardent conservationist long before ecology had become fashionable, and that each of his blockbuster historical novels involved at least a year of research.

If Graham's interests were American history and ecology, his son's seemed to be old-time religion and old-time free enterprise. Loren learned from the *Time* piece that the only child of Graham's marriage to Amanda Blair had been paid princely sums by the *Reader's Digest* for such articles as "Why I Am Not an Atheist" and "Capitalism: Man's Last Best Hope." *The*

Presbyterians was his first book. "I have no talent for fiction," Will was quoted. "My only wish is to contribute what talents I have to the preservation and betterment of our way of life. I want people to realize how grateful we should be that we live in America." His next project was to be a multivolume series on the American young, with separate books on such subjects as juvenile delinquency, drug abuse and political protest.

Time was respectfully discreet about Graham Dillaway's Mexican divorce and remarriage but expansive on the literary career of his second wife. Loren was informed that Hope Foxworth's first best-seller had been a McCarthy era tearjerker about a college professor's wife who comes to suspect her husband of Communist sympathies and winds up heroically leaving him. Married young and widowed young, she had had two children by her first husband, but *Time* gave their careers short shrift. The article merely noted that James Foxworth supported himself by writing for paperbacks under several pseudonyms and that Doreen Foxworth, a fiery activist while away at college, had settled down and recently married a retired Army Dental Corps officer.

One item buried in the write-up caught Loren's attention for a moment. It was reported that three or four times a year Graham Dillaway would leave the lavish penthouse apartment where he and Hope lived and worked and retreat to a rustic cabin somewhere in the mountains. After a few days he would come home, refreshed from closeness to the earth, and would return to work.

Loren now knew everything he had never wanted to know about America's most successful family of verbiage contractors. He turned to the movie reviews, convinced that he would not cross paths with the Dillaways again.

And for a few years, he didn't.

He noticed the *Courier* headline only by chance. On his way to lunch he happened to glance at the newspaper vending machine in front of the university cafeteria and there it was. If the headline had been below the centerfold and out of sight to passersby he might have missed the story completely.

GRAHAM DILLAWAY DEAD IN FIRE

He fed the slot a dime, yanked the machine's handle and

pulled out a paper.

Graham Dillaway, 52, this city's most prominent author, died yesterday in a blaze that consumed his mountain cabin. The distinguished historical novelist was the author of such best-sellers as *Saratoga Musket, The Eagles,* and *The Road Beyond the River,* and had also been active in organizations seeking to preserve America's wilderness areas. He had left his penthouse apartment at 1400 Delaware Avenue three days ago for one of his periodic solitary vacations close to nature. Also consumed in the blaze was Jackson Corby, 35, identified by state police as a young black writer.

Site of the tragedy was the author's cabin on the slope of King Mountain in this state's sparsely settled northwest corner. State Police Sergeant Ernest Moore, assigned to Substation 7 at the base of the mountain, told reporters that at 4:41 P.M. yesterday he received a telephone call that there was a blaze along the south slope. The caller did not identify himself. A team of state police and forest rangers equipped with mobile fire-fighting apparatus raced to the scene, arriving at approximately 5:25 P.M., and was able to contain the fire before it spread beyond the immediate area. The clearing surrounding the cabin and the cabin itself were consumed, however. Fire fighters discovered the two bodies in the charred remnants of the cabin. Although both were burned beyond recognition, authorities have identified them by means of the remains of their clothing and personal effects as well as by two automobiles, one registered in the name of each victim, which were found parked in a lean-to several hundred yards from the cabin. A forest service officer stated that had the automobiles been kept much nearer to the cabin the fire might well have caused a gasoline explosion which could have set the whole mountain ablaze.

State police spokesmen informed reporters that they are satisfied the fire was of accidental origin, probably the result of a cooking-stove malfunction. Surviving the late Mr. Dillaway are his widow, novelist Hope Foxworth Dillaway, and a son by an earlier marriage, Will Dillaway, also an author. Surviving Mr. Corby is a sister, Arlena Corby, of Centralia. A memorial service for Mr. Dil-

laway will be held tomorrow at Grace Chapel and his remains will be buried in the family plot in Spruceknoll
Cemetery.

Loren couldn't finish his lunch. The sense of what it must
be like to feel one's flesh on fire took away his appetite.

Before he locked up his office that afternoon he decided to
look into the status of the will he had drawn for the dead man
six years before. He dialed Mensing & Nalbin and asked to be
connected with Mr. Nalbin.

"I spoke with Mrs. Dillaway this afternoon," the old litigator said. "She's taking it very hard, I'm afraid. I had to
make most of the arrangements with her secretary—can't think
of the girl's name. But we shall be filing the will with the probate court tomorrow. I've decided that it would be advanta-
geous to use Section 349(b)."

Loren remembered the section from his time in practice. It
was a clause in the state probate code that authorized an expe-
dited procedure where the estate furnished bond in the amount
of a large fixed sum plus a certain percentage of the appraised
value of all estate assets. The rich, who could afford the bond,
were thus relieved of having to wait the several months others
had to wait to allow time for the filing of creditors' claims and
routine paperwork. Loren wondered when someone would
challenge 349(b) as a violation of the equal protection clause.

"We shall need you, of course," Nalbin went on dispas-
sionately, "to testify at the probate hearing as to the proper
execution of the will and all that. I will send you a note when
the hearing date is set."

Something in the old lawyer's statement struck Loren as incongruous. He dredged his memory of that chilly day in the
law library, and suddenly he knew what was bothering him.

"Stanford," he pointed out, "I never witnessed that will. I
only saw the Dillaways that one day no one else was there,
when I interviewed them and drafted what they wanted."

"Yes, but both of the witnesses—your father and Miss
Waller—predeceased Mr. Dillaway. Under the statute, in that
situation the proponent of a will must produce proof that the
witnesses' signatures are authentic. Since I should think it
would be awkward for me to call upon myself for that testimony, I would like you to come."

"You don't anticipate any trouble, do you?" Loren had

learned to hunt for ulterior motives whenever Nalbin asked him for a favor.

"Oh no, not with the will. Of course we must satisfy the court that the body found in the cabin was indeed Mr. Dillaway, but that won't be difficult. Even though both bodies were burned too badly for fingerprint identification, we have the fact that Mr. Dillaway owned the cabin, his statement to Mrs. Dillaway that he was going to spend a few days at the cabin, the personal effects found at the scene of the fire, the dental records, and so on. No, we'll have no trouble."

Five weeks later the note arrived from Nalbin and Loren marked the following Tuesday morning on his appointment calendar. Tuesday God decided to sink the city. An endless curtain of rain poured down stinging thick from a black sky. Loren fought the VW through one city block of traffic snarls after another. After three crawling circuits around the courthouse area he gave up hunting for a vacant parking meter and splashed the fastback into an overpriced lot around the corner from the city government building. Three steps away from the car and he was drenched. In the blowing wind his umbrella was not only useless but dangerous. He jogged through ankle-deep puddles and past swarms of office workers as wretched-looking as himself. He ran up the slippery stone steps of the courthouse and under the sheltering pediment with its inscription *Obedience to Law Is Perfect Freedom.*

At the end of the high-ceilinged corridor an elevator door slid open and the UP sign blinked on. Loren fought his way into the cage with more than a dozen others. The elevator lurched upward feebly, stopping at every floor to disgorge and receive passengers. The odor of rain-soaked clothing was suffocating. At the tenth floor Loren elbowed his way out and breathed long deep gulps of air. He trudged along the Romanesque corridor to DIVISION 19, JUDGE COLLISON (PROBATE), hoping that he wasn't the only one the storm had made late.

As he stepped into the hush of the courtroom he saw that Collison had not yet taken the bench. A handful of people sat in groups of one and two, and in the far right corner Loren noticed a larger group that seemed to be together. The gaunt figure of Stanford W. Nalbin sat nearest the aisle.

Loren edged into the hard pewlike seat beside the attorney and Nalbin shook his hand gravely.

Loren looked past the old man at the group. He barely recognized the woman on Nalbin's right. The years had not been kind to Hope Foxworth Dillaway. Her face was wrinkled and puffy, her body bent. Her eyes were buried in dark circles of fatigue and grief like the mouths of caves. Even with Nalbin between them Loren thought he detected the odor of liquor-under-breathmints emanating from her direction. On her other side a dark-complected man of about thirty in blue turtleneck and sport jacket held her right hand comfortingly between his own. He sported a neat British mustache under his Roman nose and combed his hair so as to minimize his growing bald spot. Loren surmised that he was Hope's son, James Foxworth, and his guess was confirmed a few moments later. Nalbin made whispered introductions and Loren expressed sympathy in conventional mumbles and James disengaged his hand from his mother's for a brief and distracted handshake with Loren.

At the far end of the pew, next to the oak-paneled wall, sat a couple Loren didn't recognize. The woman was tall and stunningly attractive in mourning, with thick chestnut hair curling below her shoulders and eyes hidden behind dark glasses. The man was taller and older, hair thinning, back ramrod straight. He sat still and stared at the empty judicial dais, detached as a statue. "Dr. and Mrs. Josephson," Nalbin whispered, "Professor Mensing. Professor Mensing drew your stepfather's will, Doreen, when he was with the firm." A handshake across three intervening bodies was too awkward, so Loren and the Josephsons nodded solemnly at each other. Loren vaguely remembered having heard or read that Doreen Foxworth had married an army dentist.

Nalbin leaned forward and tapped the shoulders of the two men in the seat in front of them. One was a short bald flustered-looking man in a hopelessly wrinkled brown suit; the other, tall and hawk-faced, wore the powder-blue uniform of the state police. "Dr. Beck and Sergeant Moore, I'd like you to meet Professor Mensing of City University Law School. Dr. Beck is the state forensic pathologist who examined the bodies," Nalbin confided to Loren in an almost inaudible whisper, "and the sergeant was one of the first officials who arrived at the cabin." The whisper was intended not to upset the widow, Loren thought. Dr. Beck turned his back on them and continued his incessant knuckle-cracking.

Sergeant Moore's muddy brown eyes brightened with interest. "Hey, you wouldn't be the Mensing who was the deputy legal adviser to the police department a couple years ago?" And when Loren admitted that he was that Mensing, the sergeant extended his hand across the back of his pew in a swift gesture of delight. "Ever since I met Charlie Hough at a law enforcement conference last year and he told me how you helped solve the Spencer English murder and that crazy dog food case, I've wanted to shake your hand." Then a look of puzzlement stole over the trooper's face, mingled with what might have been hostility. "But what's your angle here? Dillaway's death was an accident, plain and simple. Everything's all aboveboard and everyone's satisfied. I don't get how you fit in."

Loren didn't answer. A chill certainty had formed in his mind that the sergeant was protesting too much. Was there something to hide in this case? Loren's thoughts raced. Well, there was the strange anonymity of the caller who had reported the cabin fire to Moore's substation, and of course there was the unexplained presence of a young black writer named Jackson Corby in the Dillaway cabin. And now there were a forensic pathologist and a state trooper who were much too nervous.

Nalbin took up the slack of Loren's embarrassed silence to answer Sergeant Moore's unspoken question. "Professor Mensing drew Mr. Dillaway's will when he was in practice with the firm." Loren felt not only puzzled but stifled. The air of whispered gloom and the repetitions of trivia reminded him of a funeral parlor. He wished Judge Collison would finish his morning coffee and call the court to order.

The door swished open and wet rubbers slapped as a newcomer entered the seat behind Loren. Nalbin squirmed around to identify the latest arrival. "Ah," he said. "Our last man. Professor Mensing, meet Mr. Will Dillaway. Professor Mensing drew your father's will when he was in practice with the firm." Loren wondered how many more times he would have to endure that sentence. He swung around and offered his hand, which Will clasped warmly and soaked soundly, muttering apologies a moment after the damage was done. Loren noted that the head of Graham Dillaway's grim-faced son was pumpkin-round and three-fourths bald and gleaming wetly from the storm. He wondered if Will had conscientious scruples against using an umbrella or rain hat, or if perhaps he counted on faith in God and free enterprise to keep the drops away.

The door to the judge's chambers opened and shut smartly and the bailiff boomed: "All rise!" Loren stood and faced front as Collison ascended the bench. As he stood he heard the courtroom door swish open again and sensed a flurry of hesitation behind him. Then the sergeant-at-arms was escorting the newcomer to the pew he himself occupied. It was a woman. She stood next to Loren, her shoulder almost touching his upper arm, until the judge banged his gavel like a blacksmith shoeing a horse and roared: "Be seated."

There was something about the feel of her shoulder against him. Loren turned his head to her as they sat.

He knew her. He remembered her. Almost ten years had passed since he had seen her and now beyond all human expectation she was sitting beside him in probate court. He fought an urge to get up and run from the room. The next moment he knew he didn't want to run. The moment after that he didn't know what he wanted to do. He avoided her by retreating into the impersonal labyrinth of his thoughts. It's like something out of a movie, he thought wildly. Out of *Casablanca*, the famous play-it-again-Sam scene where Bergman walks into Bogart's café. But with certain differences. It wasn't the Nazis that had separated this couple, it had been he. He had broken off with her, nine years ago and half a country away, in his last semester of law school and her last of college, and he still wasn't certain why. At times he thought it had been simple cowardice, a refined distaste for assuming the responsibility for her handicap, a fear that she wouldn't be a proper wife for an ambitious young attorney and that she might hinder an otherwise meteoric legal career. At other times he thought it had been more complicated and perhaps less selfish, a sense that he did not love her but saw a chance to inflate his self-image by smothering her in paternalism and pity, so that it was better for her that they separate. He had never been able to resolve his own confusions about why he had made some ri- diculous excuse and stopped seeing her. And now here she was beside him again. He said her name silently, lips unmoving. Lucy. Lucy Martell. Same initials as his. "I won't even have to change my monograms," she'd once said.

Eyes lowered and unseeing, she sat on the hard bench next to him with that slight awkwardness which had been her birth gift from blind chance. The years had matured her loveliness. Her hair was still golden brown, worn short, fluffily curly; her

makeup was still minimal, no lipstick or eye shadow and only a
subtle hint of perfume. He noticed that she wore no rings. As
she shrugged out of an oyster-white raincoat, half turned away
from him, he watched the movement of her shoulders, her right
held stiffly about two inches higher than her left, the outline of
the finlike ridge running from below the neckline of her simple
black dress to below her right shoulder blade plainly visible to
anyone behind her. The childhood operation had corrected the
spinal curvature she had brought into the world with her but at
a price.

He couldn't help himself. As she folded her raincoat on the
back of the bench he laid his fingers gently on her shoulder
blade. She whirled around and for a moment her eyes were
hard and grim with anger, but then she recognized him. Her
mouth gaped open and she stared blankly at him as if a corpse
had come to life.

"In the matter of the estate of Graham Dillaway," intoned
the clerk of the court sonorously.

She'd be almost thirty now, Loren thought, and she was still
as uncannily attractive in her own private way as she had been
in her early twenties. He wondered whether he still looked like
a graceless woolly bear to her. She had called him that once
while they were in each other's arms in the flame-leafed au-
tumn woods.

"Ready for proponents, if the court please," Stanford W.
Nalbin called. He rose to edge his bony body past Loren and
Lucy and strode with almost military dignity through the
wicket and up to the counsel table, where he snapped open his
briefcase and began to outline the facts he expected to establish
by the testimony of his witnesses.

There was so much Loren wanted to say to her, and he
could see in her face that there was so much she wanted to say
to him. But court was in session.

"I call Sergeant Ernest Moore," Nalbin announced, and the
trooper marched smartly to the witness stand and was sworn.
Under questioning Moore recounted the circumstances leading
to his discovery of the two charred bodies in the ruins of the
cabin on the south slope of King Mountain. Loren forced himself to listen to the testimony. Except for a few details he
learned nothing the newspapers had not already told him.

"Excuse me, Sergeant," Judge Collison interrupted, swivel-
ing squeakily to face the witness box. "If both bodies were

burned beyond recognition, how can you identify one of them as that of the testator, Graham Dillaway?"

"Well, Your Honor, as I said a minute ago, there are a lot of indications. We found a belt buckle with the monogram GD under one of the bodies. It was pretty burned up but the lab was able to make out the initials."

"Do you have the remains of that belt buckle with you?" Nalbin asked.

Moore reached inside the breast pocket of his powder-blue uniform jacket and extracted a small, carefully wrapped parcel. "Yes, sir." He began to unfasten the binding, and after Nalbin had laid the formal groundwork with a series of questions the chunk of twisted metal and the laboratory report pertaining to it were admitted into evidence.

"Will the widow be able to identify that thing as Mr. Dillaway's property?" the judge asked skeptically.

"Ah, no, Your Honor," Nalbin replied, "but she can and will testify that Mr. Dillaway habitually wore a monogrammed belt buckle of a certain description. Such testimony should carry weight."

Collison nodded and swiveled back to face the trooper. "Any other indications, Sergeant?"

"Well, we found what was left of an alligator-skin wallet and were able to reconstruct a few of the papers inside it. There was a driver's license and a couple of credit cards in the name of Graham Dillaway—"

The judge broke into his testimony again. "Excuse me, but did you personally perform the laboratory tests you are testifying to?"

"I supervised them personally," Moore answered. The additional lab reports were received in evidence after the usual formalities. While the clerk marked the exhibits, Nalbin faced the bench. "Mrs. Dillaway will testify that the decedent habitually carried an alligator-skin wallet. I would also like to point out, Your Honor, that the cabin itself and the lot on which it stood and one of the automobiles found nearby were all in the name of Graham Dillaway. In due course I shall introduce certified copies of the recorded...."

The words droned on and Loren and Lucy looked into each other's eyes.

Finally Sergeant Moore stepped down. "I call Hope Foxworth Dillaway," Nalbin announced. The widow rose, moving slowly and heavily as though through water. Lucy and Loren stood with her and stepped into the center aisle to make her passage easier. The widow struggled into the aisle, tears wetting her cheeks. Lucy clung to her arm as her step faltered and Loren took her other arm as they guided her gently to the witness chair, then returned to their seats. As they sat they reached at the same moment for each other's hands.

At first Hope couldn't speak, and Collison instructed the bailiff to pour her a glass of water. When she was able to talk, she described her husband's periodic trips to King Mountain, confirming his use of an alligator wallet and a monogrammed belt buckle. She identified the will being offered for probate as the instrument her husband had signed in her presence in the offices of Mensing & Nalbin. Every answer was an ordeal. Several times during the low-voiced interrogation she sobbed uncontrollably. At the end of her testimony Nalbin took her hand and guided her back to her place. "It's almost over," he whispered to her as she sat dazedly beside her son.

Judge Collison pounded his gavel. "Court will recess for ten minutes."

"Let's take a walk," Loren suggested. He and Lucy Martell passed through the swing doors to merge with the stream of litigants and lawyers and witnesses and sheriff's deputies and harried-looking secretaries scrambling up and down the corridor. Loren led the way to the fire stairs and closed the thick steel door behind them to shut out the noise and they gazed at each other in silence. Her lips parted and he bent to kiss them gently and they whispered each other's names.

It was Lucy who broke the spell. "I know coincidences happen all the time but this is too much."

"I'm still groggy from it," Loren confessed. "The best I can come up with is What's a nice girl like you doing in a place like this?"

"I've been Hope Dillaway's secretary and all-around troubleshooter for the past year and a half, since her last girl got married."

"Isn't that wild? And I drew the Dillaways' wills for them a few months after I'd passed the bar. I wonder how much sooner we'd have bumped into each other if I'd stayed with Pop's firm."

"Are you glad we bumped, Loren?" she asked after a moment.

"Are you?" he countered.

"It's—a crazy situation," she told him, and then changed the subject swiftly. "What are you doing these days?"

"Teaching law at the university. I made associate professor two years ago. Spent one year on leave of absence as deputy legal adviser to the police commissioner's office and got mixed up in some off-the-wall cases and wound up with a reputation as some kind of detective. How about yourself?"

"Mostly drifting. One marriage that turned into a disaster. Hardening my shell."

"It must be hard as a rock. You've been living in my home city for eighteen months and never tried to look me up?"

"I did try, once. I found the Mensing & Nalbin law firm in the yellow pages and phoned. The receptionist told me that Mr. Mensing had died several years ago and that she'd never heard of a younger Mensing being with the firm."

"Goddamn," Loren growled. "Secretarial turnover. And of course my home phone's unlisted."

"I just assumed you'd married and left the city long ago."

"Life's weird," he said. "I've been here all the time. Unwed, unattached, not sleeping with anybody regular."

"It's better being unattached," she admitted. "You don't get hurt that way. I've been hurt enough."

She said it quietly and without emotion but Loren felt as if she had lashed him. He didn't know if she was referring to him and was afraid to ask her point-blank. "Uh, look, we have to get back, I think I'm the next witness," he blurted hastily. "But maybe we should get together sometime and, well, try to sort things out. Unless you'd rather not?"

"Let's," she said without hesitation, and Loren felt the tightness inside him disappear. "Taking care of Hope ties up a lot of my evenings but Doreen and her husband are staying over tonight so I think I could break free. Dinner?"

"You still like banana daiquiris with orange juice?"

"If I could ever find someone who made them right."

"Why don't you come by my place for a drink first? I'll pick up the bananas and things on the way home." He tore a sheet from a pocket notebook and wrote his address on it. "Here. We can work out dinner later. We'd better get back before Collison holds me in contempt or something." He touched

the ridge line of her back with his fingertips and as she looked
up at him he thought he could read in her eyes the memory of
long-ago caresses. He opened the fire door and they walked
back into the corridor silently.

In the courtroom Loren found that he'd miscalculated; he
was not the next witness. Dr. Beck, the forensic pathologist,
was called and squirmed out of his seat and up the aisle to be
sworn. He continued to play with his knuckles in the witness
chair even after he'd cracked all ten of them. In sentences full
of technical detail which he wove around himself like a security blanket he testified to his examination of the charred remains of the two bodies. He produced a series of X-ray photographs he had taken of the teeth of the white male corpse. He
stated that he had requested and received from Graham Dillaway's dentist, Dr. Michael Josephson, a set of Dr. Josephson's
most recent X-ray photos of Mr. Dillaway's teeth. He gave it
as his expert opinion that the two sets of photographs were so
close to identical as to convince him beyond doubt that the
white male corpse he had examined had been that of Graham
Dillaway.

Nalbin faced the judge at the end of this line of questioning.
"If you wish further testimony as to identity, Your Honor, Dr.
Josephson is also in court."

Collison shot a glance at his wrist. "Not necessary, Counselor. Can you finish this case before the luncheon recess? I
have another matter on for this afternoon."

"Yes, Your Honor." Nalbin hastily excused Dr. Beck and
called Loren to the stand. Under the ritual of questioning he
testified that he was the draftsman of the will being offered for
probate, that the will offered for probate was the instrument he
had drawn, that he knew of no subsequent will the testator had
made, that he was intimately familiar with the signatures of
both subscribing witnesses to the will, and that they were genuine.

"Where are the witnesses, Counselor?" Judge Collison demanded testily.

"Both dead, Your Honor," Nalbin replied. "My partner,
Stephen Mensing—Professor Mensing's father—died six years
ago. The other witness, Constance F. Waller, was our senior
secretary, and she died four years ago."

"Proceed, Counselor," the judge ordered in a bored tone of

voice.

Nalbin continued asking Loren the formally required litany of questions. Finally he said: "Thank you, I have no further questions," and turned to the bench to announce: "That completes our presentation, Your Honor."

The judge adjusted his bifocals and picked up the legal pad on which he had been scrawling notes throughout the hearing. "The court finds as facts the following: That the will herein offered for probate is the will of the testator, Graham Dillaway; that the said testator...." He droned on with his recapitulation of all the testimony for several minutes and finally laid down his note pad. "The court rules that the statute has been complied with and orders that the will be accepted for probate. Submit your decree, Counselor." Nalbin extracted an unsigned form order from his briefcase and handed it to the clerk, then bowed slightly to Judge Collison with a "Thank you, Your Honor" and began to return loose papers to his case. The clerk was calling the next matter before the gaunt-faced old attorney was on the spectators' side of the wicket.

The Dillaway group collected rain gear and drifted out of the courtroom and down the corridor to the elevator bank where they stood in a cluster. All but one of them. Loren noticed that Will Dillaway had hung back. Looking up the corridor, he could see the dead man's son standing very deliberately outside the probate courtroom door, smoking a cigarette. A down elevator clanked open but was too crowded for the entire party to enter. Loren and Nalbin volunteered to wait for the next car. "About six?" Loren reminded Lucy, and she nodded as the cage door slid shut between them.

Loren looked up the corridor again. Will Dillaway was still standing and smoking in the same spot.

"What do you think that little prima donna performance is all about?" he asked his father's old partner.

"The classic filial syndrome at father's remarriage, I should hazard," Nalbin said. "I doubt there is much love lost between Will and his stepmother."

"A bit shocking that he'd display open animosity at a time of mourning, wouldn't you think?" Loren suggested.

The old litigator pursed dry lips. "I daresay," he muttered. "Almost as shocking as that a professor of law would make a pass at a young lady in the halls of justice. Your advances did not go unnoticed, my boy."

"Why, you dirty old man." Loren decided that he'd rather eat live worms than tell Nalbin one word about his past relationship with Lucy. "I refuse to dignify that slur with a reply. In fact I might even sue you for slander."

"Ah, yes, but you would not win." Nalbin chuckled as they entered the next elevator and crawled downward. "My lawyer is smarter than your lawyer." When they stepped out at the main floor Nalbin shook his hand, thanked him for attending, and explained that his own car was parked in the basement garage of the courthouse. They exchanged goodbyes and Loren turned up his raincoat collar in preparation for the two-block wade to his lot.

He was still in the vestibule, staring glumly out at the river of falling water, when he heard a loud imperious voice behind him. "Mr. Mensing!" He turned and saw Will Dillaway jogging toward him across the foyer. "I was afraid I'd miss you." He steered Loren into a corner of the high-ceilinged vestibule. "If you have a few minutes to spare I'd like to speak to you privately."

Loren looked at his wristwatch. It was almost noon and he had a jurisprudence class to meet at 2 P.M. Will interpreted the gesture as a hint. "Could we have lunch?" he suggested.

They sat soaked and dripping on high stools in front of the oval bar at Hocky's, sipping drinks and nibbling on cheese and crackers while they waited for their meals. Every table in the restaurant was packed to capacity and a line of standees stretched back to the street door. Desperate-faced waitresses fought to elbow their way through the crowd without dropping their trays. The odor of wet clothing was worse than in the courthouse elevator, and whoever spoke in less than a drill sergeant's roar went unheard. It was the ideal spot for conversational privacy.

"When Mr. Nalbin introduced you as a law professor," Will shouted three inches from Loren's ear, "I decided to take advantage of a golden opportunity if you'd let me. I've got a contract for a series of books on American young people today. I've had two published so far, and right now I'm working on one about what young people value." He could not have been much over thirty himself but he spoke of the young with the detachment of a Bostonian discussing the Bantus. "What are law students thinking these days?" Will went on. "What do they believe, what do they hope for, what do they love?"

Loren bit into his steak sandwich and found it to be stone-cold in the center and tough as a shoe all over. He pulled the alleged meat out of the bread, reached for the cheese knife on the bar and spread creamy sharp cheddar over the two slices, thankful that Will was paying. "You're asking questions that are overbroad and call for a lot of conclusions from the witness," he roared, "but here goes. I believe and the best of the kids believe that nothing short of an unimaginably radical social overhaul can make conditions decent in this country. That kind of overhaul is impossible for the foreseeable future. The dreams of the late sixties are dead." On a hunch he let his voice drop. "Some people come to law school hoping that as lawyers they'll have the leverage to make some small social changes that they couldn't make in any other field. Others are in law school the way people used to be English majors, they still haven't decided what to do with their lives. Another type is in it for the money and most of them will wind up in firms like Nalbin's. As I almost did."

"I see," Will said solemnly.

"You see like a toad at noon," Loren told him. "You didn't take a single note, I don't see any battery recorder in your pocket, and a minute ago I deliberately lowered my voice so you couldn't hear me and you didn't even change expression. So what do you really want to see me about?"

Will Dillaway flushed red, then mopped his brow with a raincoat sleeve. "I was wondering about your underground reputation as a detective. I don't wonder anymore. That was why I had to talk to you. Tell me, what's your opinion about my father's death?"

Loren took another bite out of his sandwich, chewing on bread and cheese and the question. "I don't know if I have any opinion," he answered cautiously. "You heard Sergeant Moore's testimony in court. The police seem convinced that your father's death and Jackson Corby's was accidental."

"The police are fools," Will shouted. "My father was murdered. I know why he was murdered and I know who murdered him, or at least paid to have it done."

"Who?"

"My stepmother. Hope, the grief-stricken tearjerker. The stinking bitch. She did it for the money. She married him for it and she killed him for it."

Loren finished his scotch to give himself time to think. "You realize," he said as he put his glass down, "that she could sue you for slander if what you just said should get back to her? What proof do you have?"

"I'll get proof," Will vowed. "I was hoping I could persuade you to help."

Loren remembered Nalbin's comments about the classic filial syndrome, and studied the taut whiteness of the skin next to Will's mouth and the burning intensity of his eyes, and decided to perform a gentlemanly evasion. "I'm not a licensed detective," he said, "I have a job that keeps me very busy, and I certainly don't need your money. What's more important is that you haven't given me a single reason why you're so insistent your father was murdered at all, let alone that your stepmother is responsible." A deceptive maneuver worthy of a President, Loren told himself, inasmuch as he had already found at least three aspects of the deaths that seemed cockeyed.

"The heart has its reasons," Will Dillaway intoned solemnly, like a participant in a holy ritual, "which the reason knows not of."

The phrase disturbed Loren; not just its irrationality but the words themselves. He rummaged through memories of required reading in college courses and finally remembered its source. Will had been half-consciously quoting or paraphrasing Blaise Pascal, mathematician, physicist and religious mystic, the great antirationalist of the Age of Reason, who had written that line as an attack on skepticism and a defense of blind faith in the existence of God. Loren winced at its craziness in the context of his conversation with Graham Dillaway's son.

"No," he said. "I don't want to get involved. If you come up with any evidence, go to the police."

Through the rest of lunch Will tried to persuade him to change his mind but Loren stood by his refusal. Finally Will mumbled a brusque good-bye and trudged out of the restaurant, leaving the check unpaid.

A most unsatisfactory meal however you sliced it, Loren thought as he settled with the waitress.

By midafternoon the rain had subsided to a dribble. Loren was preoccupied with Lucy Martell's reappearance and Will Dillaway's obsession, so that his two o'clock jurisprudence class did not see him at his best. By the end of his lecture on Scandi-

navian legal philosophy he was convinced that he'd done nothing to help his students tell the theories of Hägerström, Olive-
crona and Alf Ross apart from each other. At the end of class
he shut himself in his office and wasted an hour making pointless revisions in his draft chapter on Hitler's *Reichsfilmkammer*
and the campaign to rid the German film industry of Jews.
Shortly after four he decided to call it a day. He swiveled to the
portable Olympia on a typing table in the corner, typed a hasty
note to Stanford Nalbin summarizing his luncheon talk with
Will Dillaway, and dropped the letter down the mail slot on his
way out of the law building. On the drive home he swerved the
fastback into the crowded lot of Sappington's Supermart and
bought bananas, a can of frozen orange juice and a bottle of
light Jamaican rum. He spent the late afternoon cleaning the
apartment, with the roar of the Khachaturian Second Symphony on the stereo almost drowning out the wheeze of his
vacuum.

Five thirty. He showered, changed, mixed the banana daiquiris in the blender and waited with a queer commingling of
tension and delight for her to ring the bell.

She didn't.

Six, six thirty, seven came and went.

By seven thirty he knew that she wasn't going to come. He
toyed with the idea of calling the Dillaway penthouse. Maybe
there had been an emergency with Hope. But he knew Lucy
well enough to know that in that case she would have phoned
him.

It followed that she must have made a deliberate decision to
stand him up. And with a shock of guilt he remembered that
that was almost exactly what he had done to her, back when he
was in law school and trying to end the relationship and she
had begged to see him again and without explanation he had
broken their date. She had set him up for this evening, to make
him feel the ache he had made for her. He cursed himself as a
bastard then and an idiot now, thinking a dead relationship
could spring back to life at a word and a touch. He poured the
banana daiquiris down the drain and went out for a late dinner
preceded and followed by several drinks. He knew he deserved
what she had done and had no comeback but to write the entire
Dillaway family out of his universe of discourse permanently.

Eight days later, sitting in his book-crammed office, with the sun glaring through the east window and Nalbin balanced primly on the edge of the sectional, Loren listened to the news that the man whose will he had drawn had been burned to death by another human being.

THREE

"WHAT letters in the newspaper?" Loren asked.

Nalbin snapped open his briefcase and extracted a cream-colored file folder which he passed across the paper-strewn desk. "Here is one of them, the one sent to the *Courier*. I am told that identical letters were sent to the *World* and the *Beacon*. None of the papers would publish such a letter sent to them without the writer's address, but nevertheless they did the job the writer intended."

Loren bent to read the letter.

> Dear Sir:
>
> The death of Graham Dillaway last month was not an accident. The tiny cooking stove in his mountain cabin could not possibly have started a fire intense enough to gut the whole cabin. Something else started it. Rather, *somebody* started it. Graham Dillaway was murdered.
>
> Why haven't the police thoroughly investigated that fire? Why aren't they hunting for the murderer? WHAT ARE THE AUTHORITIES COVERING UP?
>
> E.A. Rogers

"Whoever wrote this knows his literature," Loren commented when he'd finished. "Did you get the point of the signature E.A. Rogers?"

Stanford W. Nalbin shook his head dumbly.

"Back in the 1840s," Loren explained, "a writer named E.A. Poe—Edgar Allan Poe to you—wrote a story which included a lot of news articles and letters to newspapers about the murder of a girl named Mary Rogers. The story was called 'The Mystery of Marie Roget.' Poe thought his story actually solved that murder. Apparently the writer of this letter would like to follow in Poe's footsteps. I'd suspect it was Pious Will Dillaway, trying to make trouble for his stepmother, except that when I talked to him he couldn't give me one rational argument to support his ideas, and this Rogers does a bit better. I wonder if he visited the Dillaway cabin before it burned; that must be how he got his information about the cookstove. Tell me, where were these letters mailed from?"

"They seem to have been mailed from the central post office downtown. I don't think you will ever trace them that way."

Loren polished his glasses with a silicone-treated tissue. "How did you get a copy of the letter and what did you mean when you said they did the job Rogers intended?"

"Tom Bingham, the chairman of the editorial board of the *Courier,* is a golf partner of mine and knew I was handling the Dillaway estate. He called me yesterday morning, told me of this strange letter that had come in and of course assured me that the *Courier* would not print it. What you have on your desk is a photocopy which Tom sent to my office by messenger yesterday afternoon. At that time we had no idea that the other papers had received identical letters, nor that the *Beacon* was doing something about it."

Of the city's three papers the *Beacon* was the one most alert for any story involving official misconduct. "What did the *Beacon* do?" Loren asked, already half suspecting the answer.

"They sent Chad Corrigan to King Mountain yesterday. You have heard of him, I trust?" Loren had indeed. Corrigan was a former FBI agent, a Pulitzer Prize-winning reporter, and a bloodhound on the scent of any crime story. "Corrigan and his assistants flew to King Mountain in the *Beacon* helicopter yesterday. They went through the ruins of that cabin virtually with microscopes."

"And found?"

"Fragments of a narrow-necked wine bottle, a bit of charred oil-soaked rag, a tiny pocket of unignited gasoline. In short, irrefutable evidence that a firebomb had been thrown into that cabin, apparently through the west window judging from the laboratory analysis of some bits of shattered glass. The reports came in at dawn this morning and they seem conclusive."

"How do you happen to know all this?" Loren demanded.

"A *Beacon* reporter phoned Mrs. Dillaway early this morning. Told her the paper had evidence her husband had been murdered and asked for her reaction to the news. She hung up in terror and called my home at once. I've spent the morning running between her penthouse and the *Beacon* offices and police headquarters."

"Now wait a minute." Loren held up a palm. "If Dillaway was murdered, it's a King County matter. If the state troopers did a sloppy job of investigating, and from Corrigan's evidence it looks as if they did, somebody will get fired over it, but that's a state matter. Where do the city police come into the picture?"

"When the private laboratory employed by the *Beacon* made its report, the paper insisted on absolute certainty before it would publish the story and so they used their connections to have the evidence reexamined by city police technicians. The original results have now been verified. Furthermore, Captain Engelhorn told me in his office this morning that the city Homicide Division has received several anonymous calls over the past ten days insisting that Mr. Dillaway had been murdered—though giving no reasons—and demanding that the police investigate. The calls were all completed too quickly for tracing and the detectives who took the calls are in complete disagreement whether the voice was that of a man or a woman. They ignored the whole series of calls as the work of a crackpot. Now they don't seem to know what to think. Two state police captains are flying down today for consultations. There has been no official statement yet, but be assured there will be within the next few hours, and its gist will be that the case is reopened and the crime is murder. There will also be a special edition of the *Beacon* on the streets before long, carrying the full story. Not to put too fine a point upon it, all hell has broken loose."

Loren sat in silence a long minute with elbows planted on the desk top, nursing his temples between his fingers. His thoughts were flying in five directions at once. "All right," he said finally. "Assume Dillaway was murdered, and Corby too of course. What is the firm's interest?"

"Loren," the old litigator confessed, "I am frightened. We have absolutely no expertise in criminal law and suddenly we are in the middle of the worst kind of criminal matter. It is well known that whenever a woman is murdered the prime suspect is her husband and that when a man is murdered the police look first to his wife. In addition there is a financial motive in this case that runs to something like nine hundred thousand dollars after taxes. And also I'm afraid that—well, I won't go into that."

"You'd damn well better," Loren told him quietly, "if you want any help from me."

"You're right. I apologize." Nalbin sank back another two inches on the sectional seat. "It's been a hellish morning. I am virtually certain that Mrs. Dillaway is concealing something from me. I have no idea what it might be, but every instinct I have developed through forty-seven years of cross-examining witnesses tells me that she is hiding something. I frankly don't know how to handle the situation."

"What you're afraid of," Loren pointed out, "is that she killed Graham. Right?"

Nalbin didn't answer the question directly. "It is inconceivable," he pronounced, "that she herself could have made a surreptitious visit to King Mountain and tossed a Molotov cocktail through that window. She says she can establish that she was here in the city the entire day of her husband's death. I have verified that when the state police telephoned with the tragic news shortly after the bodies were found, she answered the phone personally, and fainted at the phone, and was revived by her secretary, Miss Martell, whom you, ah, met at the probate hearing. Even with a private helicopter she could not have returned to the city from King Mountain by the time the police phoned her at the penthouse. So it is absolutely certain that she herself did not commit murder. She told me, by the way, that she had never even seen the King Mountain cabin and did not know its exact location. That is not the problem. The problem is that it's quite conceivable that she could have paid someone to kill her husband. And I am not necessarily thinking of a professional assassin. Any child can learn how to make a firebomb these days."

"In other words," Loren summed up, "you're afraid the physical evidence isn't going to mean much in this case and you've got to fight shadows you can't see."

"I'm deathly afraid that it may become a matter not of trial by jury where the state must prove Hope Dillaway's guilt but of trial by newspaper where she must prove her innocence, which under the circumstances is impossible. How does she prove she did not hire an assassin? When is the last time you successfully proved a negative? Now you see why I had to come to you—to ask you to use those special talents you displayed as deputy legal adviser to the police commissioner."

"To play private detective for you," Loren amended. "Exactly what Pious Will wanted me to do."

"The circumstances are different now," Nalbin insisted. "Certainly you've shown yourself more than competent in the field, and surely your professorship does not preclude you from taking outside consultation work. And the estate of Graham Dillaway is far from stingy in its compensation."

Offering Loren money to do something he did not want to do was the quickest route to making an enemy of him. He hunched forward in his chair and made fists on the desk blotter. "God damn it, if I'd wanted to get rich I'd have stayed with the goddamn firm!" he shouted.

"All right, so your father left you enough money to satisfy your needs. How can you use your affluence as an objection to assisting a widow in bad health who needs help desperately?"

Even in his own mind Loren couldn't completely sort out his objections. There was his reluctance to serve the rich and powerful under any circumstances, his subtle suspicion that Hope Foxworth Dillaway might well be guilty, his fear of further involvement with Lucy Martell, his intuition that the whole Dillaway case was a Pandora's box, a cage in which no man would willingly imprison himself. He couldn't find words to explain all this to Nalbin so he remained silent.

"You claim to love humanity but as soon as a specific human being begs your help you turn your nose up." Nalbin's voice seethed with cold contempt.

Slowly Loren stood up, let his chair slide back to crash against the wall. "You have one hell of a way of asking for a favor. All right, damn you, I'll do it. What do I call myself?"

Nalbin let out a long slow whoosh of relief and seemed to crumple in his seat as the tension subsided in the stuffy cubicle. "Your title will be legal and investigative consultant. That sounds impressive enough, wouldn't you say?"

"Yes indeed. Now the next item of business is this. I'm not a licensed private detective and even if I were I wouldn't do the routine leg work myself in a case like this. I'll need to bring in an agency and I want the best in the city, which means Marc Hooft, and he comes high. Will you foot the bill and give me complete discretion as to what I engage the agency to do?"

"Of course. I shall have a memorandum of agreement between us prepared and mailed to you this afternoon."

"All right. Now leave your file here and get the hell out of my office."

FOUR

WHEN he was alone again he glanced ruefully at the broad windowsill where he kept the sheaf of Nazi legal documents he had fondly hoped he could translate this morning. Then he looked at his watch. Eleven forty. If he skipped lunch and ad-libbed his two o'clock First Amendment seminar he could devote the next two and a quarter hours to the Dillaway case. He leaned back and shut his eyes, barricading himself in the fortress of his thoughts.

When he blinked himself back into reality he shot another glance at his wrist and found that it was just short of noon. He fished a ball-point pen and legal pad from the forest of papers on his desk and scribbled furiously until four yellow sheets were covered with notes. He read his campaign plan over, added some new details, deleted others, then reached for the phone book.

"The Hooft Agency, may I help *you?*" chirped a bright female voice at the other end.

"Mr. Hooft, please....Professor Mensing calling....No, that's M-E-N, M as in mammal....Yes, he knows who I am. Thank you."

A few seconds later he was saying hello to the head of the city's best detective agency and beginning to acquaint him with what he wanted done. It was a lengthy conversation. His ear was sore long before he could hang up.

His next step was to cross the campus to the main university library and make photocopies of every available newspaper account of the double death on King Mountain. The walk was short but the wait at the front desk in the reference division was considerable. Apparently the ancient little lady librarian was having trouble collecting the six-week-old papers Loren wanted. When she returned to the front desk, reed-thin arms laden, she wore a smile of grim triumph like Hercules after his twelfth labor. Loren thanked her and took the pile to the nearest photocopying machine, which, as is the habit of photocopying machines in libraries, was out of order. By the time he completed his duplications and returned the originals to the ancient lady it was almost two o'clock and he had to race back to the law building and pick up his seminar materials. But as he pounded down the hall to Room 127, five minutes late, a scrap of remembered fact about one of the students in that seminar suggested a short cut on one of his paths of investigation. He would ask her, he decided, right after class.

"Loren, I don't *care* what the Supreme Court said, burning the flag is symbolic speech and I have a perfect right to do it under the First Amendment," Gael Irwin continued as he stuffed his materials back into his attaché case. The cedar-paneled seminar room was empty except for the two of them and the electric wall clock read 3:10.

"You're raising another jurisprudence issue, Gael. And a good one too. Suppose all the liberals on the Court conveniently die next week and the President appoints the kind of people to replace them that you would expect him to. Then the Court comes down with a ruling that the President can have anyone arrested who criticizes him. Suppose it holds this is perfectly proper under the Constitution because the First Amendment only protects freedom of speech, not license, and criticizing the President is license. All earlier holdings to the contrary are overruled. After a decision like that, does it make any sense to say that you still have a First Amendment right to criticize?"

Gael shuddered prettily. "God, Loren, don't scare me with your hypotheticals. That *could* happen tomorrow!"

"Let's grab something to eat," Loren proposed. "And change the subject while we're doing it. How would you like to prostitute that year you spent in library school and do a little bibliographic research for me?"

They stored their books and papers in the admissions office and strolled across campus to the student union. Loren settled for a cheeseburger and fries, Gael for pastry and coffee. They took a table in the far corner of the snack bar and Loren sat beneath a blown-up photo of W.C. Fields tacked to the chartreuse wall.

"A bibliography of Jackson Corby?" Gael repeated Loren's request. "Loren, that name rings a bell in my belfry, I think. Isn't that the man who was burned to death last month with that silly fascist maniac Graham Dillaway?"

"That's right. The newspapers said he was a black writer but so far I haven't learned anything else about him. Not that I've tried very hard yet."

"What do you need a bibliography for?" she asked.

"I don't know." Loren munched his cheeseburger and waited for her to wrinkle up her perky face into a cartoon like-ness of disbelief. "That's the truth. I'm into something that seems to involve Corby and have to learn all I can about him in a hurry. He and Dillaway were both writers and I'm hoping that when I know what he wrote and what other people wrote about him I may know more about his connection with Dilla-way. Whatever that connection was, the newspapers haven't said a word about it."

He watched her face with amusement as a sudden surmise grew into an irresistible idea inside her. "Loren," she said, "could all of this interest in Jackson Corby have anything to do with the crazy detective things you keep getting into?" She asked the question cautiously, speaking each word with slow deliberation.

"It could," Loren admitted, chewing on a fry.

"That-fire-was-no-accident-it-was-murder!" she squealed as if the sentence were a single word.

"If you grab the special edition of the *Beacon* on the way to the library you'll know as much as I know. Will you do the chore for me?"

She squared her shoulders under her olive-drab polo shirt. "Not unless I'm an equal partner in the whole show," she in-sisted. "I mean, just because I'm a woman and a student does not mean that I am your flunky, Loren Mensing!"

"God preserve us, it's lib time again," he groaned playfully. "Okay, I'll tell you what. If I deduce who killed that fascist maniac Graham Dillaway, I won't turn him over to the cops without consulting with you first. How does that grab you?" He thought it was a safe enough offer to make since the solu-tion of a crime by deduction happened about as frequently as a total eclipse of the sun.

"Equality of the sexes. Right on!" She grinned. "The only class I have tomorrow is yours so I don't have to study today. I'll go over to the library right away and get started. It may take the rest of the week."

"I can wait that long. Well, I've got other wars to fight, so I'll see you later. Have a cold potato." He flipped her the last of the french fries, which she caught in her mouth as he scraped his chair back and headed for the exit.

The *Beacon* extra had hit the streets during his late lunch. He fed the friendly vending machine a dime and yanked a copy from its iron maw.

Back in his office Loren cleared his desk by simply piling all the books and papers onto the fractional sectional and trusting to luck that no one would want to sit down for a few hours. Then he spread the photocopied newspaper articles fanwise across the blotter, positioned the E.A. Rogers letter at one end of the fan, raised his feet to what free space was left on the desk top, and began to read the relevant articles in the *Beacon* extra. Little in the paper surprised him. Stanford Nalbin had stated the essentials fully.

When he was finished with the current newspaper he turned to the six-week-old accounts of the King Mountain fire. Sketchy and misleading as they seemed in the light of the new discoveries, he read each of them with care, and reread the Rogers letter after each news account. At the end of his research he scrawled some hasty notes on a legal pad, then cleared the desk and tore off fresh yellow sheets and reworked the notes into a memorandum to himself.

It is now clear that Dillaway and Corby were murdered. The following questions are raised by the crimes.

1. Who was the mysterious caller who reported the fire to Substation 7? Why did he conceal his identity?

2. Why did the police perform such an incredibly sloppy investigation and then announce so quickly and assuredly that the fire was accidental? Does this tie in with Dr. Beck's nervousness and Sgt. Moore's combativeness at the probate hearing?

3. What was Corby's connection with Dillaway? Were they staying together at the cabin or was Corby a casual visitor? What do the police know about him? Why is this black writer the invisible man in the case?

4. Who made the anonymous calls to the city police, charging that Dillaway and Corby were murdered? The same person who reported the fire? The same person who wrote the Rogers letters? Why?

5. Where did Rogers get his information about the cooking stove in the cabin? Does he have evidence for his accusations, or did he just make some lucky guesses?

6. What is Hope Dillaway hiding?

He was going over the memorandum for the third time when the phone rang. He scooped it up mechanically. "Mensing,"

"Hi, Loren, this is Gael. I'm over in the library and something crazy is going on."

"Oh? What kind of something crazy? Mouse in the stacks?"

"Sexist," she said pleasantly. "No, Loren, I'm serious. I began looking up Jackson Corby and do you know what?"

"No, Gael, I haven't the foggiest what. Tell me what."

"There is no Jackson Corby."

Loren jerked his feet off the desk top and sat bolt upright. He picked up his pen and drew a circle around the words "invisible man" in his memorandum. "Now wait a minute," he protested. "There has to be a Jackson Corby. Has to have been, I mean. He just died last month."

"Silly, I don't mean the man didn't *exist*. I'm just telling you that he didn't write anything. I've checked the *Library of Congress Catalog*, the *British Museum Catalog*, the *Cumulative Book Index*, *Paperbound Books in Print*, the *Reader's Guide*, the *Black Authors' Dictionary* and everything else I could think of. If he wrote anything, Loren, it must have been with invisible ink."

Loren gripped the phone strangler-tight and thought furiously. Gael liked to play the flighty kook but he knew from her work in three semesters of his classes that when she said something was not the case, it wasn't. "All right," he told her. "Thanks for letting me know. Keep trying to track down material on Corby and give me another ring if you get lucky. I'll see you after class tomorrow."

"Okay, provided you promise not to call on me in class, because I'm not going to be prepared. After all, Loren, I'm slaving for you all afternoon, you owe me *at least* that much!"

"Closet capitalist," he hissed.

"Male chauvinist bear," she hissed, and they hung up.

Loren sat back and shut his eyes. He staunchly believed that when you are on an investigation and something crazy is dropped into your lap you must play with it and worry it like a cat with a mouse until the item has become digestible. He rooted in his bottom drawer for his lawyer's desk diary and from the back pages reserved for the insertion of important clients' names and addresses he made a list of the phone numbers of several black organizations with which he'd been involved in one capacity or another until the policy of blacks-only had forced him out. Tugging the phone to the center of his desk, he began dialing the groups in which he thought he might still have a friend who would give him information.

After seven failures he gave up. Whatever facts about the late Jackson Corby were known to the black community were going to stay in the black community.

Time for another approach. He made a long-distance call to state police headquarters in the capital and asked the headquarters operator for the records division and asked the records division operator for Sergeant Kendrick. He was lucky. Kendrick had the four-to-midnight shift this week.

"How goes it, Ken? This is Loren Mensing down at City University....Sure has been a long while, like two years....No, I'm not playing legal adviser to the commissioner this year, but I haven't forgotten all that good stuff you used to dig out of the files for me when I needed it....You called it, Ken. I've got myself sucked into another winner and I'm hoping you can dig me out some more facts."

Another few minutes of gentle arm-twisting and the records sergeant agreed to help. But when Loren explained precisely what he needed, Kendrick whistled in awed surprise. "Man, don't you know the lid's on the Dillaway case....? Yeah, I know you're one of the good guys, but I just can't give you what you want. I mean, that's the way it is."

"All right, then give me just one item. Tell me what happened to Jackson Corby's body. That has to be a matter of public record, I can get a court order if I have to," he lied.

Kendrick let out a long and soulful sigh. "Hold the line, man." Loren listened over the phone to a tinny portable radio in the records room, tuned to a country and western station. After three minutes Kendrick's Harlem baritone broke into the lyrics of "Okie from Muskogee."

"His sister claimed the remains," the sergeant reported. "Got pen and paper handy? Her name is Miss Arlena Corby." He added an apartment address in Centralia, halfway across the state. "Now you watch your step, Professor. I tell you straight, man, if you mess with the Dillaway case you've gone and walked into the stewpot."

Loren thanked him again and they exchanged good-byes. A worm of fear crawled inside him. The unflappable Kendrick did not issue such warnings lightly. He cursed himself for letting Nalbin taunt him into becoming involved but knew that it was too late to back out.

As doors began to slam along the outside corridor and the footsteps of his law faculty colleagues echoed down the stairway, Loren stowed the Dillaway papers in his briefcase and returned the other paperwork from the old sectional to the desk and settled down to the law school business on which he should have spent the business day.

FIVE

HE worked in his office late, first out of necessity and then, when the necessary chores had been done, out of choice, to put off the moment when he would run out of rationalizations. Eventually he cleared his desk of the trivial paperwork too but by then it was after eight and he had a new excuse. He locked the office and drove across town to Vecchio's, where the food was excellent and the service slow.

Over the antipasto and beef *braciole* and rich dark barolo he became disgusted with himself for not making the call. He'd known from the minute he'd allowed Nalbin to shame him into taking the case that very shortly he'd have to get in touch again with Lucy Martell. He'd known that becoming involved with the Dillaway household would be unpleasant for both Lucy and himself. He expected the worst but he had committed himself and the job had to be done. He gulped his espresso, paid the check, stepped into the phone booth by the cashier's desk, found the number in the directory and dialed.

"I'm sorry, the number you have dialed is not in service. This is a recording. I'm sorry, the number...." Loren slammed down the receiver, made an educated guess, retrieved his dime from the coin slot and dialed another number.

"Evening, Stanford, it's Loren. I don't want to take any of your time, but would you happen to know the Dillaways' new unlisted number?....Ah, I thought you might have arranged for that, considering how the media must have been harassing them since the news broke. If you want quick service from Ma Bell it pays to be famous, doesn't it?....Okay, I've got it down. Thanks much and sleep tight."

He inserted another dime and called the number. Four rings, five, six. No answer. Then he heard a woman's voice. "Dillaway residence." The voice was worn down to exhaustion, fighting for control. He had never heard it sound so desperate but he knew it was hers.

"Lucy, this is Loren. What's been going on up there, what

are they doing to you?"

"Loren! God, it's been a nightmare all day, Hope has been in hysterics ever since the first call this morning, the police and news people won't let us alone. I was just trying to get a few minutes' nap when you phoned. How did you get the new number?"

"I figured you must have given it to Nalbin so I got it from him. Did he tell you I'm working for the family now?"

"Yes, he said you'd be some kind of consultant. Welcome to the Venus flytrap," she said ruefully. She must have been through hell today, Loren thought.

"Look, I need to see Hope Dillaway tonight,'' he told her. "I know she won't be in the mood for it, but if I'm going to help her she has to talk to me, and it's probably going to be a long talk."

"Loren, that's completely impossible. She's on the point of collapse. She....Well, she put away a fifth of brandy this evening, and I don't blame her one bit. I tucked her into bed a little while ago and she will be out all night. She couldn't talk to you now if her life depended on it.''

"It might," Loren said quietly.

"Will I do?" Her voice was low and expectant in the booth's stillness. "I mean, I've been with her for eighteen months and I think I know her and the family as well as anyone. Give me an hour for that nap and a bath and change and I'll tell you anything you want to know."

"Including what happened last week?" He blurted the question without thinking, trying to keep his voice calm.

"Oh, Loren, seeing you again in that courtroom shook me up so badly I couldn't believe it was happening. You were the same and different all at once and I could feel my shell coming apart. I hit the panic button. I was afraid to go to you that night and I was afraid to call and tell you why and ever since then I've been terrified that you'd never call me."

"We have so much to make up to each other," he told her quietly.

"Let's begin in an hour," she suggested.

"Sure, kitten." He hadn't called her that old pet name in almost nine years, he realized with a shock. "Do I meet you at the penthouse?"

"No, I'm in my own apartment now. I live one floor below the penthouse, in 23 D. Mr. Dillaway rents—rented this whole floor besides the penthouse. The cook and the housekeeper live in A and B, and C is sort of a guest cottage. There's an extension of the upstairs phone here in my place and I turned off all the phones in the penthouse so Hope wouldn't be disturbed. That's how you got me. You know the way out here, don't you?"

"I'll find you," he promised. "See you soon."

"Don't get run over or anything on the way out," she begged him. "That would be just like one of life's wonderful jokes. Watch out for yourself, Loren."

"And you," he said.

The interrogation got off to a late start.

Showered and changed, Loren maneuvered the fastback into a space on the side street and walked two blocks through velvet darkness. He passed a garden apartment complex, a small typewriter repair shop with a placard in its dusty window, a few old and untended-looking houses. The one high-rise in the neighborhood was a tall slab of brick, solid and secure, no gingerbread ornamentation or futuristic splashings of glass and aluminum. In the outer vestibule he pressed the 23D buzzer and the inner door crackled open. A uniformed doorman stood by the wall-to-wall mirror in the lobby. The elevator poured out soft music from a hidden speaker as it lifted him. He turned into the carpeted corridor of 23 and pressed the creamy chime button of D. The door opened and she was standing on the edge of the rich blue carpet, a kind of hesitant brightness in her eyes.

"Hi," he said. And suddenly she was molded silkily against him. They closed the door behind them by the combined weight of their bodies. He kissed her eager lips and stroked her neck, reaching under her robe's glossy collar to caress the outthrust wing of flesh at her shoulder blade that he had not touched for so many years. Lucy's eyes flooded with tears of release. They embraced without words, only small sounds of pleasure that grew more urgent as she untied the belt of her russet robe and moved against him until the robe fell away and she was naked and moaning in his arms.

He had no idea how much time had passed when they lay

back exhausted. Absently he glanced at the alarm clock on the nightstand next to her bed. "What time do you have to get up tomorrow?" he asked her.

Lucy sighed. "Seven thirty. Have to be upstairs by eight. I never eat breakfast."

"You will tomorrow," he promised, and reached across her breasts to set the alarm for five thirty and press out the tinted light.

He woke the instant the buzzer went off and thumbed it quiet before she could stir. He washed and dressed noiselessly and searched for instant coffee in her tiny kitchen. Just after six thirty he opened the bedroom door and bent over and gently lowered the sheet and kissed her nipples till she was awake. "Ten minutes to the best meal you ever ate," he whispered. "Rise and shine." He left her to get ready and went back to the kitchen where he turned the flame low under the skillet of eggs, cheese, spices, green peppers, cream, and bite-size chunks of leftover turkey.

He was delighted to see how much his cooking pleased her. She ate as hungrily as she had made love. "Oh, no more hot rolls, Loren, I'll blow up like a balloon. I haven't had a breakfast this good since I was a little girl. You never did gourmet cooking when we were in school, where did you learn?"

"Well, I had three choices. Learn to cook, get married or shrivel. I picked number one. Here, let's get these things into the dishwasher and start talking business. You've got an hour to give me a bird's-eye view of the Foxworths and the Dillaways, beginning with Hope. And I'll start with a tough question. From sitting near her in court and from what you said last night I gather she has a drinking problem. How long has she had it?"

"I shouldn't be telling you these things," she protested. "I work for her and by and large she's been good to me. I won't be disloyal."

"Lucy, I work for her too. What I don't know won't hurt me but it may get Hope convicted of murder. I can't help her in the dark."

"I'm sorry, Loren. You're right, of course." She looked up at him thoughtfully. "It's hard to get used to trusting somebody all the way again. Be patient with me?"

He answered by kissing her lips and eyes. They loaded the

dishwasher and then took their coffee mugs to the breakfast bar where they sat on padded wrought-iron stools facing each other. "Have you ever read any of Hope's novels?" Lucy asked him.

"Never opened one in my life," he told her, "although now that I think of it, she actually autographed one for me a long time ago. Remind me to tell you that story someday."

"When she was at her best those books were good. Not great literature but good of their type. They were safe and sentimental and didn't have much to do with the real world, but Hope knew how to touch a woman's heart—when she was at her best. She could make you cry and then laugh through your tears. It's a great gift. Then she lost it. I think it happened about six or seven years ago, before I came here. Her kind of books had no place in the new world. Things like black revolution and draft resistance and drugs and communes did to her line of work what the automobile did to the blacksmith shops. Her new books stopped selling in hardcover and the paperbacks stopped reprinting her old ones. Her publishers began insisting on rewrites and nothing she did satisfied them. She started drinking heavily. She still turns out a few thousand words a week, or at least she did until this nightmare began, but it's all useless. Take it from me, I've been typing those words for the past year and a half."

"If her handwriting hasn't improved since she autographed that book for me," Loren commented, "I don't envy you."

"You get used to it after a while. It's no worse than a lot of medical prescriptions I've seen. Anyway, most of my job is watching out she doesn't hurt herself and answering correspondence from old ladies who beg her to do more of the love stories she wrote in the good old days."

"This is one you won't like but I have to ask it. Do you think her failure as a writer gave her another motive besides money to kill her husband?"

She covered her lengthy silence by taking a slow sip of coffee. "Graham's books still sell. Not as well as they used to, but they sell. There's a nice contract in the works for hardcover and paperback reprints of his Revolutionary War novels for the Bicentennial. And he gets a percentage whenever that Charlton Heston movie they made out of one of his books runs on TV. It's been his income that's supported this place for the last five years. I feel like the lowest bitch in the world for saying it,

Loren, but Hope was very jealous that Graham could still make it when she couldn't. When she was drinking she'd say unforgivable things to him."

"No wonder he had to get away to King Mountain," Loren said. "And that brings me to my next question. Apparently Hope told Nalbin that she had never seen Graham's cabin and didn't even know its location. Did she ever say that to you?"

"Let me think." She chewed her lower lip gravely. "I think she mentioned three or four times that she'd never been there. She said that cabin was like Graham's workroom away from home. She didn't go into his workroom in the apartment and she wouldn't intrude on the one in the mountains either."

"But you don't know of your own knowledge that she was telling the truth?"

"Well, I do have weekends and holidays off plus three weeks vacation a year. I can't be certain what she's done when I haven't been around, but why would she lie about something like that?"

"How about the rest of the family? How about Will?" Loren remembered the E. A. Rogers letter with its apparently intimate knowledge of the mountain retreat. "Was Will ever up there?"

"I don't see how he could have been. The whole point of Graham's going there was to get away from everybody and everything. But of course there's no way I would know for sure."

"All right, we've run into a dead end. Let's try another road. What do you know about Jackson Corby, the black writer or whatever he was who died in the fire?"

"The police asked Hope and me that yesterday," Lucy said. "They didn't like the answer. We were both honest about it."

"About what?"

"Hope told them that Mr. Corby first came to visit Graham here about two years ago. He would come every few months. After three or four visits she took a violent dislike to him and wouldn't let him come anymore. I've heard her call him—not to his face, of course, this was long after she'd closed the door on him—well, she told Graham that Mr. Corby was a....she called him some very filthy names. She was Old South, you know, and very frightened of assertive blacks." Lucy sat in stony silence for almost a minute before she went on. "There's something I didn't tell the police. I didn't dare to. But I think I'd better tell you. At least twice since I've been here I've overheard violent arguments upstairs where Hope accused Graham and Mr. Corby of—well, of being lovers."

If there had been a homosexual relationship between the two dead men, Loren reflected, then there was a whole new aspect to the case that he hadn't considered. "Did Hope admit these arguments to the police?"

"I don't know," Lucy said.

"Do you think she was right?"

"I can't believe it. Even Hope couldn't have believed it if she'd been sober. After all, he was happily married to one woman for more than twenty years and a few days after divorcing her he married Hope. That doesn't sound like a homosexual to me."

"Just what was the story behind that divorce and remarriage anyway? You must have heard some references to it in a year and a half of living with them."

Lucy drank the last of her coffee. "Do you remember what Hope looked like when she and Graham came to you to have new wills drawn? When Graham met her Hope was an extremely attractive and talented woman. Graham's first wife, Amanda, was a wrinkled little mouse. I've seen pictures of them both and talked to people who knew them both, and in those days any man would have been tempted by Hope."

"Were there any outside affairs with women since you've been here?"

"Not as far as I could see."

"Did he ever make a pass at you?" Loren shot the question at her as though she were a hostile witness on the stand.

"Absolutely never," she answered firmly.

Abruptly Loren changed the subject. "How did he react when Hope went into one of her rages?"

"He didn't hit back at her if that's what you mean. He'd either just sit and take it, or go into his workroom, or sometimes he'd go out for a walk till she calmed down. He never got angry at her in a physical way. Deep down he was a kind and compassionate man and I admired him very much."

"Did he ever try to get her to see a psychiatrist?"

"She wouldn't go," Lucy said. "And he would never have sent her to an institution against her will. He felt she was his responsibility, I guess."

Loren looked blankly at the gold-flecked Formica breakfast bar. He was thinking about what would have happened to Graham and Lucy and Hope if the fact of death hadn't intervened. In an alternate future where Graham had not yet died, he and his wife's secretary would have been drawn so close together by mutual need and by their detached compassion for Hope that a sexual affair would have followed as surely as the tides follow the phases of the moon. Loren had a sick moment of happiness that Graham was dead. He forced himself to snap out of it and think impersonally again.

"Summation time," he said. "At the very least, Graham *might* have had strong personal reasons for wishing Hope dead. Hope had even stronger motivation for wanting Graham out of the way, both personal and financial motivation. Also, Hope loathed Jackson Corby. We're not certain how much of all this the police know, but sooner or later they'll probably get hold of most of it. All right, let's talk about opportunity. You told the police and Nalbin that Hope was here the entire day of the King Mountain fire?"

"I was with her all day," Lucy insisted. "The cook was off but Mrs. Parkins, the housekeeper, was upstairs too that day. There's just no way in the world Hope could have gone there and back without our knowing it."

"But the police aren't going to proceed on the theory she did it herself," Loren pointed out. "They'll be looking for evidence that she paid someone to do it for her. They'll go through her bank statements and try to find some unusual checks or cash withdrawals. They'll go through her life looking for some contact with a hit man or someone who could line up a hit man for her. Did she have any contacts like that?"

Lucy's lips grew taut with sudden fright. "Oh, God," she whispered. *"The Heart of Julie Corrado."*

"What are you talking about?"

"It's a title, a working title. A manuscript she was working on when I first came here. It was about a young girl who fell in love and married this man who turns out to be an officer in the Mafia. What I've read of it was told from the girl's point of view, the trials and tribulations of a gangland housewife, but there was a fair amount of material about organized crime in it and I don't know where she got that material, it was before my time. I suppose she could have gotten help from a friendly Mafioso."

"Who might have helped her again," Loren added, "if she wanted to dispose of her husband. What happened to this manuscript? Was it published?"

"No. It was terrible. She couldn't even finish it. I typed up the part she worked on after I came here, about a hundred pages, and they're sitting in a file cabinet upstairs as far as I know."

"If the police ever get in that cabinet, and get a lead from the manuscript that connects Hope with the Mafia, we're hurting. All right, what other secrets might she be hiding?"

Lucy slid down from the wrought-iron stool and began pacing the peacock-blue carpet. When she swung into the living room area and threw herself onto the matching blue couch Loren followed and sat beside her. Finally she looked at him and said: "I can't think of anything else that might hurt her."

"Then let's talk about Will Dillaway for a minute," Loren suggested. "I gather he and his stepmother aren't on the best of terms?"

Lucy drew her pale pink housecoat more tightly around her. "Will hates Hope's guts," she said simply. "He blamed her for his parents' divorce and still thinks of her as the Scarlet Woman who broke up his family. They've hardly spoken in years."

"Will struck me as a good hater behind his religious veneer," Loren noted.

"He's a very earnest man," Lucy told him. "I don't think I've ever seen him laugh."

Loren wondered whether Will might have hated Graham so much for divorcing Will's mother that, years later, he would kill his father, or have him killed, and then try frantically to pin the crime on his stepmother. It sounded unlikely but might be worth looking into, he decided. "How about Hope's own children?" he asked, switching to a new subject. "James and Doreen, I think their names are?"

"Well, I haven't seen too much of them. James lives across the state line in Farmwick with his second wife. Her name is Lola and she's the cuddly emptyheaded sexpot type. I never met Marion, the first wife; she and James were divorced before my time. He doesn't say much about her but I gather she's constantly hauling him into court to get more support money out of him. He writes too, you know, mostly cheap gothics and semi-pornography under four or five pseudonyms."

"I'll have to try one someday. In fact I should probably sample all the family's work product. What can you tell me about Doreen?"

Lucy's eyes brightened. "She is the one person in the tribe who isn't a writer and doesn't want to be. I'm told she was a firebrand in college, antiwar demonstrations and student strikes and all that, but now she's just sweet and loving and unpretentious and all wrapped up in her husband. You saw him in court, Dr. Josephson or Colonel Josephson or whatever you're supposed to call him. Mike's much older than Doreen but as far as I can tell it's been a good marriage. She grew up without a father, you know."

And now she has a father figure and a lover in one package, Loren thought. "Then neither James nor Doreen nor Josephson had any personal motive for killing Graham?"

"Not that I could see. Hope never cared for Mike and gave Doreen the cold shoulder when she married him, and they haven't socialized since then, but that wouldn't be a reason for anyone to murder *Graham.* By the way, would you believe Mike is only a few feet away from us this minute?" She paused for a moment of mischievous delight at Loren's puzzlement. "After the news broke yesterday, Hope called Doreen and asked her and Mike to come over and spend the night. Begged them to come, actually. They're the kind that never say no to anyone who needs help. They came after dinner and did what they could. That's the only reason I was able to come down here at all last night. Hope got smashed anyway, but at least she had another shoulder to cry on. When I came back here last night to get some rest the arrangement was that Doreen would sleep with Hope and Mike was going to sleep next door in 23 C, the guest cottage. He had to get back early to his dental practice."

Loren laughed. "For your reputation's sake I hope he and I don't wind up going down in the same elevator. Which reminds me, you have to get dressed and go upstairs and take Hope off Doreen's hands and I have to get down to the law school. I've got work corning out of my ears today and tomorrow."

Lucy threw a glance at the gilt clock over the breakfast bar. "Oh, I'm late!" she squealed, and scurried off the couch and vanished into the bedroom, closing the door behind her.

Loren yawned and stretched and wrestled with the temptation to call in sick at the law school and catch up on his sleep. From somewhere he heard the muffled ringing of a phone. He looked into the alcove that held Lucy's petite workdesk. It wasn't the princess phone there that was ringing. He wondered if the sound could be coming from 23C, and if the sounds of his and Lucy's lovemaking had been as audible to the occupant of C as the phone now was to Loren.

The bedroom door flew open and Lucy in bra and half-slip waved her arms at him frantically. He sprang up and followed her into the room. The double bed was half made and the phone on the glass-topped vanity table was off the hook. Lucy picked up the handset and held it so that she and Loren could both listen.

"….so glad to hear you're up and about this fine lovely morning, Hope darling, because I'm going to spoil your day for you, you drunken putrid bitch." It was a man's voice that Loren didn't recognize. Lucy moved her lips silently to form a single word. "Will." They heard a gasp of outrage from the phone.

"I'm going to a lawyer today," the male voice went on. "I'm going to make sure you never see a cent of my father's money that you killed him for, you filthy stinking cunt. I'm going to have the courts take all the money away from you and then I'm going to kick your fat drunken ass into the gutter where you can rot. You murderer!" A phone slammed down, and Loren heard uncontrollable sobbing from the open end of the connection. Stealthily he lowered his handset back into place.

Lucy threw herself into his arms. "Oh, Loren, that was horrible. I thought the phones upstairs were turned off and picked up the extension here just as Hope answered upstairs. She or Doreen must have turned the phones in the penthouse on again." She shuddered and he stroked her shoulders, holding her tight. "Loren, legally what can he do?" she whispered.

"I can't commit myself without doing some research, but I advise you to get dressed right now and go upstairs and make sure Hope makes an appointment with Nalbin as soon as the office opens. We may have some messy litigation on our hands." He brushed her lips lightly. "Go and take care of Hope. I'll let myself out and call you later."

"The doorman knows who lives here and who doesn't," she said. "Maybe you'd better not go out the front way past him. When you get out of the elevator turn right and go through the steel door into the service area and follow the rubber matting out to the side door. It opens onto the parking lot and you can get through to the side street without having to answer questions."

"You sound as if you've gone through this routine before," Loren suggested playfully. She drew away from him as if he had slapped her.

"I'm sorry," he muttered. "It was a lousy joke. I didn't mean it the way it sounded. Forgive me?"

"If you'll forgive me for reacting like an idiot," she said.

"We'll get used to each other again after a while," he promised, and they shared a last kiss.

As the elevator carried him to the lobby and as he walked through the empty service corridor to the side exit, three thoughts revolved in Loren's mind. One was trivial. They hadn't had time to even begin to talk about their relationship, and he'd better make time and soon. The second was academic. On what legal theory could Will Dillaway take Graham's legacy away from Hope?

The third was dangerous. *How had Will gotten hold of Hope's new unlisted number?*

SIX

THE minute Loren got to the law school the crises began. Urgent correspondence, a heated faculty meeting, an irate phone call from a judge of the city court, ten minutes for lunch before an emergency meeting of the law library committee to consider structural weaknesses of the railings around the central well in the new building, frenzied preparation for afternoon classes, an evening meeting of the University Academic Senate that dragged on until almost midnight. By the time Loren groped his way into his apartment he was too exhausted to fix himself a decent meal and too hungry to fall asleep. He took the hottest shower he could stand and collapsed into bed.

Next day, Friday, was more of the same. Before his morning jurisprudence class he made a quick call to Lucy and learned that nothing new had happened.

"Would you want to come over and talk to Hope tonight?" she asked. "I know you can't do much until you've heard her side of things. Maybe we could go somewhere and have our talk when you finish with her."

"Oh, damn it, tonight's impossible," he said hastily. "I have to go out to Centralia tonight to see Jackson Corby's sister, and I don't expect to be back till late Saturday night. Suppose I come over about ten Sunday morning and we can go for brunch at the Cheshire afterwards?"

And so it was arranged, and Loren hung up and went back to work. The Dillaway case intruded again late in the afternoon when his office door opened and Gael Irwin stepped in and flopped down on the sectional.

"Loren, I'm finished," she announced. "Through, done, terminated. I refuse to pick up one more reference book and try to find that Corby character in it as long as I live." Her features drooped like the face of a sad clown. "I struck out! I can't find a trace that the man ever published a word anywhere."

"Okay, I was more or less expecting that after Wednesday. Tell you what. Write me a memo that tells exactly what research you did and how many hours you spent. Then I can bill the lawyer for the Dillaways and get you some money."

Gael stuck two fingers into the holes in her faded yellow sweat shirt. "These aren't here for ventilation, Loren. Give me two minutes and I'll have your memo for you. And soak the bastards hard for me, I have to start squirreling away next year's tuition."

At four thirty he locked his office, went home, packed a bag, filled up the VW's tank at the House of Gas and headed northwest on the Interstate. It was dark when he braked the fastback under the portico of the Centralia Qualitel, halfway across the state. After a late supper at the Char King across the highway and a glance at the late news on TV he pulled the blankets up to his chin against the refrigerated coolness of the motel room and snapped out the bedlight.

He sat tensely and without comfort on the plastic-covered cream settee and absently counted the doors leading out of the apartment's living room. There were seven, all painted cream-white like the walls, all shut tight, as if the woman were determined not to reveal more than a corner of herself. African carvings gleamed on mahogany shelving supported by wrought-iron brackets. He read off the names on the spines of some paperbacks on one shelf. Malcolm, Eldridge, Fanon, Baraka. He felt like an invader.

The woman on the cream divan was tall and regal and dark. She wore her hair in a feathery Afro. A necklace of carved wooden beads fell across the bosom of her flame-orange sweater. She showed no emotion, no reaction to him at all.

"The Man paid me a visit three days ago," she said. "Told me I better not talk about my brother with nobody if I know what's good for me."

"Local fuzz or state?"

"Both. They tried to impress me real hard."

"Does that mean you don't want to talk to me?"

Her shrug was a graceful gesture of pure contempt. "Day ain't come yet when I kiss the pig's ass," she said. "But now you tell me why I *should* talk with you."

"What did Reverend Owens tell you about me?" The reverend ran the black community organization for which Arlena Corby worked and Loren had met him several times at civil rights rallies.

"He told me a few things, cases you took to court for the

brothers, that kind of thing. He said you go with us about as far as a white intellectual can go and still be a white intellectual."

Loren was far from certain that this was an endorsement. "Does that mean you'll tell me about your brother Jackson?"

"Ask your questions," she said simply, and leaned back on the divan.

Loren hunched forward and looked into the woman's liquid unfathomable eyes. "Who was Jackson Corby? What was he? What was his connection with Graham Dillaway?"

Her nostrils flared in remembered anger and grief. "I begged him to quit four years ago. He told me to quit mother-in' him, he wasn't a little boy no more. Ever since then I've had a feeling that something terrible beyond imagination was going to happen to him." She closed her eyes and Loren could not be sure whether she was crying. "My brother worked for The Man. He was some kind of a spy, I don't know who with but he spied on people in this country, that was his job. I think he was in something like the Plumbers Unit."

Loren's breath caught. He'd been expecting to find some kind of underworld connection but he had not expected this. All of a sudden the Dillaway-Corby case had taken on a political dimension. Watergate, the Plumbers, Presidential secret-police units who set themselves above the law. Was Jackson Corby the token black in the outfit? Loren didn't stop to evaluate the news; it was better to keep asking questions while she seemed to be in an answering mood.

"When was the last time you saw your brother?"

"A year ago last Christmas. I never saw him but one or two times a year and he didn't stay but a few hours when he did come."

"Did he ever mention the name of Graham Dillaway?"

"He never talked about his jobs at all. Once in a while he'd tell me some places where he'd been, never more than that. I never heard of this Graham Dillaway in my life till I saw the stories in the papers about how he and my brother died in that fire. I saw his remains were buried right. I guess that was how the pigs knew to warn me to keep my mouth shut."

"You were close to him, weren't you?" he asked softly.

"I was all the family he had. Our mamma died when he was six and I had to look after him till he was old enough to take care of himself. Now is there anything else you have to know?"

From her tone he knew he could get no more answers from

her. "I think you've given me all you can," he said. "Now it's up to me. You know I'm doing this for a woman who's in bad trouble and can't help herself. She thanks you and I thank you." He stood and reached out to touch her shoulder almost guiltily. "I'm sorry about your brother. No one should have to die like that."

Tears glistened in her dark eyes.

Before checking out of the Qualitel he sat down on the unmade bed and put in a long-distance call to the Hooft Agency. He was lucky. Marc was still in the office.

"Ah, yes," the detective wheezed asthmatically. "I've been expecting you to call. My men haven't turned in all the input reports you wanted, but this morning I did have a *very* interesting phone conversation with the fellow I sent to King Mountain to talk with the late Mr. Dillaway's neighbors—if that's the right word for a handful of hermits a mile or more apart from each other. I called your apartment and the law school to give you the details but couldn't find you."

"Glad I decided to give you a buzz. What's the news?"

"First of all, it seems that my man was the first person to talk to the neighbors," Hooft reported. "The state police did not even take the trouble to interview the people who lived nearest to Mr. Dillaway. Would you call that significant?"

"If I knew what it signified." Loren thought of the strange courtroom behavior of Dr. Beck and Sergeant Moore, and of Sergeant Kendrick's insistence that the lid was on this case. "Anything else?" he asked Hooft.

"I have only begun to report." The detective made bubbly chuckling noises under his breath as if he had just perpetrated the pun of the century. "My next little tidbit starts with a question. Would you describe Hope Foxworth Dillaway as a tall, puffy, fiftyish woman with faded blonde hair and one chin too many?"

"Not to her face," Loren said, "but the description fits. Why?"

"A woman of that description was observed by at least two of the other cabin dwellers on King Mountain sometime last fall, blundering around the back roads in a black four-door Montego. One of the people who noticed her took down her license number just in case; these hermits are a suspicious lot. My man traced the number to a rental agency in King City.

The woman had put her driver's license number on the application form. If Hope Dillaway says she never went to King Mountain, she's a liar."

Loren cursed softly. Not only was he in the stewpot, but every few minutes someone seemed to be turning up the heat. "How long can you keep the police from finding this out?"

"They know it already. The rental agent made the connection when he went through the records and called the state police while my man was still in the office. They let him go after half an hour of questioning. My man had to tell them he was working for me, of course, but—and here's another funny thing—they've made no effort to get in touch with me and find out who I'm working for. But they will, my friend, they will. And when they do I've got to tell them. State license and all that."

"Okay, just hold out as long as you safely can. Anything else?"

"One more item. We identified the make of typewriter E.A. Rogers used for his letters. It's a new German make, a Griem, that has a slightly different typeface from the standard models and hasn't been too widely distributed over here yet. Griem makes only electric portables with a stationary carriage and disposable type cartridges, so there's no irregularity of touch in the letters that would tell us anything about the typist's habits."

One word of Hooft's report seemed to echo in Loren's mind. The name Griem. He had heard or seen that name before, and very recently. He couldn't recall where. Then he had it.

A two-block walk through velvet darkness, past a garden apartment complex, then past a small typewriter repair shop. There had been a placard in one of the shop windows and he had glanced at it for a second as he'd walked by. What had it said? TRY THE NEW GRIEM ELECTRIC PORTABLE. DEMONSTRATION MODELS INSIDE. Something like that.

It might be coincidence but Loren didn't dare believe that it was. He had to go to that typewriter shop first thing Monday morning. To that shop so close to the Dillaway apartment, and to Lucy's.

Loren realized that Hooft hadn't stopped talking although he himself had stopped listening several sentences ago. "Sorry," he said into the phone. "Could you run that by again, Marc?"

"I just said that I'll probably have complete reports on your people by Tuesday morning, if that's soon enough for you."

"Fine. Look, I'll be getting home around midnight. Call me if the police hassle you."

"If I have visitors you'll know it," Hooft promised. "Fortune."

"Peace." And they hung up.

The drive back to the city was uneventful. Loren kept the needle at the legal 55 mph and let the white ribbon of the divided highway lull him so that for a few hours he would not have to think about the case, which not only puzzled but was beginning to frighten him. The strange behavior of the police, the political aspect of the murders that had opened up today, these were bad enough. What frightened him even more was his own growing suspicion that several strands of the double murder case led straight to the door of Lucy Martell.

SEVEN

JUST before ten the next morning, Loren stepped out of the elevator at the twenty-third floor and through a steel door at the end of the hallway. A square foyer with peach carpeting led to a flight of iron-railed spiral stairs. On the upper landing, Lucy in a virgin-white minidress with a wide scarlet belt was holding the entrance door open for him, and they kissed with fervor in the doorway.

"It's good I don't wear lipstick," she whispered, releasing him. "Nothing to rub off before you talk to Hope. She's in her workroom, second door to the left down that hall. You don't want me in on this session, do you?" She beckoned him across the forty-foot sunken living room. The white-brick artificial fireplace was fronted by a low semicircular stone wall topped with soft brown seat cushions. The oak desk in the far corner stood piled high with letters. "I have to get back to sorting and answering these. Graham's and Hope's readers have been sending condolence cards by the bushel basket."

"No, this is private. I should be through by noon. Hope you're ready for brunch by then." He kissed her again and followed the peach carpeting through the corridor to the open workroom door. He tapped lightly and stepped in. Hope Foxworth Dillaway sat in a high-backed chair with a silver tea service on the glass-topped table in front of her. If she had aged between the day Loren had drawn her will and the day he had seen her in probate court, she seemed to have aged as much again in the few days since the hearing. Her face and body were puffier, the lines of grief and fatigue and perhaps fright etched more deeply, the smell of breathmints overpoweringly strong. Loren wondered if she had caches of liquor hidden all over the apartment. He had a curious urge to sniff the spout of the teapot.

"It's so nice to see you again, Professor Mensing." She extended a hand to him with what grace she could muster. "Mr. Nalbin told me that you are investigating this whole hellish nightmare on my behalf, and Lucy said she had given you all the background information about my family and Graham's that you desired. What is it that I can tell you?"

It was time to test her reactions with a frontal assault, he decided. If she didn't pass the test, perhaps he could take himself out of the case. "Did you kill your husband?" he demanded in his strongest courtroom voice.

She gasped, sat straighter in the high-backed chair and looked at him without fear. "I did not," she said. Anger and surprise fought for supremacy in her tone.

"Did you arrange for someone else to kill him?"

"My God, no!"

He took a blind gamble with the next question. "When is the last time you saw the gangster who gave you all the technical help on *The Heart of Julie Corrado*?"

An uncontrollable giggle forced its way through her lips. "Do you mean that funny little Luca Lomenzo or whatever his name was? How ever did you learn about him? Why, I haven't even thought of him for years—or was his name Lozano? I spent one afternoon with him something over three years ago when I was researching *Julie*. It was a rather wasted afternoon from my point of view." She giggled again. "He was drunk as a skunk! I wound up buying some books about the Mafia and doing my research from them. I never finished *Julie*. Poor girl, lying unfinished forever. Excuse me, please, my mind is wandering. It's so hard to concentrate on anything these days."

"Did you know where Graham's cabin on King Mountain was?"

"I did not. I never saw the place. I've told the police that."

"You lied to the police," Loren said, "and they know it. They found the rent-a-car place in King City where you took out the black Montego six months ago."

Hope Dillaway's face bleached white with terror. "They *what?* What are you saying?" Loren looked into her eyes knowingly. "Oh, please, please, don't do this to me! Tell me what's happening to me, tell me why my whole life is destroyed in a few days, oh, tell me!"

Loren saw a certain irony in the situation. Hope had spent her creative life throwing melodramatic crises like beanballs at her beleaguered heroines and now life was doing the same thing to her. She looked like a woman goaded beyond endurance.

"It's true," she wept. "He took one of his trips to King

Mountain late last fall. I flew to King City and rented a car and tried to find his cabin. It was while Lucy was off on vacation. I thought—a woman was living with him in that cabin. All right, I thought Lucy would be up there with him! I had to know for certain."

Loren felt icy panic. He had to ask the next question but was deathly afraid of the answer. Slowly and cautiously he released the words. "What happened?"

"I couldn't find the place! I kept blundering along the wrong roads. Finally I cursed myself for a paranoid old fool and gave up. I drove back to King City and flew home."

"Why didn't you tell all this to the police?"

She lowered her eyes in shame and fear. "I just couldn't do it, Professor Mensing. I couldn't make myself look so ridiculous. I was afraid the story would get into the papers and I had to keep what little self-respect is left me." When she looked up her face was sick with dread. "What's going to happen to me now that the police know?"

"I just can't say," Loren admitted. "They're behaving very strangely in this case. Maybe nothing will happen. All we can do is wait and see." He pulled a hassock over to her side and stroked her trembling hand. "I'm sorry I put you through the wringer that way but I had to know the truth. Now I have a few things to tell you." He gave her a brief sketch of what he had learned from Arlena Corby about her brother's domestic surveillance activities. As he told the story he saw numb horror spread over her. If her reactions are the least bit calculated, he thought, she is the greatest actress of our time.

"Now please," he finished, "try to follow this closely, Mrs. Dillaway. Jackson Corby's cover, if they still call it that, was as a writer. Graham was a writer. Corby's connection with your husband may have had something to do with writing. Did Graham ever drop any hint, at any time, that he was writing anything or doing anything that related to domestic intelligence gathering?"

Hope hid her eyes again and after a time looked at him with a sort of horrified impotence. "My memory is gone. I can't remember any hint of—of that but for all I know there may have been hundreds. We wrote in separate workrooms and he never said very much about anything he was writing until it was done."

"Could Graham have gotten involved with the Plumbers

Unit or some other secret police group if they had asked him
to?"

Her eyes turned flint-hard and her gaze cold and wary. "My
husband was a good American," she declared. "He believed in
America and he loved the American earth. He served his country well in World War II. If his country called on him again, he
would have served again. But I will tell you this, Mr. Mensing.
He would never have done anything vicious or evil or wrong.
Never."

Loren was not satisfied. No governmental gangsters ever
thought they were doing anything vicious or evil or wrong.
Their belief that they could do no wrong was the worst thing
about them.

"Now is there anything else?" Hope demanded. "I'm dreadfully tired this morning and you have upset me considerably."

Loren wondered how she had made the switch from suppli-
cant to authoritarian so effortlessly. He kicked the hassock
back in place and stood up. "Yes, just one thing. I'd like to borrow copies of your husband's writing over the last few years.
Fiction and nonfiction. Maybe that will give me a lead to his
connection with Corby."

"Take anything you want," she snapped, as though he had
become the enemy. "Graham's workroom is locked, Lucy has
the key. Leave the room as you find it. Give her a list of the
things you take. Now please let me alone so I can rest. Oh,
God, let me rest."

Loren closed the door in silence and retraced his way back
to the sunken living room. From somewhere in the large
apartment he heard the soft whine of a vacuum cleaner.

Lucy was sitting on one of the cushions atop the low wall
around the fireplace. "That didn't take long," she began. Then
she studied the lines of tension in his face more closely, the
tightness around his eyes and mouth. "What's the matter,
Loren? You look furious and I can't tell if it's with yourself or
Hope or with me."

Should he tell her anything of his crystallizing suspicions?
Reason told him that it was too soon, that all he had were two
or three scraps of trivia. A Griem demonstration typewriter two
blocks away; an unlisted phone number that Will Dillaway
could have obtained from only a handful of people, Lucy
among them; her reaction when he had playfully suggested
another man might be going in and out of her apartment

through the downstairs service corridor. Building these scraps into some kind of secret alliance between Lucy and Will was not the act of a reasonable man. He knew this and yet he couldn't stop doing the building. Was he subconsciously trying to get out of the relationship with her again? Sit tight and say nothing, he told himself. Let it fester awhile longer.

"It's nothing you did," he said. "Mostly I'm angry with myself. I didn't handle things right with Hope." Briefly he described his conversation with the widow. "After talking with her I can appreciate better what Graham had to put up with. And you."

"She wasn't always that way. She had a few very bad breaks and couldn't cope with them." Lucy shifted closer to Loren's cushion so that they almost touched. "When I want to scream back at her I look at my hump in the mirror and wonder how long it's going to be before I wind up the same way."

Something in the way she said the words made him want to take her in his arms and kiss her gently like a child, and then he realized how paternalistic and ridiculous that would be and did not reach out to her. They sat side by side without speaking or touching, as if a wall of soundproof glass stood between them.

She altered the tangle of moods with a word. "Brunch?" she suggested. "I can eat five of everything."

"Mind if we run a little errand first?" He needed to keep his mind on the case. He was afraid to think about his relationship with Lucy. "Hope said I could borrow some of Graham's writings from his workroom. I want to take a boxful back to my place."

"Wonderful! I still haven't seen your apartment, you know." She rose from her cushion with fluid grace. "I have the key to Graham's study in my desk. I'll have to tell Hope I'm going but the housekeeper can watch her for a few hours. This is supposed to be my day off."

Thirty minutes later they dropped twenty-three flights, a cardboard carton full of Dillaway materials on the elevator floor between them. The Muzak box played "Never on Sunday." Loren hoisted the carton into his arms and they took the service corridor to the side exit. They said nothing as Loren drove to his apartment. He dropped off the carton and showed her around and they went out to eat and he drove her home and went back to his place alone. He felt that he was killing the relationship between them again just as he had years ago. He felt like a poisonous insect.

Late in the afternoon his phone rang. He put down his third drink of the hour and lurched for the receiver.

"Marc," said the voice on the other end. "Well, it happened. I had a visit from Captain Engelhorn today. They know you're in the case now."

EIGHT

MONDAY morning when he left the apartment he drove in the opposite direction from the university. Two blocks from the Dillaway apartment building he fed coins into a meter and walked half a block to the typewriter repair shop. The placard was still in the front window. TRY THE GRIEM, GERMANY'S NEW ELECTRIC PORTABLE SENSATION. MODELS INSIDE FOR YOUR INSPECTION.

There was another sign in the window, one he hadn't noticed on his earlier walk up the block. OPEN MONDAYS TILL 10 P.M.

It had been a Monday night that Lucy had not kept her date with him. Could she and Will have gone to this shop that night to type the Rogers letters?

He opened the door and stepped in past the jangling bell. A long counter on his left cut off a third of the shop. An open doorway behind the counter led to a small cluttered office. Typewriters of all makes, models and ages filled unpainted wooden shelves, awaiting repairs. Newer models, gleaming bright, rested on steel racks and tables. Over a machine on a tiny folding table in an alcove at the far end of the store hung the sign GRIEM—LATEST MODEL ELECTRIC PORTABLE. Loren sat in the cold folding chair in front of the table, fed a sheet of paper into the carriage and flipped the ON button. He typed with the deliberate speed of the self-taught.

The slow blue wolf crawls under the industrious rattlesnake.
The death of Graham Dillaway was not an accident.
He was murdered. What are the authorities covering up? E. A. Rogers
    LM   LM   LM   LM   LM   LM

A shadow darkened the page. He looked up to find a tall potbellied fiftyish man in shirt sleeves staring at him. "Can I help you, sir?"

Loren yanked the sheet from the carriage and pocketed it as

he stood up. "If you're the proprietor, perhaps you can." He opened his cardcase to a plastic window displaying a card from the State Board of Bar Examiners, on one of whose subcommittees he had once served a term. "I'm an investigator for the Bar Examiners. We do security checks on law students before they're admitted to the bar. I've been assigned to look into something we think happened in this store a few Monday nights ago. Could you remember whether some people were in here if I described them?" He began to formulate descriptions of Will Dillaway and, though he despised himself for doing it, of Lucy.

"Nuh-uh," the proprietor grunted. "I'm not here Monday nights. Five o'clock Monday I go home just like any other night."

Loren stifled a curse. "Who is on duty Monday nights? Could I talk to him?"

"Sorry, mister. I had a college kid clerking for me afternoons and Monday nights but he quit me last week and took off. At least he said he was in college. Never seemed to do no reading. Didn't work much neither if you ask me."

"What was his name? Where did he go?"

The fiftyish man shrugged. "You don't think he'd tell me, do you? Kids don't tell nothing to people over thirty these days. They just live in their own world. Long hair, dirty clothes, pot and sex. Makes me glad I never had a kid of my own. Break my heart if a kid of mine turned out like the punks around the schools nowadays. Come on back to my office, I'll get you his name from my books."

Loren took down the name and address and left. He would have Hooft check it out but expected nothing to come of it. There wasn't even any evidence that the Rogers letter had been typed here. He squeezed behind the wheel of the fastback and headed for the law school.

The new law library was a futuristic cylindrical structure designed by the dean of the university's school of architecture— probably during an LSD trip, Loren thought. He stood in the geometric center of the ground floor and looked up the egg-shaped central well to the domed skylight six stories above him. From somewhere over his head he heard a faintly bookish clatter. He pocketed his key to the building, strolled across red and green checkerboard carpeting to the elevator built into the outer wall. The cage was a cube of darkness. The electricians who were supposed to install the light fixtures were on strike. He felt for the 5 button and the car lifted him while a bud of amber light swept across the rising numbers in the floor indicator. As he was stepping out of the elevator on the fifth floor the steel door sprang shut and almost sliced him in half.

He forced himself to keep calm. Every new building has its bugs. That was what the contractors said every time something went wrong. Each time he came over to inspect the new law building he found himself liking the old one more.

The fifth floor was a beehive. About two dozen students were hefting book cartons, shelving law reports in the tall blond wood stacks, arguing heatedly about where certain reference works belonged according to the law librarian's master plan, taking smoke breaks in the study carrels. Loren heard a familiar voice around a corner and headed toward it.

"Henry, that's *ridiculous*. If we put all the decennials on one or two units they'll fall over and crack somebody's skull. We have to spread them over the bottom shelves and put light books on the top. I don't *care* what the master plan says!"

"Hi, Gael," Loren said. "Fighting another good fight?"

"Loren, come over here," Gael Irwin demanded. "Don't you think it's *asinine* to put all these heavy books on these shelves?" She planted her hands in the pockets of her tie-dyed jeans and gave an I-told-you-so look to the harassed male student who had been so foolhardy as to argue with her. Loren reached out to embrace the book stack, shook it between his outstretched arms and felt it sway.

"God damn it," he muttered. "Something else wrong in this bloody building."

"Maybe I should get Ralph Nader to investigate the place," Gael ventured. Loren almost believed she could do it.

"How many shelves are as bad as this one?" he demanded.

"All the blond ones on this floor, Professor," Henry said. "The dark wood ones all seem okay. Do you think something can be done about getting them replaced?"

Loren had no chance to answer. Across the central well the elevator door banged open and a man in a tan suit stepped out and walked around the railed well in Loren's direction. He had Marine-cropped graying hair and the face of an unlucky prize-fighter. A dime-sized scar bleached his left temple. "Are you Professor Mensing?" he grunted.

"I am."

The man flashed a crooked grin, displaying a full set of tobacco polluted teeth. He pulled a square black leather case out
of a pocket and a badge flashed. "I'm Detective Sergeant
Guerra from headquarters. They told me at the law school
you'd probably be here. Guard downstairs at the door let me in.
Captain Engelhorn wants to see you downtown. Right now."

The name rang a bell. That was the one who had questioned
Marc Hooft yesterday. And—yes, Stanford Nalbin had also
mentioned the name when he had first pleaded with Loren to
work on the case. He decided he had better obey the summons.
"Okay, Gael, I've got to go. I'll tell the library committee
about the shelves next time we meet. Thanks for letting me
know."

Loren and Guerra descended in the dark elevator. "Cute little broad," the sergeant's voice rasped. "Nice tits." Loren said
nothing. The unmarked police car was parked in a delivery slot
at the rear of the building. Guerra drove downtown expertly
and in silence.

Police headquarters was a gray stone fortress. Men and
women in and out of uniform filled the high-ceilinged corridors, striding with file folders under their arms between in-
terchangeable cubbyholes. Engelhorn's office was on the
eighth floor. Guerra opened the outer door, then trotted away
down another hall. A uniformed clerk led Loren to the balsa
wood door lettered with the captain's name and knocked twice.
At the command to enter the clerk opened the door and announced, "Professor Mensing, sir," and shut the door smartly
behind him. Loren was trapped in the small stuffy room.

The steel desk and file cabinets were painted battleship
gray. Engelhorn sat behind the desk, thick-bellied, hard-faced,
balding, with eyes that believed nothing and hoped nothing. He
motioned Loren to a chair and stared at him steadily with a
look of cold contempt, letting the oppressive atmosphere build.
Finally he broke the silence.

"I understand you've been playing supersleuth in the Dillaway case," he began. Loren did not even nod. "I also understand," Engelhorn went on, making the weight of each word
register, "that you found out some things about a certain Mr.
Corby that you weren't meant to know."

Loren felt a wave of fright in his belly. If Engelhorn knew
what Loren had learned about Jackson Corby, it was probably

because Arlena Corby's apartment in Centralia had been illegally bugged. The old old story. When the police say law and order they mean selective lawlessness. He knew his rights as a citizen and part of his profession was to teach the meaning of those rights but as he sat in that hard chair he knew cold fear.

Finally he cleared his throat and spoke. "Mrs. Dillaway's attorneys have retained me as legal and investigative consultant." He tried to speak without inflection but his voice sounded to himself like a croak.

Engelhorn leaned back, lit a cigarette, inhaled, gave Loren an expansive smile. "Fine, fine. I think I understand the situation, Professor." He paused long enough for another puff. "I didn't send for you to give you a hard time. I want to relieve your mind to a certain extent."

Loren stared at the midget American flag on a corner of the police captain's desk.

"I simply want to assure you that we have no intention of accusing Mrs. Dillaway of any crime," Engelhorn went on. "There's just not enough evidence. I know that, the state boys know it and the prosecutor up in King County knows it. So you see, there's no reason for you to be in the case at all." The captain smiled bleakly.

Loren gathered his nerve for a dangerous question. "You say that after what the King City car rental people reported the other day?"

"Oh, yes," Engelhorn assured him. "Mrs. Dillaway's little trip to the mountains last fall has nothing to do with the murders. That's what you'd say if you were defending the lady in court, isn't it, Professor? And you'd be perfectly right, of course. We're rational men here. We don't go after people unless we have solid evidence."

"Suppose you find more evidence?" Loren wondered if they had yet come across the alcohol-loving Mafioso in Hope Dillaway's past.

The captain tapped a chewed-looking pencil against his thumbnail. "Maybe I didn't make myself clear. We know Mrs. Dillaway didn't kill her husband or Corby. We're a hell of a lot more certain of it than you can be."

"Why?" Loren demanded.

Engelhorn raised his palm like a crossing guard halting traffic. "Now there I have to draw the line. I've told you all I'm going to tell you. Your client is in no danger. You can drop your investigation." His voice hardened to cold ruthlessness. "You damn well better drop it, Professor. Now." He rose from behind the metal desk, walked around Loren to open the door to the outer office. "Nice meeting you," he said tonelessly. "My clerk will show you to the elevator."

"No police car to take me back to the law school?"

Engelhorn cracked another smile but this time he seemed to be enjoying himself. "Why, Professor! Haven't you heard about inflation and the energy crisis? Do you know what it costs in gas alone to keep a squad car on the streets? I can't waste the taxpayer's money to give you a private limousine back to the law school." He paused a moment. "Don't make me send for you again." He shut the door slowly and carefully behind him.

Loren fought to hold back a shudder. He had known in his mind for several years that 1984 had come early, but until now he hadn't felt it so vividly in his bones. He walked slowly through the corridors, past another parade of people carrying files—*What was in those dossiers? Was he in one? How many others like him?*—and out into the warm spring sun. A cab took him back to the university.

He checked his slot in the faculty mailboxes on the ground floor of the law building. The cubicle was half-filled with junk correspondence and buff phone-call slips. He thumbed through the slips and began to run for the stairs. Lucy Martell had been calling all morning, every fifteen minutes. Her call slips were marked Urgent.

Loren took the stairs three at a time, threw open his office door, flew to the phone. "It's me," he said when he heard her voice. "What's wrong?"

Her voice was torn with anxiety. "Oh, thank heaven, I've been trying to get you all day! Loren, first thing this morning I went back to work on that pile of condolence letters to Hope. One of the first I opened was—it was from Graham!"

Loren took the news poorly. "From Graham? Graham Dillaway? You mean he's *alive*?"

"No, no. The letter was dated more than a year ago. It sounds as though Graham arranged to have it sent to Hope a few months after his death. I think you need to see it. Before Hope does."

"I'll be right over," he said. "Keep it out of sight till I get there. Don't tell Hope I'm coming." He hung up, slammed the office door behind him, stuck his head into the dean's office to have a note posted on the bulletin board canceling his one o'clock class, and raced toward the parking lot.

He read the note for the third time.

> Dear Hope,
>   By the time you read this I will be six months dead and buried. I've arranged to have it mailed to you after that period of time. I have to tell you certain things I couldn't say in my lifetime. I've kept a private diary which you'll find inside the stuffing of the old green divan pillow on the daybed in my study. Please take apart the other pillows too, but very carefully. You will understand shortly. Please don't hate me.
>
>   Graham

"Since he actually died less than two months ago," Loren remarked, "whoever was holding this letter for him must have read in the papers that he'd been murdered and decided to drop the hot potato. Hope hasn't seen this?"

Lucy shook her head. "She couldn't sleep last night. The doctor who lives downstairs came this morning and gave her something to keep her under till late in the afternoon. I didn't want to do anything about this letter without you. I haven't even looked at the pillows in the study."

"Let's go look at them," Loren said.

Lucy reached into a desk drawer for her key ring and led the way through peach-carpeted halls to a fumed-oak door. Graham Dillaway's workroom was furnished with a sort of drab tastefulness. Paintings of wilderness scenes cluttered the walls between high walnut-stained bookshelves. The bare workdesk in the center of the room was filmed with a coat of fine dust. In a corner a blue-upholstered daybed was piled with faded multi-colored pillows.

Loren plucked the green pillow from the heap and stood hefting it from hand to hand. A foolish grin spread over his face. "Hey, kitten, how do you take apart a sofa pillow carefully?"

Lucy ran her hands over the nubby surface of the cushion. "They never taught us that in home ec. Let's go out to the sideboard and get a carving knife."

"No, let's keep this private. Why don't you see if you can sneak the knife in here? And a wastebasket for the scraps."

Two minutes later at her conspiratorial knock he whipped open the study door and she dashed in, holding in front of her a lacquered wastebasket in which nestled an ivory-handled saw-toothed knife. "No cord or plug. It's battery-powered," she explained breathlessly. They took lotus positions on the carpet and held one edge of the pillow over the lip of the basket while Loren made a gingerly incision. The blade whirred and the pillow covering sliced apart. They peeled it back like a banana skin and began pulling handfuls of gray stuffing into the basket.

Lucy reached in for another handful. Suddenly her fingers froze inside the material and she looked at Loren with a glance of wild puzzlement and withdrew her hand. It emerged holding six ten-dollar bills.

Loren let out a long incredulous whistle. "What have we here, the Maltese pillow or something? Let me try." He plunged his own hand into the stuffing. It came out with three more tens and two fives.

Two more handfuls apiece and the pillow was gutted. Three hundred forty dollars in used tens and fives lay in a stack on the fuzzy peach carpet, and on top of the bills lay a tiny brown spiral-bound notebook.

"Loren," Lucy demanded, "what are we going to do with this money? Whose is it?"

Loren picked up the notebook and then reluctantly put it down. "Before we know what to do with it we should see if there's more. Remember, Graham told Hope to take the other pillows apart too. I think I can stretch my jurisdiction as legal and investigative consultant to do it for her."

Lucy glanced at the heap of cushions on the daybed. "We're going to need another wastebasket. The biggest one in the house." She rose to her feet and left the room.

After half an hour of unstuffing pillows the small pile of bills had grown to several stacks. When the last cushion was cleaned out, Loren and Lucy totaled up their find. Almost seven thousand dollars in crinkled fives and tens and a few twenties lay spread on the peach carpet. Loren separated the bills by denomination and divided them into segments of five hundred dollars each. Then he turned to Lucy again. "I need some rubber bands and envelopes to seal the money in. No, don't leave the room. Find the things in Graham's desk if you can. We've got to protect ourselves in this kind of situation."

"Protect ourselves from what?"

"Suppose Hope decided there was originally twenty thousand dollars in those pillows and accused one or both of us of socking away the rest? Suppose Hope died today and one of her legatees got that notion? Suppose the state inheritance tax people got the notion? Do you know where we'd be? Up the creek with no riparian rights. Look, the more I think about this the less I like it. Let's call Nalbin and get him over here as a witness." He strode to Dillaway's desk and sat in the dead man's black leather chair. As he reached for the dust-filmed phone he looked at himself and saw that his dark suit was stippled with carpet fibers.

"I'd like to speak to Mr. Nalbin, please....Professor Mensing....Thank you....Yes, this is Loren. Things have been popping up in the Dillaway case and I...."

"Loren, where in the name of reason have you been?" Stanford W. Nalbin's querulous baritone cut in. "I've been calling your office and apartment for hours. I need you down here instantly. We have a crisis."

"Stanford, you're speaking more truth than you know," Loren told him. "Miss Martell and I just found sixty-eight hundred dollars in Graham Dillaway's sofa pillows. What do we do with it?"

"Oh, dear God," Nalbin groaned. "And I sent the estate inventory to the tax bureau three days ago. Tell me exactly how you came to find this money." When Loren had finished, Nalbin issued instructions. "I will dictate affidavits for you and Miss Martell to sign, stating what you have just told me, and one for myself attesting to your delivery of the money to me. That should protect us in the event the money is found to be subject to estate tax. We might be able to argue that it constitutes an *inter vivos* gift from Mr. Dillaway to his wife, in which case we must pay gift tax but no federal or state inheritance tax. However, that problem can be dealt with when the need arises. Meanwhile my crisis persists and I need you at once. Bring Miss Martell so that she can sign her affidavit, then she can take a cab home and you and I can talk."

"See you in half an hour," Loren promised.

"And don't forget the money!" Nalbin repeated as they

hung up.

Loren returned to Lucy amid the wastebaskets. "We have to go downtown, and my suit's a mess and yours isn't much better." He ran his eyes appreciatively down her peach-spotted forest brown pants suit. "Let's clean up." They spent a pleasant ten minutes rubbing each other's clothes with a swatch of masking tape. Loren found an inordinate amount of peach fuzz around Lucy's breasts and hips.

The electric clock above the entrance to the paneled law library in the offices of Mensing & Nalbin showed 4:50 P.M. The offices were quiet now, the machine-gun staccato of the electric typewriters muted, the stenographers on their way home. The firm's young associates remained at work in their brightly lit cubicles with desks stacked with file folders and law books as Loren's had been in his time with the firm. When he had put Lucy into a cab, Loren followed Stanford Nalbin down the corridor into the library and they sat at the small round conference table near the doorway. Nalbin laid a folder from his attaché case on the table between them.

"No, don't read it yet." He held up a pale bony hand in warning. "Let me explain the situation in slow stages and solicit your opinion at certain points." The old attorney reached to a shelf for a green-bound volume of the annotated state statutes, which he opened to a dog-eared page. "Please read Section 747(b) (3)," he instructed, handing the book to Loren.

Loren had never been able to break either his father or Nalbin of the habit of dog-earing pages. He took the volume and read the statute aloud.

" 'Section Three. If any surviving heir or spouse or legatee or devisee shall feloniously and with premeditation do murder upon the decedent, said surviving heir or spouse or legatee or devisee shall not be entitled to any benefits under the will of the decedent nor under the statutes governing descent and distribution of intestate property, and the estate of the decedent shall descend and be distributed as if the said surviving heir or spouse or legatee or devisee had predeceased the decedent.' So what? It's the standard criminal divestiture statute. Every state in the Union has one like it. If that's what you're worried about, I can relieve your mind right now. Captain Engelhorn sent for me this morning to warn me off the case. He told me the police are certain Hope is not guilty of murder."

Nalbin's face lost a measure of its pinched tension. "Now that *is* good news, but I'm afraid it does not solve my present problem, which is civil not criminal. If you will reread 747(b)(3), you will see that it nowhere says criminal conviction is a condition precedent to divestment." Loren skimmed the statute again while Nalbin droned on. "It does not read 'shall be convicted of having done murder' but simply 'shall do murder.' If you will turn to the legislature's historical notes, you will see that the draftsmen used that phraseology because of some cases in other states with statutes that did require conviction. The cases were those tragic but all too common ones where husband kills wife and then himself or wife kills husband and then herself. Where both murderer and victim are dead there can be no conviction, and the courts in those states held that the statute did not apply and that the legatees of the killer took both the killer's estate and that of the killer's spouse. To avoid that result our legislature rejected the criterion of conviction."

"I think," Loren said, "I can figure out what your crisis is. Will Dillaway has made his move, hasn't he?"

"He has," Nalbin answered gravely.

"And the argument his lawyer is making is that they don't need a criminal trial to take Graham's property away from Hope. They can bring a civil action contesting the bequest to her on the ground that she—what's the phrase?—did murder upon Graham. And of course in a civil suit they have to persuade the jury only by a preponderance of the evidence, not beyond a reasonable doubt. Wow! A civil prosecution for murder against our client."

"We were served with the papers today," the gaunt-faced attorney said. "I must say their brief in support of the theory of action seems well researched."

Loren whistled. "What a wild cause of action! What authority are they using to support it?"

"Most of their precedents deal with the situation where both the alleged murderer and the alleged victim are dead. In a few cases the murderer was alive but had been found legally insane and incapable of standing criminal trial. I will argue, of course, that inability to stand trial either by reason of death or insanity is an indispensable prerequisite to such an extraordinary proceeding. I think our chances of success are quite good."

"As far as the civil side is concerned I tend to agree," Loren said. "Allowing that kind of action, a civil murder trial, would open up the biggest can of worms this side of Joe's Bait & Tackle Shop. Imagine how many disappointed heirs would take that short cut to divest the relative who got the money! But you may be overlooking something."

Nalbin raised his fatigue-worn eyes in a question.

"If this civil suit gets enough publicity in the media, even if it fails in the end, it may generate pressure that will force the prosecutor to go for an indictment," Loren explained.

Nalbin's tone was that of a man neck-deep in a sea of troubles. "How am I going to explain all this to Mrs. Dillaway?"

"That is not my problem, thank heaven," Loren told him. "Now let me give you a rundown on what I've been doing." Leaning back and crossing his ankles, Loren summarized his discovery of Jackson Corby's background, his interviews with the black spy's sister and Captain Engelhorn, the letter from the dead Graham Dillaway to his widow, and the pillow hunt. Near the end of his summation he took the small brown notebook from his breast pocket and held it out to the older man.

"When I get a chance to read this," he said, "we'll know a lot more. You wouldn't think there'd be much in a book so small but he wrote in a very tiny handwriting and I may need a magnifying glass. Graham certainly didn't want this read by any casual eye."

Nalbin glanced at the six-hundred-dollar Swiss watch on its flexible gold strap around his bony wrist. "I have a dinner engagement with Judge Kittredge at six thirty. Why don't you make yourself comfortable here, examine the diary at your leisure, and we can confer when I return at, say, nine P.M.?"

"And what do I do about supper?" Loren asked plaintively.

"The cheeseburgers in the coffee shop downstairs are considered gourmet treats by the office girls," the old man replied dryly.

Loren found them somewhat less appetizing. If it hadn't been for the prospect of reading the diary he would have gone home in disgust and cooked himself a decent meal. He let himself back into the Mensing & Nalbin suite with Nalbin's borrowed key and settled himself in the senior partner's corner office. Three minutes after opening the diary he found he needed the reading glass in Nalbin's drawer. As he inched through the micrography he scribbled notes on a legal pad. By eight he had read the diary twice through. He turned out all the lights in the office and began to think about what he had read.

There was a frantic pounding from far away. Loren snapped on the desk lamp and shot a glance at his watch. Nine ten. Had Nalbin been pounding on his own front door for ten minutes? Loren trotted down the corridor to the front door and let in a Nalbin whose expression resembled that of a dyspeptic Baptist elder who had just swallowed a lemon.

"We scored," Loren announced. "The diary's a gold mine." Nalbin's face returned to its usual look of cold baleful intensity. They went back to the corner office and Loren hitched forward in the black leather client's chair.

"Graham was a long-winded writer," he began. "It probably came from writing six-hundred-page historical novels most of his life. There's no reason for me to read you anything from the diary verbatim, you can ruin your eyes on it later if you want. I'll make it short and simple. He was homosexual."

"Oh, no," Nalbin breathed, as if a close friend had died.

"Rather, he was bisexual, to be precise. He'd had to hide it for most of his adult life. A whole lifetime of contrivance and deception and feelings of guilt. He became an expert at covering his tracks. There's enough pain in his picture of his secret life to keep you awake nights thinking about the society that forced him to keep it a secret.

"Corby learned that secret.

"His job was domestic surveillance for the government, just as his sister told me. I get the impression that most of his assignments had to do with spying on black activists but he was put on other missions too. The diary doesn't tell what kind of assignment brought Corby in touch with Dillaway but I can make an educated guess. Wasn't Doreen Foxworth a pretty fiery activist herself when she was in college? Peace demonstrations, sit-ins at draft boards?"

"I'm not intimately acquainted with the entire family history," Nalbin confessed.

"Well, either because of Doreen or for some other reason, Corby kept the family under surveillance for a while. That's how he learned about Graham. And do you know what our homegrown James Bond did with the proof he got that Graham was bisexual?"

Stanford Nalbin half shut his eyes as if bracing himself for a shock.

"He sat on it," Loren said. "It wasn't the first time he'd dug up private dirt on people he'd been spying on and it wasn't the last time either. He didn't report it, he just tucked away the evidence until he had enough people on the hook. Then he quit the CIA or whatever piece of alphabet soup he worked for, made a private visit to each of the marks and began putting the black into blackmail."

"My God," Nalbin breathed.

"Graham was his richest victim. Corby was hitting him for five thousand every quarter, in small bills. Dillaway had to accumulate the payoff in dribs and drabs to avoid suspicion. He kept the money sewn into those sofa pillows till rendezvous time at King Mountain, then he'd transfer the money to his bag and sew up the pillows again. He must have learned how to use a needle and thread when he was in the Navy."

Nalbin shook himself out of a deep meditation. "Then that is the explanation for the money you found in those pillows."

"Exactly. *On his last trip he didn't take the payoff money with him.* What does that suggest to you?"

The ancient attorney remained silent and motionless as a mummy.

"The diary doesn't answer that question," Loren continued. "It comes to a dead stop three and a half months before Dillaway's death, and with several blank pages left so he didn't just run out of paper. But while he was still writing, two or three times he thought about going to the FBI or the CIA, telling them all he knew about Corby's operation in the hope that they'd—what's the term they used in Vietnam?—terminate him with extreme prejudice, if for no other reason than to keep the extent of the government's domestic spying from coming out. But he could never bring himself to do it because he knew he'd be destroyed in the process. The market for his books is Middle America, and Middle America doesn't like faggots."

A vein in Nalbin's neck began to pulse.

"And so every three months Graham Dillaway goes to King Mountain to pay off Corby and listen to him brag about how many suckers he's got on the hook and how he can travel around like a circuit rider, collecting money from all the marks. And finally, the one time Graham does not bring money with him, he and Corby die on that mountain. Does that give you any ideas?"

Stanford Nalbin shook his snowy head sadly.

"All right, let's go over the possibilities. One. Dillaway

made up his mind to murder Corby on that last trip. That's why he stopped making entries in his diary. He did kill Corby, but in trying to make it look as if he'd died in an accidental fire he clumsily burned himself to death. Plausible?"

"I suppose it could have happened that way," the old man muttered absently.

"Two," Loren went on. "Dillaway went up there without the money because he'd finally steeled himself to make the break with Corby. He told Corby to go to hell, they had a fight and Corby killed him. Then *he* tried to make it look like an accident and burned himself up in the process.

"Three. This is simply a combination of elements from one and two. They killed each other and the cabin caught fire during their fight."

"I see no way of choosing among your theories," Nalbin commented, "especially with the physical evidence reduced to ashes."

"I'm not through yet," Loren said. "There are more than three possibilities. Why couldn't an outside party have killed both Dillaway and Corby? Maybe one of the other blackmail victims followed Corby to the cabin, or maybe someone who had it in for Dillaway trailed *him*. The remains of a homemade firebomb suggest a third party, not one of the two victims trying to make the death of the other look like an accident. And the third party could be almost anyone."

The old attorney's eyes seemed to sink deeper into their pits, where they glowed with a kind of helpless fascination.

"Let's look at another interesting thing about this case," Loren suggested, "namely the absolutely bizarre behavior of the police ever since that fire was reported. They don't bother to question the other people who owned cabins on King Mountain. Sergeant Moore practically throws a fit when he sees me in Judge Collison's court. The ashes are hardly cold before they issue a statement that the fire was an accident—even though the remains of a firebomb were still on the scene when Chad Corrigan went up to investigate. After the newspaper story forces them to admit that Dillaway and Corby were murdered, they learn about Hope's secret visit to King Mountain last fall. Do they even bother to ask her why she lied to them? No! They ignore the whole thing and go on their merry way. When they learn I'm in the case Engelhorn tries to scare me off and then tells me they know Hope is innocent but refuses to tell me *how* they know. Stanford, this is not normal police procedure. They're covering something or somebody.

"You haven't said anything. Does that mean you agree or disagree?"

Nalbin slouched forward, his arrowhead chin nested in his bony hands, and licked his arid lips. "It's weak, Loren. Very speculative, very circumstantial. But perhaps it's unreasonable to demand greater certainty. At least we know Mrs. Dillaway will not be indicted now."

"You're forgetting something, Stanford. The main threat against Hope right now is a civil trial for murder, not indictment. If the standard of proof is a mere preponderance of the evidence rather than beyond a reasonable doubt, I don't think there's anything in this diary which proves Hope couldn't have paid someone to kill Graham. If the court upholds Will's theory of civil murder we'd better have a good credible alternate suspect before we go to trial. Remember the anonymous caller who reported the King Mountain fire? Remember the calls to the city police insisting Dillaway and Corby were murdered? Remember the details in the Rogers letter that indicated the writer was familiar with the Dillaway cabin? Those pieces in the puzzle can't be accounted for unless there's a third party in the picture. We don't know his name or his game but we have to find him if we want to protect Hope.

"Your job now is to fight Will's theory of a civil murder suit. Mine is to flush out Mr. or Ms. X." Loren reached his hand across the desk top to cover the hand of the old man facing him. "Partner," he said softly. They sat silent in the chill of the spring night.

NINE

ABOUT ten thirty the next morning, halfway through his con-stitutional liberties class, Loren became aware that something about the crowded lecture hall in front of him was not quite right. Near the end of the period, when he picked up his glasses and balanced them on his nose before reading a passage from *Palko v. Connecticut,* he saw what the problem was. There was one student too many in the room.

"....So you see, Cardozo begged the question. The test of whether a federal constitutional right binds the states through the Fourteenth Amendment can't be what Justice Cardozo said it was, can't be whether the right is 'implicit in the concept of ordered freedom,' because there's no such concept as ordered freedom, any more than there's a concept of tall shortness or strong weakness, or civilized war. Order and freedom are op-posites, they conflict in every society, and a win for one is a loss for the other." The end-of-class bell rang just as he was building up to a thunderous peroration, and the students col-lected books and papers noisily. "My preference is for free-dom. Next class we'll watch the Supreme Court of the McCarthy era tromp on my preference. Let's try to get up to 472 in the casebook." The class surged out through the swing-ing rear doors and within two minutes the vast lecture hall was empty except for Loren and the extra student.

He was an immensely fat man with hair and a suit the color of wet sand. A paperoid accordion file was tucked under his left arm. He moved slowly down the slope of the center aisle between the rows of trestle tables. He seemed to be moving in slow motion, as if he were afraid of rolling down the incline like a basketball down a hill.

"Greetings," he wheezed when he reached the professorial lectern, his chins wobbling gently. "I had a light morning so I thought I'd drop in early and soak up some legal knowledge. I bring you the latest snoop reports from my shami, which as all intellectuals know is the Latin plural of shamus."

"Hi, Marc." Loren returned the eraser to the chalkboard

ledge and extended his white-powdered hand. "There's another class in here next period. Let's go up to my shop." He piled his lecture materials under his arm and they climbed three flights to Loren's office. Marcus Jaan Hooft, panting furiously, lowered himself onto the fractional sectional like a drowning man climbing into a life raft and dumped the contents of the accordion folder on Loren's desk.

"I think you'll find these satisfactory," he beamed, and checked off their subjects on sausage-shaped fingers. "Hope Foxworth Dillaway; Will Dillaway; James Foxworth; Lola Foxworth, present wife of James; Marion Binns, ex-wife of James; Doreen Foxworth Josephson; Dr. Colonel Michael Josephson; Amanda Blair, divorced wife of the late Graham Dillaway; Lucy Martell; and last but not least, Miscellaneous."

"You didn't approach any of these people directly, I assume?"

Hooft lifted a pudgy hand as if to halt such a thought in its tracks. "Oh no no no, that would have been terribly unprofessional. None of the subjects knows of this investigation, that is to the best of our knowledge. We can't ensure that our sources won't mention something to a subject, of course. We take what precautions we can without doing anything too illegal. License, you know."

Something about Hooft's words made Loren disgusted with himself. He felt as if he had deliberately climbed into a field latrine. This damned case was turning him into the same kind of intelligence bureaucrat who had sent out Jackson Corby and hundreds of other agents to compile secret dossiers on dissidents.

Hooft penetrated Loren's stony silence. "Those reports cover all the matters you asked us to look into. Personal data on each subject, subject's relationships with the other subjects and with Mr. Dillaway, financial condition of each subject, whereabouts of each during the murder period, possible connections of subjects with hit men. Can I be of any further assistance?"

What kind of sick son of a bitch must he be, Loren wondered, to have ordered a secret dossier on Lucy?

"If not, I'll be on my way." Hooft struggled out of his seat. "It was a slow morning but I expect a brutal afternoon. My bill is under the bottom file."

"Wait," Loren grunted. "I want you to get me another file.

Everything you can find on him, and I mean everything. The name is Jackson Corby. He must have had a headquarters somewhere. Find it. Girlfriends, boyfriends, spending habits. I'm very interested in any safe-deposit boxes he may have rented. Did he leave a will? I want the works. And I also want you to find out how much of his trail the police have uncovered and why they've put the lid on. If you have to bribe people to get the answers, do it."

"Shocking instructions from a member of the bar," Hooft burbled. "Ah, this Watergate mentality!"

Loren wondered if he could convince the fat detective, or anyone else for that matter, that there was a difference between Watergate and what he was doing. Then he tried to formulate the difference and couldn't. He roused himself from self-contempt long enough to give Hooft the name and address of the former student assistant at the typewriter repair shop and ask him to try and locate the young man.

"I'll call if I learn anything important," said Marcus Jaan Hooft, and shook hands gravely with Loren and made an elephantine exit.

Loren gazed bleakly at the ten files. They seemed to hypnotize him. They attracted and repelled him so that he felt like an adolescent of strict religious upbringing among a rack of pornographic magazines. He tried to rationalize away his misgivings by telling himself that he was acting in a good cause. He didn't convince himself. He had heard that on the lips of too many war criminals. He told himself that the files would probably not tell him much more than he had already learned from his long talk with Lucy. That sounded better but still not good enough.

He couldn't think up a justification that satisfied him but in the end he read the files anyway.

First he went through them rapidly, then he reread them in detail. After the second reading he drew a fresh legal pad out of the desk and set to work capsulizing the papers down to essentials. An hour later he leaned back, tried to knead the writer's ache out of his hand, lifted his feet to a stack of Supreme Court advance sheets at the corner of the desk and read his abstract over.

DILLAWAY, HOPE FOXWORTH

Report confirms Lucy's account of Hope's literary downfall and alcohol problem. No hint of any other man in her life. Hooft's sources knew of no personal troubles between her and Graham (fat lot they know). Very close relationship between Hope and her son James. Hope's relationship with daughter Doreen cooled when she married Josephson who is old enough to be her father. Hope's behavior toward people runs in cycles: abuse them, bawl for understanding and forgiveness, abuse them. Personal finances wretched since her writing went downhill. Was definitely here in the city when Graham killed. Still possible that she could have hired a hit man. Mafioso called Luca Lomenzo or Lozano can't be located.

DILLAWAY, WILL

Unwed, unattached. Lives beyond what he makes as a writer. Second mortgage on house, heavy bank loans. One best-seller or big bequest and he'd be above water. Loved Graham intensely, hates Hope like the plague. Makes frequent visits to his mother, Amanda Blair. No significant contact between Will and Hope's children or their families. Was in Georgia on research trip when Graham was killed, but cannot rule out possibility of side trip to King Mountain at crucial time. Will is a licensed pilot and flies own plane. Has written articles on organized crime and no doubt has contacts who could have lined up a hit man for him. No known contacts between Will and Lucy.

FOXWORTH, JAMES

Moderately successful writer for paperbacks under several pseudonyms: private eye, Gothic, porno, etc. Best known for Steve Dusk private-eye series as by Angelo Anovella. Lives across state line in Farmwick where he seems to spend substantially more than he makes. Has borrowed large amounts from Hope without paying interest but Graham may have been about to crack down on Hope's generosity with what was essentially Graham's money. No significant contacts with Will, not much with sister Doreen since her marriage. James is presently on his second marriage. No children. Physically quite attractive in raffish Errol Flynn way. Was out of state at time of murders. Told police he was at Jersey seaside cottage of his literary agent for informal discussions about how to attract new publishers. Wife stayed home. Literary agent confirms James' alibi. Through researching his private-eye books James just might have met a professional hit man.

FOXWORTH, LOLA

Present (second) wife of James. Clinging blonde who likes expensive toys. Used to be stripper in New York City. If she had mob contacts from that time in her life they might have helped her speed money into her husband's pockets. She herself was definitely in Farmwick during the murders.

BINNS, MARION JEAN

Ex of James. Resumed maiden name after divorcing him (adultery, uncontested). Tall, dark, skinny, severe, intense looking—exact opposite of Lola. Married James before he broke into writing game, supported him first couple years. Persuaded court to make James pay her tuition and other expenses of getting advanced degrees in abstruse sciences, in her pursuit of which she had been interrupted when she married James and went to work to support him. She gains nothing by any inheritance of James, hence no apparent motive for her to kill Graham. Relations between her and Graham while she was married to James were okay. No present contact between her and any member of Dillaway family. Lives in upstate New York, completing degree at Canandaugus University.

JOSEPHSON, DOREEN FOXWORTH

Hope's daughter but not very friendly with her in recent years due to Hope's attitude toward Doreen's marriage to Josephson. Patching-up may be in progress since the Josephsons spent at least one night recently at Hope's penthouse. Doreen welcomed Graham into family when he married Hope. After Doreen's own marriage Graham tried unsuccessfully to reconcile Hope and Doreen. Doreen's own marriage seems very happy, no children. She is very much involved in community work. No contacts with underworld, no known contacts with the radical groups she was involved with in college. One source says that Doreen once before her own marriage slapped Will's face in public after Will insulted her mother. She sees her brother James seldom. Was definitely at home during murder period. Speeding along a large bequest is a powerful motive.

JOSEPHSON, MICHAEL, D.D.S.

In his late forties. Served as colonel in Army Dental Corps, retired after twenty years and second Vietnam tour. Moved to city, built up nice practice. Got involved in civic work, named to several mayor's blue-ribbon committees. Met Doreen after Graham came to him for dental work. Two years ago after strike threat from police over fringe benefits, city put Josephson on substantial retainer to handle dental work for all non-uniformed department personnel. Since then has curtailed his private practice drastically. Spends much time fixing teeth of ghetto children free. Was at dental convention in St. Louis at time of murders but could have slipped away and flown to King Mountain area. Was disliked intensely by Hope, but this may be healing. Finances quite sound. No prior marriages, no extracurricular sex life.

BLAIR, AMANDA

Graham's ex-wife, divorced in Mexico seven years

ago. Received generous settlement and returned to home in Nebraska. Confined to wheelchair since auto smashup two years ago, right leg paralyzed, living in private nursing home near Omaha. Hated Graham intensely but gains nothing financially from his death and has no underworld contacts. Never met any members of Foxworth family. Is visited regularly by Will but never was by Graham. Could she have incited Will to murder or arrange to murder Graham?

Loren hesitated before rereading his summary of the tenth report. The facts and inferences seemed too cold and dead.

MARTELL, LUCY

Worked as editorial assistant in various New York publishing houses, came here after marriage and divorce, got job eighteen months ago as secretary-assistant to Hope. Sources queried do not believe there was any sexual affair between her and Graham. Finances adequate. No known underworld contacts. Was in city with Hope at time of murders. No financial gain by Graham's death. No covert contacts discovered with Will.

But damn it, how if not from her had Will gotten Hope's new unlisted number within hours after it had become effective?

Suddenly Loren saw an answer to that question. *Why couldn't Will have done exactly what Loren himself had done?*

He clawed for the phone and dialed Mensing & Nalbin, identified himself to the office manager who had taken Connie Waller's place and asked him to speak to each and every secretary in the firm and find out whether any of them might have given out the unlisted number of a client named Hope Dillaway to the client's son Will Dillaway.

"Will you hold, please?" the office manager requested.

Five minutes later Loren had the answer. It was Yes. One of the secretaries remembered having done just that, late last Wednesday afternoon.

"Thank you very much," Loren said, and hung up.

So that was that. Will must have tried to call the penthouse
and had gotten the same recorded message Loren had heard
when he had attempted the same call that night from Vecchio's. Will guessed as Loren had that his stepmother's attorney would know the new number and had wangled it from an
office girl, although he'd waited till the next morning to make
his call.

The only concrete basis of Loren's misgivings about Lucy
had vanished as in a gust of wind, and with it the rest of his
doubts vanished too.

He felt lighthearted as a child, liberated, carefree, tempted
to shout with delight, tempted to call Lucy and tell her what a
flaming ass he had been and how happy he was now. He tossed
the dossiers and his own summations into the bottom drawer of
a file cabinet beneath a three years' accumulation of old law
examination papers. He bounced down the stairs and spring-
stepped across the scented green campus in an orgy of solitary
delight. Lucy filled his thoughts and he lost track of where he
was walking.

When his mind returned to the real world, he saw that he
was on a street just off campus. The block bristled with businesses catering to students: a rock music shop, several fast
food places, an art movie house, a used bookstore. The Book
Worm. He liked the name, and wondered if it stocked any of
the work of James Foxworth.

The bell jangled raucously as he stepped in. It took less than
a minute to find them, neatly arranged on the mystery-fiction
shelves under the letter A. Loren took half a dozen secondhand
adventures of Steve Dusk to the student behind the cash register, paid his dollar-plus-tax, and retraced his steps across the
campus.

He got no further schoolwork done that day. In fact he even
forgot to go to lunch. At the end of the afternoon he still sat in
his office, transfixed with laughter. He did everything but roll
on the floor. The walls echoed his roars of delight. Steve Dusk,
private eye, had reduced him to rollicking helplessness.

Long after dark he decided that he had to share his experience with someone and that only one particular person would
do. He dialed the unlisted number of the Dillaway penthouse.

"Hi, hey, hello there, kitten, this is Floren, the Loctor of
Daw!" That was as far as he got before a wave of uncontrollable laughter swept over him.

"Loren? Are you all right?" Sudden alarm gave an edginess to Lucy's voice.

"Oh, I'm in excellent health! Couldn't be better. I've spent most of the day purging myself of every worldly care in the company of a fellow called Steve Dusk. You know Steve?"

Lucy hesitated. "The name does seem to ring a bell but I can't...."

"He's a private detective. Not a real one, a fictional character, like Bogart. Oh, hell, I didn't mean like Bogart, he's twisted my brain around like a pretzel and everything's coming out silly. Steve Dusk is the character in some books by Hope's son. He's incredible! I happened to pick up half a dozen paperbacks about him before noon and I've been consuming them like peanuts ever since. James Foxworth is either the worst writer kicking his heels on this sorry old planet or else he's a genius so far ahead of his time it'll take us till the twenty-first century to catch up with him. I've got an irresistible itch to talk about this guy to somebody. Can you come over to my place in about an hour? Which reminds me I haven't eaten since breakfast. It's about time I cooked something for you in my own kitchen."

"Let me see if Mrs. Parkins will watch Hope for a few hours. I'll be right back."

Ninety minutes later Lucy and Loren were flinging cutlery around the Mensing kitchenette in the process of improvising a casserole. Soft chamber music from the stereo speaker was drowned out by Loren's excited tribute to the fabulous universe of Steve Dusk. Every few minutes he would snatch one of the six paperbacks from the counter beside the blender, refilling their glasses with banana daiquiris along the way, and read aloud from a page picked at random.

"'An engraved fresco of the Last Judgment hung in a wooden frame on the wall, laughing at we poor mortals.' 'Rocco Bonabuoni cradled the muzzle of his gat and looked across at me with a face full of irk.' 'With a touch of miff on my puss I turned away from the patio overlooking seven stories of sidewalk and glanced toward Dr. Scrot's office which was partly ajar.' Wait, wait, you ain't heard nothing yet. James writes his own rules of anatomy too besides his own rules of grammar and art and logic. Here's the great strip scene from *The Dead Have No Ears.* 'She unearthed one of her gorgeous breasts from the folds of her miniskirt.'"

"Oh, God, stop!" Lucy gasped in the middle of a swallow of daiquiri and rushed blindly for the sink. She bent over, choking with laughter and banana fragments, and Loren burped her like a baby until the strangled coughing died away and a semblance of normal color returned to her face.

"Oh, Loren, don't read me any more, my heart will give out. He's a madman! He's totally insane. No one could write lines like that and get them published. I've worked for publishers."

"You never worked for his publishers. Look, they're here, every glorious word I read. And his plots are just as crazy. They don't make the first bit of sense from one chapter to the next. He must sit down at the typewriter and reel these things off like a school kid making up a story as he goes along. But by God it works! Look, *The Dead Have No Ears,* Steve Dusk pitted against a mad strangler who cuts off the quote naked ears unquote of his lovely victims—I suppose clothed ears don't turn him on. *Chew My Flesh, Nibble My Bones,* with Steve Dusk versus three nymphomaniacs, two lesbians and a Mafia don who keeps piranhas in two little water tanks sewn into his coat sleeves. Don Fuo Manchuone no doubt. *Death and the Naked Ghouls,* that's the one where Dusk proves the killer walked around a nudist camp in full view of everyone, stark naked and carrying a Thompson submachine gun that no one ever noticed! I'm not kidding, Lucy, the man's a mad genius. He's created a whole universe the way the British used to say they got their empire—by inadvertence. How's the casserole coming?"

Lucy bent to inspect the glass door of the wall oven. "The cheese is just beginning to turn gold. Another ten minutes. Are you hungry?"

"Ravenous. I could eat your naked ear." He nuzzled her neck and caressed the wing of her back as he would have stroked a kitten. After a while he mumbled something into her hair.

"Didn't hear you," she breathed, wriggling against him.

"I said how about taking your shoes off so I can kiss your gorgeous elbows?"

That the cheese was burnt coal-black before Lucy remembered and squealed and jumped naked out of bed to turn off the oven was a regrettable accident for which neither of them was more to blame than the other.

TEN

FINALLY, Wednesday night, he told her.

After dinner they drove out of the city to a quiet hilltop above a lake. They wrapped themselves in blankets and looked down at the silken waters jeweled with light. He turned to her as she lay nestled beside him. "There's something I have to tell you." Quietly, not knowing how it would affect their future, he explained why he had had misgivings about her, why he had ordered an investigation of her, how his doubts had vanished. She did not change expression except that her eyelids lowered a bit as if she were sleepy.

"I guess I'm sorry," he finished. "I don't know. I committed myself to help Hope if I could, and getting that report on you was part of the job. I hated myself for doing it but I did it. I guess it was part right and part wrong. Everything is, except the things that are all wrong. I had to let you know." He bent closer to her. "Think we can still make it work between us?"

Slowly but without hesitation she molded herself against him and they shared a long quiet kiss.

"I've never been any good at relationships," he told her. "I got straight A's all through school, I'm a good lawyer, a pretty good teacher, anything that has to do with concepts or intellectual work I've always had a knack for. I'm one of those types that bleeds for the poor and oppressed as a class but I'm an absolute clod when it comes to relating to a specific human being."

"Oh, don't run yourself down—" she began.

"I have to say this. Even back in school I worked like a horse to keep things all light and casual and on the surface with you because I was sick in my gut with fear of really getting deeply involved with another person, and when things sort of got out of control between us I, well, I bugged out on you. For a while I told myself it was because I was ambitious to be a big-shot lawyer in those days and I thought having a cripple for a wife would get me about as far as marrying a black woman. I really believed that for years. But I was letting myself off too easy. I licked the money-and-success hangup but I haven't licked what made me run out on you. I get involved with all sorts of causes I believe in but it's still like pulling teeth for me to get involved with a person. You have to know that about me." He laughed softly. "The FTC makes people label all sorts of products with their true ingredients but doesn't say anything about labeling themselves."

"I'm the same way, Loren," she said. "I wasn't when I was younger but I told you my shell hardened, remember?" Their faces almost touched in the scented grass. "Do you know how my first marriage ended?"

"I gathered it wasn't very pleasant. The report didn't go into the subject."

"Everyone did a good job of covering it up," she said. "I got a job in New York in a publishing house and I met this man and we were married and then he was drafted and something happened to him. He volunteered to go to Vietnam. After he was shipped there he stopped writing me almost completely. He extended his tour an extra six months.

"When he finally came home he was someone different. He was hard and cruel and he loved to degrade people. Especially me. He said the only reason he married me was because he thought screwing a hunchback would be kinky. He told me things he did to women and children over there. Horrible things, things that still give me nightmares. Loren, I wouldn't wish the two months I stayed with him after he got back on the lowest vermin in the world."

"You left him then?"

"As soon as I could walk without falling over. When I filed for a divorce he got worse. He threatened to disfigure me so that my own mother would vomit at the sight of me. He really believed he had a license to maim and kill whenever he pleased."

"He couldn't understand that license only applied to gooks," Loren said.

"Then one day I was walking along Madison Avenue on the way back from lunch and he was behind me and I didn't know it. He spun me around and threw something out of a little bottle at my face but it was a windy day and he missed me. The acid hit a twelve-year-old girl who happened to be passing. She wound up being blinded for life. The police caught him and they tell me he'll spend the rest of his life in a hospital for the criminally insane. That's what hardened my shell."

Loren stroked her hair and kissed her eyes.

"When everything was over I came out here and got my job with Hope and there I was again, only this time it was somebody else's rotten marriage. I died a little inside every time she went after Graham because he was so quiet and understanding with her but she was the one who was sick and frustrated and desperate for help."

It was then that Loren realized that if he had been a different sort of person, if he hadn't run out on her nine years ago, none of those horrors would have happened to her. He held her in his arms and mumbled over and over: "Oh, Lucy, I'm sorry, I'm sorry, I did it to you, I did it."

"We'll build harbors for each other," she said. "It may take us awhile but we will." They lay back and listened to the birds and looked up into the empty night.

Thursday afternoon Loren was in his office, frantically trying to catch up with paperwork before the law library committee meeting, when the phone shrieked. He cursed and reached out, speaking his name into the mouthpiece in what he hoped was an emotionless tone.

"Oh, hi there, Mr. Mensing," a smooth affable voice greeted him. "Jim Foxworth speaking. You remember, we met in court the day they probated Graham's will."

Loren found it difficult to keep from breaking into a spontaneous literary homage to the ebullient creator of Steve Dusk but by calling on the self-repressive instincts built into him by years of legal training he avoided the temptation. "Oh, yes. What can I do for you, Mr. Foxworth?"

"A few days ago Mother happened to mention that you were doing some investigating for her lawyer on this pile of crap we've all fallen into."

"That's one way of putting it," Loren conceded. "The case seems to be stalled up several blind alleys right now."

"Well, it's the case that I'd like to talk with you about. Could you come out to my place in Farmwick tonight after dinner, say around eightish?"

Loren debated whether he could afford to take an evening off from the law school busywork that had been piling up. He decided he couldn't pass up a chance to spend the evening with the mad genius of the Foxworths. "Yes," he replied judiciously, "I think I could make it. Could you, ah, give me some idea of what you'd like to discuss with me?"

"Not-over-the-phone!" The words streamed out of James Foxworth like waters over Niagara. "Look, Mr. Mensing, I'm in sort of a bind and I don't know what the hell to do and you know the ropes so I'd like to pick your brains. Okay?"

"You're on." Loren sighed, wondering what development lay in ambush for him. "How do I get out to Farmwick?"

"Aw, I'm a clod when it comes to giving directions. Let me put my wife on the extension."

Loren heard a muffled request to someone named Lola to pick up the phone and then a female voice trilled brightly. "Oooh, hello out there, Mr. Whoever You Are!"

Loren remembered the characterization of Lola Foxworth in Hooft's report and chalked up another point for the fat detective. "Hello, Mrs. Foxworth," he said neutrally. And shortly he was taking down her instructions how to get to Farmwick— instructions which he had to ask her to repeat twice and which even the third time made no more sense to him than the plots of her husband's novels. "See you tonight," she finished, and "Thanks again, Mr. Mensing," James added, and they exchanged good-byes and broke connections.

Loren lost his way driving out to Farmwick but considering the directions he'd been given he expected to get lost and was not greatly upset.

At 8:22 P.M. by his dashboard clock he turned left off Walkers Lane and followed the serpentine bends of Hillcrest Drive past neatly spaced suburban split-levels. Tricycles stood parked in driveways, lawn sprinklers arced fine spray, television sets and squabbling children made noise. Loren braked the VW in front of 4179 and followed the fieldstone pathway to the front door. On the horizon the last of the twilight deepened to evening. The door opened before he reached it and a man held the outer aluminum screen door with one hand and extended the other in greeting.

"Loren Mensing? Hi, Jim Foxworth. Good to see you again, come on in." He looked the way Loren vaguely remembered him from the probate hearing. Medium height, trim build, high forehead, Guards mustache. He wore a blue Madras shirt and matching slacks and smiled as though he meant it. His voice was casual, relaxed, velvet-smooth. He led Loren up three steps into a red-carpeted living room that looked lived in rather than displayed. A small but delightfully curved blonde uncurled herself from the corner of the claret couch.

"Loren Mensing, my wife, Lola," James said.

"Hi, Loren Mensing," Lola welcomed him. "Come sit by me while Jimmy builds us some drinks."

James took their orders and bent over the liquor cabinet for bottles and glasses while Loren and Lola sat thigh to thigh on the couch and chatted about nothing. There was a warning glint in James' eye as he handed Loren a J&B on the rocks but Loren didn't need the warning. He had already decided not even to hint at the purpose of his visit in front of the seductive little emptyhead. Lola's next words helped keep the talk light and safe.

"What do you do, Loren Mensing?"

"Just Loren. I'm an attorney," he equivocated.

"Oooh, Jimmy, that bitch Marion isn't taking you to court again, is she?" Lola stared wide-eyed at her husband.

Loren noticed that James seemed to wince at the question. "Let's hope not, kid," he said in gruff Bogart style, and gave her long gold hair a paternal pat. "No, honey, Loren's not that kind of a lawyer. We've got some contracts with a couple of publishers to look over, that's all."

Loren decided to take advantage of the cue. "You know," he remarked, "it's only recently that I actually began reading some of your books for enjoyment. The Steve Dusk series, I mean."

"Oh, you like Steve Dusk." James' words may have been a statement or may have been a command. They certainly weren't a question. His eyes lit up as if someone had turned on a switch. "Yeah, everyone says old Steve's my best character. My Gothics and movie tie-ins and porno sell better but hell, I can write those sure-fire sellers in my sleep. When I do a Dusk the sky's the limit and I let myself go wild."

He stood up and beckoned Loren to join him at an old-fashioned secretary-desk against the west wall. "Here, let me show you the complete works," he offered guilelessly. Loren saw that the shelves were crowded with well over a hundred paperbacks. On the top shelf sat his old friends *The Breastless Bodies, Ship of Ghouls, The Dead Have No Ears, Chew My Flesh, Nibble My Bones,* and all the other adventures of the private eye to end all private eyes. The next shelf held translations of the Duskiad into French, German, Italian, Japanese, and at least two languages Loren couldn't identify. On the lower shelves were paperbound Gothics under five female by-lines—"They're all me," James said proudly—and movie and TV series novelizations. Beneath eye level on the lowest shelf stood *Harem Pussy, Lust Fever,* and a dozen similar titles. "Mine are the healthy heterosexual ones," James said. "Don't get the wrong idea from them. I'm not a sex maniac, except in bed of course ha-ha. The only erotica in my house is what I've written myself."

"You certainly have turned out a lot of books," Loren said, completely at a loss for anything else to say.

James Foxworth shrugged modestly. "It's in my blood. If I don't write, I dry up."

"Jimmy can write a book in four days!" Lola cooed.

"That's only when someone shoves a deadline under my nose," the creator and sole proprietor of the Duskiverse added. "Most of these take ten days to two weeks. I do ten or twelve a year, the rest of the time I swim, play golf, loaf around, write letters to my fans, putter around the playroom—it's a great life. I just have one problem. Sixty-seven books in six years, and still if I walk down Main Street and somebody says 'Hey, there goes Jim Foxworth' somebody else says 'Jim who?'"

"Jimmy threw an autograph party for himself last year and no one came!" Lola interpolated brightly.

The subject of his own anonymity suddenly seemed to pall on James Foxworth. He picked up his scotch glass and nodded knowingly at Loren. "Well, you don't want to hear my troubles. Honey, will you excuse us? I'm going to take Loren into the den and get our business done. Bring your drink, Loren."

Loren followed his host up a red-carpeted mini-staircase to a room on the upper level. STEVE DUSK in raised white letters glowed on the door. Foxworth turned the knob and palmed the lights on. Loren saw a desk, typewriter on a folding table, day-bed, file cabinet. The typewriter was not a Griem, he noted. A few bookshelves held standard reference works which looked dusty and unused and extra copies of James' own output. James sat Eisenhower-style in the straight-backed chair while Loren took the daybed.

"Life's weird," James began. "Here I've written umpty-ump scenes where people get involved with the cops, I never have any trouble turning them out and they read smooth as honey, but ever since this afternoon I've been trying to figure out how to tell this to you and it's still got me whipped. Look, let me do it the way I do the Dusks, I'll start in the middle and work my way around to both ends."

Loren silently filed away this tidbit of insight into the Dusk man's methods of composition.

"I asked you out here," James went on, "because I know a bit about you. You cleaned up some toughies for the city cops a couple of years ago when you were legal adviser or whatever. And of course Mother told me that her lawyer had brought you into our own mess as some kind of investigator.

"Now let me ask you a question. Your friends on the force must have given you the poop on all of us, right?"

Loren wondered how to answer without giving away the Hooft Agency's private surveillance of the Dillaway and Foxworth families. "You might put it that way," he said finally.

"Then you know I was supposed to be out on the Jersey shore at my agent's place when Graham's cabin was hit."

Loren nodded with what he hoped was an expression of quiet wisdom.

"I wasn't," James said. "The cops don't know that yet but I think they're going to find out pretty soon. My agent's getting scareder by the day about giving me a phony alibi and I don't think he can hold out much longer before he spills it."

Loren leaned forward on the lumpy daybed and fought to keep one curve ahead of the twists and turns of James' account. "Why are you telling me this?" He tried not to let his face reflect the pace of his thoughts.

Foxworth laughed. "You won't believe this, Loren, but it's the God's honest truth. I don't know how to go about persuading the cops what really happened. I've never had any serious dealings with cops or murder in my life."

Which explains something more about the adventures of Steve Dusk, Loren saw. "And you want to use me as a sort of middleman?"

"Something like that. You see, actually I've got a perfect alibi for the whole day but I can't prove it and I'm afraid it'll bollix things up royally if I use it."

"All right," Loren said. "I'm on the hook. Where were you?"

"Upstate New York," James told him. "Canandaugus University. Screwing the legs off my first wife."

Loren adjusted his head against the daybed cushions as though to protect it from shock and waited for further enlightenment.

"Look, you have to understand the background." James emptied his drink with one swallow. "When Marion and I got married I was a kid with no money and too much pride to let Mother support me and a dream of being the next Hemingway. She was the intellectual wizard type, working for some kind of advanced degree in science. She had to quit school and take a job in a crummy little medical lab to support the both of us while I tried to break into the lit biz. It was tough sledding at first but then I began to make it and the marriage started to go sour. We broke up and she got a divorce and there's where I blew it. I guess I felt guilty so I didn't fight it when she asked for a clause in the property settlement that would make me pay the rest of the way for her degrees. I've been paying for three years now and she's still in school. It's always another semester or another science, or the tuition has gone up, or she needs an increase because of inflation. She's hauled me back to court five times since the divorce and gotten five increases, plus I have to pay my lawyer and her lawyer every time we get on the merry-go-round. I'm so deep in the hole I can't keep my head above water. I've had to borrow from Mother just to pay our living expenses.

"Okay, that's the background. Two months ago Marion comes up with a new nifty. She wants me to finance a post-doctoral degree in some new area in physical chemistry. Her lawyer says there's an ambiguity in the property settlement and the court will make me pay up.

"Now that was the straw that put my back to the wall. I made up my mind I had to fight her. And between you and I, Loren, I had the right weapon." James exhibited a wide virile grin. "I figured she just hadn't been getting enough of what every woman wants since we split. Now I knew I could take care of that, but the problem was I couldn't let Lola know what I was doing. She's a great kid, in and out of the sack, but she just wouldn't understand the bind I was in.

"So I arranged this phony trip to Jersey. I told my agent I had to get away for a few days on extremely private business. Well, Steve Dusk has put a lot of coin in old Harry's jeans so he went along with the gag. I flew out to Jersey and rented a car at the airport and drove to Canandaugus and stayed in the sack with Marion for three days and nights. Nonstop."

Loren decided that it would be impolite to question the literal truth of James' last statement. Instead he chose a safer question. "Did it work? Did she back off on her threat?"

James Foxworth shook his head in a frenzy of frustration. "I thought the old persuader had persuaded her, but then this damned murder story broke in the papers. The cops came and I gave them the Jersey story. Then two days ago Marion went puritan on me. She called long-distance and said that if I told anyone I'd been shacking up with her while someone was making a piece of toast out of Graham, she'd call me a liar and swear she hadn't seen me since the last time we were in court. Then old Harry called up to tell me he was getting colder and colder feet about confirming my phony alibi to the cops. So that's when I knew as sure as I know I'm a good writer that I was going to be in hot you-know-what before many more days went under the bridge.

"Now you tell me, Loren, what the hell should I do?"

Loren scrambled up from the daybed and paced the small room, sorting out possibilities. On the one hand, Foxworth just might be an extremely clever murderer who saw his original alibi in danger of exploding and was desperately trying to replace it with an alternate. But it was just as possible that he had been telling Loren the truth, or that truths and lies were hopelessly intermingled in his story.

He swung back to face the author. "Can you prove you rented that car in Jersey?"

James nodded. "Yeah. I used my credit card. But the outfit I rented from doesn't charge by the mile, it's a flat rate by the day plus gas. I can't prove how many miles I drove and I don't know if they keep mileage records after a guy returns a car. Anyway, even if they do, how can I prove I didn't drive from Jersey straight out to King Mountain and set back the speedometer before I brought the heap in?"

"If you can establish what you were doing while you had the car it might help," Loren advised him. "Did you see anyone at all in Canandaugus? Go out to get food or liquor? See any movies? Did anyone ask you for your autograph or when the next Dusk would be out? Anything that might prove you were actually there."

Foxworth knitted his bushy brows together so that they made a single dark trail across his creased forehead. "Well, let's see. I did stop at...."

"It won't do you any good to tell me," Loren interrupted. "Get it all down on paper, every detail you can remember. What your wife wore, the furniture where you stayed, everything. Pretend you're Theodore Dreiser or something. When the police come to find out why you lied the first time, you'll have a complete record to give them. Maybe with a little luck they can dig around in Canandaugus and locate someone who can confirm your story or break down Marion's."

James looked up at Loren, his eyes wide with anxiety. "But suppose the cops don't buy my story? Suppose they claim I made it up?"

"In that case," Loren suggested angelically, "you might consider hiring a private eye...."

ELEVEN

AT five o'clock Friday afternoon Loren was making a rough translation of Nazi judicial decrees for his book and debating whether he should cook his own dinner or go out when the phone rang. He snapped shut his Brockhaus lexicon and scooped up the receiver. "Mensing."

"Nalbin here. I thought I should bring you up to date on the legal situation in re Dillaway's estate."

"You know, with a little bit of work on the meter that would be a poem," Loren pointed out. "I'm sorry, Stanford, I was wool-gathering. I've been too swamped to give you a ring and find out what's happened since Monday night."

Nalbin cleared his throat loudly. "Our answer to their petition to set aside probate of the will is being typed this afternoon. We are moving to dismiss their petition and our supporting brief is along the lines I laid out in our last discussion. So far the press has not picked up the story but I am afraid they may when our papers are served on the other side. The next motion day is a week from Wednesday and I assume our case will be set down for argument at that time. Needless to say that whoever loses will appeal all the way to the state supreme court."

"Have you explained things to Mrs. Dillaway yet?"

"The day before yesterday," Nalbin replied. "She literally turned white with fury when I told her what her stepson was doing. Today her secretary called to ask me to attend a sort of war council in Mrs. Dillaway's penthouse tomorrow evening at seven thirty. I gather that Mrs. Dillaway's children by her first marriage and their spouses will be present. I would like you to attend also since you've been involved in the legal aspects of this affair from the beginning."

Loren salvaged his appointment pad from the maze of German documents on his desk. "What do you think Hope has in mind? Any reason to believe I'm really needed?"

"I am not sure what is on her mind," Nalbin said. "But if certain fears of mine are well founded, your presence is absolutely essential."

"All right. Thanks for filling me in. See you tomorrow." As soon as they had hung up Loren dialed for an outside line and called the Dillaway number.

"Hi, Lucy, me again. How are things going? What's this I hear about a strategy meeting tomorrow night?"

"I don't know, Loren. Hope has been acting deviously the last day or so. Whatever she's planning, she wants to spring it as a surprise. She had me call Mr. Nalbin and the Josephsons and James and Lola Foxworth. Was it one of them who told you?"

"Nalbin. Not only told me but wants me to come. I was hoping we could go somewhere tomorrow night but I guess this meeting ties you up."

"Maybe she'll finish early and we can get a drink or a snack later," Lucy suggested.

"Deal," Loren said. "See you at seven thirty."

He decided to eat out and work on his translations after dinner. It was after ten when he went home. He had mixed himself a drink and put a Shostakovich symphony on the record changer when the phone rang. He lowered the volume to where it was barely audible and picked up the receiver.

"Mr. Mensing?" It was a woman's voice, young and vibrant. "I'm Doreen Josephson. We met in court when my stepfather's will was probated, I don't know if you remember."

"I remember distinctly." Loren leaned back in his easy chair and reached to the end table for his drink. "What can I do for you, Mrs. Josephson?"

The woman seemed uncertain how to phrase what she wanted to say. "Well, actually I'm calling for my husband. Mike's really a very shy man, but he wanted to tell you how impressed he was with your work as deputy legal adviser to the police commissioner when he was on the mayoral commission two years ago. And now that you're working to help my mother, we'd, well, we'd like to get to know you better, if that's all right with you."

"I'd be delighted." Loren's answer was mechanical. Something in Doreen Josephson's voice told him that more than social amenities were involved in this call.

"Could you have dinner with us tomorrow, say around five thirty?"

"Rather early for dinner, isn't it?" Loren asked casually.

"We have to go somewhere later in the evening."

"Same place I'm going," Loren told her. "Mr. Nalbin asked me to sit in on your mother's powwow. But I'll be very happy to have dinner with you. Any particular place?"

"Mike's favorite is La Ronde, it's about a mile from our house. Why don't you take a cab out here and we'll drive you to Mother's and back to your own place when the meeting is over?"

An arrangement that would make it difficult to get any privacy with Lucy later in the evening, Loren realized. "Thanks very much but I may have another stop to make after the meeting. I'll bring my own car. Now how do I get to your place?"

Doreen Josephson gave him directions to a hillside suburb just inside the city limits. "Why don't you come by around five so we can all have a drink before dinner?" Loren agreed and they exchanged thanks and good-byes.

Sipping meditatively at his drink, he wondered what might be on the minds of the dentist and his wife. Another guilty secret like James Foxworth's? Could Michael have been in some woman's bed instead of at the dental conference in St. Louis at the time of Graham Dillaway's death? Was Doreen the secret mistress of a forest ranger and had she had a sylvan tryst with her lover coincidentally near the King Mountain cabin at the time of the fire? Was it chance that both James Foxworth and the Josephsons wanted to talk with him before the conference with Hope?

Naturally these baseless speculations led him nowhere. After a while he gave up, killed his drink with a gulp and raised the volume on the record changer for the third movement.

Loren's Saturday morning breakfast dishes were rinsing merrily in the washer when the downstairs annunciator buzzed. He stepped to the wall and depressed the talk button. "Yes?" he called loudly into the metallic speaker.

Mksft, the thing crackled back at him.

"Can't hear you!" Loren shouted, cupping his hands around the tiny microphone.

Mksft! Mksft! Prtnt! squawked the machine.

Now that his ears were accustomed to the extraterrestrial sounds of the annunciator, he understood that the visitor downstairs was Marcus Jaan Hooft and that he had important news. Loren pressed the door release button impatiently. A minute and a half later, standing in the doorway in shirt sleeves, he waved a hand in greeting as the fat detective wheezed out of the elevator.

"You're too late for a lovely breakfast, Marc. Beautiful fluffy pineapple pancakes, roast beef hash, the juiciest cantaloupe I've had in years....Would you like the other half of the cantaloupe?"

"I'm too busy to eat," Hooft stated without the slightest hint that his tongue was in his cheek.

"The millennium!" Loren proclaimed. "All right, what has made you too busy to eat? Don't tell me the Corby matter's put you off your feed!"

"I've made progress," the chubby sleuth burbled. "It has cost you a small fortune in bribes but I know a bit about what the police have been doing. They found three safety-deposit boxes, each under a different name, and there was dynamite in them. Not only the evidence on which he was getting his hush money but the names and addresses of the victims. There were seventeen besides Dillaway. I wasn't able to learn their names but the police are investigating thoroughly, if quietly, and if any one of sixteen out of those seventeen names is responsible for the deaths on King Mountain, he will be caught."

"What about Number Seventeen?" Loren demanded.

"Number Seventeen as you call him is a *very* special case. It was because of Number Seventeen that the police have behaved so peculiarly in this affair." Hooft paused to beam with pleasure at the effect he was creating. "Number Seventeen has an office in Washington, D.C.," he went on. "Pennsylvania Avenue. I needn't tell you the street number."

"God," Loren breathed.

"Or one who would love to be thought such," Hooft added. "Now I have no details but I've been told on good authority that some of the late Mr. Corby's—ah—intelligence operations were on special assignment to, well, indirectly to Number Seventeen. And that some if not all of these operations were *extremely* illegal. And that Mr. Corby ran true to form and eventually after leaving the service of his country put in a bid for some hush money."

"Just like E. Howard Hunt," Loren muttered.

"What? I don't follow."

"Did you read the Watergate transcripts? When everyone was talking about how to handle Hunt's demands for money, don't you think it's surprising that none of them ever suggested the obvious recourse of killing him?"

"Inaudible," Hooft burbled.

"Exactly. Now obviously it wasn't safe to kill Hunt. But suppose the decision was made that it *was* safe to kill Corby?"

"Now you see why the police have acted so queerly." Marcus Hooft blew delicately on the lenses of his thick glasses. "They don't know it happened that way, they can't prove it happened that way, but if it did happen that way they don't want any part of it."

Loren was too stunned at the news to say anything. He sat with his head buried between his hands and thought furiously.

"Let me share a rumor with you," Hooft offered generously, "since you were so kind as to offer to share your cantaloupe with me. Two investigators from the staff of the House Judiciary Committee flew to the capital early this week. Apparently they also made a visit to King Mountain. Now this is only a rumor."

"Wow!" Loren said stupidly. "Expletive deleted."

"Now of course there is no positive evidence so far to suggest that Number Seventeen wasn't just as docile a victim as all the other marks. On the other hand...."

"My God," Loren cut in. "He murdered a couple of million innocent Vietnamese, he's run roughshod over the Constitution since the day he took office. Wouldn't it be ironic if they nailed him for having a lousy blackmailer zapped? No, that's just too beautiful to be true." He lapsed into another stunned silence.

"Well," Marcus Jaan Hooft lumbered out of his chair, "I just thought you'd like to know." He bobbed his chins by way of advance warning. "My bill will be very high for this one."

Saturday afternoon, 5:07 by the dashboard clock, Loren swung the fastback into Cedar Crescent Drive. Pastel split-levels lined both sides of the street. Flowering bushes divided the manicured green lawns into parcels. He parked in front of a corner lot. A neat white post in the grass read MICHAEL JOSEPHSON, D.D.S. He followed a path of tinted stone to a doorway and, obeying the directions on a printed card, rang bell and walked in. An air conditioner hummed in the clubby pickled-pine waiting room. A heavyset black woman in a flowered print dress sat on a low couch, the skin around her eyes tight with tension, fingertips pressed together as if in prayer. The only other person in the room was a chunky fiftyish white man on the edge of a chair in a corner who was rubbing his palm tenderly against his puffy jaw.

"Sergeant Hackett, isn't it?" Loren dropped to the chair beside the man and held out his hand. "We met when I was legal adviser to the commissioner, remember? Loren Mensing."

The older man took the hand absently. "Oh, yeah, sure, how's tricks?" he mumbled. "Don't mind the way I sound, the doc pulled an abscessed tooth last week and my mouth still ain't back to normal. Came for some more pain pills."

Loren tried to take the sergeant's mind off his misery. "How are things in your shop?"

"Rough," Hackett growled. "Shake-up's afoot. Five guys were suspended this month. They're charged with running their own vice ring on off-duty time. More are going to get nailed before the month's out if you ask me."

An inner door opened and a tall chestnut-haired woman entered the waiting room. Her starched white laboratory coat fell to her knees and her arm was around the shoulder of an adolescent black girl who walked as though in a trance. Doreen Josephson helped the girl to the couch where the older black woman was sitting.

"Odetta was a wonderful patient, Mrs. Simms, and that tooth will never bother her again. The anesthetic will wear off in an hour or so. Now do you remember what the doctor said about the pills, Odetta?"

"Yes, ma'am," the girl said weakly. "Red pill every four hours the next three days and take a white pill if the pain act up."

They chatted for another minute, then the black mother and daughter left. Doreen watched them through the curtained window as they walked up the street to the boulevard bus stop. She turned and took a small paper-wrapped packet from her lab coat and handed it to Sergeant Hackett. "Please forgive the delay." She smiled. "My husband just finished emergency oral surgery on that girl."

"No sweat, Mrs. J, but I tell you straight, I need these bad. Thank the doc again for me, will you?" Hackett tore open the wrapping, unscrewed the bottle cap and swallowed two pills without water, then pocketed the bottle and extended a moist hand to Loren. "Good to see you again, Mr. Mensing," he muttered, and let himself out. Doreen locked the entrance door behind him.

"I hope you'll forgive the disorder too. We didn't expect to be working this late." Doreen shrugged out of the lab coat. Beneath it she wore a sleeveless black cocktail dress with a sparkle-studded belt at the waist. "The poor girl came in an hour ago after suffering the tortures of the damned for a week and Mike said that tooth had to go. He's washing up now. Come this way and we'll have a drink."

She led Loren through an inner hall that smelled of antiseptic. Small cubicles along the corridor were lined with instrument racks and white-painted metal filing cabinets. She tossed her lab coat down a laundry chute and opened the steel door at the end of the hall. The living quarters on the other side looked like a good place for a medical man to relax in. Wall paneling glowed dully and the forest-green carpeting set off the pale green of chairs and couch. An oak bar fronted by black leather high stools dominated one corner. Loren mounted a stool and Doreen stepped behind the bar. He was sipping a scotch sour when the steel door creaked open behind him and he half turned on the high seat.

Michael Josephson walked in with his head lowered as though lost in thought. Loren thought he seemed older and more tired than when they had met in court, but perhaps Josephson always looked worn out after oral surgery. The dentist's sideburns and mustache were trim and flecked with gray but his shoulders were still straight and his belly reasonably under control.

"Ah, Professor Mensing." He held out a pink freshly scrubbed hand. "Glad you didn't have to sit and wait for me. Darling, make my sour a double, after that cliff-hanger with Odetta I need it....Ah, that's good. If our taxes go up again you can get a job tending bar at La Ronde. Did Doreen tell you that's where we're dining tonight, Professor?"

"Loren," he corrected.

The conversation over dinner flew from current movies to Watergate to the manufacture of material for dental fillings. But through the salad and hot cheese bread and chicken Kiev a question plagued Loren like a splinter under a fingernail. Why had he been invited to this meal? Josephson seemed to be watching him with a sort of sophisticated wariness as if Loren were an enemy general at a negotiating session. The scrutiny made Loren feel subtly disoriented.

"....God? Of course not." The dentist made a precise incision with his fork into the cream pastry. "Whoever believes in God denies the horrors he has seen with his own eyes. One is born in pain, lives in pain, dies in pain, and when I die the worms won't know what kind of man they're eating."

"Oh, Mike, how morbid." Doreen Josephson turned to Loren as if to apologize. "Mike had a year in Korea and two in Vietnam. He still won't talk about them much even to me. Personally I'm more of an optimist. Things get better little by little. You just have to be patient." She smiled at Loren across the table and her necklace glinted in the soft tint of the light. "Mike and I don't always agree, you see, but then whoever said you have to agree with someone you love?" The way she looked at her husband said more about her feelings toward him than a hundred books could say. Loren felt empty and alone and envious. He wondered just what Colonel Josephson had seen in Asia, and how much he had had to do with his wife's deradicalization.

"Religion is a form of escape," Michael went on, spacing his words with solemn care. "A very effective form. Everyone finds life intolerable in one way or another. Who wouldn't escape completely from what he is and remake himself if he could?" He sipped coffee, wiped his lips with the snowy napkin. "The essence of religion is that anyone can. Mistakes are not final. God will forgive. I find that escape route too easy."

"You sound like an expert," Loren remarked casually.

"I've taken the hard route," the dentist said, and behind his hooded eyes Loren sensed an agony beyond words. He felt he had to change the subject drastically.

"You were Graham Dillaway's dentist, weren't you?" he asked.

"Both the Dillaways started coming to me shortly after I left the military and moved here," Josephson replied absently. "Hope stopped when Doreen and I started seeing each other but Graham stayed with me. Small loss." He grinned ruefully at his wife. "Hope's teeth were in wretched shape but Graham always took better care of himself, brushed after meals, kept away from sweets...."

"How many girls wind up marrying their mother's dentist?" Doreen wondered, and reached under the tablecloth to squeeze her husband's hand.

And amid the hum of other diners' conversations and the glidings of waitresses and the chink of silverware Loren wondered again what he was doing here. What was the point of the invitation? Or was the point that there was no point? Or had the point not been reached yet? Loren felt like a theatergoer who is uncertain whether the players were going to remember to perform the third act.

But the talk over second cups of coffee remained trivial, and as they drove separate cars to the Dillaway apartment Loren decided that there had been no ulterior motive behind the dinner.

Even with the VW he couldn't find a parking space within six blocks of the apartment building. When he pressed the penthouse buzzer he didn't know if the Josephsons had already arrived or were behind him somewhere. Lucy opened the door, lovely in a brown knit dress. She stretched upward to kiss his lips and he held her tight and breathed in the enticing scent of her hair.

"We can't do anything wicked just yet," she whispered, her soft brown eyes gleaming. "Everyone's waiting for you. Meeting's about to be called to order."

"Afterwards?" Loren fondled her back. He wished they could forget the meeting and race to her bedroom instead.

"If I'm in the mood." She laid his hand on her breast for a moment and then eased it away. "Come on now, we can't look mussed."

In the huge front room Loren exchanged greetings with Hope Dillaway and Stanford Nalbin and James Foxworth and nodded again to the Josephsons. He noticed that Lola Foxworth was not in sight and assumed that James had cajoled her into staying home.

The creator of Steve Dusk turned to whisper in Loren's ear like a conspirator. "Old Harry hasn't spilled the beans yet but I wrote up everything I did in Canandaugus like you said. Reads terrific. I might turn it into a story when this is all over."

Loren found a place on a divan with its back to the low stone wall around the fireplace. The Josephsons sat on a matching divan across from him, Nalbin occupied three inches of the seat of an overstuffed chair on Loren's right and James Foxworth lounged in a black leather reclining chair beside the old lawyer. Lucy rolled a peach hassock into the arc of seats and placed it next to Loren.

Hope Foxworth Dillaway sat in her high-backed plush chair which blocked the opening in the stone wall. She sat motionless as a carved image. Loren twisted in his seat and studied her, trying to penetrate the intense mask of her face.

When she cleared her throat the undercurrents of small talk died and the room fell still.

"I asked you here this evening," she began, "because I believe you are all on my side. Some of you may not know what my—stepson has done this week. Mr. Nalbin?" She bowed slightly to the ancient attorney and bared her teeth in a smile that reminded Loren of Dracula.

Stanford W. Nalbin coughed importantly and strode to the center of the group. Then, as if realizing that no matter whom he faced his back would be to some of the party, he returned to his overstuffed chair. With the precision of a pedant he summarized the events leading up to Will Dillaway's action to prevent his stepmother from taking under his father's will and the legal theory behind that action.

"....So much for the legal issues." The old man's voice had begun to crack during the presentation. "As I stated before, we have filed a motion to dismiss. The matter will be argued a week from next Wednesday and it is a foregone conclusion that the loser will appeal. Mrs. Dillaway will not have to submit to interrogatories or depositions or the like until and unless the Supreme Court rules that this kind of suit can be maintained against her. My opinion is that the matter will ultimately be decided in our favor, but we will be in the courts with it for many months before it will be resolved." Nalbin took a raspy breath and darted glances around the arc as if looking for questions in the faces of his audience. Finding none, he allowed himself an extra inch of the chair seat.

"I am not so confident," said Hope Dillaway in a voice of venom.

Instantly every eye focused on her. She drew herself erect and glared malevolently at the room. Loren sensed that something was about to happen.

"I need a more reliable weapon than legal oratory," she went on. "And I know a good one." She paused again and held the pause to let the tension mount. Loren saw that she still had some of the storyteller's arts built in her.

"Mr. Nalbin," she demanded. "If by chance my stepson should win, and I should be found—what was your phrase?—civilly guilty of the murder of my husband, how would Graham's property be disposed of?"

Nalbin snapped open the attaché case at his feet and consulted a sheaf of papers. "As for all but one class of property the law seems quite clear," he replied. "Mr. Dillaway's estate would be distributed as if you had predeceased him. And you will recall that under the reciprocal wills you and Mr. Dillaway executed, if you had died first he would have inherited your estate for his lifetime, and on his death both of your estates would have been divided equally among Will Dillaway and your own two children." He nodded toward Doreen and James as if pointing them out to their mother.

"Suppose I revoke that will?" Hope said.

Dead silence followed her question, and Loren's mind raced.

"Because that is exactly what I intend to do, and at once." She bit out the words through lips taut with fury. "I am going to make a new will. Lucy, dear"—her voice softened for a moment to a semblance of humanity—"you will receive a very generous bequest for putting up so long with an annoying old lady. James and Doreen, you will share what is left." Her tone hardened to steel and broken glass. "My beloved stepson will get nothing."

A buzz of excited comment broke out. Loren scanned the arc for the family's reactions. Doreen and Michael Josephson were talking in low intense whispers, Doreen's eyes narrowed into slits of concentration. The dentist rolled a half-smoked cigar between his long spatulate fingers and his face was an introspective mask. James Foxworth sank into the depths of the black leather reclining chair and expelled a low ecstatic breath, and Loren recalled how deeply the young author was in debt.

He turned to see how Lucy had taken the news. She sat hunched forward on the hassock, and he thought there was an edge of sadness in her eyes.

Stanford Nalbin barked a loud cough. He seemed distressed but not really surprised by what the widow had said. "I was afraid that was what you had in mind," he said to his client. "But I must advise you that you cannot do it."

Hope hurled herself out of the chair and for a second Loren was afraid she would physically attack the old man, like the ancient king who executed messengers with bad news. "What the hell do you mean I can't do it?" she shrieked. "It's my money! I inherited Graham's property under his will and I can leave it as I please. This is still the United States of America and I can change my will as often as I damn well choose to!"

"Ah, but there are exceptional circumstances here." Loren had to admire his coolness under fire and suddenly felt a closeness to his father's partner that he had never experienced during his time with the firm.

"What are you talking about?" Hope demanded harshly.

"Well, first of all let me return to that one special class of property I mentioned a few moments ago. You may not be aware of this, but Section 24 of the Federal Copyright Act places a part of Mr. Dillaway's estate—of any author's estate—beyond his control. Would you happen to know in what year your husband's first book was published?"

Hope Dillaway looked blank and swiveled her head in Lucy's direction.

"In 1948, I think," Lucy replied. "A few years after the end of World War Two anyway."

"As you know, Mrs. Dillaway, the term of copyright is twenty-eight years," Nalbin went on, "which is renewable for an additional twenty-eight years."

A look of scorn passed over the widow's dissipated features. *"Of course* I know that," she said.

"Ah, but did you know that Section 24 gives an author's widow *and children* all the unvested renewal rights in his work and provides that no will can disinherit them?"

The mask of scorn began to crack. Loren wondered what would replace it on Hope's face.

"And since the first renewal on Mr. Dillaway's books does not come up until 1976, the result is that once the renewal period of any title commences, then you as the author's widow and Will as his only child share the proceeds on that title until the work goes into the public domain. Of course, during the initial copyright term and before renewal, the author's will governs, but after the first twenty-eight years the author has no say in the matter."

If looks could repeal statutes, Loren thought, Section 24 of the Copyright Act would now be as dead as the fugitive slave laws. He had never seen such a look of naked rage as the one that possessed Hope.

Nalbin adjusted himself more comfortably in his chair. "Now let us consider Mr. Dillaway's rather substantial assets apart from the value of his writings. Even if you should change your will so as to cut out your stepson, the change would obviously be null and void if he should win the suit he has commenced. As I explained before, in such an event he would be awarded one third of Mr. Dillaway's estate."

"I'll take that chance," Hope declared. "They can't prove I killed Graham."

"Yes, but even if the suit fails I think you must still let those reciprocal wills stand. You came into your husband's estate on the strength of the understanding between you that upon the death of whoever died later, your children and his child would share both your estates. Now that Mr. Dillaway's estate has passed to you it would be unconscionable for you to divest his only child."

"There was no understanding between my husband and me," Hope said, "except what was written in our wills. Mr. Mensing." She glared balefully at Loren. "You drew those wills. Does either of them say they can't be revoked?"

Suddenly Loren felt the eyes of everyone in the room focused on him. A clammy feeling that he had made some horrendous blunder crawled over him. He thought back to that cold November afternoon when he and Graham Dillaway and Graham's radiant bride had sat around the oval table in the Mensing & Nalbin law library and worked out the disposition of the two estates. With the clarity of perfect hindsight he cursed his own incompetence, his failure to guard against this possibility by putting an irrevocability clause in those wills. He knew that some courts would not enforce such a clause but the knowledge didn't make him feel better.

When he was ready with the best answer he could devise on the spot, he stood and paced into the center of the circle. "The wills don't say in so many words that they are irrevocable," he began slowly. "But don't you see what Mr. Nalbin is driving at? Suppose Will loses his suit and you change your will to cut him out. Nothing happens till you die. Once you are dead, Will contests your new will on the lines Mr. Nalbin has just laid out. And *that* case he'd probably win."

Hope kept her malevolent glare trained on him. "It is my property and my decision," she thundered. "I can put in a clause setting aside enough money to fight all the way to the

Supreme Court."

James Foxworth bit his lip as if distressed at the thought of a reduction in his own share. His sister Doreen jumped to her feet. "Mother," she said, "you're being a bitch again. I'm no fan of my stepbrother's but he has a right to his father's property. You can't cut Will out of your will."

Loren expected Hope to react with fury or contempt. Instead her face turned beefsteak red and exploded with sudden laughter. She burst out in a fit of maniac mirth and plopped into her chair like a boulder plummeting into the ocean. She clutched her middle and shook back and forth until she was too weak to laugh anymore and then she fell limp and gave her daughter a basilisk look. "Oh, I can't, eh? Well, my dear, I will cut Will out of my will!" And she began to laugh like a madwoman again.

James Foxworth gave a polite little giggle as Doreen's face turned the color of dirty snow. Lucy ran to the bar for a glass of water and tried to hold the roaring woman's head steady enough to drink. Dr. Josephson stubbed out his cigar into an ash stand, his face wooden and empty.

Loren went back to his chair, wishing that he had never been sucked into this clan of demented pen people.

When Hope had finally recovered she stared at Nalbin with inflexible determination and issued an order. "I want you to go to your office tomorrow and draw me a new will with the provisions I have outlined. I want it ready for my signature tomorrow evening. I know it's Sunday, you can bill me accordingly."

Nalbin bowed his head in sorrow. "I cannot do it. Tomorrow or any other day. My firm drew the first will and I think it would be unethical to become involved in any attempt to circumvent it."

Hope's head snapped back as if she had been struck and she looked at him with withering contempt. "All right, then you're fired. You will not touch one piece of the Dillaway estate work from this moment on. I'll get a new lawyer Monday morning and you can submit your bill to him. Now get out of my home." Her voice rose and her sow eyes blazed at the room. "All of you get out! I'm tired," she said. "Dreadfully tired." Whatever energy source had carried her through the evening, she no longer had it. Her voice had grown worn, exhausted like the voice of someone dying.

James Foxworth crossed the arc of peach carpeting and bent

to kiss his mother's wrinkled cheek. Doreen rose and said: "Good night, Mother," in a cold emotionless voice. Michael Josephson stared at the old woman like Zeus on Olympus studying some particularly foolish mortal and took his wife's arm and led her with studied haste to the door. Nalbin had already vanished, and Loren followed the Josephsons to the entranceway. He shook hands with them both and thanked them again for dinner.

When the door had closed behind the dentist and his wife, Loren reached into the foyer closet for the light raincoat he had brought. He turned around and Lucy stood there, calm but almost in tears at the same time. "I have to take care of her," she said simply. "I've never seen her this bad. Oh, Loren, I'm sorry, I didn't know anything like this would happen tonight. Give me a rain check?"

"How about my place for breakfast tomorrow, say about eleven?"

"If I can't get away I'll call and you can cook for us in my kitchen again." She pressed herself against him for an open-mouthed kiss and he stroked her neck and the wing of her back and her upward straining hips. They broke away breathless as James Foxworth's voice approached the front door. Loren shut the door behind him and trudged down the iron-railed spiral stairs and over to the elevator bank on 23 where he gouged the button savagely.

On the street, breathing the crisp night air, he realized that his wish had been granted. Now that Nalbin was out of the case, in effect Loren had been fired too. He was free! Never again! He almost whooped with relief as he strode along the residential streets to the fastback.

Tomorrow, he resolved, he'd make Lucy get out of that madhouse too.

TWELVE

ELEVEN o'clock. No Lucy. Eleven-thirty and still no Lucy.

Loren paced his living room like a prisoner in a cell. Every minute he expected the phone to ring or the annunciator to buzz, expected to hear something from her, anything. A disquiet sucked at his nerve ends.

He dialed the Dillaway number. Ten rings. No answer. Twenty rings and still no answer. He waited five more minutes that seemed like five days and tried again. Nothing.

He took the elevator to the basement garage, gunned the VW up the ramp and out to the boulevard. The stoplights kept turning red as he approached intersections. Streams of cars around the churches slowed him to a crawl.

He twisted the wheel right, turned into Delaware Avenue, spun into the parking crescent outside the Dillaway high rise. He raced into the glass box entranceway and pressed the penthouse buzzer savagely. Once. Twice. Again. No crackle of a voice and no buzz of the inner door in reply. His stomach knotted tighter.

He pounded on the glass of the inner door. A tall white-maned doorman uniformed in gray and brown rose from a chair in an alcove and laid down his Sunday paper and moved slowly toward Loren across the foyer. Loren kept up his frantic pounding. The doorman seemed to be wading through snow. He stared at Loren through the thick plate glass. Loren beat on the door, his face gray with fear.

Finally with a slow and cautious movement the doorman depressed the lock and opened three inches, keeping his hand on the door as if ready to slam it shut and throw the lock in a microsecond. "Is—something wrong, sir?" he asked hesitantly.

Loren rushed his words together. "I'm an attorney. I've been working for Mrs. Dillaway since the death of her husband. There's been no answer from the penthouse for the last hour. Could Mrs. Dillaway and Miss Martell have gone out for some reason?"

The doorman shook his head in puzzlement. "No, sir. They

didn't go past me at any rate and I've been on duty since eight this morning. I can't answer for before then."

"I think something may have happened up there," Loren said. "Is there a security guard who can go up and make sure they're all right?"

The other squinted in thought for a moment. "No security guard Sunday mornings. Mrs. Kelvin the building manager's gone to church. She'll be back in maybe half an hour, forty minutes."

"This can't wait." Loren knew he had no logical reason for his certainty something had happened but he also knew that unshakably certain he was. "Will you get a passkey and go up with me?"

"I don't know if that's such a good idea, sir. Mrs. Kelvin and Mrs. Dillaway both might be very unhappy if I did, and I do like this job, sir."

"Please," Loren begged him. "If you've ever loved anyone please for God's sake get a master key and come with me."

The doorman's eyes filled with an ancient sadness. "My son died in an auto smash on the coast a long time ago," he said slowly. "The night it happened something told me, something inside me. They didn't notify me till late the next day. You look the way I felt that night. Come on in." He held the door wide and Loren entered.

They ran down the hallway of 23 and through the door to the private foyer and up the spiral stairs, the carpet muffling their footfalls, the key ring jangling in the doorman's hand. At the top of the stairs he fumbled with the keys, trying each in the lock. Loren lifted his fist over the doorman's bent head, rapped furiously. The lock clicked. The doorman drew back hesitantly from the opening door.

Loren threw it open all the way. "Lucy?" he called into the apartment. "Mrs. Dillaway? Lucy?" No answer. With the doorman behind him he turned the corner into the front room.

A woman's body was sprawled on the far side of the room, the head touching the low semicircular stone wall surrounding the fireplace.

"Oh, Christ, no," the doorman whispered.

They ran to the wall and fell to their knees. Loren felt for a pulse and there was none, listened for a heartbeat and there was none. Hope Foxworth Dillaway was dead. Her head lay at a grotesque angle against the jagged stonework and her eyes bulged hideously. Blood had dried around her nostrils and mouth. Tiny cuts and a few dark inky smears stood out on her ghost-white hand.

Strewn near the body like the remnants of a paper chase was a pile of mail. The trail of letters and envelopes stretched across the room to Lucy's desk in the corner. A letter opener lay on the white sheets near the center of the jagged paper trail. A black-tipped felt pen stood out against the peach carpet near the dead woman's fingers.

Loren bent to study the sheets closest to the body. He saw black scrawls on two or three of them but couldn't decipher them.

He got to his feet and called out again. "Lucy!" No answer. He strode through the corridor leading to the other rooms, keeping his hands carefully in his pockets. Without touching anything he went into every room in the apartment. No other signs of disturbance. No signs of Lucy.

At least she hadn't been killed here. When he was sure of that he felt relieved and frightened. He went back to the front room. The doorman was using a pencil to turn the finger-slots of the telephone dial. "I want to report a murder," Loren heard him say. His voice was calm, as though death was not a stranger to him.

Detective Sergeant Charles Hough shuffled lugubriously into the penthouse foyer and saw at a glance that the crew was well into the usual tasks of body-examining, photographing, dusting for prints, measuring, note-taking and questioning. He was long-faced and sandy-haired and professional enough to know how to work with intellectuals when he had to, having shared many cases with Loren during and after Loren's year as deputy legal adviser. He strode to Loren's side and told him that the department was searching for Lucy throughout the city, then he set up a command post in a low-backed armchair and sum- moned the technical people one by one. Scrawled notes filled the pad on his shiny-suited knee as each man gave a quick and concise report on his own aspect of the investigation. Finally the last evidence technician was gone and the morgue men who had come for the body were gone and Hough and Loren sat alone in the cavernous room and talked. Loren told him every- thing that had happened up to his discovery of Hope's body. It was a long recital. When it was over the sergeant reread his notes. His breath was loud and harsh in the silent room.

"Okay," he said at last, and slouched back in his seat. "It looks like a pretty safe bet that whoever killed her did it because of what happened here last night. But on the other hand every single one of the people who were here last night would have been crazy to kill her *today,* before she made her new will. The Josephsons and the Foxworths lose the difference between a third and a half apiece, the Martell girl loses the money the old lady promised her. Nalbin and you never did have a motive."

"But you've checked where everybody was this morning just the same," Loren ventured.

"That was those phone calls I took," Hough said, and referred to his notes. "Between nine and eleven, which is when the prelim medical report says the old lady was killed, Mrs. Doreen Josephson claims she was at the non-denominational church services she always goes to on Sunday mornings. Detective Abrams confirmed that with other people who were at the service. Dr. Michael Josephson never goes to church. He was home all by himself and has no alibi. Mrs. Lola Foxworth was also home by her lonesome. James Foxworth was out playing nine holes at the Farmwick Country Club. Detective Edwards verified that Foxworth checked out a golf cart at eight forty-two A.M. but that don't prove he stayed on the course all morning. He claims he played alone. No partners. The boys are running down other people who were out on the course to see if anyone saw him. Stanford Nalbin and his missus slept late this morning but no outsider can alibi him. You have no alibi for yourself, Professor."

"Thorough men," Loren murmured.

"I try to be a good cop," Hough said. "That means doing a lot of useless work. None of you people seem to have had a motive to kill the old lady. But we've got a much better suspect who *wasn't* here last night."

Loren completed the thought. "Will Dillaway."

"I'd lay money on it," Hough said. "Somehow he found out his stepmomma was about to cut him off. Maybe Hope called and told him just to gloat about it like you say he did to her when he started his lawsuit. Maybe someone who was here last night tipped him off for a reason we can't figure yet. Once he learns what she's going to do, he has two motives for killing her. It stops her from changing her will and it ends his worries about his own suit against her, which you say was sort of shaky anyway. So he comes over here this morning."

"How did he get into this apartment?" Loren demanded. "How did he even get into the building? I told you the trouble I had."

"We'll work that out later." The sergeant's hand made a trail in the air from Lucy's desk to the low stone wall. "Those heel marks the boys found in the carpet and that line of papers from the girl's desk to the body show that there was a fight. The paper knife got into the fight and the old lady's fingers got cut up. The knife drops. He shoves the old lady hard or else he decks her one. She falls back and hits her head the wrong way against that stone wall. Exit one female authoress. Will ducks out."

The phone rang. Hough grabbed the receiver and held it to his ear for a long minute. He barked into the mouthpiece. Loren saw his face darken and his grip on the phone tighten as the answers came back to him. The sergeant slammed the phone into its cradle and threw himself down into the chair in a rage of frustration.

"Scratch Will Dillaway," he growled. "Make it X. Will's out of it."

"What happened?" Loren demanded

"That was Detective Scanlon. His job was to check out Will's movements this morning. You wanta know what Will Dillaway did this morning?" He gritted his teeth in disgust. "He was teaching Sunday school, that's what he was doing! He runs a class every Sunday. Three clergymen and a roomful of kids back him up. He was lecturing on what the Bible says about smoking pot or whatever. Now that is one hell of an alibi."

"If we can prove it was his name Hope wrote," Loren suggested, "we may be able to crack his alibi."

"Okay, let's get back to work, but for Will we gotta say X now. So X ducks out. But as it happens the old lady isn't quite dead yet. She reaches out for the felt pen from the desk that got thrown on top of the papers while they were fighting. She tries to write X's name. But as luck would have it she dies before she gets done."

"Even if she'd written the entire name it wouldn't have helped," Loren insisted. "I told you before, her handwriting was atrocious. I don't think more than a few people in the world could read it."

"And one of them is your girlfriend," Hough added savagely, "who is conveniently among the missing. My God, what a god-awful case I got handed!"

"You and me both," Loren said. He paced back and forth to the rhythm of his fears.

Hough looked up with eyes that seemed to have lost some of their professional coldness. "You don't have to be so uptight about the girl being gone. That's the easy part of this mess. She can't disguise that spinal curvature and no one can hide it for her. We're pulling out all the stops and by tonight we'll have her."

"If she's alive?" Loren said.

Hough stood up and threw a gruff paternal hand across Loren's shoulders. "If you start that kind of thinking, Professor, you won't be any help at all, and I need all the help I can get." The glow of an idea lit his features. "What say we sit down and go over the whole works together? Take your mind off your troubles."

"Okay, let's." They sat half facing each other and Hough opened to a fresh page of his notebook. Loren closed his eyes and tried to arrange his thoughts in some kind of logical sequence.

"Problem one," he began. "Why is Lucy gone? Did X kidnap her *because* she could read the message Hope left? Ridiculous! If he'd stayed around long enough to know Hope *had* left a message, he could have torn up the sheet of paper she wrote on or taken it with him, which is a lot simpler than taking Lucy with him and then having to worry about what to do with her. No, it's much more likely that Lucy saw something about the murder or about X himself that forced him to risk abducting her."

"If she was a witness, why didn't X just kill her too?" Hough demanded. "After all, if this is the same guy who killed Dillaway and Corby besides the old lady, why would he get squeamish about making it a foursome?"

"We don't know and I don't think reasoning about it will give us the answer. All we know is that he didn't kill her. At least not here."

"God damn it," Hough rasped, "if we could only read what the old lady wrote, we wouldn't have to keep saying X, X, X. I ....hey, what's the matter with you?"

Loren's eyes blazed with sudden excitement. He leaped from the chair and paced like a dervish again. "You just reminded me of something," he said. "A long time ago I owned a sample of Hope Dillaway's handwriting. A sample that just happened to include the word 'will,' with a small *w*. After I drew the Dillaways' wills for them, Hope autographed a copy of one of her books for me. The inscription said 'Thanks for drawing a lovely will' or something like that. If I had that book we could compare the way she wrote the word 'will' and what she wrote with that felt pen this morning. We'd either eliminate Will Dillaway as a suspect or nail him!"

Hough flew out of his chair as if propelled by a hidden spring. "Where the hell is that book?" he shouted.

"I don't have it. I threw it away right after the Dillaways left the office. Soap operas never were my bag."

"Damn it, damn it, damn it!"

"But I think I know what happened to it," Loren added.

An image came back to him. He remembered Connie Waller's look of horror when he had tossed an inscribed copy of her favorite author's latest novel into the Mensing & Nalbin umbrella stand. Quickly he described the incident to the long-faced sergeant.

"I think she took the book out of the stand and kept it for herself," Loren concluded. "She must have."

"Where is this woman?" Hough demanded.

"Died of cancer four years ago," Loren said.

Another string of oaths exploded from the sergeant like a string of firecrackers.

"But when you were talking back there," Loren interrupted, "I suddenly remembered something. I don't know who told me this because Connie died long after I left the firm. Maybe it was Nalbin who mentioned it."

"Mentioned *what*, for God's sake?"

"That Connie Waller had left everything to her sister, who also lived in the city and who was married to a man with an unpronounceable Greek name. *A name that began with an X!*"

Loren raced to Lucy's desk in the corner of the huge room and tore open drawer after drawer until he found the telephone directory. He opened the book from the Z end and thumbed backwards to the X's. "There can't be many Greek names beginning with X in the city. I think I'll remember it when I see it. Here we go, Xanos, Xanthos, Xenopoulos. Xenopoulos, that's it! 555-7457. Quick, call him, find out if he's Constance Waller's brother-in-law and ask him what happened to Connie's books." Loren collapsed into the black leather reclining chair while Hough bent over the phone and dialed frantically. The dull whistle of unanswered rings came over the wire. One. Two. Three. Four.

A voice croaked something on the other end.

"Mr. George Xenopoulos? This is Sergeant Hough from the homicide detail...."

Two minutes later Hough replaced the receiver with a sense of infinite weariness and turned to Loren disgustedly.

"Washout," he reported. "They took all her books and gave them away to the Crippled Children's Fair two years ago. God knows who's got it now." The sergeant delivered a long and obscene diatribe on the unjust way in which the world in general was managed.

"All right," Loren said. "Let's take up where we left off." They retraced their steps across peach carpeting now dirty with the footmarks of many investigators.

"Problem Two," Loren continued. "How did X get into this building and into the penthouse? Now in general there are only two ways he could have got in. Either he had a key or someone let him in. Let's go over what the doorman told you."

Hough flipped back several pages in his note pad and squinted at a cluster of pothooks. "Here we go, statement of Edgar Bates. He was on duty at the front door downstairs from eight A.M. till the time you showed up. He was in that front lobby every minute, didn't even have to go to the john. He said the only people who came in by the front door during that time were people who lived here, coming back from church or whatever. He swears that neither Mrs. Dillaway nor Miss Martell went past him out the front door while he was on duty."

"We have to assume that X doesn't live in this building," Loren insisted. "At least for now, till we see where it leads us. That means X was a visitor. Now the only authorized way for a visitor to enter this building is by buzzing the person he intends to call on and getting the inner front door opened from upstairs. But of course no visitor intending to commit murder would come into the building that openly. And anyway, Bates told us that in fact there were no visitors at all between eight A.M. and the time I got here. That is, no front-door visitors. Now, how many other ways into this building are there?"

Hough flipped more pages of his notebook. "Just one," he said. "The side door, the one that leads through the storage areas and past the fire stairway and freight elevator and the room where the doormen change into their uniforms. It opens onto the side parking lot. Didn't you say you and Miss Martell left the building that way once?"

"Right. Now, let's go over what Mrs. Kelvin and the doorman told us about the keys."

Hough read silently in his notes, then lifted his head and wet his lips. "Anyone already inside the building can get out the side door just by twisting the knob. That has to be how X and the girl left after the murder, he probably took her down the firestairs that open into the side passage where the doorman couldn't see them."

Loren nodded in agreement.

"But you can't get *into* the building by the side door unless you have a key," the sergeant continued. "Every tenant has one, of course, and the same key that works the inner front door works the side door of the building *and* the front door of the tenant's apartment. But each apartment lock is different so a tenant can't just walk into somebody else's apartment with his own key."

"You verified all that?" Loren asked.

"Detective Hooks checked out every word of it."

"Then we know one of two things happened," Loren concluded. "Either X had a key and used it to get in by the side door or he had an accomplice on the inside who knew when he was coming and waited in the side corridor and opened the side door for him when he came. I think it's much more likely that X had a key." His voice dropped on the last sentence as if he hoped it would escape the sergeant's notice.

Hough grunted as he lit a cigarette from the butt of his last. "If there was an accomplice," he pointed out dryly, "the likeliest suspect is your girlfriend."

A nerve twitched in Loren's neck and he moved toward Hough as if to attack him.

"No, don't get sore, Professor, I'm just sorting out possibilities like yourself. I don't think the inside accomplice idea's very hot either. Let's assume X had a key. Now we're also assuming the killer is not a tenant in this building, right? So who are we narrowed down to?"

"We have to go back to the number of keys Graham and Hope Dillaway were originally given."

Hough riffled back through his notes to the statement of the building manager. "Mrs. Kelvin said as far as she knew they had three keys. One for Dillaway, one for his wife and one they had made when the Martell girl came to work here. Those are the only three keys to this penthouse."

"Now what happened to those keys? Where are they now?" Loren asked. "We can assume Graham's key was destroyed at King Mountain. We found Hope's in the key container in her purse. Lucy's must be in her purse but her purse is not up here and it's not in her apartment so it's probably with her, wherever she is. All right, if none of those three keys could have been the key X got into the building with, what other keys could he have used?"

"Well," Hough offered, "Mrs. Parkins, the housekeeper, had a key to the penthouse."

"Yes, but she left Friday evening to spend the weekend with relatives downstate. Bates told us he saw her leave with her suitcase late Friday. You're not going to suggest *she's* X, are you?"

"Not hardly," Hough agreed. "How about the Martell girl's key to her own apartment, 23 D?"

"No good, no good," Loren muttered. "We started out with the assumption that Lucy is not the killer and is not an accomplice."

"Meaning no offense, Professor, but that assumption may just about have outlived its usefulness," the sergeant complained. "Because the only other key I can think of is the dead woman's key to the guest apartment downstairs, 23 C, and if you'll recall, we found *that* key in her key container too, right next to her key to this place. So what do we have left? A goose egg. A big fat zilch. A...."

"No," Loren said. He felt as if a heavy weight had been lifted from him as he said it. "No. What we have left—I think—is the answer. I think I know who killed Hope Dillaway."

Sergeant Hough stared at him in frank disbelief and puffed furiously at his cigarette. "Suddenly you see the answer where all I see is questions?"

"The key to the solution," Loren said, "is the key." He hunched forward, elbows planted on knees. "X had to have a key to get in by the side door. X is the King Mountain murderer as well as the killer of Hope Dillaway. Which is the most likely key for the King Mountain murderer to have in his possession? *The only key that was ever on King Mountain. Graham Dillaway's key.*"

The sergeant sat silent, turning the thought about, poking at its edges. Finally he spoke again. "You mean X could see so far into the future he took Dillaway's key out of that fire with him just on the off chance he might need it later? Bullshit."

"Not if you grant me one condition," Loren insisted.

"What condition?" Hough demanded suspiciously.

"That X equals Graham Dillaway himself."

Hough's head snapped back as if he had been struck. "Oh my sweet Christ," he said very softly.

"That Graham Dillaway is alive and well," Loren went on, excitement making his voice a croak. "That he killed some vagrant who superficially resembled him, stuck his body in that cabin, killed Jackson Corby, set fire to the place, and took off to start a new life free of an intolerable marriage and free of blackmail. It was probably Dillaway himself who put in that anonymous call to the state cops about the fire. With his feelings about the wilderness and ecology, he wouldn't want the whole forest to be burned up without reason.

"Since the fire he's had a few lucky breaks. First when the police passed everything off as an accident, then when they apparently got the idea that Corby had been killed because he'd tried to blackmail, well, let's call him Number Seventeen, and put the lid on the case.

"Now we don't know what Dillaway's been doing for the past several weeks but we can do some educated speculation. One, he didn't care very much whether his wife was suspected of instigating his murder. If she'd ever been charged, well, we don't know what he'd have done. Two, he definitely did not like Hope's plan to cut his only child out of *his* money, since that threat must have been why he killed her—to keep her from writing a new will.

"All right, somehow he hears of Hope's scheme. He comes here this morning, gets in the side door with his own key, takes the firestairs to 23 and the spiral staircase to the penthouse. He gets in here with his own key. He comes upon Hope, they get into a fight around that letter opener, he hits her, she falls back and hits her head against the stone wall. At this point Lucy comes in, and of course recognizes him."

Loren thought back to the things Lucy had told him about Graham, and the way she had said them. "I admired him very much," she had said. He remembered his own intuition that only Graham's death had prevented the eventual ripening of an affair between him and Lucy. He thought he understood how each of them would have reacted to a confrontation this morning, in this vast room, with Hope dying in their sight. He thought he saw now why the murderer had not been able to kill Lucy here.

"So far Dillaway has killed to free himself and to save his son's inheritance." Loren muttered the words so low that Hough had to strain to hear them. "He hasn't killed merely to save his own skin. He could have killed Lucy right here but he didn't, he took her with him instead." Did she go with him willingly? Loren didn't dare think about that question. He dropped it down his private memory hole. "I don't think he wants to harm her but he may get scared and decide he has to. Charley, for God's sake we've got to find her!"

Hough took a long breath and hunkered down on one of the seat cushions along the jagged stone wall, massaging his thick neck in his hands. He tugged another cigarette from a crumpled pack and jammed it between his lips without striking a match. "I'm not convinced," he decided. "It sounds good but you've got no solid proof. All you've done is build a castle in the air. There's too many other possibilities you haven't ruled out. Suppose Lucy Martell's X? Suppose she's X's accomplice and let him in by the side door? Suppose one of the other tenants in this building is X? Suppose the doorman or the janitor's X?"

"I want verification as badly as you do," Loren said. "Will you do something that will either prove I'm right or prove I'm crazy?"

Hough stared at him as if suspecting a booby trap. "What do you want me to do?"

"The papers said Graham Dillaway's remains were buried here in town. Get them exhumed. Have the medical examiner go over them with every test he has at his disposal. Let's nail this down one way or the other."

"That's going to take the permission of the next of kin or a court order," Hough grumbled. "I don't know if I can dig up a friendly judge on Sunday afternoon and I doubt if Will Dillaway's going to cooperate."

Loren grabbed the sergeant by the arm and almost dragged him to the phone. "Come on, let's get moving! You call the golf courses and I'll try the Lawyers' Club. We'll pick up Will on the way out."

The late afternoon shadows deepened to twilight as the three men sat in Hough's cubicle at headquarters and waited.

Loren paced to the dirt-crusted window. He stared out at the police parking lot, off-duty squad cars at one end and the private autos in which the officers came to work at the other. A chain-link fence enclosed the lot and an armed guard patrolled each entranceway.

He turned away from the view. Will Dillaway chain-smoked as he sat tensely in the time-gouged straight chair. Sergeant Hough lit one cigarette after another behind his battered desk. The air was thick with clouds of stale tobacco smoke that had massed around the harsh overhead light.

"You can't be right." It was at least the tenth time Will had said that since they had taken him downtown in Hough's squad car. "I don't pretend to mourn my stepmother, but this fantastic opium dream about my father being alive and a multiple murderer is—it's just insane!"

"Maybe," Hough muttered. "We should know soon."

Will bowed in agonized concentration. "I can't believe this is happening," he said over and over.

The phone screamed. Hough snatched it in mid-ring, spoke his name. He reached for a pencil and pad, nodded, listened, jotted notes. With brusque thanks he hung up. He let out a long sigh and threw a look of slightly cockeyed admiration at Loren.

"You called it," he said. "That was the medical examiner. There's not a Chinaman's chance in hell that that body is Graham Dillaway."

Loren studied Will's face as he heard the news. Joy that his father was alive fought with revulsion at what the discovery implied. He seemed not to know whether to laugh or weep.

"The M.E. did something no one did before," the sergeant went on. "Called the Pentagon and coordinated what he found on the burned body with Dillaway's medical records when he was in the Navy. Turns out Dillaway broke his leg on an aircraft carrier in 1944. The M.E. swears the body he's got never had a bone broken in its life. There are other things too but that's the clincher. He's going to keep working just to make sure all the bases are covered but hell, that's enough for me."

Hough paused to mash out his cigarette in the overflowing tray. Then he stared at Will Dillaway with cold contempt.

"Your father got hold of some wino that was built more or less like himself. He killed the wino, killed Corby, set fire to the cabin and started a new life for himself. Then you got cute and started a lawsuit to pin the murders on your stepmother and she decided to break that mutual will she had. And you told your father about it and he came out of the woodwork and killed her too."

"I didn't! I didn't!" Will's voice was almost a shriek.

"You going to tell me he found out by ESP or something? Come on, boy, you knew what he'd done and you got in touch with him last night and that makes you an accessory to murder and by God I'll nail you for it if it takes the rest of my life!"

"His rights," Loren Mensing said loudly.

Sergeant Hough stared at him with mixed incredulity and malevolence and Loren glared back defiantly. The silence in the smoky room was a form of combat, a test of strength.

When Hough let loose a torrent of obscenities, Loren knew he had won. The sergeant dug into his wallet sullenly and from a printed card he read out the Miranda warnings. He advised Will Dillaway of his constitutional rights in a flat dull voice. Will sat stunned through the reading as if still unable to believe this was happening to him.

"I want a lawyer," he mumbled when Hough put away his card. "I want to talk to my lawyer."

Hough barked something into an interoffice communicator. A uniformed man came into the room. "Take this man to one of the detention rooms and let him call his lawyer," he snarled. The uniformed man seized Will's arm and hustled him out.

Hough held the door open and motioned for Loren to follow him. They followed a grimy-floored tile corridor, passed men in rumpled suits and men in crisp blue uniforms. Loren thought he recognized a few faces but it was hard to be sure. The role depersonalized them, made them indistinguishable.

At the ice-water fountain Hough bent over and gulped long swallows. He cupped his palms in the chill water and shot a stream of it over his face and hands. Dripping, he straightened and looked at Loren with naked disgust.

"You and your fucking rights," he rasped. "Back in the old days I could have put so much heat on him he'd have melted like an ice-cream cone in the sun. Anything he knew we'd know inside of an hour. Just keep this in mind, Professor. If Dillaway kills your girlfriend, and we could have found her alive by breaking his son, blame yourself and the Supreme Court."

He spun on his heel and started to walk away. Loren reached out for his jacket sleeve, pulled him around.

"Don't you think I know the consequences of what I did back there? Do you know what it cost me to do that?" Desperation made his voice hoarse.

"Suppose his rights turn out to be the difference between life and death for the girl?"

Loren squeezed his eyes shut. "For God's sake don't ask me that. Just find her!" A wet mist blurred his sight and his head throbbed so that he almost cried out with the pain. "Find her," he mumbled.

Hough put a rough hand around Loren's shoulder. "You've paid your dues, Professor," he said. Somehow it was like a career soldier's tribute to a totally dedicated enemy general. "Now why don't you go home? I'll be here all night. If anything breaks I'll call you. You've got to get a decent meal and some sleep. Look, if it takes a bottle to put you out tonight, kill the bottle. You've pointed us in the right direction, now it's our baby. Come on, man, I'll scrounge a ride home for you in a squad car."

"I don't want to go home," Loren told him.

He wasn't sure why he wanted to stay away from there. Was he afraid he'd find traces of Lucy, a few strands of her lovely hair on a cushion, the faint perfume of her body between the sheets? If he could keep control, if he could keep the fear and uncertainty and grief from overpowering him, maybe he could do more to help find her. That was what he told himself. That was what he hoped. Deep inside he didn't believe it but he was afraid to abandon the hope.

"Will you tell the squad car to take me to the university and drop me off at the new law library?" he asked.

He looked up the oval well. Through the skylight six stories above, he could see the pinpoint glitter of stars. Arcs of metal railing at each level receded upward toward the transparent dome and the night. There was something alien and awesome about the place, like a cathedral built by creatures of a distant planet. The indifferent immensity of the sky dwarfed him. After a while he was able to think again.

He walked slowly to the ground-floor study area and sank into a futuristic swivel seat of foam cushion and tinted plastic. He swung left to right and then right to left in the crescent of work space scooped out of the huge round metalloid table. Cold air whispered through invisible ducts. Once or twice a frenzied light pattern flew along the black wall, making hideous shadows: car passing on the road outside. He sat wrapped in a cocoon of thought.

When his ideas had begun to take shape he snapped on the tiny tensor lamp beside the workspace and laid his pocket notebook in the pool of hot bright light. He wrote a single sentence. "Assume Will Dillaway is completely innocent and has had no contact of any sort with his father since Graham's apparent death."

He squinted his eyes shut and thought again, and when he opened them he added another sentence to the page. "But if Will didn't tip Graham off to Hope's disinheritance plan, who did?"

He turned the page and set down, each on a separate line, the names of all the persons who had known of Hope's plan.

Michael Josephson
Doreen Josephson
James Foxworth

The first three he dismissed. All of them had every reason *not* to hinder the execution of a new will under which their share would increase.

Hope Dillaway
Stan Nalbin
Me

The next three names were ridiculous. That left only one person who was at that meeting. He printed the name in large block capitals.

LUCY

He underlined her name, extended the line into a box, dark-

ened the edges of the box until it enclosed her name like a
cage.

All the old suspicions of an alliance between Lucy and Will
flooded back, except that now Will had been replaced by Graham. All his old doubts that had fed the suspicions rekindled
them again. It made even more sense with the substitution of
the father for the son. Hadn't he sensed as early as that first
morning over coffee at her breakfast bar that an affair between
her and Graham would have inevitably grown? It had. She was
going to be part of his new life. There had been no kidnapper
but only two conspirators.

He thought it but he couldn't write it down and he couldn't
make himself believe it. It made not just a mockery but an ab-
surdity of the times they had lain in each other's arms and
taken their first faltering steps at building harbors for each
other. Every instinct in him revolted at the idea that all that was
a fake. He remembered her moving frantically against him until her robe lay in a pile at her feet and he was caressing her
silken nakedness. He remembered the night he read to her from
the adventures of Steve Dusk and their casserole burned. He
remembered the day they had taken the electric knife to Graham Dillaway's sofa pillows.

That thought froze him.

Graham Dillaway's money-stuffed sofa pillows, and the secret diary in which he had revealed himself.

God, God, God! Of course! Dillaway hadn't come back to
save his son's patrimony. He hadn't known about Hope's
threat to change her will. *He'd come back for the diary and the
money.* Not knowing that the depository of his posthumous
letter to Hope had gotten cold feet and prematurely mailed the
letter that had led Loren and Lucy to the hiding place, Graham
Dillaway had come back for the contents of those pillows. That
had to be it.

But that only led to another question.

Why hadn't Dillaway taken the diary and the money with
him on that last trip to King Mountain? What countervailing
risk made him decide that it was less dangerous to slip into the
penthouse weeks after he'd been reported dead?

Suddenly Loren saw what might be the answer.

He asked himself two more questions.

How had Dillaway obtained, and transported to King Mountain, the body that was to pass as his own? How had he planned

to get out of the area after the fire?

Loren shut off the tensor lamp and sat in the cathedral hush. Now he had it. Not the specifics, but he had the answer in principle.

He decided that he would let himself out of the library and lock the door behind him, walk across campus to the boulevard and find a cab to take him home. When he was home he'd call Hough if he thought the answer still made sense.

He unlocked the entrance door and once outside he turned facing inward to rattle the lock and make sure it had caught. He heard the chirp of crickets in the grass. A car door slammed, footsteps tap-tapped toward him, running. He turned in the doorway. A man was coming toward him along the inky path. Behind the man a single car stood in the parking area midway between two lightpoles. The man ran into the ell of the doorway. In the faint light from the bulb in the overhang of the entranceway Loren recognized him.

He had graying Marine-cropped hair and the battered face of an unlucky prizefighter. A dime-sized burn scar bleached his left temple.

"You're Sergeant Guerra. You picked me up here to take me to headquarters last Monday."

Guerra's lips parted and his teeth gleamed white in a hideous grin. He stuck his tongue into the single gap in the row of teeth and wagged it as if in a mock salute. He drew a short-barreled pistol from a shoulder rig and trained it on Loren's middle.

"Step back in, Professor," he ordered. "Fast."

This was the answer. To carry out his plan Dillaway had to have an accomplice. Now the specifics were filled in too. The accomplice was Guerra. That was how the substitute body had gotten to the mountain and how Graham Dillaway had left the mountain. That was why he hadn't brought the money: so as not to tempt Guerra into killing him for it. That was why he hadn't brought the diary: so that Guerra couldn't take Corby's place and blackmail him all over again.

Loren stared down stupidly at the gun and felt his spine turn to ice. Guerra snatched the key from him, twisted it in the lock, backed him into the library at gunpoint and locked the door again. They stood in the faint gray light of the inner vestibule. Guerra motioned him to step backward.

"What the hell are you trying to do?" Loren demanded.

"Shut up. Over to the elevator." Guerra spoke through taut lips. A vein throbbed in his temple and his scar seemed to shine with a dull glow. "Move! We're taking a ride to the top floor of this joint. If you believe in a next life, you're going to see your chick in a couple minutes."

Something inside Loren crumbled to powder. "You killed Lucy," he said. It was not a question.

"You can die here now or upstairs a minute from now," Guerra snapped. "Move!"

The instinct to live a few moments longer forced his legs back along the corridor. His mind flailed wildly, useless like his body. They reached the elevator bank and Guerra stabbed a button. A door flew open with a fierce metallic bang, loud as cannon fire, loud as a head-on collision, *someone had to hear it.* He backed Loren into a corner of the dark cage and pressed the iridescent button marked 6. The door banged shut and the cage lurched upward. Loren felt heavy weight under his feet. They rose in near-total darkness. The bud of light behind the floor indicator panel was all they had to see by. *Why hadn't the goddamn electricians put the bulbs in?* Guerra was a shadowed bulk and a rasping breath.

"If I even think you're making a move toward me I empty this into you. At this range I can't miss."

The hollow cube lifted them, three, four, five, and in the muffled darkness Loren knew with all the certainty of immediate experience that in less than a minute he would be dead, dead, dead, nothing, nothing.

The hum of rising stopped. The metal door banged open. Dim light poured into the cage from the skylight above the railed well. Guerra backed into the elevator doorway, beckoned Loren out with a slow waggle of the pistol barrel. "Come on, Professor, let's find a quiet broom closet and get it over with." There was an undertone of boredom in his voice.

Loren tried to make his legs move. He couldn't. He didn't want to die but his body would not help him live. He stood rooted in the corner of the cage. Cold sweat covered him. His own stench made him sick. The pistol like an extension of Guerra's arm pointed at him. Guerra's finger tightened on the trigger. Loren felt his knees giving way.

And then the door banged again.

It slammed shut, sharp and swift as the guillotine. It smashed into Guerra's upraised arm and drove it against the wall. Loren leaped, clawed for the gun. From elbow to gun the arm writhed against the wall like an obscene insect. The gun boomed. Loren twisted the fingers cruelly. The gun slid from them, clattered to the floor. Loren seized the arm in his two hands and snapped it down, down, with all his weight pinning it against the cold smooth wall of the cage. He heard the crack of bone. Muffled by the door came a hoarse animal scream. The door flew open. Loren's foot lashed out, caught him in the groin. He shrieked and doubled up, mewling. Loren hauled him upright, drove a savage uppercut into his face. Guerra's nose crumpled. A stream of sticky blood dyed Loren's hand. Guerra snapped back under the punch. His arms flailed backward wildly. His body rammed against the metal railing around the open well. The rail buckled. Guerra's feet danced on empty air. He grasped for a handhold with his ruined arm. The metal ripped apart under his weight. He dropped. The crunch of his landing cut his scream like a knife.

Loren sank to the floor and trembled. His body jerked in epileptic spasms. Tears of rage and grief and sheer joy at being alive flooded him. He sprawled on the cold tile of the library floor and shuddered and wept. When he thought he might be able to walk again he groped blindly to his feet and fell into the elevator and stabbed at the ground-floor button. He crawled past the smashed insect in the central well and croaked into the phone on the reference desk that he wanted the police.

He sat on the bottom step of the firestairs, head in hands, rocking back and forth. From the library he heard footsteps, muted voices, the click of cameras. Uniformed figures crossed the doorway in blurs of motion. Time crept but he did not sense its passage. Finally he saw a shadow in front of him, blocking the light from the doorway. He looked up. Hough sat on the cold stone stairs beside Loren and lit a cigarette. He squinted his eyes half shut against the smoke.

"We found her," he said softly. "She was in the trunk of Guerra's car. Strangled sometime early this afternoon. From the postmortem lividity marks it looks like he put her in the trunk right after killing her and kept her there until he had a chance to figure out a good place to dump her."

Loren stopped rocking. It was over. It had been over even before they'd begun looking, and nothing he or the police or anyone in the whole putrid world could have done would have

saved her. He propped his back against the night-chilled concrete wall and studied Hough's hard stoic face and said nothing.

The sergeant stubbed out his cigarette against a step.
"Guerra died in the ambulance but the facts tell the story pretty
good. He had the midnight to eight A.M. shift this morning and
worked overtime till almost noon. We checked the duty roster
and logbooks. He was with between two and five other cops
during the whole time Hope Dillaway could have been killed
so we know he personally didn't kill her or snatch Miss
Martell. Which means Graham Dillaway must have got hold of
him right after he came off duty and they decided the girl knew
too much. Where they did it and which one actually strangled
her we don't know."

Loren looked up at the break in Hough's story. His red-
blotched eyes felt like lead balls. The detective was tearing the
paper of his cigarette butt into tiny shreds, releasing a trickle of
golden brown tobacco to the cold floor.

"I don't know how to tell you this," he went on. "Guerra
had an emergency recall this afternoon to help look for the girl.
He was on duty from five to nine P.M. He drove his own car to
headquarters and drove it out again when he got off. We were
sitting in my shop turning the city upside down for Lucy
Martell and she was stuffed in a trunk in our own parking lot."

Loren began to laugh wildly. He pressed himself back into
the corner against the wall as if something was tearing at him.
He couldn't stop the sharp maniacal laughter. Hough bent over
and rocked him gently in his arms. Someone handed a container of coffee to Hough and he held it to Loren's lips. It was
scalding hot and tasted like liquid cardboard and Loren drank it
greedily, savoring the burning sensation it brought to his
throat.

"We don't know how Dillaway and Guerra got tied up in
the first place," Hough said. "I don't suppose it matters much.
We did find out that Guerra took a week of his annual leave
during the time Dillaway's substitute and Corby were killed on
King Mountain. His landlady told us he wasn't home that week
so it's a safe bet he was up in the mountains helping Dillaway.

"His ass must have been warming the panic button all day,
carrying the girl's body around in his own car like that. He
could never have gotten all the traces of her out of his trunk, no
matter where he ditched her in the end. It was a dumb play but

under enough pressure anyone will panic and get stupid." He held Loren's eyes with the gaze of tough-minded compassion that comes to one who has seen much death.

"Anything else I can tell you? Oh, yeah, almost forgot. After you left headquarters Will Dillaway made a statement. Freely and voluntarily and with his lawyer right next to him. He admitted he was the one made those anonymous calls claiming Dillaway had been murdered. Also that he wrote those E. A. Rogers letters. He made up the details out of whole cloth, including that cookstove thing that was bugging you. Wrote 'em up on a German-make typewriter he'd borrowed overnight from a neighbor. He said he was so sure his stepmother was behind his old man's death he was willing to go out on a limb to see justice done. After the medical report sank in and he realized that wasn't his father's body, he broke down and cooperated. We might or might not charge him with something." Hough pushed himself to his feet and took a step in the direction of the library.

"Wait." A strange look came into Loren's ravaged eyes. "Why did Guerra want to kill me?" His tone was professorially detached, as if he had asked a student why Brandeis had dissented in a certain case.

"He was getting afraid of you. At least since Monday when he picked you up here, he knew you were in the case. When you were down at headquarters tonight he was there. He must have seen you. He probably kept an eye out and saw you leave in the patrol car and figured you were going home and it'd be a good time to kill you. You gave him a break when you came here instead. He sat out front and waited till you were leaving. When he was in this building Monday he must have seen it wasn't officially opened yet. He probably thought he could find a spot in the basement or somewhere for the girl's body and yours. Instead it turned out to be his own coffin. He died a damned rough death but the son of a bitch deserved a hell of a lot worse. All we have to do now is find Dillaway. Or his body. The way Guerra was killing off people today, he just may have gotten rid of Dillaway too." He reached down to Loren's shoulders, lifted him to his feet. "Come on, I'm driving you home and feeding you as much booze as you can take and putting you to bed."

Loren followed Hough into the blinding light of the library, shuffling like a zombie. He didn't want to go to bed but he

didn't want to stay here either. It didn't matter a damn whether
he went home or didn't go home, went to sleep or didn't sleep,
woke up in the morning or never woke up. He thought it would
be better if he did not wake up.

They passed through groups of officials completing their
routine. Hough guided Loren like a seeing-eye dog leading a
blind man. At the front door Loren stopped short.

"Is Lucy...." he began.

Hough shook his head. "The morgue wagon took her away
hours ago. Look, the sun's going to come up before you know
it. Life goes on."

"Not my life," Loren said.

THIRTEEN

TWO days later, in a gray and sullen rain, she was buried. Loren stood by the muddy gravesite, apart from the handful of others who had come, relatives of Lucy's he'd never met, people who had known Lucy but not him and whom he knew not at all. He watched them lower the coffin into the dark neat hollow and tried not to think of how lovely she had been nor of how good they would have been for each other. He remembered something Michael Josephson had said at dinner the evening before Lucy's death, that when one dies the worms won't know what kind of person they are eating, whether cruel or compassionate, rich or poor, executioner or victim. He wished Guerra had killed him too.

The pock-pock of footsteps came toward him through the sodden grass. He looked away from the grave and saw Doreen Josephson, tall and straight in a black trenchcoat, her face pinched and brooding. She took his hand and held it and they stood together without words. He didn't want to wait any longer, didn't want to see the rain-dark earth shoveled on the coffin. He bent on one knee and plucked a wild flower from the grass and tossed it into the hole and rose and shuffled blindly away.

He knew that the search for Graham Dillaway or his body was still going on but after the first few days it wasn't news any longer. He thought Dillaway must still be alive. If Guerra had gotten rid of Graham, and disposed of the body so well that the police had found no trace of it, why wouldn't he have disposed of Lucy's body the same way?

Dillaway had to be alive somewhere. The need to see him pay for what he had done was all that kept Loren going.

After enough time had passed to dull the ache he set himself an intellectual exercise. He would reconstruct everything that had happened from the viewpoint of Graham Dillaway. It was a kind of discipline, an overcoming of himself and his grief, to re-experience the whole bloody tangle from the murderer's perspective.

There was still no indication how Dillaway and Guerra had first come in contact. In any event they had, and Dillaway had decided to use Guerra to help rid himself of Jackson Corby and of his own past. Certainly he hadn't told Guerra what hold Corby had on him since that would have meant exchanging one blackmailer for another. Most likely he had simply offered Guerra money, hired the cop as a hit man.

At the right time Guerra had procured a body. It might have been alive or it might have been dead when Guerra had procured it. Either way, it would not have been difficult for him. Skid row was full of derelicts whose disappearance would never be reported. Guerra had taken the corpse to King Mountain where Dillaway had already gone to meet Corby. On Guerra's arrival they killed Corby and set the stage for the fire. Then the sergeant had driven Dillaway to safety, with one stop along the road so that Dillaway could anonymously report the fire. Guerra went back to the city and Dillaway went underground, whereabouts still unknown, neither of them realizing that the authorities would have their own reasons for covering up Corby's murder nor that Guerra in his haste had left behind enough evidence to prove to the first really thorough investigator, Chad Corrigan of the *Beacon,* that the fire was no accident.

Dillaway had not taken the diary and the money from his sofa pillows into hiding with him, no doubt because he was afraid of tempting Guerra. But he needed that money to start a new life, and finally, that Sunday morning, he had taken a chance and gone to get it. Knowing nothing of Hope's showdown conference over the mutual wills, unaware that the depository of his own posthumous letter to his wife had mailed the letter prematurely, Dillaway had used his own key to enter the apartment building by the side door and to reenter the penthouse. He had found his workroom completely empty of sofa pillows. And then on his way out he had been seen by Hope and there had been a struggle over the paper knife and Hope had fallen and hit her head the wrong way.

And then Lucy had come in.

Why had she gone upstairs just then? Loren wondered. Probably just to make sure Hope would be all right for a few hours by herself while Lucy was with him. If she had gone straight down in the elevator from 23 D she would be alive and in his arms today. One of life's little jokes.

He thought Graham would have killed her on the spot if he had really wanted to protect himself. Dillaway must have gone through the tortures of the damned that morning, seeing himself sinking deeper in blood with every step he took. He hadn't wanted it that way. He had only wanted to begin over again. He couldn't kill Lucy. Somehow—had he had a gun?—he made her leave with him. She had been too shocked and frightened to resist. If she had resisted she might be alive now. By then Dillaway must have been crumbling apart inside. He might not have been able to stop her if she'd put up a fight. If only she had gone to the phone and called Loren or the police. If only she had done *something* different! But she hadn't. They had gone down the firestairs together and out the side door and away. What they had said to each other, what their thoughts had been, no one would ever know.

In panic, Dillaway had contacted Guerra—his last mistake, and one that sealed Lucy's fate. Loren was sure it was Guerra who had strangled her. Dillaway could never have done that. The two murderers had separated again but before Guerra could dispose of Lucy's body he'd been recalled to duty in the search for her and the body had lain in the trunk of his car in the police parking lot while officers hunted for her in three states.

And then Guerra had followed Loren to the new law library, and when Loren had stepped out of the futuristic building the sergeant had run up, gun in hand, and grinned at him.

Grinned at him.

That was when Loren realized that he would have to begin the reconstruction all over again.

On another Sunday morning, with fleecy clouds dancing in the sky, mellow church bells pealing, birds chattering brightly in the green treetops, Loren sat behind the wheel of the fastback parked at the curb and gazed steadily at the corner house half a block ahead. At 8:40 she opened the front door and came out. She wore a flower-print blouse and tan slacks. She stepped into the Lincoln Continental in the carport, backed into the street and drove away.

Loren waited five minutes against the possibility that she might come back for something she'd forgotten. Then he locked the VW and walked slowly up the tree-shaded block, savoring the breeze and the warm sun. He turned in at the path to the front door of the corner house and pressed the bell.

Five minutes later, sitting across the paneled living room from the murderer, Loren told him.

"I thought I was safe for a while yet." Michael Josephson's voice was surgically calm.

"I haven't told anyone else yet," Loren said. "There are reasons why I had to come to you first."

"How did you know?"

"Guerra grinned at me," Loren said.

A look of polite puzzlement crossed the other's face.

"The first time I saw Guerra he had tobacco stains all over his teeth and he wasn't missing any teeth that I could see. The second and last time I saw him, a week ago tonight when he tried to kill me, his teeth were clean and one incisor was missing. He even stuck his tongue in the hole, as people do when they've just had a tooth pulled. Teeth cleaned, one tooth pulled—obviously he'd seen a dentist during the week.

"And the dentist that has the contract with the city to take care of non-uniformed police is you."

Josephson sipped steaming black coffee from a thick mug. "Of course he came to me for his dental work," he murmured after a minute's thought. "I don't see how that brought you to the truth."

"In itself it didn't. But it got me thinking about you. And then I remembered something that clinched it.

"Do you recall the day we all met in court for the probate hearing? Remember Dr. Beck, the state forensic pathologist, the one who kept cracking his knuckles? He testified that he'd examined the remains of that burned body and that he'd taken X-ray photographs of its teeth. He also testified that he'd gotten a set of X-ray photos of Dillaway's teeth from his dentist— that is, from you. *And Dr. Beck swore that the two sets of photos matched perfectly.*

"But we know that in fact that dead body was not Graham Dillaway! Dillaway had broken a leg while he was in the service. The burned man in the cabin had never broken a leg. But then how did his teeth come to match Dillaway's perfectly?

"There was only one way to explain this discrepancy. The X-ray photos you had sent Dr. Beck as Dillaway's were not Dillaway's at all. Furthermore, since you did have X-rays that matched the corpse's teeth, it followed that he must have been a recent patient of yours.

"Put that together with the Guerra connection and it proves that you were in these murders up to your neck. You weren't there at King Mountain when Dillaway and Guerra killed Corby and left him to burn with the other body. You made sure you were in St. Louis at a convention when the dirty work was done. But you were part of it. You had to be. They couldn't have done it without you.

"Dillaway was being bled to death by Corby, he was trapped in a loveless marriage, he desperately wanted to start over again. You were of his generation, you loved his step-daughter, and death didn't faze you. He confided in you and begged you to help him. You were supposed to get hold of some derelict who superficially resembled Dillaway. You'd fix his teeth for him free, making X-ray photos as part of the usual routine. You'd destroy the real photos of Dillaway's teeth which you'd made as his dentist and file these substitute ones under Dillaway's name. You'd keep tabs on the derelict, and when the time came, you'd take him to King Mountain. The derelict and Corby would be killed and cremated up there and Dillaway would take off for his new life. That or something pretty close to it was the plan. You didn't want to do the dirty work yourself so you brought in Guerra. Had you dug up some dirt on him while you were on those mayoral commissions? Is that how you kept him in line?"

Josephson set down his cup on the coffee table next to the thick untouched Sunday paper. He said nothing but began to lick his lips as if he were still thirsty.

"But you had a few ideas of your own, didn't you, Doctor?

"With Graham Dillaway accepted as dead, Hope would inherit his estate for the balance of her life. On her death everything, both his and her property, would be divided three ways, among Will, James and your wife. One third of almost a million dollars, plus whatever interest in both Graham's and Hope's copyrights might go to Doreen under Section 24 of the Copyright Act.

"Enough to tempt even a dentist with a colonel's pension. All you had to do was kill Hope Dillaway for it.

"But you were afraid of one thing. Your motive would be too obvious. You, along with Will and James and Doreen, would be prime suspects if Hope were murdered. That didn't sit well with your plans but you could afford to take your time and wait for the right moment.

"And a week ago last night, at the conference in the penthouse, the moment came."

Josephson picked up his coffee mug and tapped a fingernail absently against its side.

"Hope announced that she was going to change her will," Loren went on, "so as to disinherit Will and increase James' and Doreen's shares. If you could kill her *at once,* before she had a chance to make out a new will, you would have the most beautiful psychological alibi I've come across in my life. Who would believe you killed her on Sunday for a third of the estate when by waiting till Monday to kill her you'd get control of half? Not only that, but by killing her at once you make Will Dillaway the prime suspect! An absolute brainstorm, and incredible returns on a little self-restraint. It was so beautiful you didn't even need a physical alibi.

"And the breaks stayed with you Sunday morning. Doreen went off to services as she does every Sunday and you took off for the Dillaway building. One thing that bothered me was how you got inside. In fact, last week I worked out a very plausible argument to show that only Graham Dillaway himself could have killed Hope! But I'd forgotten one thing. The week after the probate hearing, you spent a night in the guest apartment downstairs from Hope. The key to that apartment, like the key to any other apartment in the building, also works the locks on the front and side doors. Was it your idea to stay over that night, and did you conveniently forget to return the key until you had a duplicate made?"

Josephson said nothing. His silence was answer enough for Loren.

"That's how you got into the building, through the side door and up the firestairs. You got into the penthouse itself just by knocking, I suppose. You knew she'd be alone at that hour. But she must have suspected something before you had a chance to catch her off guard. She put up a fight, you struggled over that letter opener, and finally you hit her and she fell very hard against that low wall around the fireplace.

"And then Lucy walked in."

Josephson gulped more coffee, leaned back in his chair. "I keep a gun in the house for self-defense," he said slowly. "I took it with me that morning. I didn't need it till Miss Martell walked in."

Loren let out a breath of relief. He'd been right and now Josephson had admitted it, at least privately. That was one long step taken.

"I held the gun on her," the dentist went on. "I suppose I should have killed her on the spot but all I could see was that I was getting in deeper and deeper every step I took. I didn't want to kill her. I made her come with me. We went out the side door to my car. I took her away from there and got hold of Guerra. We met out in the woods beyond the city. It was Guerra that strangled her. He said he'd get rid of the body but the papers said he was called back to duty to help hunt for her before he could dispose of her and it was in his trunk all afternoon."

Loren stared at the other flatly. "So it was Guerra and Dillaway who killed Corby and the derelict, and Guerra who killed Lucy, and all you did was to kill Hope in self-defense. Do you expect me to let you off or something? I'd like to cut your heart out with a dull knife."

"I have to tell you why I did it...." Josephson began.

Loren sprang from his chair and towered over the other. "You destroyed the only person in this whole stinking world that I really loved and you expect understanding from me?"

The dentist's eyes were moist with supplication. "Please hear me out," he said simply. "I've never been able to tell this to anyone, not even Doreen. She would have hated me. You hate me already. It doesn't matter how much more you hate me. Please listen."

Loren sat down again, tense, waiting, fists clenching and unclenching.

The dentist's eyes seemed to retreat into the shadows of the past. He spoke as if in a trance, without tone or inflection. "Twenty-three years ago, after dental school, I took a direct commission in the army and was sent to Korea. My specialty was facial reconstruction. They would bring children, women, old people with faces half blown apart by bombs or grenades or artillery. I would try to give them some of their faces back. Every minute I worked I could hear the explosions that were making the next shipment of patients for me. Most of them were maimed by our side, some by the other side. It wasn't my job to distinguish, just to heal if I could. Most times I couldn't. That was where I learned detachment.

"I stayed in the military after the Korean war. I wanted to—make up for what I wasn't able to do to help all those mutilated people. And then Vietnam came and I was sent. And one day, a few months into my first tour, something happened." He paused and flicked a glance across the room as if to see whether his story was holding Loren's attention.

"I won't give any names or places or details. A field officer had some Viet Cong suspects and it was absolutely vital that they give us certain information within a few hours. I was in the area and had some dental equipment with me. I was asked to use that equipment to make them talk.

"It was a boy and a girl, no more than fifteen years old either of them. I was told that American lives would be lost if I didn't get the information. I worked on them. They talked. I can still hear them screaming in my sleep."

Loren stared at the other with a mixture of fascination and loathing, as if Josephson were a spider bloated with poison.

"Two months later something similar happened and someone remembered me and they flew me into the area in a chopper and I did the same kind of job again. And then a third time and then a fourth. God help me, I'd gotten myself an underground reputation as the best torturer in the Saigon area. After my second tour I couldn't stand it any more, I got out of the army and came here to open up a practice. I've tried to make up for it, I've fixed the teeth of more ghetto children than I ever worked on in Vietnam. It didn't help. I still wake up in the night with a cold sweat that's like the blood of all those people I did things to.

"I didn't dare talk to anyone, not to Doreen, not even to a psychiatrist. I knew I had to get away. I had to get out of dentistry completely, start all over again, wipe away almost a quarter century of my life. That was my only chance of stopping the nightmares.''

"And then Graham came to see you with his problem," Loren said.

The dentist nodded somberly. "His situation was eating him alive just as mine was tearing at me. And I saw that just a few more deaths, just a few more, a man on the brink of suicide, a vicious blackmailer, a filthy-minded old woman and a bum, just four more and I'd be free, I'd have the money to start over again at forty-nine. And—so I did it."

"Wait a minute." Loren stood up again, strode over to him. "You said four murders. Corby and the derelict on the mountain, Hope later....I see. The fourth was Graham Dillaway himself. Of course you had to kill him too, because if he ever came back from his new life, or was caught, you'd be stuck."

"Guerra killed him," the other muttered. "Weeks ago, in the fishing shack where he was hiding."

Loren sank back into his chair. That was another giant step forward. Now he knew that Dillaway was dead. Only one matter was left, and that was what to do with the man who sat opposite him, stoically detached, sipping coffee from a tall thick mug.

"Josephson," he said, "you're something else. You really believe deep down that torture and murder are all right when *you* have a reason. Does Doreen have a will? Does it leave everything to you? How long do you think you'd have waited after she came into all that property before you killed her?"

The soldier-dentist lifted his eyes eloquently. "You don't understand," he protested. "I love Doreen, I'd never do anything to hurt her."

Not unless you had a reason, Loren thought.

Michael Josephson took a cigar from a hammered-silver case, tapped it unlit against the edge of a tall metal ash receiver. He seemed abstracted, lost in his own thoughts.

"How much evidence do you have that will stand up in court?" he asked after a time of silence.

"Probably not enough," Loren admitted. "Guerra may have a safe-deposit box somewhere with more evidence but no one's been able to find it yet. We may be able to convict you with what I have if the prosecutor plays his cards right and runs into luck. We can ruin your life even if we can't put you away. A jury has to find you guilty beyond a reasonable doubt. Your wife doesn't. And I'm going to make it my business to turn her against you and make her see you for what you are even if I have to frame evidence against you to do it. No new start for you, Josephson. You'll stay in your sick filthy skin and wake up screaming in the dark till the day you drop dead."

Colonel Josephson lit his cigar. He took one puff and sighed with a sort of resigned contentment and laid it in a holder built into the smoking stand. They both watched the thin brown cylinder consume itself into ash.

"You don't need to do that," he said calmly. "I still have that gun and bullets for it. Perhaps it's about time I—test-fired it. It's not a very good answer but the best available."

Loren leaned back again and let a slow exhalation of breath escape him. He felt drained and exuberant at the same time. It was almost over now. Just a few more minutes.

Josephson stood erect, paced over to Loren, stared down at him. "Will you get somebody to take over the care on the black children's teeth?"

"I'll do what I can," Loren promised. "The School of Dentistry faculty should be able to spread the kids among your colleagues."

"Thank you," the other said simply. "I need a few minutes to think what kind of note I should write for Doreen. You'd better go now. You don't want to be seen in the neighborhood when I'm ready."

Loren forced himself to his feet. He felt a strange whistling noise in his head. He wondered if the top of his skull would fly off.

"Do what you can to make it easier on Doreen," Josephson said.

Loren remembered how she had taken his hand in the graveyard. "I will," he said.

"I'm sorry it happened this way," Josephson said.

"Things always happen this way," Loren said.

The dentist turned, strode toward the corridor leading to the back of the house. He moved briskly, like a well-trained soldier carrying out an order. Loren went to the front door and let himself out and walked slowly through the soft bright air of the morning to his car and drove away.

He knew the pain of losing her would last for a while but in time it would pass away and life would go on and from the security of his newly hardened shell he would go on too in his blundering way. But he knew that she would come to life as a sudden stab of loss within him whenever late at night he saw the glimmer of starlight on dark water.

CORRUPT AND ENSNARE

ONE

IT WASN'T A NIGHT for hospital visits. Soft wet flakes sifted past the sodium-vapor streetlamps, covering the mounds of hard dirty snow from the past week's accumulation. Loren backed the VW into a space at the edge of the city park, across the boulevard from Stoner Memorial. He locked the car and half ran across the all but deserted street, through the powdery orange glow of the lights. Falling snow stung the back of his neck. Recorded music over a loudspeaker sounded faintly from the depths of the park. Loren recognized the tune: "God Rest Ye Merry Gentlemen." The tan-brick hospital complex stood bathed in saffron light behind the transparent curtain of snow. He mounted the stone steps and an electric eye slid back twin glass doors.

A tall young nurse with shell-rimmed glasses sat inside an octagonal information post. Loren slapped snow off his gloves as he approached her. "Professor Mensing," he said, "to see Justice Richmond."

The nurse rotated a Wheeldex file mechanically and stopped at a card. "Oh, yes, Professor," she said gravely. "Room 3013, that's on the third floor. The judge's wife and daughter went back up a few minutes ago. They said you'd be coming." She pointed at the tiled corridor to her left. "The elevators are that way." Loren thanked her, trudged down the white hallway, pressed a buzzer. A huge antiseptic whitewalled cage lifted him two flights. He found the closed oak door of 3013 and twisted the knob softly.

It was a small private room. Bed, bedside table, three chairs. Walls painted dull green. No private bath, no television, none of the amenities. It was the room they took you to when they decided they could do nothing more and that another patient could make better use of the space you were filling in the intensive-care unit. The place where you were to say good-bye to your loved ones and die.

The man lying under the bedcovers looked less like a man than a pale empty shell, ancient and drained. The two swollen-eyed women sitting on one side of the bed looked up as Loren entered, releasing the old man's hands so that he could grasp them. The fingers felt cold as the snow.

"Merry Christmas," the dying man whispered as his hand stirred loosely in Loren's embrace.

"And to you, Ben," Loren muttered without thinking. He functioned poorly in hospitals. The disinfectant smell, the ugly labored breathing sounds behind curtains, the maimed people trudging or wheeling themselves through the halls, the sense of death in the air—everything reminded him too vividly that the house of concepts in which he lived and worked and hid himself was a paper fortress and that he owed the worms his own death. He looked down at what was left of the man who for a while had been more of a father to him than his real father and he remembered how Ben Richmond had been at the peak of his powers—sturdy bodied, mind like chrome steel, with a voice that could roll out over a courtroom like a thunderclap one moment and could be as gentle as a small child's an instant later. Loren looked into the judge's almost vacant eyes and his own eyes moistened. He pressed Richmond's hand more tightly, as if to hold off the end a few seconds longer.

"Thanks for...coming." The voice was so weak Loren could scarcely make out the words.

"I wish I could do the last few years over again," Loren said. "Spend more time with you. Try to tell you how much I...."

The judge cut him off, thrashed about in the bed, trying to lift himself, to raise his mouth to Loren's ear. He gasped and fell back and Loren bent over him. "What is it, Ben? What's the matter?"

"Tape." Richmond formed the word with his mouth. "Listen ... tape...just...you...." The words trailed off into nothingness and the judge's eyes went empty. Iris Richmond gave a little cry and threw her arms about her husband and pressed her lips against his and whispered, "Oh, Ben, I love you so much, so very much." Tears fell down her cheeks onto the judge's cold face. Jeanette ran blindly into the hallway calling "Nurse! Nurse!" in a high tight voice.

At 12:03 A.M. the doctor pronounced Justice Richmond dead. From somewhere in the distance Loren heard the muffled peal of church bells.

It was almost nine and a half years since Loren had returned from law school in the East and taken the state bar and gone to work in his father's firm. But even before the examination results were announced and he was fully licensed to practice law, he knew that he did not want to spend his life in this profession. The incessant pressure to bring in business, the technically legal but distasteful trickery, the obsession with property rights, the competitive ethos, created a world which he found repugnant in direct proportion to his growing certainty that he was incompetent to work in it. Yet he knew his father expected him to stay with the firm and eventually to become a partner, to put down roots in the legal community of the city. Loren was programmed to be a lawyer and he dreaded to let his father know how much he had grown to hate the life to which Stephen Mensing had dedicated both of them. It was agony to come to work every morning, not just because he couldn't stand the job but because he lived every day with the fear that his division against himself would lead him sometime to do or to fail to do something crucial and that his father's firm would suffer the consequences. He had no one to share his agony. He took to drinking too much and too often.

And then Ben Richmond's mother died and a door opened.

The old woman's will had left half her substantial estate to various charities and the rest to her son, who had been appointed a judge in the state court of appeals five years before. Judge Richmond had retained the firm of Mensing & Nalbin to settle the estate and Loren's father had assigned him to prepare the federal and state tax returns. "The experience will be good for you," Stephen Mensing had said. And so night after night Loren had sweated over the paperwork, sometimes literally banging his head against the wall in desperation, until finally the worst was over and he slipped the returns into his neat little attaché case and cabbed to the courthouse to get the judge's signature where it was needed.

In Richmond's chambers he had sat stiff and tense in a high-backed leather chair to the right of the judge's glistening desk. Richmond was tall, lean, with cobalt-blue eyes behind thick reading glasses, and hair graying at the sideburns. He looked strong as a redwood, and just as unbending. He finished scanning the tax returns and placed them in the exact center of the immaculately polished surface of the desk and leaned back in his black leather executive swivel chair and tapped a ballpoint pen against his thumbnail. He could have been posing for a portrait of a Wise

Judge Pondering; it struck Loren as too theatrical. Then he broke the pose, tossed the pen onto the sheaf of papers and took off his glasses and looked into Loren's eyes with a hypnotic gaze that for a moment made Loren want to run.

"You are about as miserable in that firm as if you were in a Siberian salt mine," the judge had said.

Loren's eyes widened and he hunted frantically for something to say in reply. Instinct told him not to deny it; if it was so obvious Richmond had seen it, pretending he was happy in his work would do no good anyway. "Is it that transparent?" he asked, and tried to cover a nervous little laugh.

"I have an instinct about people in traps," the judge said. "Perhaps I could help. Suppose we talk it over tonight at the Boatmen's Bar."

For two hours that evening they sipped scotch in the nautical ambience of the Boatmen's and discussed Loren's situation. Within the first half hour together in the brown leather booth Loren had told the judge things about himself that he had never dreamed of telling his father. He talked of how he had loved the intellectual challenge of law school but had become disgusted at how the system translated theory into practice. He even mentioned his ambivalence about his father and his distrust of his own competence.

"You're twenty-four years old already," Richmond had said. "Every day you wait is going to make it harder when the break finally comes. And it will come someday, believe me."

Loren grinned halfheartedly, like a gambler resigned to making the most of a poor hand. "But, Judge, all I'm qualified to do is use my law degree. How can I support myself if I don't practice?"

"I need a clerk," the judge said. "Someone who can do research in the library for me eight to ten hours a day, draft some opinions, sit around a table with me and help me clarify my thinking when I have to decide a tough one. There's pressure but not like in an office. And you'll have some time to help find yourself. Quite frankly, I made a few phone calls about you this afternoon and from what I learned I'm satisfied you'd be good in the position."

Loren resigned from his father's firm the next morning.

Before he had completed a month as Richmond's clerk, Loren knew that he had made the right choice. For the first time since law school he could wake up in the morning and shower and shave and dress and make his breakfast of orange juice and coffee and a chunk of hot French cheese bread in a spirit of looking forward to the day's work instead of dreading it. He would walk the twelve downtown blocks, dense with office buildings and coffeeshops and parking lots, that separated his cramped studio apartment in a riverfront highrise from the courthouse across Broadway from the city government complex. He would ride the elevator to the eighth floor where the Court of Appeals had its chambers and unlock the door to the judges' law library at the end of the paneled corridor, and across the glossy surface of one of the long mahogany tables that dotted the room he would spread the briefs and memoranda and the volumes of the state judicial reports that dealt with the case he was working on. A little before nine, when Loren was surrounded by his notes and jottings on the case, Richmond would poke his head in the doorway and invite Loren into his chambers for a conference, and for half an hour or an hour or as long as current business required the two of them would sit on the judge's overstuffed couch and sip coffee out of stoneware mugs and talk law. Richmond was gently critical of a good deal of Loren's early work for him but it took only a few weeks for Loren to get the feel of what the judge expected. Within three months he was enough in tune with Richmond's thinking to be able to draft opinions for the judge on almost any legal issue that might confront the court, and more often than not Richmond would make only minor editorial changes. Richmond was brilliant at drawing intricate distinctions to avoid applying higher court precedents that he felt would work injustice in the matter before him, and Loren soon became proficient not only at making such distinctions himself but at discovering or inventing distinctions that Richmond had overlooked and persuading him that they were sound.

The Richmond home was an elegant showplace built in 1906 at the foot of Boxwood Drive, in an affluent suburb west of the city. The corners of the high ceilings were decorated with frescoes of cherubs and roses. Opulent chandeliers and mantel-topped fireplaces and full-length pier glasses graced most of the rooms. Loren was welcomed into the house as a frequent guest. Iris Richmond, slender and gracious and perpetually aflutter, as though a thousand lovely little knickknacks were constantly smashing into fragments around her, took him under her wing as if Loren were the son she had never borne. With her outrageously selective memory for exact visual and verbal details of incidents that had occurred months or years ago, she was a never-failing source of amazement and delight. And Jeanette, who was dark and softly curved and enticing at sixteen, developed a fondness for Loren

which was not at all that of a sister for an older brother and which
Loren neither sought nor encouraged but had no idea in the world
how to deal with. Only her subsequent passion for the right half-
back on the local university's football team relieved Loren of an
involvement that had begun to embarrass him. Throughout the
difficult weeks Richmond prudently refrained from mentioning the
matter.

On a storm-soaked summer morning in the fifteenth month of
his clerkship Loren hung up his raincoat and umbrella in the law
library closet and strode to the shelves built into the north wall to
take down a volume of the annotated rules of civil procedure.
Richmond stepped into the book-lined room from the corridor
leading to the judges' chambers, the perennial stoneware coffee
mug in his hand.

"Got a few minutes?" He motioned Loren to follow him back
to chambers, where they took their usual places on the couch and
Richmond poured Loren a steaming cup from the percolator on the
table. "How does the name Professor Mensing sound to you?" he
asked.

Loren had not thought of his father for weeks. He stared at the
judge, uncomprehending. "Some law school wants Pop to teach?"

"Not your father," Richmond said. "You."

Loren almost spilled the coffee into his lap.

Richmond went on. "When I was in law school my best friend,
the guy I roomed with, was Conor Dunphy. He used to practice
criminal law but a couple of years ago he became the associate
dean at City University Law School. Right now they're hurting
very badly for new faculty. Ken Cole had that heart attack last
month and Dick Patterson just got a Fulbright to spend a year at
the University of Iran. I think you'd make a damn good law
teacher, Loren, and I want to phone Conor and tell him so, but I
had to check with you first to see if you'd be interested. With your
academic background and my recommendation, I think the job's
pretty much yours for the asking."

Loren felt a rush of almost unearthly lightheadedness. In law
school he had looked on the best of his own professors as almost
godlike in their wisdom, in the skill with which they explained the
law, the mastery with which they could direct the intellectual en-
ergies of classes of more than a hundred students. They fielded
whatever questions might be asked, framing their own questions
and making use of whatever answers the students gave, right or
wrong or indifferent, to carry the analysis further. At times Loren

had dreamed of being that kind of Socratic questioner someday.

"You want to get rid of me that bad, huh?" he said to the judge, and lay back on the couch and laughed uncontrollably.

He went out to the law school that afternoon and spent an hour talking with Eli York, the fierce and white-haired dean. Their conversation seemed to begin nowhere and end nowhere, like a random doodle on scratch paper. Then Loren spent an hour and a half with Associate Dean Dunphy, a big hearty Irishman with wild thatches of reddish-gray eyebrows above his bifocals, who kept a bottle of Tullamore Dew in the lower left drawer of his desk like a private eye in a 1940s movie. An interview with the full faculty was arranged for the following week.

By the end of the month Loren had been offered a position as assistant professor of law, which it took him less than ten seconds to accept. He continued with his work at the court until Richmond had hired a replacement clerk he felt comfortable with. Then he called Dean Dunphy's office and read off the titles of the casebooks he wanted the law-school bookstore to order for his first semester's courses and spent his last day at his old job cleaning out his desk in the courthouse library. That night Richmond treated him to dinner at Poe's, one of the most lavish restaurants in the city, and they sipped scotch as they had in the Boatmen's Bar and laughed and reminisced and tied up whatever loose ends remained in Loren's work. In the restaurant parking lot they shook hands for the last time, and Richmond threw his arms around his young clerk and embraced him like a father. And after a ten-day vacation cruise in the Virgin Islands with a petite and passionate young blonde who would shortly be returning for her senior year at Yale, Loren reported to Conor Dunphy's cluttered office in the fading brickwork wreck that was the administration building of City University Law School.

"You'd have to be a blind man to miss it," the associate dean thundered heartily as he tossed Loren a key. "Third floor, right above the law library, second from the end. Ken Cole's name's still on the door but his widow cleared away Ken's personal things last week, poor girl. I hope you stay with us a long time." Dunphy gave Loren a brisk clap on the shoulder. "And when you have a few minutes free, come down and visit with a poor devil of an administrator and share a drop of Dew with me. I'm editing a criminal procedure casebook and could use a bright young partner. This book will revolutionize the field, young Mensing, and you can be in on the ground floor."

"Sounds interesting," Loren said without committing himself. "What approach are you taking?"

"The Supreme Court, bless its collective soul—not to mention all the lower federal courts—has been cranking out decisions for four or five years now, applying constitutional rights to more and more corners of the criminal justice system. More power to them, says Dunphy! But how are the law schools going to find time to teach all these brave new concepts? I'll tell you how. They're going to take the traditional crim-law curriculum and split it into one course on substantive concepts and a second on straight procedure, stressing constitutional aspects. My casebook, or rather our casebook if you want to join the team, will be the first one on pure procedure, which means for a while at least it stands a fair chance of being the only book a school can use once it decides to bifurcate crim-law. And"—he grinned slyly at the prospect—"at the rate the courts are grinding out new decisions in the field, we'll need to do annual supplements of current developments as far ahead as the mind can foresee, with nice piles of the glorious green stuff that makes the world go round for you and for me. And by the way, if there are any faculty committees you don't want to serve on, let me know and I'll see that you avoid them."

"Doesn't the dean have anything to say about that?" Loren queried innocently.

Conor Dunphy looked around his office as if suspecting an eavesdropper, then lowered his Irish tenor to a conspiratorial wheeze. "Eli York," he said solemnly, "has been the dean of this institution since the memory of man runneth not to the contrary. Respect him, defer to him, think of him as you would think of General Patton if you were a second lieutenant on his staff. But don't forget that he has long ago passed the usual age of retirement, and don't be surprised if now and again he acts, well, just a wee bit erratic."

"Thanks for the tip," Loren said. "See you after I've moved in." And he walked down the echoing corridor to the rear stairway that led to the law library and above that to faculty offices, wondering what he had let himself in for.

Loren like most beginning law professors was given a light teaching load his first year, but before many weeks had passed he found himself thrust into a life radically different from anything he had experienced before. Frantic preparations for each class. Hopeless attempts to anticipate and prepare answers for any conceivable student question on the cases assigned for the day. Interruptions, invariably timed to take place at Loren's busiest hours, when a student would knock on his office door with a problem or a complaint or just to pass the time. Wrangles with Dean York over certain rather unenthusiastic comments Loren had made in class about the foreign and domestic policies of the United States. Endless committee meetings and endless faculty meetings. (Loren discovered that law professors had an uncanny ability lo debate for hours what an ordinary person could resolve in five minutes flat.) Working on law-review articles which had not the least connection with his ability as a teacher but which he had to grind out if he hoped to receive promotion and tenure. Preparing final examinations. Grading final examinations. Long bitter encounters with students who had received D's and demanded C's, or who had been awarded B-pluses and insisted stridently that they had earned A's. Skimming the advance sheets that reported Federal court decisions, carefully reading every case on criminal procedure involving constitutional claims, conferring twice a week with Dunphy over what materials should and should not go in the casebook. Every few weeks he would resolve to call Judge Richmond when he could snatch a few spare moments but he never seemed to find the time. Days, weeks, months, the semester itself, passed in a blur as if he were living on a rollercoaster.

On a Thursday morning late in the spring term of his first year, Loren sat in Dunphy's office with the working copy of the embryonic Dunphy & Mensing casebook on the desk between them. "Damn it, I want those cases in there!" Loren insisted. "*Ex parte Starr* and all the other outrageous decisions I dug out. Students have to get a sensitivity to the infinite capacity of the legal system to dispense with basic decency and fairness, and it's part of our job to give it to them."

"Well, maybe we could squeeze some of your material into Chapter Seven," Dunphy conceded wryly, "if we knock out those radical hypotheticals you posed at the end of the police perjury section."

There was a hesitant tapping on Dunphy's door and Ellie, Dean York's secretary, stood nervously in the doorway. "Has either of you seen the dean?" she said.

Loren shook his head no. "Not since nine or so," Dunphy replied. "Wasn't he supposed to meet with Judge Mills here at eleven?" He threw a glance at the electric clock on the file cabinet, which read 11:14.

"The judge has been waiting for twenty minutes," Ellie said, "and he's getting impatient. Dean Dunphy, would you please help us try to locate Dean York?"

Conor Dunphy sprang to his feet. This kind of problem had arisen before, Loren knew; all too many times before. Dunphy had become an expert at sniffing out where his superior might have wandered on any given occasion. "Loren, we'll have to continue pounding each other's heads against the wall another time. I have an illegal search of the building to make. If you're not doing anything, could I draft you to try the other usual spots?"

"No trouble." Loren pushed himself out of the visitor's chair and headed out of the law-school building and across the fragrant green meadow to the center of the campus. He checked the main library and found no dean. He tried the school bookstore and found no dean. He half ran along the cindered pathway that connected the bookstore and the venerable old mansion that had been turned into the faculty club.

The cool dim hallway of the club building led to the faculty dining room and three high-ceilinged lounges furnished with easy chairs and divans and tables stacked with current issues of popular and scholarly magazines. None of the downstairs rooms had the dean in it. Loren mounted the grandly sweeping staircase two steps at a time and tried the lounges on the second floor.

In the smallest and most remote room on that level he found York, lying prone on the floor, not breathing, not moving. Loren bent over him, took his pulse, listened for a heartbeat, then ran out the door and downstairs for help.

By the end of the afternoon Eli York was in the coronary care unit of Universal Hospital and Conor Dunphy was acting dean of the law school.

And the semesters and the years rolled past. The administration launched a nationwide search for a successor to York and eventually returned to home base and offered the permanent position of dean of the law school to Dunphy. Loren's father had a heart seizure during the negotiation of a corporate merger and died instantly, leaving no will, so that thanks to the laws of intestacy Loren became a moderately wealthy man all but overnight. Within two years of its publication the Dunphy & Mensing casebook had been adopted by three dozen law schools. Loren's festering sense of outrage at the America of the late sixties and early seventies came to a boil and propelled him into deeper involvement in the marches, the demonstrations, the protests, the massive quixotic lawsuits on behalf of the government's victims. He was denied tenure twice.

The university rule was that any professor failing to be granted tenure three times was discharged at the end of the academic year of his third attempt. During the weeks when Loren's third application for promotion and tenure was before the appropriate committee, he spent most of his off-duty hours in his office, wrestling with his thoughts. He knew that the committee was stacked with "America: love it or leave it" types and expected to find himself canned in short order. He had thought for months about beating them to the punch, resigning from the faculty and working full time and without pay as a lawyer for the peace movement. On a certain Friday afternoon late in the spring he sat slumped over his desk, scanning the latest U.S. Law Week listlessly, half listening to the Mendelssohn Symphony Number Five, the "Reformation," over the university's FM station on his tiny radio. He came close to making up his mind to go downstairs for a heart-to-heart talk with Dunphy about his future.

The phone rang. He let it blare three times while he lowered the volume on the radio to a whisper, then he lifted the receiver. "Mensing."

"And a glorious afternoon it is, Loren. Just wanted to make sure you were in. May I run up for a minute?"

Dunphy's tone told Loren that something had happened but whatever it was, the dean would not want to break the news impersonally over the phone. "Sure, Conor," he said quietly. "I'll be waiting."

He hung up, adjusted the radio volume again and irrationally began to straighten the office clutter, picking student seminar papers and advance sheets and junk mail off the windowsill and the seats of the chairs, removing a pile of law reviews from the segment of an old gray sectional sofa he had bought at a secondhand store for ten dollars, rummaging in his desk for a cloth to dust with. When the knock sounded five minutes later and Dunphy walked in, the office was more orderly than it had been in months. The dean closed the door and dropped onto the sectional and set his attaché case flat on the faded shag rug. Loren swiveled around to face him, awaiting the verdict.

"I have sad news for you," Dunphy said solemnly, and sat back, savoring the pregnant pause like a ham actor. "The damn fools decided to keep you. Welcome to the ranks of the tenured!" And he beamed and bounced up from his seat and clasped Loren's hand between his own and then, as if ashamed of displaying his emotions, he sat down again and snapped his attaché case open. Nestled inside were two squat glasses and a half-full bottle of Tullamore Dew. "No ice, but what the hell, it's a cool day." With due ceremony he poured two generous drinks and they touched glasses.

By 4:30 the bottle was dead, and Dunphy squinted at its emptiness against the light and sprawled back against the sectional's single arm. "I'll tell you, Loren," he said, "I had the devil's own time fighting for you in that rank and tenure committee. Your views on the war and the other evils of the system are distinctly unwelcome in certain quarters. I don't always see eye to eye with you myself and I've never made any bones about admitting it but damn it, that sly old frog was right about defending to the death somebody else's right to express different ideas."

"You might not have gotten tenure here yourself, spouting the views of a godless degenerate like Voltaire in Middle America," Loren said. "I...don't know quite how to tell you this, Conor. You put yourself on the line for me and I owe you. I hope we spend a lot of years here together so I can begin to pay you back."

"Ah, but we won't." Dunphy laid his glass on Loren's desk. "You see, this little celebration isn't just for you. It's for the two of us." He indulged himself in another pregnant pause, then cleared his throat as if in prelude to an important announcement. "You knew that the governor had two vacancies to fill on the supreme court?"

Loren nodded slowly. "I haven't stopped following the state news just because most of my crusades are federal. The advisory committee's been screening names since Chief Justice Edwards died." Then the significance of what the dean had said penetrated the Irish mist, and Loren blinked in amazement behind his glasses. "Conor, do I understand that....?"

"You are now looking at the noble countenance of the next chief justice." Dunphy made a comic monster face. "I was at the top of the advisory committee's list. The governor had me on the phone for an hour this afternoon. He'll make the official announcement at a press conference tomorrow morning."

Loren stumbled over to the sectional and threw his arms around the dean in a burst of joy. "Congratulations! Bravo! Wow!" he shouted stupidly. "My God, what a crazy day this has turned into for both of us. So I guess you'll be packing your bags and moving to Capital City?"

"Not just myself either, Loren. You forgot to ask me who the governor picked to fill that other opening on the court."

"All right, Mr. Bones," Loren said. "Who did—no, strike that—whom did Thornton pick to fill the other opening on the court?"

"My best friend from law school," Dunphy told him. "Ben Richmond."

"Oh, God," Loren muttered. "And I haven't even said hello to him in ages. This is just fantastic news, Conor, and I've got to call him right away before court closes and wish him my best." He lurched off the sectional and across to the phone, kicking over the empty bottle of Tullamore Dew as he went, while Dunphy beamed indulgently and sprawled back in his corner.

That night Loren hosted a dinner at Poe's in honor of his own good fortune and that of the two new supreme court justices. In a cool dim booth curtained in blue they feasted on caesar salad tossed at their table, filet mignon and lobster tails, champagne, an obscenely rich Black Forest cake, and coffee with Grand Marnier. Dunphy and Richmond produced twenty-dollar bills and bribed the five-piece orchestra to play music from the big-band era, the slow sentimental danceable tunes they had grown up with. Richmond and Iris rose from the table and moved in a stately waltz across the gleaming floor. Mischievously sensuous at twenty, Jeanette Richmond in a backless white evening gown reached out for Loren's hand, motioning that she wanted to dance. "You don't need your glasses," she said, and Loren obediently set them on the tablecloth for Dunphy to watch over. As they glided about the open floor amid other dancing couples, she molded her body tight against him, letting him feel her warmth and enjoy the loveliness of her breasts. "Oh, Loren, I don't think I've ever been so high, just so high I want to fly around the room and kiss everyone I see and tell them I'm so happy, not hut for Daddy and Mother and Conor and you but for the whole beautiful world."

"I know." Loren held her close and smelled the fragrance of her long dark hair. "I know. It's all I can do to keep from busting out myself."

Jeanette pressed even closer against him. "Let's bust out together," she whispered into his ear. "Later, after the party. After we drive Conor home." Across the dimly lit room the dean beamed like a drunken angel and poured liqueur into his coffee. "I'll tell Mother I want to spread the news among a few girl friends. I know the way to your place. If you want me?"

"There are some invitations even a law professor can't refuse," he said.

A month later Loren made the 130-mile drive upstate to the capital for the swearing in of the two new justices. The governor administered the oath of office to Dunphy and Richmond in the vast high-ceilinged courtroom on the fourth floor of the State House building where the justices heard oral arguments. Afterward coffee and creamy petits fours were served from tables covered with snowy cloths and set up in the corridor outside the courtroom. The mob of judges, lawyers, state functionaries, media people, friends, relatives and strangers surged around the two men of the hour. Loren squeezed his way into the center of the throng just long enough to shake the justices' hands and give them his best wishes.

"And how do you like your new house?" he asked Iris Richmond.

"It's a lovely old place." Iris kept her arm entwined in her husband's as if afraid the crowd would carry him away. The fine lines and wrinkles of early middle age had crept into her patrician face since the last time Loren had seen her. "Not quite as large as the one we had before, but I've fixed up a suite for Ben so that his bedroom and study are right next to each other. We'll have to invite you up for dinner once things settle down a bit."

"I've got an apartment in town now," Jeanette told him. In a bright-orange knit skirt and jacket over a scoop-necked brown top, and with her hair falling softly below her shoulders, she seemed to Loren the loveliest woman in the building. "And a job with the Bureau of Community Affairs Uncle Norm got for me. You've met him, haven't you, Loren?"

"My brother, Norman Abelson," her mother explained, and tried to point through the mass of bodies toward one of the refreshment tables. "There he is, standing next to Justice Lutz. The tall well-built bald man in the gray suit. He's the deputy administrator of the Department of Institutions and Agencies. I'm sure I've mentioned him a hundred times."

"Oh yes, of course," murmured Loren, who had never seen the man before.

"Loren!" Chief Justice Dunphy called out. "Come on over here a second....What's this I hear about your taking leave from the law school and going to work for the police?"

"Not really leave." Loren had to shout to make himself heard over the babble of legal and political small talk that surrounded them. "A sort of shared-time arrangement. Comes of getting a liberal mayor in November's election, I guess. Bill Sturm's always been concerned about abuse of police power, and a few weeks ago he called up and asked if I'd be interested in a part-time appointment as deputy legal adviser to the commissioner's office. I'm supposed to root out illegal practices by persuading the brass they're counterproductive. It may turn out to be a waste of time but I said I'd give it a whirl. As if I didn't have enough complications in my life already."

The complications multiplied as Loren's involvement with the police deepened. Over the next year, almost in spite of himself and by means he was never sure he understood, he was credited with having helped the department solve a number of bizarre crimes, including a few murders, and developed a kind of underground reputation as the man to call in when a situation seemed too crazy for normal procedure to be of much use. Before too many months had passed he found himself the object of a strange amalgam of attitudes on the part of the police, even of Sergeant Hough, who had worked with him on several cases. They had nothing but contempt for his social philosophy and for the minor restrictions on their power that he had bulldozed the commissioner into imposing, but they couldn't help but respect him for his detective abilities. Sometimes he thought that this astuteness and his connection with the mayor were all that saved him from being framed on some charge, beaten to raw meat in some station-house back room, and railroaded into prison by a friendly judge. At least three officers had subtly threatened to do just that. After a year Loren resigned in frustration and disgust and returned to law school to concentrate on battles he stood a chance to win.

And as the early seventies turned into the middle seventies, and the hideous war had ended as it deserved to end and the White House pigsty had been cleansed as it needed to be cleansed, Loren began to tire. There seemed to be fewer issues of good against evil these days, and the social problems were not as clear-cut as they had appeared a few years before. He was uncertain whether it was society or he, and a lot of burned-out rebels like him, that had changed. The campus grew quiet; the students were cool, better groomed, self-seeking and uncommitted, worried about jobs and their own futures. Loren no longer felt guilty about his inherited money and was only vaguely uncomfortable about his lack of guilt. He sensed his life winding down into a cycle of mechanical academic ruts. Except for Christmas cards, and a get-well note to

Dunphy after he'd heard that the chief justice had lost a foot in some grotesque auto accident, he fell out of touch with his old friends on the state's high court. When he was promoted to full professor, he didn't bother to celebrate. His fortieth birthday was still years off but getting uncomfortably close.

The call from Jeanette that he received in his apartment that snowy December evening stunned him like a blow in the face. "He hasn't got long, Loren. He wants to see you badly."

"Stomach cancer," Loren repeated grimly. "And he's known for a year or more and didn't tell you or your mother till last month?"

"He just kept working," Jeanette said, and he could hear the grief in her voice. "Like a demon. We thought he was pushing himself too hard but we never suspected, or at least I didn't, and I don't think Mother or Uncle Norm did."

"And it's been so long since I've seen him or even talked to him," Loren said. "God, I feel putrid inside....You say he's in Stoner Memorial, the intensive-care unit?"

"Since Tuesday," Jeanette told him. "We tried to call you at the law school but they said you were out of town and wouldn't be back till tonight."

"Tell me how to go after I get off the Interstate." Loren reached for the pad and pencil beside the telephone on the coffee table. "I'm leaving right away."

TWO

FORTY-EIGHT HOURS before Christmas, on a bone-chilling morning of leaden-gray skies and sifting snow, Justice Richmond was buried. Loren had stayed in the capital to help Dunphy and Norman Abelson with the funeral arrangements and to serve as one of the pallbearers. A line of black limousines, headlights ablaze, crunched in stately procession through the snow-packed city streets from the funeral home to Eternal Rest Cemetery. A shivering clergyman stood under a hastily erected canopy and read words over the grave and a forklift device lowered the polished casket into the hungry earth. Loren and a ghost-faced Jeanette stood on either side of Iris Richmond, their arms tight around her, supporting her, trying to shield her from the bite of the wind. Her eyes were raw with grief and she sobbed quietly against Loren's snow-crusted overcoat.

At the other end of the knot of mourners the six surviving justices of the court stood wind-whipped and erect. Chief Justice Dunphy took a few hesitant steps toward the lip of the grave as if to look down and say a last farewell to his old friend. He moved slowly, planting his thick heavy cane into the treacherous ground before venturing each step. His eyes were hooded with a bitterness Loren had not seen there before these last few days.

It was the accident, Loren thought. In the downstairs lounge of the funeral home, the first night of Richmond's wake, he had seen the chief justice sitting in a wine-colored armchair in the far corner, playing with an unlit pipe, the knobby cane propped at an angle against the paneled wall. Loren had crossed the lounge and dropped onto a hassock nearby Dunphy. Conor looked older and more tired than Loren had ever seen him during their years together at the law school.

"Just your usual garden variety auto negligence case," he had said, trying to treat the loss of his foot lightly and failing so miserably Loren almost winced. "And the hell of it is that I hadn't drunk a drop that evening, except two bloody marys. It was a Sunday, around nine I guess, pitch dark, downtown was pretty much deserted, and I was just leaving the bar and jaywalking across

Broadway to the parking lot when this state police car comes tearing out of nowhere at seventy miles an hour without even its siren on and roars by within a couple of inches of my face. Have you ever been stepped on by an elephant, Loren?"

"Not to my recollection," Loren said.

"Well, I've been stepped on by a police cruiser," Dunphy said, "and it smarts. Where my right foot had been looked like a basket of crushed strawberries. And mind you, I was still standing upright somehow, as if my brain hadn't gotten the message yet. Well, they rushed me to the hospital and the doctors had to cut off the whole foot and a chunk of the ankle and give me a plastic contraption I still haven't learned to walk on properly. It didn't cost me a cent. The state gives us complete insurance coverage, and I even got them to pay for the cost of Sean Patrick here." He clutched the lethal-looking cane in his powerful hand. "This is an authentic shillelagh from the old country, I'll have ye know. Made in 1824 by Seamus O'Fearna of Dublin, the finest woodcraftsman of his generation. Just what I've always wanted to have." Loren didn't know whether or not to believe Dunphy's account of the cane's history; it was the kind of blarney Conor had a talent for improvising at a moment's notice. The chief justice squeezed his eyes tight shut for a moment as if to hide something. "But I didn't want it like this," he whispered hoarsely. "Oh, Christ, not like this." There was the sound of squeaky-shoed feet descending the staircase into the lounge and Dunphy sniffed hastily and straightened in his high-backed chair. "Ah, Jonathan, I could tell you were coming a mile off. Come on over here and meet a young friend of mine. Professor Mensing, Justice Lutz...."

After the funeral there was a quiet luncheon at the Richmond house for Loren, the family, the justices, Norman Abelson and his wife and a few friends. Loren picked absently at the cold turkey and potato salad on his plate, remembering that on the day Ben Richmond had been sworn in, Iris had promised to have him up for dinner sometime and it had never happened. Late that afternoon he drove back home on the Interstate, keeping the VW at a safe forty miles per hour as it slid through the softly falling snow, the auto heater turning the interior into an oven. He thought about Richmond's last moments, that night in the hospital, when he had thrashed about in bed, forcing his dying body to sit up, straining to whisper those last desperate words in Loren's ear. "Tape," he had croaked, so softly it was almost as if he had said nothing. "Listen...tape...just...you."

Loren wondered, not for the first time, what the words could have meant. He had debated whether he should ask Iris or Jeanette if either of them knew anything about a tape but it was the wrong time for questions. Let the grief subside first, let their life return to some kind of normal pattern. There would be time enough in the weeks and months ahead. But would the judge have wanted him to ask the other members of the family? "Just...you," he had said, as if perhaps the tape involved some private secret.

Loren put the puzzle out of his mind and concentrated on the road. He noticed that the gas gauge was low, remembered the Benneco station just off the next exit and hoped it was open. The VW's tires slithered through the sea of slush.

And then another semester began, and as new problems fought for his attention, Richmond's dying words receded from his mind. Late in the spring a large cardboard box arrived at the law school for Loren, postmarked CAPITAL CITY. An envelope bearing the letterhead of a Capital City law firm was attached to the upper side of the box with strapping tape. Loren lugged the box up to his office, set it on the floor and used a paper knife from his desk to cut the letter free.

Dear Professor Mensing:

Enclosed please find one (1) calf-bound set of the 1833 edition of *Commentaries on the Constitution of the United States*, in three (3) volumes, by The Honorable Joseph Story, Justice of the United States Supreme Court. These books come from the personal library of the late Justice Ben Richmond of our own high bench and were specifically bequeathed to you in the will of Justice Richmond dated June 14 of last year. We trust that you will be happy with this memento from the distinguished jurist.

Very truly yours,
LATIMER, MARTIN & GASH
SIDNEY J. LATIMER

Loren attacked the industrial tape that secured the bulky carton. Piled firmly inside the box were three heavy volumes bound in rich calf, each wrapped for protection in a swatch of clean white cloth. Loren arranged the books on his desk, sat in his swivel chair and rubbed the luxurious bindings with an almost sensual delight.

He opened a volume at random and read a few pages and remembered that Story's three volumes had occupied the top shelf in Richmond's chambers when he had been an appellate judge and Loren had been his clerk. He must have eyed them fondly even then, and the shrewd and gentle judge had remembered. Loren took down some legal texts from the top shelf of one of his own bookcases and reverently installed the Story volumes in their place. When he had cleared away the remains of the box and the tape scraps, he sat down at his desk again and placed a long-distance call to Capital City, to tell Iris how much he appreciated Ben's gift and to find out how she was feeling.

He thought of asking if the judge had ever mentioned a tape recording to her, but the fear that the matter might be a completely private one kept him from raising the question. The meaning of those cryptic words of Richmond's had begun to nag at him again, like the ache of an old wound. Someday, he thought, he'd mention the matter to Dunphy and see if the chief justice could shed any light. Someday.

When he finished grading the spring semester examinations, and made his ritual appearances at the university graduation exercises and the weekend round of student parties that followed, he felt drained and purposeless and alone. He wanted to go away somewhere but knew that he would feel more isolated than ever if he went off to a strange place by himself, and there was no one he felt like asking to go with him who he thought would be free and willing. He spent a week staying in his high-rise apartment like a hermit, systematically listening to his classical music albums, fussing with minor maintenance chores he had never been able to get the building's handyman to attend to, reading a few bestsellers desultorily, feeling at loose ends and sorry for himself. When he had worked the melancholy out of his system he went back to the office for the first time in ten days and read his accumulated mail. Then he crawled under a scratched old conference table in the corner and exhumed a thick fiberboard carton and tore the tape from its edges. Inside the carton were the research materials and the seven unfinished chapters of one of his major scholarly projects, a legal history of the Third Reich. He hadn't touched the project in more than a year. He rummaged through the papers and reread a chapter he had begun to draft three years earlier and made up his mind that since he had no summer classes to teach he would spend the hot months working on the history again.

The law school was all but deserted after graduation. A few professors stayed around the campus, as did the law review candidates and some recent graduates who were cramming for the bar examination. The summer session wouldn't start for another three weeks. Loren carved out a new daily routine. He slept as late as he wanted, and made himself pork roll and a cheese omelet for breakfast or stopped at a quick-service restaurant on the way to school when he felt too lazy to cook. He would whirl the VW down the circular ramp that led to the depths of the university's underground parking facility, and maneuver into the tiny slot on the fourth level stenciled MENSING, and stroll through the long underground tunnel that connected the garage with the basement level of the new law library. From there he would take the self-service elevator to his office on the fourth level and sort through the notes and rough drafts in his files, selecting the materials to be worked on that day. He would pack what he needed in his gray Samsonite attaché case and lock the office and take the elevator down to BB, the subbasement level, where most of the foreign legal materials were kept. And there he would enclose himself in one of the cell-like study carrels and read and think and scrawl on pads of yellow paper, sometimes all day, sometimes just for a few hours. Once in a while he could hear through the thick ceiling the muffled scrape of footsteps or the blur of voices from overhead. It was rare that anyone came down to the subbasement between semesters. The few who did moved so quietly he didn't hear them.

That Tuesday the work was going well. He was revising the chapter on a curious phenomenon of Hitler's Germany, the secret statute, the law whose existence was unknown and unknowable to the people but whose violation was punishable by imprisonment, conscription, forced labor, torture or death. He had hunted for parallels in recent American legal developments and found them with little trouble. He read and wrote through the day in the cool dark carrel, oblivious of time.

In a corner of his consciousness he noted the hum of the elevator descending, the snap of its door sliding back. He wondered idly if it could be one of the maintenance crew, come to dust the shelves. He listened for the sound of footsteps echoing on the concrete floor and heard none. He thought nothing of it and bent over the legal pad on the carrel table and kept writing.

Until a prickling at the back of his neck told him to turn around.

He almost didn't do it. He had been alone in empty cavernous places before. He had experienced sudden feelings of insecurity, an urge to run, and had known they were irrational and had resisted. He resisted again. He was in the law library of a major urban university and he was a grown man, built like a bear, able to take care of himself if he had to. He was alone. He must have imagined the elevator noises, or else the cage had stopped on the floor above.

He thought he heard a quiet cough behind him, the shuffle of feet. *Someone was watching him.* He whirled out of his chair. He half ran into the nearest aisle, sighted down between the ranks of gray steel shelves to the elevator at the far end of the corridor. Nothing. He laughed at himself and turned back toward the carrel.

Two men stood in front of him.

Loren felt a stab of cold fear.

There was nothing to be afraid of. They didn't look like street muggers. They wore shirts and ties and summer-weight business suits and their neatly polished shoes glistened under the recessed lights. There was a vaguely Latin look about them: visiting South American lawyers perhaps. One was tall and slender with eyes slightly hooded and a trim tiny mustache and a look of cool self-possession as if he would refuse to sweat even on the hottest day. The other was shorter, chunky but sturdy of build, with a receding hairline and a rumpled suit jacket. They stared levelly at Loren as if they were laboratory scientists and he was the experimental animal. No one moved. No one breathed.

"Professor Mensing?" The slender one finally broke the silence. His voice was velvet smooth, evoking soft lights and seduction.

Loren said nothing. He wrestled with a wild impulse to run down the aisle in the opposite direction.

"You are Professor Loren Mensing, sir, is that not so?" the slender one said. "The two young women on the main floor said that you were working in the subbasement."

"I'm—I'm Mensing." It came out half a stammer and half a wheeze. Loren felt panic and disgust with himself for being panicky. Nothing was wrong here. Nothing.

"My name is Moraga," the other said. "This is Mr. Rojas." Moraga reached tapered fingers into the breast pocket of his jacket and extracted a tooled leather card case, hinged at one side. He flipped back the lid and displayed an identification card. Printed in dignified-looking type at the head of the card was UNITED STATES OF AMERICA and beneath it CENTRAL INTELLIGENCE AGENCY.

"Would you mind coming with us, sir?" Moraga said politely.

Loren was a veteran of the peace movement. He had learned that encountering a CIA operative was like running into a cotton-mouth in a swamp. But his irrational fear was gone now that the enemy had shape and identity. "Would you mind telling me where you'd like to take me," he demanded, "and why?"

"We would mind very much, sir," Rojas replied. His voice was hoarse, deep, froglike. Loren stored its sound in his memory. "Just come along with us, okay?"

"You characters must be out of your skulls." Loren raised his voice, hoping against hope that someone would hear them. "I am not going to budge an inch unless you give me a damn good reason. Now come on, what the hell is this all about? Or do you want me to call a security guard?"

Moraga and Rojas exchanged sharp glances. Rojas dug into his jacket. A small polished revolver materialized as if by magic in his hand. He trained the pistol on Loren's middle. Loren backed away a step.

"This is not a request, sir," Moraga said politely. "And please don't think too harshly of us. We're simply following instructions."

Rojas edged closer, held the revolver two inches from Loren's middle. "Over to the elevator," he croaked. They marched single file past the twin rows of tall musty lawbooks to the green door at the end of the aisle. Moraga pressed the second joint of his finger against the plastic circle set in the wall. The button glowed and a motorized hum descended the shaft, snapping off when the cage dropped into place and the green door slid back. Moraga's eyes darted about warily, like the eyes of an animal sensing a predator. Rojas' breath was an unhealthy rasp. Loren heard no other sound.

"In you go, Professor," Moraga said, too loudly. "And press the button for B. We're not going far, just to the underground lot." The cage door clanked shut and the motor hum rose with them, then shut off. The door opened and they motioned Loren out. Rojas walked beside him, Moraga five steps ahead like a scout. A heavy fire door gave onto the tunnel to the parking lot. They strode down the walkway briskly, in silence.

From the far end of the long tube Loren heard the echo of approaching footsteps. His heart pounded wildly. His brain raced. The sweat of fear drenched him. *Let it be security guards coming this way.*

"You'll keep our business private, sir, I hope," Moraga said politely, and chewed his lip. Their shadows flowed along the whitewashed tunnel walls. The steps from the other end boomed loudly and the people they belonged to came into sight, small at first, growing in size as their steps grew in sound.

They were two young men in sloppy shirts and jeans, talking animatedly of baseball. Loren had never seen either one of them before. The groups passed without contact and the young men's steps receded behind Loren.

"Speed it up, Professor," Moraga muttered. He stayed a few paces ahead, arrived at the door to the parking garage, opened it by pressing his forearms against the steel bar. "After you," he said. They passed through the door and Moraga let it clang shut behind them.

"Bottom level?" Rojas asked.

"Affirmative." Moraga pointed to a flight of concrete steps leading deeper into the earth. "Take him down those and prepare him. I'll get the wheels." He pivoted smartly like a soldier on parade and marched across the dark empty garage. Rojas motioned Loren to precede him down the steps to the lowest level. "Watch you don't trip," he said. "You'd think a school would spend some of our tax money for decent lighting in this damn place." They reached the foot of the stairs. Loren thought about running. He thought about trying to take the gun away from Rojas. He kept walking.

Between semesters the lowest level of the underground garage was as empty as a graveyard at midnight. None of the few people who came to the university between semesters wanted to wrestle his car all the way down the spiral auto ramp and then back up again to the street level when he left. Bright bulbs in triple clusters like electric fruit threw long shadows across the concrete floor as they walked. Loren felt dank and clammy and helpless.

"Okay, Professor," Rojas said. "Lie down. Right there. On your gut or on your ass—I couldn't care less." He pointed with the pistol barrel to one of the empty slots, its borders marked in faded yellow paint. "Your legs sticking out into the aisle, the rest of you in the slot like you'd park your car."

Loren knew then. Every muscle in his body and every bead of sweat that ran down him told him the truth. These CIA agents were going to kill him. He would be a twitching pile of dead meat in a few moments. His body refused to move. He stood there, frozen.

"Lie down, God damn you!" Rojas shoved him with his foot. Loren sprawled onto the cold dank floor. Somewhere he heard the hollow drip of water in a pipe. He concentrated on the sound, clung to it as if it were a life raft. Rojas kicked him with the toe of his shoe, made him stretch his legs out into the aisle, raise his arms over his head.

Loren couldn't hear the dripping anymore. A motor gunned into life on one of the upper levels, killing the sound, roaring nearer, down the ramp at the other end.

"That's him," Rojas said. "Now if you'll just lie still, Professor, it won't be all that bad."

Loren began to twitch uncontrollably. His mouth was bone dry. It was agony to speak. "What"—his voice sounded like the rattle of a dying animal—"what are you going to do to me?"

"Well, Professor, Mr. Moraga is going to train the car on you like you were a target on the firing range." Loren made himself turn his head to face the distant ramp. The car was reversing, running forward a few feet, reversing again. Getting into position. "Then he's going to put on the gas and fly down this lane." Rojas traced a swift line with the pistol across Loren's ankles. "It doesn't really hurt as much as you think it will if you try to relax and put it out of your mind."

Loren imagined the bones of his legs crunching into fine powder under those wheels. He saw himself trapped in a wheelchair for the rest of his life. Vomit rose in his throat. He gagged, coughed. Helpless now, no way to make a break from flat on his back. He would have given anything—ten, twenty years of his life—if he could relive the last few minutes and try to escape back in the tunnel or on the stairs.

"Why are you doing this?" He forced the words out through the vomit on his lips.

Rojas shrugged quizzically. "It's a job." The sound of the car grew louder. Loren turned his head toward the car again. "It's easier if you don't watch," Rojas said paternally. "And, look, uh, don't worry about, you know, losing too much, like not being able to make it with women when you're healed up." An auto horn honked once, short, crisp. "He's ready," Rojas said, and started to move out of the way.

A door boomed somewhere in the garage. Running steps echoed—two, three sets of steps. Loud, furious, urgent. "Loren!" A falsetto screech tore through the air. Rojas whirled about, pistol raised, searching for the sound.

Loren snaked his left foot behind Rojas' heel, kicked at the knee savagely. Rojas hit the concrete with a grunt. Loren sprang up, stamped on Rojas' hand as if it were a poisonous insect, ground it into the floor. Rojas shrieked, let go the gun. The car roared down the lane toward them. Loren kicked the gun across the garage and began to run, frantically. Rojas stumbled to the car. The car shuddered to a halt; the passenger door flew open. A tall man in uniform leaped to the bottom of the concrete steps. "Halt!" he roared. The car rocketed forward to the ramp at the far end of the level, raced up the spiral, tires screaming.

Loren clutched a concrete pillar for support. The red-bearded young man in a university security guard's uniform ran up to him, halted a few steps away, holstered his pistol.

"You okay, Professor?"

"Yeah," Loren panted. "If I ever see those goddamn pigs again I'll tear their hearts out."

"Get the make or license number?"

"Just a dark blue sedan," Loren said. "Late model. They were going to run over my legs, cripple me." He began to shudder un-controllably, his body rocking against the damp pillar. The guard whipped a walkie-talkie from his leather belt, spoke into it low and urgently. Loren heard the word "doctor." He sank into a sitting position on the floor, knees drawn against his chest.

Steps raced toward him and a young woman in jeans and a man's white shirt slid down beside him, landing like a baserunner stealing second. "Oh, Loren, did they hurt you?"

"Not bad," Loren mumbled. Gael Irwin wiped his face and mouth.

With her high childish voice, her perky clown face and tangled mop of dark curls, her lovely body and impossible causes and her total lack of awe before anyone and anything on the planet, Gael had always been a very special student for him. He looked at her and drank her in and wanted to crush her against him just out of the sheer joy of still being alive.

"You got here," he said brokenly. "And the guard. How did you?"

She seemed to understand what he meant. "Loren, Adjoa and I were in the library working on that project for Legal Aid and two men walked in who looked like contract killers in a Godfather movie and stopped us and asked where they could find you. After I told them they started to leave and I saw a gun under the short one's jacket. I told Adjoa to get a cop fast but she had to run half-way across the campus before she found a security guard and then the two of them started hunting for me and I was trying to leave a trail of dropped lawbooks for them and follow you. Loren, what have you done to make the Mafia want to take you for a ride?"

"Not Mafia," he said. "CIA."

"Jesus!" Gael screeched. "We're back in the sixties again!"

A high keening sound stabbed through the garage and a blue and white sedan with city police emblems on the doors twisted down the ramp with siren screaming and slid to a halt twenty feet from Loren. Two uniformed men raced out with revolvers drawn and scanned the vast empty area. A tall young black woman with an Afro and the red-bearded security guard converged on Loren from opposite directions.

Loren struggled to his feet. His legs were like putty, refused to support him. He sank back to a squat against the pillar and told the officers what had happened. They took down his story dutifully and exchanged polite skeptical glances when Loren reported the CIA credentials the hit men had shown. The younger officer went back to the patrol car and used his radio to request a plainclothes team and the lab truck.

An hour later it was all over. The uniformed men were gone, the detective team was gone. The evidence technicians had collected what they could find, which was nothing, and departed in the square white lab truck. Only Loren and Gael and the black girl were left in the garage. The two women helped him to his feet. He was shaky but he could stand now. He took a few steps experimentally, tottering like a small child. The image flashed into his mind of Conor Dunphy trying to learn how to walk on an artificial foot.

"Gael," he said, "is your car around here somewhere?"

"I drove us in today, Professor," Adjoa said. "My car's on the upper level."

She had been at the law school only since spring semester, a transfer student from the East. She had not attended Loren's classes but Gael had brought her in to see him four months ago and asked for his help when the university registrar refused to process the new student's records under her self-chosen name, which was Ghanaian and meant female born on Monday.

"Would you mind dropping me off in front of the library?" he asked. "I...don't think my legs want to walk much yet."

When the ancient Honda braked at the main door of the library, Loren turned to Gael, squeezed her shoulders gratefully. "Thanks again," he said. "I owe you one. Both of you." He wobbled to the door and went inside and followed the corridor around the circumference of the building, walking clumsily. His watch read 4:36 as he stabbed the UP button. It seemed weeks ago that he had taken the elevator from his office to the subbasement. As the cage lifted him, he remembered that his attaché case and the day's research were still sitting in that underground study carrel, but he was reluctant to go down there alone to retrieve them. At the third floor he left the elevator and crossed the hall to the faculty secretaries' office. All but two of the desks were empty, their typewriters shrouded for the day. He checked his mail slot, which was piled with papers and buff-colored message slips.

"Professor Mensing, what mischief have you been up to?" Rose, the senior secretary, took in his disheveled appearance with equal measures of amusement and disapproval. She had been with the law school longer than the oldest faculty member and she delighted in the prerogatives of seniority. "You've been getting urgent messages from the capital all day. We've tried your office, the dean's office, your apartment....You get right over here and sit down and call Chief Justice Dunphy. Don't stop to read your mail. This is an emergency! Here, I'll dial for you." Her fingers poked the buttons as Loren approached her stunningly uncluttered desk and sat in her leather-padded chair. When she had the connection, she put the phone to his ear and retreated to the stationery cabinets, out of hearing range.

"Conor?" Loren said.

"Loren, where in God's name have you been all day?" The chief justice's voice was tight with anxiety.

"You wouldn't believe me if I told you," Loren said. "A couple of goons tried to turn me into a cripple....No, no. I'm all right, just a little shaky. Tell you more about it later. What's all this about an emergency?"

Dunphy answered with another question. "Are you free tonight? Can you get up here right away, this evening? We're having a special meeting of the justices and I think we're going to need you."

"Conor, I'm not really up to that long a drive tonight. Could you give me some idea what the meeting's about?"

"No," Dunphy said. "But it's urgent, vital. It's state business and it involves people you and I both care about very deeply. If you don't want to drive, take a plane. Transstate runs flights up here every hour on the half hour and the court will pick up the tab. And, oh yes, are you teaching summer school this year, or do you have any other firm plans for the next few weeks?"

"Just working on a book. You know, that Third Reich thing I began when you were still dean. Why?"

"Pack a bag then," Dunphy said. "We may ask you to stay awhile. And I think you'll want to stay when you hear why. Now, what flight do you think you'll make?"

Loren made quick calculations in his head. Clean up his desk here, retrieve his papers from the subbasement, drive home, pack, grab a bite to eat, drive to the airport. "Eight-thirty's about the earliest I can take off, Conor."

"Then ye'll be landing at nine-fifteen. A limousine will be waiting to pick you up. If you don't make that flight, call me collect at my private number at the court." Loren tore a sheet from Rose's calendar pad and scrawled the unlisted number Dunphy gave him. "Thanks for obliging us this way, Loren. I hate to be so mysterious about what's happening but—Well, more about that when you get here."

"See you tonight," Loren said. He hung up, stood, waved thanks to Rose, crossed to the mail slots. His legs felt firm again. He looked through the mail, threw the pile of phone slips and all but one envelope into the wastebasket and went out to the elevators.

THREE

THROUGH the plane window the dark brown hills and scattered white pinpoints gave way to a panorama of fixed and moving lights, thousands of microdots of brightness that grew in size and brilliance as the Transstate commuter flight swooped to the airfield. Loren unsnapped his seat belt, lifted his two-suiter from the carry-on luggage bin and strode briskly down the steel steps to the tarmac. The cool night air lifted his somber mood. He entered the terminal and paused to study the knot of men and women and cranky children who milled about the arrival lounge, waiting to greet deplaning passengers. A tall powerful-looking bald man in a tailored leisure suit separated from the crowd, surged forward purposefully. "Mensing, right?" Loren nodded. "Norman Abelson, Department of Institutions and Agencies. I'm Iris Richmond's brother. You remember—we met during poor Ben's wake."

"Oh, of course." The hand Loren held out was crushed in the other's grip. "I'm sorry I didn't recognize you but this has been a hellish day for me."

"Likewise up here," Abelson said. His voice was so deep it seemed to be coming from a cavern. "Come on. I've got a state limo waiting in the VIP parking area. I'll take your bag." He scooped up the heavy suitcase as if it were a handful of balloons and marched along the airport corridor and past the security checkpoint at a pace Loren had to jog to keep up with. The man must be a physical-fitness nut, Loren thought. They came out of the terminal into the breeze-scented night and stopped at a long sleek car parked against the curb, its chauffeur smoking patiently, oblivious of the chaos of taxis and airport buses and private cars disgorging travelers. Abelson entered by the rear door, leaned forward to give terse instructions to the driver, then beckoned Loren in. The car hummed into quiet life and glided smoothly out of the bedlam around the airport. The driver turned into the ramp to Capital Expressway West.

Loren jerked forward in his seat. "I thought downtown was east of the airport. Aren't we supposed to be going to a meeting of the justices?"

"Not in chambers," Abelson said. "Out at Ben's house." His eyes were grave and brooding, his bald head glistened in the dark. The limousine's headlights sprayed the highway. Loren thought of demanding to know what was going on but something told him it would be a waste of time. He leaned back in his corner and watched the wooded ridges glide past the windows.

The limousine turned off the highway, wound among two-lane blacktop roads through the hills. Lights from isolated houses glowed dimly in the thickening night. The chauffeur turned left into a private lane and drove up a steep hill. The massive stone house stood at the end of the drive. Abelson climbed out of the car, took Loren's two-suiter from the trunk, carried it to the front door and pressed the bell. Light flamed in the vestibule; someone approached; the door opened. "Loren." Iris Richmond held out a frail and withered hand. "It's good of you to come."

She seemed to have aged ten years in the six months since the judge's death. Her patrician face looked defeated, her figure shrunken. Her hand seemed to shudder in his grasp. Behind her look of welcome the pale blue eyes were bright with a kind of horror.

Abelson set the suitcase down in the cloakroom off the vestibule and Loren deposited his attaché case alongside it and followed Iris to the huge front room. Nothing about the room had changed since Loren's last look at it on the afternoon of the funeral: high white ceiling; walls painted doeskin; landscapes in wood frames blending with the soft colors; parquet floor, walnut stained, dotted with bright-patterned area rugs; clusters of couches and easy chairs and tables and floor lamps. Jeanette rose from a hassock and kissed Loren on the cheek. She wore a tan sweater and slacks and a mint-green vest decorated with gold frogs and chains. Her eyes were raw and swollen.

Six men and a middle-aged black woman sat on facing couches at the far end of the room. A wheeled cart beside the white marble fireplace held an assortment of bottles: whiskies, mixers, wines. Bowls of crackers and plates heaped with sliced cheese and cold ham and dips and a gleaming stainless-steel coffee urn cluttered the end tables that framed the couches. The buzz of conversation died as Loren and Abelson and the Richmond women strode into the group. On the glass-topped coffee table between the couches a magenta shoebox stood. None of the group touched it, none had placed cups or glasses or saucers on the table, but their eyes couldn't leave it alone.

Conor Dunphy shifted his thick walking stick to his left hand
and stuck out his right. "Pardon me for not rising, this couch is just
too soft. Professor Loren Mensing, you've met most of my colleagues before, I'm sure. But just for the record: Justice Lutz, Justice Berendzen, Justice Goldner, Justice Colasanto, Justice Lawless—don't laugh—and the most recent member of the court, Justice Hale." Loren nodded, shook hands, murmured amenities.
Then he turned and sank into a barrel chair. Jeanette poured him
coffee and with a tiny smile set the cup on the arm of his chair.

"The court," Dunphy said, "is aware of your reputation, Loren,
as a sort of detective without portfolio. We've asked you to join us
because we can't think of a better way to handle this...awful mess
that's been dropped into our laps." He swiveled his head to indicate Iris, who sat rigid and tense on the couch beside him. "Mrs.
Richmond can best tell you what's happened."

Loren had noticed that even while Dunphy was speaking, the
other justices and the Richmonds kept darting glances at the magenta shoebox on the table, as if they were birds hypnotized by a
snake, and then turning their eyes away in revulsion. Iris reached
out for a water tumbler and ice tinkled as she raised the glass shak-
ily to her mouth.

"I found the box before breakfast this morning," she said, lick-
ing her lips. "I was sorting through Ben's clothes. There's a charity drive this week and I was asked if there was anything I could
contribute. You've been upstairs, Loren, haven't you?"

"No, but I remember you said something—I think it was the
day Ben was sworn in—about making a suite of rooms upstairs
into a combined bedroom and study for him."

"That's where it was—wedged behind his suitcases on the upper shelf of his bedroom closet. I'd never seen it before and
couldn't figure out why it was there so I took it down and put it on
the bed and opened it. I think my heart skipped a beat when I
looked inside. For a second I was afraid I was having a seizure.
Norman always goes early to his office. I called him at once and
asked what I should do. He canceled his morning appointments
and drove out and we talked it over and called Justice Dunphy and
told him the whole story."

"Luckily we haven't scheduled oral arguments this week," Justice Goldner put in. He was the oldest member of the court, lean,
soft-voiced, with wispy white hair and a mustache. The word in
judicial circles was that he would retire at the end of the current
court term. "We held a quick meeting and Conor proposed that we

call you in, Professor, to be...well, to be a sort of detective for the court. To conduct your own investigation outside of official channels and report to us on the origins of this box and what action the court should take. Will you do that for us?"

Loren leaned forward, his own gaze fixed on the box. "No one's told me yet what's in it," he said. "I'm afraid I can guess."

"You don't have to guess. Gentlemen, if I may." Justice Aldona Berendzen, the only black female appellate judge in the Midwest, drew a pair of dainty white gloves from her purse, delicately raised the lid of the box by two of its corners and set it down on the coffee table, its underside facing up. Loren bent on one knee beside the table. The inner surface of the shoebox lid was creamy white, with one word printed in ornate gold script: RADISSON.

Piles of crisp green paper filled the interior of the shoebox. Twenties, fifties, one stack of hundreds. Loren leaned over the box, almost unwilling to believe his eyes.

"You'd better not touch, Professor," Abelson said. "My prints and Iris's are on the box and the bills already. We counted very carefully. The total is forty-nine thousand dollars exactly. I've made a list of the serial numbers." He drew several folded sheets of paper from his breast pocket and handed them to Loren. "There are several consecutive runs of numbers, if that means anything."

The crisp green bills glistened evilly in the lamplight, like snakeskin.

"Loren." The voice of Conor Dunphy broke Loren's concentration. "You know as well as we do that that amount of money, hidden away in Ben's closet so carefully, suggests one thing and one thing only."

"Bribe," Loren said.

Iris flinched at the word as if she had been slapped. Her brother, who had been leaning against the mantel, came forward and put an arm around her shoulders.

"Sometime before he died Ben took a bribe to decide the way he did on one of the cases before the court. Is that what you're suggesting?" Loren said.

"My God, Loren, *I'm* not!" Dunphy protested. "Ben was my best friend for thirty years. I knew that man as well as I know myself, and I'd stake my other foot and both my hands he'd never do that. And he was your mentor too. I remember—oh, nine years ago—when he called me at the law school. This was right after Ken Cole had died and we had a faculty slot we needed to fill in a hurry and Ben called and said he had this bright young clerk with an incredible legal mind and that he'd hate like hell to lose you but he thought you'd make a first-rate teacher."

Loren stared emptily at the neat stacks of bills. He had no illusions about public officials and had long ago reached the conclusion that the kind of person who is appointed to office is the kind of person who more likely than not will abuse his power sooner or later, often or rarely. But Loren had always made exceptions for the people he knew and trusted: Mayor Sturm back home, Sergeant Hough, Dunphy, Ben Richmond. Loren couldn't believe the obvious meaning of that shoebox. He didn't want to believe it but he was desperately afraid that if he investigated the matter for the court he might in time be forced to believe it. And yet if it wasn't true, if there was another explanation, Loren wanted to be the one to find it. He owed the judge that and so much more.

"I don't know," he said. "Maybe the police ought to handle it. they can be more objective."

Jeanette Richmond went down on one knee beside Loren. "I need you, Loren," she said softly. "We all need you. Please don't say no to us. Please?"

"There must be an innocent explanation." Her mother's voice was a broken whisper. "Loren, I'll give you anything, anything in the world, if you find it. You can't know what I'm going through. You can't know what it's like to live with someone, and love him for half a lifetime, and suddenly lose him, and then find something like this that threatens to turn the whole life you shared into a wreck and a lie." Abelson slung a protective arm about her shaking shoulders as she dabbed a handkerchief at eyes that looked fragile as blue glass.

"Please," Jeanette said again, in a hoarse and frenzied whisper that conjured up incongruous memories in Loren—memories of that feverish night after the dinner party at Poe's, when she had tapped on the door of his riverfront apartment long after midnight and they had made love until dawn, tenderly and savagely, in violent explosions of need and longing. The others in the lavish front room waited for his answer, silent now, intent. Loren felt as if a chain saw were tearing him apart. He wished he had never come to this meeting.

"Sure," he said quietly, and let out a long breath. "If you want me, I'll do it."

"Thank you, Loren," Conor Dunphy said, and leaned back with a sigh of contentment. "We'll work out a per diem arrangement, of course, to compensate you for your time." The other justices and

Iris and Abelson murmured words of gratitude in unison, and Loren sprang to his feet and paced to the mantel and studied the relieved faces of his ten clients.

"If"—the word came out a quack, and he cleared his throat—"if it turns out to be as bad as we suspect, I will not tolerate a cover-up. Understood?"

The justices bent their heads together and consulted buzzily. Dunphy's flamboyant boom broke through their undertones. "Understood," he answered proudly. "This court is not going to repeat the mistakes of certain other public institutions."

"Good enough," Loren said. "Now, Iris, this may be rough on you. I have to ask you some questions about the arrangements here when Ben was alive."

The judge's widow raised her head to Loren's and held it high. "I'm ready," she said simply.

"Who had access to Ben's rooms besides you and Ben himself?"

She thought for perhaps ten seconds before she answered. "Well, no one, really. There's only one entrance to the suite; in the old days it used to be a sitting room and boudoir, I suppose. Ben used the outer room as his bedroom and the inner as a study. He kept the door locked whenever he wasn't inside because he did a lot of work evenings in the study and at times he had things there—drafts of opinions, confidential memoranda that had to be kept secure. The suite has been locked since he died, except for cleaning of course."

"Who actually did the cleaning? The luncheon we had here after Ben's funeral was catered, but I seem to recall a maid taking our coats and overshoes as we came in." He thought back, tried to capture the image of that gray and snow-laden noon. "A black girl I think she was. Very pretty, with sort of a button nose."

"Angella." Iris put the accent on the second syllable. "Angella Carmer her name was. She was our maid then, and she did the cleaning too."

"Is she available tonight? I'll need to talk with her."

"She quit to get married last month," Iris said. "But she lives in the city, or at least she did when she worked here. I don't know if she and her husband stayed or not. I'll give you her address later."

"Then she didn't live in?"

"Oh, no. With the cost of this house and all, we couldn't afford a live-in maid. She drove out three days a week to do the heavy cleaning, and on special occasions, when we were having a lot of dinner guests, things of that sort."

"How long was she working for you?"

Iris cupped her chin in her hands and lowered her eyes. "Let me think. It was, yes, a year ago last March that we hired her." That couldn't have been very long after Ben first learned that he had cancer, Loren thought. "So she was here about fourteen months in all. A lovely girl, hardworking and ambitious and helpful. I liked her very much."

"Jeanette, how did you feel about Ms. Carmer? The same as your mother did?"

"I barely ever saw her," the judge's daughter replied. "I haven't lived here for three years, you know. I have my own apartment in town. Angella was always very nice and pleasant the few times I did speak to her. Why are you so interested in her?"

"Isn't it obvious? From what you've told me, Iris, she's the only person besides you and Ben himself who had the opportunity to put that shoebox in the bedroom closet."

"Oh, that's impossible!" Iris protested indignantly. "I let her in every day she came to work and all she ever brought to the house with her was a tiny purse. You'd need something large to hold that shoebox—a shopping bag or a small suitcase."

"There wasn't a single day you can remember when she brought a package of any sort into the house?"

"Not one," she replied. "When Angella began working here she told me very frankly that a few years ago a cousin of hers had unjustly been accused of stealing things from the house where she was the cook. Angella had always been extremely careful ever since that incident not to give even the appearance of dishonest intentions. That's why she wouldn't bring any shopping bags in with her when she came to work."

"How about Christmas presents?" Loren asked. "Could she have smuggled the shoebox in, wrapped up like a gift?"

"I think I'd remember something like that," Iris insisted.

"But you didn't actually watch over her when she'd clean the judge's suite?"

"Of course not." She swung her Dresden-shepherdess head vigorously from side to side. "Why in the world would I do that?"

"Did Ben ever complain that papers or anything else were missing from his study? Or did you ever notice anything missing from any part of the house during the time Angella worked here?"

"Never," she said, then paused to think back and repeated, "No, not once."

Loren whirled to Chief Justice Dunphy. "Conor, did Ben ever complain to you about anything missing from the house? Or to any of you on the court?"

"Not to me," Dunphy said. The other justices murmured agreement except for Justice Hale. "I wasn't on the court yet," he said in a high mousy falsetto.

"All right," Loren concluded. "For now it looks as if Ms. Carmer couldn't be responsible for the box. But I'll take her address and talk to her later anyway. Now, who else had opportunity to get the box into Ben's rooms? You spoke of sometimes having a lot of dinner guests, Iris. Did you and Ben entertain often?"

"Very little, really. This house is such a long way from the suburbs where everyone else seems to live. Norm, I suppose you and Blanche were our most frequent guests, wouldn't you say?"

Abelson relaxed from the strange tensed position in which he had been sitting, and Loren suddenly realized that throughout the questioning the man had been doing isometric exercises. "About once every six weeks on an average," he told Loren carefully, "my wife and I would come out for the evening. Most of the time it would be just the four of us, or occasionally another couple or two would be invited also. Lawyers, professional people mainly."

"Did you ever stay for the night? Bring suitcases with you?"

"We'd have no reason to," Abelson said. "Our place is only twenty minutes east of here. And besides, as Iris told you, Ben kept the door to the suite locked whenever he wasn't in there."

"We'd have other members of the court occasionally," Iris continued. "And the governor came once, I think. But I'm certain none of our guests ever brought anything into the house large enough to hold that shoebox." Her eyes swerved again toward the box as if it generated an evil magnetism. "Why, it wouldn't even fit into a large attaché case."

"In all the time you've been living here you've never put up a single guest overnight?" Loren asked incredulously.

"I've stayed over a few times," Jeanette Richmond volunteered. "Mainly when Dad was out of town, to keep Mother company. It can get pretty lonely out here when you're by yourself. I'd generally bring an overnight case when I came. I suppose it's big enough to hold that box, but not with my nightie and slippers and toilet things crammed in too."

"How about visitors since Ben's death? You must have had a lot of people who dropped by to pay condolence calls."

"Oh, there were dozens," Iris acknowledged. "But no one carried anything that could have held a shoebox—except boxes of flowers perhaps. But when anyone brought flowers he'd take them out of the box right away to show them to me and we'd put them in a vase then and there. No, I don't think anyone could have brought the box in that way. But there was one strange thing...." Her voice trailed off into a vague silence.

"Even if you think it can't possibly help," Loren urged, "tell me."

"It was...in March, I think. About three or four months after the burial. A man from Ajax Exterminators in a van with a dead insect painted on the side knocked at the front door. He said Ben had called their firm late in November and ordered an inspection of the house for termite damage and the order had gotten misfiled and no one had come. The man was so apologetic it embarrassed me. And then I told him Ben had passed away in December and he got embarrassed and said that under the circumstances he'd see to it there wouldn't be any charge for his services. Well, he went through all the rooms on this floor, tapping and doing whatever these exterminators do, and then he took his toolbox and spraying equipment down to the basement to check down there. When he came up he said everything was safe and sound. He hadn't seen a sign of a single termite. A week or so later the company sent me a bill marked 'canceled.' Wait a minute—I think it's in one of those drawers." She scurried across the room to an ornate secretary-desk against the wall and leafed through pigeonholes full of loose papers. Finally with a little sound of triumph she yanked a sheet from the pile and brought it back to Loren. The letterhead of the bill read AJAX EXTERMINATORS, INC. and gave a city address he didn't recognize. Beneath the rubber-stamped cancellation of the charges was a brief hand-printed note:

> Sorry about mixup. If you see any signs of termites in the future, please appraise me and I will reinspect.
>
> C. ADESE
Inspector

"Peculiar," Loren said. "Do you know of your own knowledge that Ben had called an exterminator?"

"He didn't do it in my presence, no. But—" She turned to Dunphy, who was polishing the head of his cane with his palm. "You remember, don't you, Conor, that time you and Norm and Blanche and Ben and I had dinner at the little Lebanese place in town and you and Ben were talking about some case where a man sued because he bought a house that turned out to be infested with termites, and that made Ben worry about the possibility of termites in our house and he said he was thinking about having someone come out and look things over?"

"That's right," Abelson cut in. "Saleem's. That was the name of the restaurant. This must have been last fall, I suppose. September, maybe October. My wife could probably give you the exact date if you need it, Professor, and a complete rundown on what everyone was wearing too. Blanche is like Iris, she has that kind of a memory for little things."

"He could have called the exterminators from his chambers," Dunphy pointed out. "Most of us take care of routine items of business from our offices when nothing urgent is happening on the court."

"Did this exterminator go upstairs to inspect the judge's suite?" Loren demanded. So far the big question of the night, he thought.

"He never went upstairs at all," Iris answered firmly. "I was sitting right there on that divan by the door, the gray one with all the pillows, and I could see the stairway every minute and he never used it. And"—she anticipated his next question—"there is no back stairway."

"He didn't go upstairs even to use the bathroom?"

"He used the one on this floor," Iris said.

"Another dead end," Norman Abelson said, and drained the last of his coffee and took a conspicuous glance at his watch. "Gentlemen, it's late, and I have a miserable day at the office tomorrow. If I'm not needed any longer, I think I'll head for home." He jackknifed up from the soft low couch, bent to grasp his sister's hand, shook hands with Loren. "I can let myself out," he announced, and marched briskly to the foyer.

"Before you go," Loren called after him, "one more question."

The administrator whirled and faced Loren, waiting.

Loren pointed at the lid of the magenta shoebox. "What is Radisson?" he asked. He looked around the circle of faces. "Can anyone here tell me?"

"I can," Jeanette Richmond said. "It's an exclusive women's shoe store in the city that opened about a year ago. The corner of Twelfth and King. An excitable little Frenchman named Albert Radisson owns it."

"You've shopped there? Do you own a shoebox like this one?"

"Not that color," she told him. "But I've bought two pairs there,

I think, since the place opened. And, Mother, you bought me a pair of slippers for my last birthday that came from there, didn't you?"

"Yes. Yes." The answer seemed to terrify Iris as she stammered it, and she took another gulp of water from her tumbler.

"Have you ever bought shoes there for yourself?" Loren asked the widow.

"No!" she shrieked. Then, more calmly, "There's a very nice shop in the Spruceknoll Mall, about ten miles from here. I've bought all my shoes there since we moved to Capital City."

The justices were shifting restlessly in their seats, finishing their whiskey or wine or coffee, checking watches. Justice Goldner cracked his knuckles, Justice Berendzen played with her white gloves. Loren sensed that it was time to call it a night. "Let's wrap it up for now," he proposed. "But I want all you men to do one thing before we meet again—call it a homework assignment." Justice Colasanto fought to suppress another of his giggles. "Check with your wives tonight and find out if any of them have bought shoes from this Radisson. If they have, see if any of the boxes they came in is missing. Report to Conor in the morning. Conor, I'll call your chambers to get the results. Jeanette, if any of your shoeboxes are missing, you call Conor too."

The justices rose and the hum of their conversation drifted across the large front room as they moved toward the foyer, shaking hands again with Loren as they passed him, some leaving at once, a few waiting to use the bathroom. Dunphy stayed behind until he had placed the shoebox in a brown paper bag. Then he lurched to his feet and trailed behind his colleagues, leaning heavily on his shillelagh, the bag nestled protectively under one arm.

"Jon Lutz drove me out here," he told Loren, "and is dropping me off at the State House so I can lock this damned shoebox in the court's safe, and then he's driving me home. Like a lift into town with us? My secretary made a reservation for you at the Belvedere Inn downtown and you'll want to rent a car in the morning." He shifted his weight to his good foot, put down the paper bag and drew a cracked cowhide wallet from a hip pocket, removing a plastic rectangle from one of the wallet's compartments. "You can use this credit card to charge your expenses to the court." He pressed the card into Loren's hand.

"I'll be with you in a minute," Loren said. "Iris, before I go, would you mind giving me a quick look at Ben's suite? I want to see exactly where you found the shoebox."

Iris and Jeanette led him up the carpeted staircase to the second floor. The key shook in Iris' hand as she unlocked the door to the place where her husband had worked and slept. Loren spent five minutes exploring the rooms, feeling among the suitcases neatly arranged on the shelf of the walk-in closet, sensing the women's eyes watching him from behind as he rummaged.

And found nothing.

With his back still turned to them he thought of the bizarre words Judge Richmond had fought to whisper in his car in the moments before his death. Now was the time. There just might be a connection. He faced them, stepped out of the closet, shut the door. "Iris," he said, very carefully, "you didn't happen to find anything else hidden in there, did you? A letter, a record, maybe a tape of some sort?"

A look of puzzlement and anxiety held the widow's exhausted face. Loren would have sworn her emotions were completely genuine, that she was hiding nothing and had no idea what he was talking about. "No, Loren," she said. "Just the box."

"God," Jeanette said, "wasn't that enough?"

They locked the suite behind them and descended. Loren found his two-suiter and attaché case set outside the foyer closet and Justice Lutz waiting patiently on an antique wooden chair near the front door. He exchanged farewells and quick kisses with the women and hefted his luggage and followed the justice into the thick warm night. Ragged clouds raced across the star-sprinkled black sky. Cricket chirps sounded in the tall grass.

With Lutz behind the wheel and Dunphy and Loren riding in silence in the backseat, the paper bag between them, the Fleetwood sped east on the Expressway with a blithe disregard for the 55-mile-per-hour limit. At 12:25 A.M. Loren said goodnight and stumbled wearily out under the portico of the Belvedere Inn. He dragged his suitcase into the empty lobby and registered under the indifferent gaze of the night clerk, a tired heavyset woman. The elevator shot him to the fourteenth floor. Inside his room he double-locked the door, set the chain, braced a plastic-covered armchair against the knob. Then he threw off his clothes and scrubbed himself under the hottest shower he could stand, letting the roaring water redden his body, relax and unwind his nerves, so he could forget the shoebox and the encounter in the subbasement of the law library for a few hours and get some sleep. He toweled himself dry and lifted his two-suiter onto the luggage rack and unzipped it and pulled out of it a sport jacket and two pairs of slacks. Something fell out of the suitcase and onto his bare foot. He bent over to pick the object up. It was a small white cassette, and through its tiny plastic window he could see a stretch of tape.

Loren paused, then went to the phone and dialed the desk clerk. Apparently the hotel didn't have a cassette recorder. It would have to wait until morning. Almost relieved, he turned to bed.

He tossed fitfully through what was left of the night. As first light crept through the heavy drapes he fell into a frenzied half doze that was worse than no sleep at all. He dreamed that he was stretched out paralyzed on a highway, his back and arms on the gravel shoulder, his legs extended into the road, and that hundreds of automobiles roared over his legs, one after the other, an endless parade of autos, Fords and Chryslers and Lincolns and Hondas and Cadillacs and Buicks and Volkswagens, all systematically pounding his lower body into a bloody pulp.

FOUR

BY SEVEN he was awake but as exhausted as if he hadn't slept for a week. His muscles felt stiff and cramped. A numbing fog dulled his thinking. The bedclothes were a frenzy of twists and tangles. He stumbled to his feet, showered again—this time with ice-cold water—shaved and dressed, then went to the hotel restaurant off the lobby and fueled himself with tomato juice and French toast and roast beef hash and eggs. After a fourth cup of black coffee he paid his check and walked to the front desk where he picked up a complimentary map of the city and asked the clerk for directions to the nearest budget car-rental office. He walked five blocks through auto-choked downtown streets, rented a Volkswagen, inquired how to reach the nearest audio store. At Elston's Soundarama he bought a battery-powered Japanese cassette player and, yawning lustily, fought inbound traffic back to the Belvedere. In his room he hung the cardboard Do NOT DISTURB tag on the outer doorknob and double-locked the door and took the cassette from his pocket and inserted it in the player. He lowered himself into the stiff armchair, put his feet on the bed, pressed the PLAY switch. Listening was not going to be easy, not if this tape was what he thought and feared it was.

The tape wound through the player heads but for a minute there was only silence. Then a little static—sudden, crackling. And then the voice came on. A deep familiar voice but speaking low, as if afraid someone might be listening.

"Testing, testing," it said.

Loren could not mistake the voice. It was Richmond's. There was another half minute of silence before the voice returned, stronger now but hurried, running words together as the judge never had when Loren had known him.

"I'm dead now, Loren. If you're listening to this, it means I've been dead for a year. I am making this recording in my chambers. It is 11:20 P.M., the date is April tenth. I've been thinking all evening how to go about this. Loren, I have to tell you some things no one else knows. Please don't be hurt by what I'm going to say.

"Last month my doctor told me that I have inoperable cancer."

His voice did not lose a fraction of its strength or dignity as he said it.

"In all likelihood this is the year I'll die. I have decided to tell nobody but one person, and to continue my work on the court until I reach the point where my illness may affect my judgment. But meanwhile I have to get my life in order. Loren, I need your help.

"I'm going to put it bluntly; there's no time to waste words. Iris and I have not been together—we haven't been lovers—for nearly twelve years now. She developed what I can only call a refined disgust with the physical side of a relationship. I've done some reading about this condition and found it isn't unheard of for women in their mid-thirties. There was nothing I could do about it. She wouldn't even discuss it with me. She didn't want a divorce, she didn't want to have to raise Jeanette alone, and I didn't have the heart or the guts or whatever you want to call it to divorce her."

So that explains the separate bedrooms, Loren thought.

"Eventually we worked out a kind of tacit understanding. We'd continue our lives as normally as possible, and as far as other women were concerned I would be...I guess you could say...a free agent. Iris knew I would be extremely careful, and I was. The proof of how careful is that unless you are a hell of a better actor than I think you are, this is all a ghastly shock to you. I won't go into details, Loren. Not now, not ever."

No wonder he had such empathy for people caught in traps, Loren thought.

"Most of the women were casuals. Some were in impossible marital situations as I was. I never even hinted to any of them what I'm telling you straight out now. By being very selective and very cautious I avoided even a hint of scandal all the time I was on the court of appeals.

"When I was named to the supreme court and moved here, I knew I'd have to redouble my care. The suffering that my family would endure, and the other justices, and the people who entrusted this responsibility to me, the tortures they would go through if any of this should ever leak—when I thought about that I was ready to give up the physical side of my life if it meant jeopardizing so much. And then, Loren, it happened.

"I won't tell you her name or anything about her, not now. But about eight months after I came on the court I met a woman. It was almost as if a miracle had happened. She was everything I ever wanted and needed. She wasn't a teeny-bopper or anything.

She was a grown, experienced woman, poised, sophisticated, liberated, loving, understanding....It was magic, Loren. I don't know if it's ever happened to you that way. I hope it has."

Loren thought of Lucy, of how he had loved her and thrown her away and how he had loved her again years later and lost her again. It was all he could do to keep from shutting off the tape and tossing it into the trash. But he had made a commitment. He had to know what Richmond would say about the forty-nine thousand dollars.

"We were lovers within twelve hours of the time we met. It wasn't just physical desire, Loren; it was everything. We each had our separate lives and neither of us intruded into the other's world but we built a world of our own, just for us, as often as we could see each other. We—oh, Christ, I can't go on with this. ..."

Loren's nerves tautened at the sudden silence. Was that the end? Had he or someone else erased whatever came later? He studied the sweep second hand of his watch. Ten seconds, fifteen, twenty....Richmond's voice faded in again, strong as ever. Loren released a long-held breath.

"She is the only person I've ever told about my...domestic situation until now, when I'm telling you. I loved her so much I had to tell her. She accepted it. It changed nothing between us. Then, about a year after we'd met, one night she cried in my arms and told me something she had been keeping from me but couldn't any longer. In the first few months she had been careless. She'd gotten pregnant."

Another pause, two, three, four, five, six seconds.

"She knew we couldn't have the child. She had gone away and had an abortion."

Pause, two, three, four.

"She said she'd done it for the sake of both our separate lives and our life together. And she hadn't told me because she didn't want me to feel guilty....And tomorrow evening I have to see her and tell her I'm dying. Making this tape is like flaying myself alive, Loren, but tomorrow's going to be worse.

"I can't say any more. Just this: I have to make sure she knows how much I cared. Obviously I can't leave her anything in my will. In the time I have left I am going to liquidate certain securities I own, turn them into however much cash I can obtain without making waves. Somehow I'm going to arrange for that money to reach you after I'm gone. This money will be yours, Loren, in trust to convey it to her. To my woman. I'll have to arrange for you to know her identity after I'm gone too. Loren, I know I can't compel you to do this for me, but please, remember the night at the Boatmen's Bar when I asked you to come to work for me, and that rainy morning I called you into my chambers and told you about the faculty opening at the law school that I had recommended you for, and please, Loren, do this for me. Good-bye, and thank you."

The player made a sharp clicking sound and silence flooded the room again. On the chance that there might be more at a later part of the reel, Loren kept the machine running. The high whine of a vacuum cleaner sounded from the corridor. After seven minutes of silence from the tape he no longer expected anything but didn't dare turn it off prematurely. He sat in the stiff green chair and thought about what he had heard, and what he hadn't.

Who was the woman, and how could he find her? Was the recording genuine? Was that in fact the voice of Ben Richmond, speaking of his own volition? Loren would have wagered his career that it was. The precisely detailed references to the time the judge had hired Loren as his clerk and to the time he had worked behind the scenes to secure him a faculty position proved the authenticity of the tape more surely than a dozen witnesses.

Had Richmond actually obtained the money he expected to raise? Unanswerable. But Loren could make a reasoned guess. The forty-nine thousand dollars in the Radisson shoebox might very well be the funds for the nameless woman, raised legitimately but in secrecy. If Loren could somehow trace those bills and tie them to property transactions in Richmond's last months, the circumstantial evidence that the judge had taken a bribe would vanish like morning dew. He would have to get hold of a private detective who could be trusted, retain him to trace the money without explaining why. Then, if the hunch proved out, he would have to tell Dunphy, but perhaps no one else would need to know and the money could still be transferred as Richmond had wanted.

The cassette player gave another click. Loren saw that the tape had been played through. He reversed the cassette in the machine and pressed the PLAY button again. The opposite side of the tape began its silent journey through the player heads.

Of course, there was another possible explanation for the money. Suppose Richmond had found he couldn't raise the amount he needed without leaving too broad a trail. Might he not in desperation have solicited an under-the-counter cash payment to guarantee a favorable vote in some pending case? Another unanswerable. Loren felt a sick emptiness in the pit of his stomach.

Then there was a further puzzle: Who had slipped the cassette into his luggage, and why? The possibilities fell within a tight circle. The only time his two-suiter had been out of his control, from the time Norman Abelson had carried it to the limousine until Loren had unpacked it in this room, had been the period when it had been stowed away in the foyer closet of the Richmond house. The case hadn't been locked, and anyone at the meeting—Iris, Jeanette, Abelson, one of the justices—could have ducked into that closet and slipped the tape into the two-suiter within fifteen seconds. And there had been enough confused milling about when the meeting had broken up that almost anyone in the group could have done it while Loren had been upstairs with the women, inspecting the judge's bedroom closet.

And a final question: Where was the balance of Richmond's communication to Loren? How had he arranged for Loren to discover the whereabouts of the money and the identity of its intended recipient? Or had that part of the plan gone haywire?

The ruby button glowed in the base of the telephone and a harsh ringing scattered Loren's thoughts. He stretched in his chair and grabbed the receiver. "Hello."

"Top of a lovely morning, young Sherlock!" It was the lilting brogue of Chief Justice Dunphy. "Just wanted to report that all the men justices checked with their ladies on your shoe question. Mrs. Lawless and Mrs. Goldner are the only ones who've bought footwear from the elegant Monsieur Radisson, and neither of them found a shoebox missing. And Jeanette says none of hers is gone either."

"Okay, Conor, thanks," Loren muttered absently.

"I detect a note of distraction in the voice. Did you go barhopping after we dropped you this morning?"

For a moment he considered telling Dunphy about the tape at once, then he decided to keep his mouth shut until he had more facts. "Just worn out," he said. "I never sleep well the first night in a strange bed....Thanks again for calling. I'll be in touch." The chair's cushion hissed as he stood to replace the receiver in its cradle. He perched on the unmade bed and resumed his thinking.

There was no way of knowing whether Richmond had worked out a satisfactory plan to give Loren the rest of the needed information. But if he didn't want to throw up his hands and abandon that part of the puzzle, he had to assume for now that there had been such a plan. Somewhere outside this hotel room there was a message from a dead man, waiting for Loren to find it. Where?

Loren thought back to the time between April 10 of last year, when Richmond had sat in his darkened chambers and made the tape, and the raw December evening when Jeanette had called from Stoner Memorial Hospital and told Loren that her father was on the edge of death. Had he had any letters or phone calls from the judge in those months, any contact at all that might have contained a clue? He tortured his memory and couldn't recall a single letter or conversation. Well, if not before Richmond's death, then how about afterward? No, he had received nothing after the judge's death, nothing except the set of Story's *Commentaries on the Constitution* the judge had left him in his will.

Lawbooks. Will. That was it! That had to be the answer.

He snatched the phone, dialed eight for long distance and a number back home that he knew by heart. After two rings a chirpy female voice came on at the other end. "The Hooft Agency. May I help *you*?"

"Marc Hooft, please....This is Loren Mensing....No, that's M as in mnemonic, E as in eiderdown." Ms. Chirp giggled wildly into the mouthpiece, as she did whenever Loren played that game with her, and said she'd see if Mr. Hooft was free.

The voice on the line after a series of harsh clicks was the musical burble of Marcus Jaan Hooft. "And how may I serve the distinguished legal scholar this morning?"

"Hi, Marc. I'm up in Capital City today, and you may serve me by going down to the law school right now and breaking into my office."

"What violent behavior for a mild June day!" The voice of the oversized private detective remained unruffled. "May I use a skeleton key or do I have to kick the door in? And what do I do when I'm inside?"

"The first thing you do is search for a folder labeled 'Richmond, Ben.' It's probably in the second drawer from the bottom in the file cabinet up against the window. When you've found it, call me from my office." He read off the digits typed on the center of his dial. "And before you go, one more thing. I'm going to need a Capital City detective, a good reliable person who doesn't mind working in the dark. Got any suggestions?"

Hooft's singsong hum drifted over the wire as he thought. "Tremaine Investigations," he pronounced finally. "I don't have the number handy but they're listed. Tremaine is as tough and competent an operative as, um, as you'll desire. May I ask what unholy brew you are fermenting?"

"Later," Loren said. "Much later. Call me as soon as you find that folder, Marc. And my expenses are covered on this one so bill me what the job's worth....Thanks much." He hung up, dug the phone directory out of the bottom bureau drawer, found TRE-MAINE INVESTIGATIONS, dialed nine for a local line and then the number.

"Good morning, Tremaine's." Judging by her voice, the woman on the other end might have been a TV pitchperson. Bright, cheery, eager to sell the world. Not quite what Loren expected from a detective agency.

"I'd like to make an appointment to see Mr. Tremaine today if possible," he said. "My name is Mensing."

"Well, you can't see Mr. Tremaine," the woman told him zest-fully. "He doesn't exist. I am the Tremaine of the business, Mr. Mensing."

Stupid, stupid, Loren berated himself. Assuming that a private operator recommended as tough and competent had to be a man. Hooft had set him up for this. In fact he had even dropped a subtle hint with that comment about Tremaine being as competent as Loren would desire. He wondered how attractive this woman really was.

"I'd be delighted to have the appointment with you then," he said, "and tell you in person that I'm sorry. That is if you don't mind a client who's still tainted with sexism."

"If I did I'd starve," she told him. "Eleven-thirty this morning?"

Loren's watch read 10:23. He could give Hooft till eleven to call back and still make it. "Looks good. See you then, Ms. Tre-maine. And thanks."

With thirty-five minutes to occupy before he left for the ap-pointment, he hauled the sticky armchair in front of the portable color TV and turned on the set. Twisting the channel selector, he discovered that the city was served by four stations. Two were running game shows, one a cartoon-frolics festival and the fourth an old Charlie Chan movie. He settled back to enjoy the proverb-spouting Chinese who made detective work look so damned easy.

At 10:49 by his watch the phone shrilled. Loren snapped off the set in the middle of a Confucian aphorism and caught the call on the second ring. "Marc?"

"Speaking. From your office and with file in hand. What do I do now?"

"Look through it for a letter from a Capital City law firm. I for-get the name but it's dated a couple of months ago and talks about some lawbooks Judge Richmond left me in his will."

"Momentito." Loren heard the crackle of paper behind the Hooft hum. "Found it."

"When does the letter say Richmond executed his will?"

"Hum hm, hum hm....dated June fourteenth last year," the detective said.

Which confirmed what Loren had dimly remembered: that the execution of the will postdated the making of the tape. "All right," he said. "Now look up at the top shelf of the bookcase that faces my desk. Do you see a three-volume set of books with calfskin binding?....Fine. Take them down to your office and search them for some kind of communication....No, I don't know what kind. Maybe a letter, maybe one of those new miniature tape cassettes stuck into the spine, or it could just be that some printed words are dotted or pricked with a needle to make a code message. It could be anything. If you find it, keep calling me here till you get me in."

"How roughly may I treat the books?" Hooft asked. "They look to be rather rare."

"Rare and valuable. Treat them as gently as you can. And by the way, Marc, I've got a date with your macho colleague Tremaine. You didn't really think I'd miss that blatant hint of yours about her being a woman?"

He depressed the phone button long enough to get a dial tone, then drew a scrap of paper from his wallet and dialed a number he had scrawled the afternoon before: the private line of Chief Justice Dunphy.

"Good morning again, Conor. Things are moving. Didn't you say last night that you were going to stop at court after you dropped me off and put the Radisson shoebox in the court safe?"

"Yes, and that's just what I did."

"I have an eleven-thirty appointment," Loren went on, "and I want to take the box with me. Without the money, of course. If I come by in, say, fifteen minutes, can you have it ready for me?"

"Can and will," Dunphy promised. "I trust you won't drop it down a convenient sewer."

"You know me better. Thanks, Conor. See you soon."

FIVE

IT WAS the first time he had heard of a private eye who kept an office in a shopping center.

Loren drove along the pavement that fronted Midwood Mall. The macadam field to his right held parking slots for more than a thousand cars but seven out of ten spaces stood vacant in the bright June morning. On his left, the supermarket and two discount stores and the cafeteria and the cheese shop and the movie house and several specialty stores waited for hordes of customers who never came. Some plutocrats had sunk millions into building a suburban-style shopping center carved out of what had been five square blocks at the edge of the black ghetto until the bulldozers had leveled the neighborhood to rubble. The hundreds of empty spaces in the parking lot showed that the idea had been a disaster.

Loren parked the rented VW, picked up the shoebox in its protective paper bag, locked the car and followed a side pathway through the heart of the mall, past a record shop and a plant store and a sewing center and a soft ice cream emporium. 37 Midwood Mall was the last building in the row. He turned the shining brass knob and stepped in. A rush of chill air greeted him.

Chairs and low tables were arranged along one pine-paneled wall and a government-gray steel desk took up the center of the reception room. Loren could hardly make out the furniture for the greenery that choked every spare inch of space: in pots, in windowboxes, in wall brackets, in terraria, hanging from hooks in macrame slings. Giant plants, dwarf plants and all sizes in between. Phoenix palms and zebra plants, calamundin and angel princess and goldenrain trees, krimson queen, African violets, Boston ferns and the lowly begonia, all neatly labeled as in a store or a public garden.

A woman rose from a kneeling position between two mismatched armchairs as Loren entered. There was a long-spouted watering can in her left hand. She was tall, slender, fine-boned, and her blue-gray eyes were alight with laughter. She wore her long pale-blonde hair in a ponytail. Her office attire was a thin beige shirt and blue jeans, with nothing beneath the shirt. Loren guessed her age at twenty-eight.

"Hi," she said. "I'm Val Tremaine and it's eleven-thirty so you must be Loren Mensing. You know, it wasn't till after you'd hung up that I recognized your name. My God, you're practically a celebrity!" She held out a strong but delicate hand. "Just let me finish nursing my babies and we can go into my office and chat."

There was something so disarmingly natural about her that even before he had said a word he was glad he had come here. She finished her circuit of the reception room, watering plants, smoothing their leaves, talking to some of them, ignoring Loren completely until the job was done. Then she set the can under a table piled with out-of-date business magazines and beckoned him to follow her.

The first piece of furniture in the inner office that caught Loren's eye was a corner worktable that had obviously once been a door, lying on its side and supported by two low file cabinets. The walnut desk was bare except for several small plant pots along its edges, and another group of plants was arranged in a row on top of the supply cupboard. Loren and Val dropped into the room's two armchairs. "Brown-bagging lunch today?" Val shot a glance at the paper sack in Loren's lap.

"That's no lunch," Loren said. "It's your job. The first part of it anyway. But maybe I'd better tell you a little bit more. You may want to kick me out when you hear how little."

"I used to go with a man who was a cop downstate while you were legal adviser to the commissioner," Val replied. "He told me a few stories about cases you got involved in. If you're on one of those again and can pay a reasonable price, I'll be glad to work with you."

"Even if you have to do things without knowing why?"

She leaned forward, her bright eyes serious now. "Mr. Mensing, a woman private detective doesn't have the world beating on her door offering jobs. I don't like to work in the dark but if you say there are reasons I'll accept that—for now anyway. So where do we start?"

Gingerly Loren slid the magenta shoebox out of the paper bag and onto his chair arm. "Don't touch," he warned. "I want you to dust this for fingerprints. Inside, outside, all surfaces. Then I want you to trace whatever you can about its history. It came from an exclusive shoe store in the city, run by a Frenchman named Albert Radisson. I'll have more jobs for you later." He reached into his breast pocket for his checkbook. "And a retainer now of course.

How soon can you get started?"

She rose and took a fresh yellow legal pad from her desk and slid it under the shoebox. "I started when you walked in. If you'll give me five minutes I'll dust this right away." He leaned back and watched her clear a space at the corner table and set the box down. She rummaged in the supply cupboard for a brown leather kit and sat on an old kitchen stool in front of the workbench and spread magnetic black powder on the shoebox lid with a camel's-hair brush. She seemed to know exactly what she was doing. While she worked, Loren made a mental list of people whose prints might legitimately be found. There was Iris Richmond, who had first discovered the box; and her brother, Norman Abelson, who had counted the money with her; and Loren himself, if he'd been careless handling the box either the night before or this morning. He would have to call the court again and ask if Conor had handled the box.

"Nothing but smudges," Val Tremaine called from the workbench after five minutes of dusting and brushing. "And not a whole lot of them either. Come on over, take a look." Loren crossed the office and stood behind her, looking down at the powder-speckled box. Val began to replace the implements of her fingerprinting kit as she talked. "So it's on to Radisson's, right? But, you know, I don't think a shoe store is likely to be able to tell who bought the shoes that came in any particular box."

"Neither do I," Loren admitted. "Someone has to check it out anyway and I've got other business this afternoon. When you finish at Radisson's, lock the box where it's safe and call me at the Belvedere Inn, room 1419. I should be in this evening."

"Is there time to grab a sandwich before I go? I never eat breakfast and I'm starved."

After his own hearty brunch the idea of another meal left Loren profoundly disinterested. But he wanted to know this young woman better and convinced himself that he could at least nibble at a salad. "My treat," he said. "Name the place."

They dawdled over their plates in the cafeteria on the main avenue of the mall and Loren asked casually how she had got into the detective business. "Inherited it," she said, sipping iced tea. "My husband started the agency six years ago, right after we got married. Just a little business: bodyguard service and some industrial-security work, nothing fancy. I did the bookkeeping and helped out when Chris needed an extra person in the field. We were growing very nicely for a year or so, then—well, Chris died."

Christopher Tremaine. Loren remembered the name now, and the story in the papers five years ago. "He was murdered, wasn't he? One of those unfancy cases turned out to be connected with political graft and somebody got afraid he'd learn too much?"

"We were on a surveillance together." Her voice was a low monotone, all emotion screened out. "It was a clammy drizzly night and we were sitting in the car together. I had to go find a pay phone and call the office on another matter. When I got back I found him slumped in the driver's seat with his hands clenched over his middle, trying to keep his insides from spilling out. They'd shot him four times with a silenced .45 and he died on the operating table. No one was ever arrested for it. That's how I inherited the business."

"I'm sorry," Loren said. "I shouldn't have asked."

"It was a long time ago and I'm over it," she said. "For a year after it happened I'd wake up in the night screaming like a banshee. I knew it was only pure dumb luck that I wasn't in the car and shot with Chris. Eventually I recovered enough to reopen the business, but before I did I went down to the police firing range and practiced and practiced till I was better than half the cops in the city. I still visit the range once a week. Then later I located a runaway daughter for a Japanese immigrant who runs a dojo and took my fee in martial arts lessons. Every morning as soon as I'm up I do twenty minutes of belly dancing and twenty of karate exercises. No one's going to catch me off guard the way they caught Chris."

Loren lifted his water glass in a sort of tribute. "You're remarkable, Val. Aggressive, competent, fragile, and you love those plants as if they were your children. I'm delighted Marc Hooft recommended you. So would I."

She took the last bite of her roast beef on rye and the last swallow of her iced tea. "Which means you think I have a fantastic body and don't know how to say it inoffensively." She laughed. "Your eyes say it for you. Okay, now that you've torn the scabs off my sores, tell me about yourself. Married, living with someone, celibate, gay?"

"None of the above." He plunged his fork into the remnants of his salad and tried to hide his embarrassment. "Sort of alone. There was a woman I cared for very much but I lost her. Twice. The second time was final." He told her a little about Lucy, who had died because she had walked up a staircase at the wrong moment.

"Oh, Loren, forgive me." Her hand reached under the table for his. "This seems to be the day for opening old wounds, doesn't it? Uh, look, I'd better hit the road for Radisson's I guess." She rose awkwardly to her feet and Loren stood a second later.

"I'll call you after dinner, right? Thanks for the sandwich," she said.

He pushed the revolving door for her and they left the cafeteria and headed for their cars, not even saying good-bye when they separated in the sunbaked parking lot. An observer would have taken them for total strangers.

Loren kept the VW at 55, heading east on the Donovan Parkway, exited at the Fenton Boulevard ramp, took Fenton along a three-mile stretch of factories and polluted air. Just beyond the smokestacks the state university campus began and he swerved among narrow streets until he found a parking lot that was open to visitors. He locked the VW and hiked six blocks north to the red-brick fortress of the law school. The building was all but deserted, like his own school downstate. A few students and faculty secretaries wandered aimlessly through the high-ceilinged halls. Loren bought several pads of legal paper in the tiny bookstore and followed the main corridor to the swinging oak doors at the far end that gave on to the law library. Orienting himself with a diagram on a bulletin board just inside the doors, he climbed narrow stairs to the mezzanine and settled into a deep alcove. Behind and on both sides of him were high steel shelves that held the volumes of the official state reports of appellate court decisions. Loren thumbed through the numbered reports until he had located the first book to contain decisions in which Ben Richmond had taken part, four and a half years ago. Systematically he took down one volume after another, working his way forward, skimming every decision the court had handed down during Richmond's time on the bench.

The justices decided perhaps a hundred cases a year, so that Richmond had voted in nearly four hundred decisions. Which cases would have been most likely to lead to an offer of a $49,000 bribe in return for his vote? The only way Loren could answer that question was to read the court's decisions, eliminate those that seemed improbable and hope not too many remained. He began with two assumptions that were reasonable but not, he knew, airtight. One: only a case in which far more than $49,000 was at stake would lead to a bribe in that amount. That eliminated almost all of the court's criminal rulings; the vast majority of defendants were indigents, represented by public defenders, and couldn't have raised that kind of money if their lives depended on it. It also eliminated many of the cases interpreting state statutes or procedural rules and a lot of the negligence cases, in which, win or lose, an insurance company footed the bill and passed on the cost to the consumer. Two: assuming that a bribe had been offered to Richmond and to him alone, the case must have been a close one, with Richmond likely to have the swing vote.

Loren read, skimmed syllabus paragraphs, took notes, eliminated, read more. In the relevant four-year period he found only a handful of high-stakes cases that had been decided by 4-3 or 5-2 votes. At 4:10 he went down to the main floor, asked the student attendant at the front desk where he might find the books on business history and law, snatched three fat volumes from the shelves housing the business materials, returned to the mezzanine. He forced his bloodshot eyes to study more pages and scrawled more notes that he could barely decipher.

By 5:30 he was bone tired, fiercely hungry, his eyes so bleary he half believed he was going blind, and he was almost certain he had found the case he wanted.

In re Bennell's Will. July 1976. The majority opinion had been delivered by Justice Richmond.

> The issue to be decided on this appeal concerns the premature termination of a testamentary trust established under the will of the distinguished industrialist Stanford Ives Bennell, who died a domiciliary of this state in 1919. The facts are complex, the legal issues close and difficult, the amount of money involved prodigious. After full consideration we hold that the termination of the trust within the lifetime of one of the life beneficiaries named therein is not permissible under the terms of the trust or the applicable law, and consequently we reverse the decision of the court of appeals to the contrary....

Loren looked at the notes on the history of Benneco Industries that he had taken from the business books. All he could make out were dark scratch marks on a yellow surface, meaningless as ink smears. He laid his glasses on the table, rubbed his tortured eyes. A dazzling phantasmagoria of shapes swam and cavorted against inner darkness. With his head buried in his arms he rested his eyes and thought about what he had read on the life and times of Stanford Ives Bennell.

The founder of Benneco Industries had been a 19th-century robber baron in the grand style, a ruthless and expert player in the game of capitalism. Like his peers he ruined competitors, manipulated markets, bought and sold politicians, hired goons to maim and kill union organizers. Unlike his peers he diversified his holdings before it became accepted business practice. His companies held the oil rights to thousands of Texas and Oklahoma acres and to lucrative petroleum concessions in Venezuela. Brazilian coffee, tropical fruit, tin, rubber—there was hardly a Latin American export that a Benneco subsidiary did not control to one extent or another. To guarantee a steady supply of cheap native labor and the right to do business exactly as they pleased, Benneco and similar large corporations shoehorned friends of free enterprise into the seats of power in the Central and South American countries in which they operated. If a popular movement should arise that seemed to threaten the companies' profits, the friendly authorities would call out troops, fire into crowds, beat a few of the leaders to death, jail the rest and disperse the movement in short order. If radicals should gain footholds in the local government itself, Benneco had enough influence in Washington to demand that Marines be dispatched to crush the evil forces. That was the way things were done. By the time Stanford Ives Bennell died of lobar pneumonia at the age of 78, his personal fortune amounted to more than seventeen million dollars. According to the most recently published of the business histories Loren had consulted, Benneco was still a power south of the U.S. border, at least in the dictatorships of the right. And when he thought back to certain newspaper columns he had read over the past few years, he remembered rumors of connections between the corporation and the CIA that set his teeth on edge. The Latin American and CIA elements just might explain why Moraga and Rojas had tried to cripple him yesterday afternoon.

He knew that his theory was far from irrefutable but it was the most likely hypothesis available. All of the criteria were met by the Bennell case more completely than by any other. Even the date of the court's decision fit the pattern: July of the previous year, three months after Richmond had made that tape and spoken of secretly raising money. He couldn't be certain his theory was right but he knew it had to be tested.

Loren checked his watch. Through a blur of mist the hands seemed to read 5:52, eight minutes before the library's closing hour when school was not in session. He needed more time, had to refresh his basic knowledge of trust law and form an opinion as to whether the Bennell ruling squared with the general principles in that field. If it didn't, his theory would be much stronger. Then Loren remembered that he had read in a legal-education newsletter last year that Jerome J. Deckler had accepted an appointment at this law school. And Jerry was both a specialist in trusts and estates and an old compadre of Loren's.

It was worth taking a chance on. Jerry had always been the hard-driving type, the kind of person who never took a vacation, never knocked off early, had to be accomplishing something every minute or pay the penalty of feeling guilty. He was one of the few professors who was likely to be in his office at six o'clock on a beautiful summer evening. Loren gathered his papers, made a photocopy of the Bennell decision at a coin-operated machine and pushed through the doors out of the library. The faculty directory in the entrance foyer gave him the number of Jerry's office. He took the stairs to the second floor and found 238 and rapped on the gray door. "Come!" a fierce familiar drawl called out, and Loren entered.

He almost didn't recognize the man. In the summer after their first year as professors Loren and Deckler had spent a frantic two weeks living on cheeseburgers and three hours' sleep a night while grinding out a tactical manual for lawyers representing conscientious objectors and draft resisters. In those days Jerry had been a vibrant energetic maniac, with a rangy Gary Cooper build and a deep cowhand accent and long thick hair and beard and an insatiable lust to exhaust himself in the good fight. The man who sat at the desk surrounded by mountains of blue examination books was clean shaven, and only a few strands of hair were left across the center of his head. He wore a gray three-piece sharkskin suit with hand-knitted tie, and the Swiss gold watch on his wrist gleamed in the late sunlight. "Loren!" he thundered, and leaped up and squeezed his hand in the grip Loren remembered of old.

"Eight years," Loren said. "My God, that's a long time. And they seem to have turned you into a Wall Street groupie. All out of righteous causes?"

"Oh, years ago. The firebrand from Arizona's burned out. Been through two marriages, changed faculties twice, and I'm going to be forty in August. It's time for peace and stability. As Hegel or whoever it was said, 'Let pass in contemplation what occurs.' The sixties are dead, chum. There's nothing left worth crusading for.

Why, do you realize how many contradictions there are just in the Bill of Rights? All those B-Western-movie good-guy-against-bad-guy fights are over. Now it's just the good guys fighting the good and the coyotes eating each other. Deal me out." His words came in a torrent. At least the old excitable motor-mouth delivery that drove students into hand-crippling frenzies of note-taking had survived the acid of the years.

"Jerry," Loren said, "I need your expertise for a few minutes. And I'm going to collapse if I don't get supper pretty soon so let's talk over grub, okay?"

They sat in scooped-out orange plastic chairs at a table in a remote corner of the student-union cafeteria and concentrated at first on the food and small talk. The coffee was tepid and muddy and Loren had eaten better mostaccioli in frozen TV dinners but he was too hungry and preoccupied to care and he chewed his meal mechanically.

Over wedges of tolerable lemon pie he brought up the reason for his visit to Deckler. "Jerry, I've got a problem," he began, "and I can't tell you what it is. But I'd like you to give me a rundown on a case the supreme court decided in your area a year ago. *In re Bennell's Will*. Know it?"

"Lovely case," Deckler muttered through a forkful of pie and swallowed hastily. "Probably get printed in half the T&E casebooks over the next ten years. Lays out the policy considerations on premature trust termination better than anything I've seen lately."

"Go over the case for me. I want to make sure I understand the situation."

"You asked for it." Instantly Deckler was transformed into a professorial lecturer—precise, analytical, speaking in a rush of words and almost defying the listener to follow the line of argument. "Bennell's will directed that most of his estate—and this included several thousand shares of Benneco Industries, which he founded, so it was a huge estate—was to be transferred in trust to a foundation he created in that same will: the Bennell Foundation. It still exists, by the way. The headquarters is here in the city. The will named several trustees and set up procedures for replacing those who resigned or died during the life of the trust. Now the trustees were directed in the will to invest and reinvest the trust assets and use the proceeds to pay annuities in various specified amounts to each of...I think it was 43 different members of the

Bennell family, which was a pretty widespread one. Each of these 43 annuitants was to receive this amount every year as long as he or she lived. When the last annuitant died, the trust was to terminate, and the will directed that at that time the trustees were to divide the property equally among eight remaindermen, all of them Bennells of course but different people from the 43 annuitants. And if any of these eight lucky dogs should happen to be a dead dog at termination time, that one-eighth share was to be divided among his or her next of kin as in intestacy. As fate would have it, all eight of the remaindermen died while some of the 43 life annuitants were still kicking. Got all that so far? I haven't seen you take a single note."

"Photographic memory," Loren said. "Okay, what precipitated the lawsuit?"

"The last living annuitant," Deckler went on. "A guy in his eighties named S. Gordon Bennell, who lived in St. Louis I think. This old bird signed some documents relinquishing his midget annuity to a descendant of one of the eight original remaindermen, and that descendant transferred what had been S. Gordon's share to the trustees of the Bennell Foundation. Well, obviously these transfers had been set up so as to cause the trust to terminate and get the corpus distributed right then rather than wait till old S. Gordon hung it up. That's what started the suit. On the one side you had those descendants of the eight original remaindermen who'd share in the assets if the trust were terminated then and there. That group argued that you didn't have to wait till S. Gordon died to end the trust, that his signing away his rights amounted to the same thing. On the other side you had the children and grandchildren of the living descendants of the eight remaindermen who wouldn't get cent one if the trust terminated right then because their own living parents would bump them, but who just might wind up with shares through the intervening deaths of their own ancestors if the trust was left intact till S. Gordon's death."

Loren held up his hand like a traffic policeman. "Whoa, boy. That last sentence of yours lost me. Remember, I haven't studied property law since I was in school."

"Okay, let's call one of the eight dead original remaindermen B. He has three living children, X, Y and Z, and they each have two kids, X^1 and X^2, Y^1 and Y^2, Z^1 and Z^2. If the trust ends at that point, X, Y and Z each take one twenty-fourth of the total pot. Their kids would take nothing because there's a basic principle of intestacy law that a living parent bumps a child from an intestate share of an ancestor's estate. And remember, old Bennell specified that the descendants of dead remaindermen should take as in intestacy. But if the trust ends at a later point, and if, say, Mr. X dies before S. Gordon Bennell, then X^1 and X^2 split their parent's share and each takes one forty-eighth of the property.

"And so the X group and the X^1 and X^2 group fought it out. There were issues about whether S. Gordon's interest was properly conveyed to the trustees—who might or might not have legally accepted it—and issues about whether the trust instrument allowed termination in S. Gordon's lifetime. The district court said terminate, the court of appeals affirmed and the supreme court reversed, four to three. Richmond wrote the opinion of the court. Dunphy and...I think it was Lutz and Ms. Justice Berendzen dissented."

Loren forced himself to swallow the last of the coffee. "How good technically was the court's opinion? Was it sound, consistent? Anything, er, askew or off key about it?"

"That's a bizarre question if I ever heard one. Well, personally I think Dunphy's dissent is the better view. I don't believe in the dead hands controlling property from the grave, but I guess you'd call that a policy disagreement I have with the court. I could be a nitpicker and punch some technical holes in Richmond's reasoning but by and large it's a good sound piece of judicial craftsmanship."

They pushed back their chairs and carried their loaded trays to the conveyor belt inside the hatchway that led to the dishwashing area. "So," Loren summed up, "the trust still exists and the Bennell Foundation still runs the show."

"Unless S. Gordon curled up and died recently," Deckler said as they pushed through the turnstile at the exit. "Okay, Loren, I've opened up for you. So how's about you doing the same? Why this sudden interest in a case that's been *res judicata* for a year?"

"The blue spruce in front of this building is the loveliest I've seen on any campus," Loren explained.

Deckler frowned. "If I didn't have a bar association meeting in half an hour," he said, "I wouldn't take that for an answer. Well, my Ferrari's over in lot G. Tell me what you're up to when you can, okay?"

"When and if," Loren stipulated, and they shook hands and separated. As Loren headed back to the visitors' lot he made a resolution that tomorrow, whatever else he did or did not accomplish, he would pay a visit to the headquarters of the Bennell Foundation.

Pale blue dusk was blanketing the skyline when Loren swung the car into the Belvedere Inn parking lot. There was nothing left to do till morning and bone-numbing exhaustion held him in a vise. When he crossed the parking lot to the side entrance of the hotel he walked like a man in a straitjacket. He swore that he would fall straight into bed and sleep like a corpse for twelve hours minimum before he would think about or touch the damned case again.

At the front desk he asked if there were any messages in his box. The gray-haired woman clerk handed him six pink slips of paper. Loren almost cursed her aloud but offered polite thanks and trudged blindly to the elevator. On the ride up he spread them in his palm like a poker hand. Two were from a Miss Tremaine, who had called at 6:15 and again at 7:00 P.M., leaving no message and no number for him to return the calls. The other four were from a Mr. Hooft, who had phoned every hour on the half hour from 4:30 on. Loren let himself into room 1419, locked himself in, shucked off his clothes and crawled into bed.

He was just drifting off into sweet oblivion when the harsh ring of the phone jolted him awake. He said some words he was glad there was no one to hear and groped blindly for the handset. "Unkh," he muttered into the mouthpiece.

"No, this is not your uncle," the familiar amused burble sang in his ear. "In the best Sherlock Holmes manner I deduce that I woke you."

"Sort of." Loren focused on his watch on the bed-table, which read precisely 8:30. "Should have known you'd call now. All the phone messages must mean you found something."

"Merely a sheet from a thin three-by-five scratch pad, folded over and sealed around all the edges with strapping tape. There seems to be a key inside, and some writing, but I haven't tried to make it out. It was inserted in the spine of Volume Two, held in place with a few dabs of glue. It, ah, took a bit of doing to find and free the thing, and I'm afraid your precious books are going to need rebinding. Should I cut the tape and read you what's inside or just mail it to you?"

Loren held a brief donnybrook with himself over the answer. If that paper contained a second message from Richmond he wanted desperately to know what it said, but he was simply too exhausted to wrestle with any new problems tonight, and he didn't dare have the paper and the key entrusted to the tender mercies of the United States Postal Service or risk their lying exposed in his hotel mail slot for the hours between the time they would arrive and the time he would return to pick them up. "I know it's asking a lot," he said finally, "but I want you to send the thing up here tomorrow morning with an operative you can trust not to open it. Have this person drive or fly up and meet me in this room between nine and ten A.M. I'll hang around waiting till ten."

"It will cost you," Marcus Jaan Hooft trilled cheerily, "but if that's how you want to play it....Which somehow reminds me, I happened to be down at headquarters this afternoon on another matter and bumped into your old amigo Sergeant Hough. What's this I hear about two men with forged CIA credentials trying to unleg you yesterday?"

So the official line was that the credentials were forged. That meant either that Moraga and Rojas were private hit men and the police had a lead on them or that they really were CIA and a cover-up was in the works. Loren knew that he could never hope to learn which was the case by making any more long-distance calls tonight. "Oh, just one of the routine incidents in a busy law teacher's day," he answered lightly. "You didn't tell Hough you were on a job for me or where I was staying?"

"Have I ever betrayed a client's confidence?" Hooft declaimed. "All right, I'll have Tommy Novo drive up first thing in the morning. May I be of further assistance?"

"Let you know later," Loren said.

"Then nighty-night and pleasant dreams," Hooft chimed, and broke the connection. Loren dialed the front desk and left word that any further callers should be asked to call again after eight the next morning and, to make doubly sure, he set the phone in the bed-table drawer before he snapped off the lamp.

When he woke again the window drapes were lightening from black to dirty gray. He stayed under the covers, listening to the hum of the air conditioner, wriggling his toes under the sheets, luxuriating in a slow languorous adjustment to the waking world. After a while he showered and shaved, straightened the room, switched on the TV and absorbed half an hour of national and local news. By eight he was ravenous. Visions of the sumptuous breakfast buffet downstairs danced before his eyes but he was afraid to risk leaving the room because Novo and the second Richmond message might arrive at any time. He studied the room-service menu propped against the bureau mirror, winced at the tripled price of every item, then remembered his credit card and pulled the phone out of the drawer and called downstairs with an

order for orange juice, the international omelet, toast with marma-
lade and a pot of coffee. Waiting for his breakfast, he fidgeted in
front of the TV and wished he had thought to pick up some paperbacks to fill the empty time.

A light tapping shot him out of the chair and over to the door to
let in the room-service boy.

Who wasn't a boy at all. A tall slender young woman with
pale-blond hair in a ponytail and steel-blue eyes gleaming with
delight wheeled in the service cart and made him a butlerlike bow.
"Breakfast is served," she intoned. "I'm sorry, Loren, I couldn't
resist coming up unannounced after I tried to call last night. And
then when the kid with the tray stopped at your door I paid for it
and tipped him and told him I'd do the honors. He probably thinks
we're lovers or something."

"I was dead on my feet last night, Val." Loren deposited the
covered tray on the round table by the windows. "Sit down, grab a
bite if you're hungry, we can share the silverware."

"I told you—I never eat in the morning." She perched on a corner of the bed and with a look of pleasure watched him eat, as if
seeing someone else devour a hearty meal satisfied an appetite of
her own. "Want my report now?"

Loren washed down a mouthful of eggs and melted cheese and
chili relleño with the last of his juice. "Ready when you are," he
said.

"Well, I told you I'd probably strike out and I did. Albert
Radisson is a darling little gray-haired Frenchman in his fifties
who wears Nehru jackets and an ankh around his neck. He opened
the shoe shop two years ago and does very well weez eet. There is
no way he or anyone else can trace who bought the pair of shoes
that box of yours originally held. He tried to date me three times in
less than an hour and insisted that I take a complimentary pair of
sandals when I finished interviewing him."

Loren debated asking whether she planned to go out with
Radisson and decided that it was none of his business. "Where's
the box now?"

"Locked up in my office desk," she said. "What's my next assignment if any?" She swept her hand back through her silky hair.

Loren sipped coffee, thinking how he could use her help today,
savoring her company but wanting her out of the hotel before
Novo might pop his head in the door. "How are your contacts with
the city newspapers?"

"Couldn't be better. My best girl friend is sports editor of the

Demagogue....I mean the *Democrat*. Local joke. Want some tickets to a ballgame?"

"I want everything you can dig up for me on an institution here in the city that's called the Bennell Foundation. They run the estate of Stanford Ives Bennell, the guy who founded Benneco Industries."

"God," Val whispered. "The Bennell syndrome."

Loren tossed her a look of incomprehension. Not only had his research into the history of Benneco and the litigation over the old pirate's trust uncovered no such entity as a Bennell syndrome, he wasn't even sure what precisely a syndrome was.

"You haven't heard of Bennell's disease then?" Val asked.

"Well, I knew Stanford Ives Bennell had died of something," he said, "but I understood it was some kind of pneumonia."

She shook a playful finger at him, like a grammar-school teacher correcting a child who spelled cat with a k. "No, no, Bennell's disease is something that runs in that whole family. There was an article about it in the feature section of the Sunday paper a couple of years ago." Her voice grew serious and a little strained. "It scared me," she said.

Loren glanced at his watch: 8:42. He didn't want Val and this Novo to see each other but the disease sounded worth pursuing. He finished his coffee and shifted his chair around to face her directly. "Tell me what you remember," he said.

"All I can recall is that it's a very rare form of degenerative nerve disease that goes back to the first Bennell that settled in America, early in the 1800s. He had a mess of children and passed it on to them and they passed it to their kids and here we are. It's a genetic disease and there are supposed to be about three hundred descendants that have had it. No one realized what it was till recently. All through the generations the family thought it was congenital syphilis and kept it hushed up."

"What are the symptoms?" Loren asked.

"You lose your coordination and start to walk with a stagger like a drunk and your speech gets slurry. That's the beginning of the end. Once you have those symptoms you've got a year, maybe a year and a half, to live. If you call watching your body break down living."

Loren fought to hold back a shudder. "God," he said. "What a birthday gift for your children. Makes you know there's a lovable old man watching over us from the sky....But wait a minute. Stanford Ives Bennell didn't die of this disease, and there's an old

Bennell in St. Louis who's over eighty and still healthy as a horse. How many people in the family get hit with it?"

"I don't know," she told him. "So much of the medical history over the generations has been hushed up by the family and the doctors that probably it's impossible to tell. One in two, one in three. But in every documented case the first symptoms struck before the person was thirty. I remember reading that."

No wonder certain members of the Bennell family might be desperate to take their share of the trust immediately rather than count the crawling days until S. Gordon Bennell would die. If he had happened to be born into that family, Loren wondered, and if he were still in the under-30 danger zone, would he have offered Ben Richmond a bribe in order to secure a measure of comfort and perhaps specialized medical care for himself and other members of his family? Had Ben known anything about the disease? If he had known, compassionate man that he was, how could he have resisted voting to terminate the trust at once, letting those millions be spent on research to cure this hideous sickness? Or was he thinking primarily of the litigants on the other side, the younger ones, who would take nothing if the trust were distributed at once? Purely in human terms, which was the better decision? And might not Richmond's position be rationally defensible even if he had been paid to adopt it? Loren was suddenly very thankful that he was not a judge.

"Knock knock." A soft female voice scattered his thoughts. "Anyone home?"

"Got carried away, I guess." He shook himself like a drenched dog. "Imagine what it would be like to carry that damaged gene with you day after day, knowing that any morning you might wake up and start staggering on your way to the john and that once that happened you had a year or so of physical degeneration to look forward to and then you'd be dead....I almost said a thank-you that neither of us and no one I care for is a Bennell."

"So did I," she confessed, "and I don't like myself for it. Loren, something in your face tells me you want a lot more information about Bennell's disease."

"I think it may be relevant," he said slowly. "Yes, that's exactly what you'll do next. If you find that article you mentioned, copy it for me, and make copies of anything else that's been written on it. Check the State U Medical School library, there might be some specialized stuff in one of the journals. Plus I want some general background on the Bennell family and the foundation, and last but not least, if you run across any hint of CIA involvement in Benneco Industries operations below the border, copy everything you find."

She sprang from the edge of the bed with a bound of eagerness. "I feel like I'm back in school and you've just assigned a term paper, Professor," she said, grinning. "Not the usual PI work but I can cope. Anything else?"

"Would you happen to have a portable printing press in that supply cupboard of yours?" Loren asked. "The kind you can use to print up phony business cards?"

"No good eye would be without one," she said. "Need a new paper identity?"

"I think I might. Tell you what: On your way to the newspaper morgue, stop at the office and print me something that makes me a journalist." He thought for a moment. "From *Businessways* magazine. And my name will be—oh, make it Jack Mackenzie."

Val nodded her head. "I've got someone office-sitting today so you can drop by later and pick the cards up. Anything else?"

She seemed to want him to ask her for some additional item, and Loren screwed up his courage and decided to take a leap. "Oh, yes," he said casually. "Why don't you give me a number where I can reach you after hours? Uh...just in case it becomes necessary."

"Thought you'd never ask." He sensed a provocative glimmer in her eyes as she dictated the number but she might have been teasing or he imagining. "That's my apartment in town," she explained. "It's a dump. I've got a house I built myself out in the sticks forty miles from here but there's no phone so I can't be reached when I'm there."

"I'd like to see the place sometime," Loren said. He had a sudden fantasy of lying in her bed in that isolated house after a night of lovemaking and watching as she did her morning belly-dancing exercises for him. He lowered the curtain on that scene instantly and hoped she hadn't guessed what he'd been thinking.

"Uh, look," she said carefully, "I'd better hit the road for the *Democrat* morgue before we both get sidetracked. This job should work out better than the disaster yesterday. Give me a ring tonight and I'll let you know." They said good-bye at the door and Loren watched her walk smoothly down the corridor. He felt a racing inside him and ordered himself to be cool and skeptical and lawyerlike. His body ignored the instructions and his mind kept conjuring images of her. He paced to the bed and sat down and realized he was sitting precisely where she had sat and jumped to his feet and paced some more.

Novo, Novo, where the hell was Novo? He dropped into the hated plastic armchair and flicked the TV on savagely and beat a tattoo against the Formica-topped table and forced himself to sit through kiddie cartoons and reruns of ancient situation comedies until at 9:42 the phone shrilled. He leaped up and caught it on the first ring. "Hello," he barked.

"Good morning, Herr Doktor!" The honeyed tones of Marc Hooft sang in his ear. "I have a disturbing message to convey to you from Tommy Novo."

"Okay, let's hear it," Loren said, bracing himself for the worst.

"Tommy had the misfortune of two simultaneous blowouts on the Interstate a little before eight. It seems that a farm pickup dropped a load of tenpenny nails on the rural stretch halfway between here and the capital and two of those nails wound up in Tommy's front tires. The nearest garage is in a village several miles from the spot and he wasn't able to get a tow truck till a short while ago. What would you like him to do?"

For a wild moment Loren considered driving south and picking up the Richmond message from Novo at the garage. Then on second thought he dropped the notion. He had other things to do in the city today and, desperately as he wanted to see that message, it could wait a few more hours. "When will Novo be on the road again?" he asked.

"Oh, an hour, maybe two, maybe three. You can't rush these hayseed mechanics, Tommy tells me."

"All right. Call him at the garage and tell him to keep coming. When he gets here he's to check in at the Belvedere and wait. He is not to leave his room unless there's a fire. I'll contact him when I get back this afternoon." He thought of the two hit men who had almost crippled him. "And tell him to be damn careful if he sees any Latin-looking strangers. Thanks for the call, Marc. See you later."

When he had broken the connection, he scooped up the directory from the niche below the night table and found the address and phone number of the Bennell Foundation.

SIX

THE HOUSE was a beautiful monster, a soot-blackened limestone castle set on a half acre of meticulously landscaped grounds at the end of one of the private streets off Duke Boulevard. Loren parked the VW and stood in the narrow roadway and marveled at the place. Stone steps led under a double archway supported by granite pillars. Gable roofs stabbed the sky, Romanesque sculptures decorated the elaborate façades and half the front windows seemed to be stained glass like the windows of a cathedral. The edge of what must once have been a coach house was visible through a screen of birch and elm. From somewhere behind the mansion Loren could hear the whine of a power mower.

He climbed the front steps, passed under the archway, pulled at the bell. A polished bronze plaque to the right of the oak door read THE BENNELL FOUNDATION in proud but not ostentatious capitals. The door inched open the length of a chain bolt and a wedge of female face peered out at him.

"I'm Jack Mackenzie." Loren smiled salesmanlike and handed a freshly printed card through the opening. "With *Businessways* magazine. I've been assigned to do an article on the foundation. May I come in?"

"Journalists usually make appointments with people they want to interview," the woman told him. Loren sensed the undertone of suspicion in her voice. He had expected to hear it and had prepared for it in advance.

"Why, my office did that, ma'am. My editor in New York told me that I had an appointment at the foundation for this morning at eleven." He stole a glance at his watch and gave her a sheepish grin. "Sorry I'm a few minutes late, that crosstown traffic jam was murder....Why, ma'am, you don't think a *business* magazine would have flown me all the way from New York without setting up an appointment first?" He allowed a look of befuddlement to invade his expression, as if she had seriously suggested that the moon was made of caviar.

"Well, I can assure you, Mr. Mackenzie, that no appointment was made." The woman unchained the bolt and threw the door open to the bright summer morning. "But as long as you've come all this way I suppose we can spare you a little time. I'm Lillian Bennell." She switched her half-smoked cigarette to her left hand and held out her right. Loren shook her hand with just the right smile of awkward thanks for her graciousness. She was below average height, somewhere in her fifties, her face lined like a well-used map, her hair dyed silver and cut mannishly short. Her body was still firm and attractive. An armada of silver bracelets clashed on her wrists. There seemed to be an immobility about her eyes, as if she had trained herself never to look to the left or right of her but only straight ahead.

"Boy, will there be a flap at the office over this screw-up," Loren muttered darkly. "Fire someone for sure....I can't tell you how grateful I am for letting me talk to you, Ms. Bennell." He gawked at the gleaming mosaic floor of the entrance foyer, the profusion of paintings and tiny sculptured figures on shelves in the broad corridor, the sweeping oak staircase at the end of the hall with a minstrels' gallery at the landing. "This is the most gorgeous house I've seen in my life," he said.

"It's a nice place to work," the woman admitted, making swift nervous gestures with her cigarette. "It was built by my great grandfather's brother in 1889 at a cost of half a million dollars—that's 1889 dollars—and was two years in the making. Stanford Ives Bennell imported a sculptor and two woodcarvers from England, traveled all over Europe picking out different woods for the floor of each room. At one time twenty-three people lived here, and that included eight maids, a butler, a carriage driver and a live-in doctor for the family."

In view of the Bennells' medical problem Loren could see the need for the doctor. "You sound as though you've given people the grand tour before," he commented.

"I have to," she said. "The place is a damn landmark, the best surviving example of Richardsonian Romanesque architecture in the United States. It's open to the public one morning a week and I take them through the display rooms. Come on along, I'm doing the pitch again tomorrow and I could use a rehearsal." She led him through room after high-ceilinged room, cluttered with period furniture and artwork. The library was filled with built-in bookshelves fronted with glass, presided over by a gold-framed wall portrait of a mustachioed ancient. "My great-granduncle," Lillian said. "Stanford Ives Bennell. A noble American and a noble man."

Mirrors decorated with ornate filigree; grandfather clocks, polished and ticking loudly; a monumental Flemish breakfront from the seventeenth century; rich Oriental carpets on the waxed and gleaming floors—only the chattering of an electric typewriter somewhere in the distance broke the illusion that he had traveled centuries into the past.

Lillian Bennell ended the tour by stepping into a small office next to what had been the servants' dining hall. She sat behind the antique desk, lighted another cigarette from a hammered-silver table lighter and looked expectantly at Loren, who dutifully dropped onto a mohair divan and plucked a spiral notepad out of his breast pocket.

"What my editor is looking for is a portrait of a private foundation in action. That's his way of putting it, not mine," he said with a slight laugh. "But that's my assignment so here goes. How many people are actually involved in administering the Bennell trust?"

"There are five trustees including myself." She puffed spasmodically on her cigarette between sentences. "We're scattered all over the country, however, and meet only twice a year. I am the president of the board of trustees and the active head of the foundation. We employ a full-time lawyer, an accountant and an investment adviser, plus two secretaries—that's their typing you hear—and of course the domestic help. And then there's a young woman who is a graduate student in American history, doing her master's thesis on Stanford Ives Bennell and the golden age of capitalism. We gave her a little office in the basement and access to the Bennell family records but she's been out with the flu for the last two days. Otherwise she could fill you in on the family history like nobody else in the world."

Loren braced himself for a crucial question. "Would it be possible for me to interview the other professionals? It would add tremendous depth to my article."

Lillian Bennell pressed a switch on the interoffice speaker and ground her cigarette butt into an overflowing tray at the same time. Four minutes later her tiny office was bursting with people and she herself was darting around the room like a silver firefly, introducing everyone, pouring sherry from a Victorian sideboard, gesturing compulsively, bracelets clicking.

"Harlow Emmet, our accountant; Mr. Mackenzie, from *Businessways*." The balance-sheet man looked about fifty, with the windburned face of a sailor, a stocky body and a vanishing hairline. He had a way of clearing his throat before everything he said that grated on Loren's nerves. When he was not talking he would crack his knuckles loudly.

"And this is Roy Taylor, who handles legal matters for the foundation." The lawyer's hair was brown flecked with gray, trimmed precisely. He was compact of build, with a delicate and almost feminine way of moving and a voice that was a hoarse whisper. "Bullet in my throat when I was in the service," he explained as he gave Loren's hand a gentle shake. "Korea, 1950."

"Corinne Kirk, our investment counselor." The woman was slender and subtly tantalizing, with naturally wavy reddish-blond hair. She wore a tailored gray pantsuit and carried a briefcase-size bag under her arm and moved in a self-created aura of cool poised competence.

Loren had prepared a battery of questions on the drive from the Belvedere Inn. What was the present amount of the trust corpus? How much in annual income did that corpus generate and in what kinds of securities was it invested? What percentage of the income of the trust was spent on administrative expenses, the upkeep of the magnificent house, the salaries of the professional staff? What was done with the balance of the income? Was the last surviving annuitant, S. Gordon Bennell, still enjoying good health? Loren felt his way carefully, like a soldier advancing inch by inch through booby-trapped terrain, accumulating information in small fragments without risking any of the direct questions that might be met with tight-shut mouths and the statement that the interview was over. And after nearly an hour of undermining their resistance he asked the questions that most concerned him: questions about the litigation to terminate the trust; questions about the last surviving annuitant, the man from St. Louis whose signing away of his rights under the trust had precipitated the termination suit. "Just who is this S. Gordon Bennell anyway?" he inquired of the room at large.

"A dear old gentleman," Corinne Kirk replied. Her high musical voice reminded Loren of Japanese wind chimes. "He'll be eighty-five years old in November and I understand he still plays golf and squash once a week and works out for fifteen minutes a day on one of those rowing machines."

"An old fool," Lillian Bennell corrected acidly. "And senile no doubt despite all that exercise. There's no other explanation for the way he relinquished his interest and started all this furor. We were just extremely lucky that the supreme court reversed the lower courts' decisions about breaking up the trust. But the life of the foundation depends on his life so we have been subsidizing a combined bodyguard and nursing service for him round the clock over the past several years."

Loren cleared his throat carefully. "Er, I take it you're all happy with the outcome of the litigation?"

"Oh, there's no question the court came to the right conclusion," Roy Taylor croaked softly.

"It's not my field," Corinne Kirk said. "But I like this foundation, I like my job very much and I'm glad we're staying in existence awhile longer." She raised her sherry glass to the light that filtered in through the stained-glass window, almost in a toast to victory.

"Silly suit," Harlow Emmet stated bluntly after clearing his throat. "Not economically justified. The group that wanted to break the trust should have run a cost-benefit analysis first."

"I've told you over and over, Harlow, it wasn't a group!" Lillian Bennell slammed her palm against the desk blotter. "It was that disgusting degenerate John Philip Wood. I know it was. He would do anything to tear down this foundation." Her long red-nailed fingers curled into talons. Loren sensed a piece of the puzzle he hadn't yet encountered and decided to pursue it.

"Uh, that name's a new one on me, ma'am," he ventured politely. "Who is this John Philip Wood?" He turned his notepad to a fresh page and prepared to summarize her answer.

"John Philip Wood is the only son of Harold and Roberta Wood. His mother was one of the eight original remaindermen— or should I say remainderpersons—in my great-grand-uncle's trust. She died fifteen years ago. John Philip Wood is a long-haired bearded filthy hippie, a Communist, a degenerate, a draft dodger, a fugitive from justice, a radical journalist who was in five or six guerrilla wars in South America. He is everything this great country of ours stands *against*. He is a dangerous maniac and belongs in prison or an asylum, or in front of a firing squad. If I ever see him again I think I would shoot him on sight."

Loren wrote frantically and fought to keep a sympathetic look on his face. "Well, ma'am, uh, that's a pretty strong statement and my editor doesn't like libel suits. But maybe we can express your, uh, point of view without running any risk if you'd let me ask a few more questions about this man Wood. What makes him so eager to break up the trust anyway?"

"His reason is very simple." Lillian swiveled her tan leather chair to face him and let her diamond-bright eyes burn into his. "A considerable block of Benneco Industries stock is in the trust corpus. Wood wants as many of those shares as he can get for his one-eighth interest, and he can use the balance of his interest to purchase more shares from the other distributees or on the open market. With control over enough stock he hopes to dictate certain policies to management and perhaps even to put himself on the board of directors."

"But for what purpose?" Loren insisted. "What can he gain?"

Lillian Bennell tapped the desk top with her nails, studying Loren in cautious silence as if deciding whether he was to be trusted. When she had made up her mind, she leaned back in the swivel chair, lighted another cigarette, crossed her legs. "Mr. Mackenzie, I'm sure you're familiar with the published news stories, the rumors, the innuendos about Benneco's operations in certain Central and South American republics that are friendly to the United States. That muckraker Frank Bolish has devoted several of his columns to the subject, and Jack Anderson, and I forget who else."

"I've heard of the stories," Loren admitted, "allegations that Benneco's had a long history of letting the CIA use company facilities in friendly countries as cover for...I think the term is destabilizing operations in countries that aren't so friendly."

"This foundation has nothing to do with managing Benneco Industries," Lillian said. "But I believe those stories have some truth in them and I am proud of the company if they do. That is what Comrade Wood is determined to sabotage. And there is enough Benneco stock in the trust so that he has a chance to succeed if the corpus is distributed. I believe that he would stop at nothing to break up the trust, not even at murder. Which is why this foundation is paying a private detective agency in St. Louis to guard Mr. S. Gordon Bennell twenty-four hours a day."

Harlow Emmet cleared his throat but said nothing. Roy Taylor shifted uneasily in the straight chair he had carried in from the rear hall. Corinne Kirk's face wore a look of embarrassment, as if she wanted to disassociate herself from her employer's opinions without giving offense. Loren felt a strong urge to cross-examine Lillian Bennell until she withered but he restrained himself and struggled to preserve his dispassionate journalistic front.

"Uh, you indicated that you had met this Wood at least once, ma'am. Did he tell you at that time that this was his intention?"

"Oh, no! The Party trains its agents better than that. I'm sure we met four years ago when the entire Bennell family had a conference about the disease but I literally cannot remember a thing about him from that occasion. But about two years ago, shortly before the lawsuit was filed, he came to see me on the pretext of asking what position the foundation would take if S. Gordon Bennell should relinquish his annuity rights, whether we'd fight the termination of the trust. Well, his clothes and his appearance and his manner and the comments he dropped about America and the Third World gave away his true purpose. He disturbed me enough so that I retained the Kurtz Detective Agency to run a check on him, and that report is the source of what I've told you about his background."

"Do you know where he's living now?"

"Anywhere. Nowhere." Her hands made nervous gestures in the air. "The agency couldn't find a permanent address for him. He had been a college student in the late sixties, a leader in the so-called peace movement. His draft board reclassified him 1-A and he never showed up for induction. Vanished into the underground. Apparently he spent some time in South America and perhaps in Cuba. Eventually he was amnestied like all the other draft dodgers, and I don't believe there are any charges against him now, but he's an elusive man who seems to prefer living in the shadows."

"I wonder," Loren mused, "if my article would be more, uh, in depth if I tried to find him."

"I advise you not to bother," Lillian said. "But if you should encounter him, Mr. Mackenzie, watch yourself. He's a smooth-tongued spellbinder and can talk very glibly about oppression and torture by fascist juntas and the suffering millions of the Third World. He could convince you white is black if you were gullible."

"Oh, Lil, international intrigue has nothing to do with it!" Corinne Kirk broke into the conversation impatiently and bent forward to touch Loren's arm with her forefinger. "Mr. Mackenzie, are you aware that every member of the Bennell family is subject until they're over thirty to a very rare genetic disease that science just doesn't know how to treat?"

"Uh, yes, I researched that a bit before I flew out here," Loren said, and hoped the investment counselor wouldn't question him further on the subject.

"A big share of the trust income goes to fight the Bennell syndrome," Corinne went on. "We've endowed chairs in genetic medicine in the three leading medical schools in the country and we are underwriting experimental research at the National Genetics Foundation. Four years ago, when the doctors identified Bennell's disease, we financed a gathering of every member of the family we could trace, paid expenses for 300-odd people to go to a medical center in Los Angeles and get all the information there was about the syndrome. Ever since then we've been paying the cost of an annual checkup at the center for every person in the danger zone—air fare, doctor's bills, lab fees, the works. It adds up to several million dollars a year. When the trust terminates, the corpus fragments into dozens of shares and all that effort to end this awful curse is over. That's why I'm so delighted that the trust property is now worth almost two hundred million dollars. That's why I put in fifty to sixty hours a week, trying to make the trust as profitable as I can. That's why this foundation fought the lawsuit." Her eyes were bright with the zeal of a crusader.

Loren wondered how much of this background Ben Richmond had known before he had voted to preserve the trust. He asked himself whether Lillian Bennell, with her contempt for John Philip Wood, might have offered Richmond a bribe to decide the case her way. He speculated whether Corinne Kirk, with her desire to see the fight against Bennell's disease go on, might have offered a bribe of her own. His impression of the accountant Emmet and the lawyer Taylor was that they were professionals who couldn't care less in a personal sense what the outcome of the suit was but who just might have tried a bribe if they were afraid their own lucrative jobs with the foundation would end with an adverse ruling. But something more than these possibilities puzzled him. He closed his notepad and drew himself closer to Ms. Kirk.

"I'm confused," he said. "Are you suggesting that all the dozens of Bennells who would each take a piece of the trust property wouldn't get together, pool their resources and keep supporting the research?"

Harlow Emmet cleared his throat. "Some would, some not," he cut in. "Simple matter of cost-benefit analysis. If you're under thirty, or if you're over but have kids or want to have them, you probably would. Otherwise you might prefer to enjoy yourself with the money."

"The Bennell descendants are a microcosm of America," Roy Taylor croaked. "They are rich and poor, young and old, selfish and caring, liberal and conservative. They are divided among themselves as we all are. They have to die eventually as we all do. The difference is that they know this in their bones every day."

"Yes, Roy, but remember, some of the people who brought the suit were under thirty," Corinne Kirk insisted. "You see, Mr.

Mackenzie, the ones in the danger zone are dissatisfied with the doctors' not having found how to control the disease. Some of them prefer to protect their health in their own ways, or just to forget it, have a ball, and if they die they die."

"Wouldn't you love to marry a Bennell woman?" Harlow Emmet asked Loren without clearing his throat.

About ten minutes later, in the midst of a string of innocuous questions whose answers did not concern him in the least, Loren read the body language of the others in the room as telling him he had stayed long enough. Their shifting in chairs, glancing at their watches and one another—everything conveyed the message that they were tired of being interviewed and wanted lunch. He tapered off with some final pointless queries, thanked everyone profusely, promised to send an advance copy of his article to the foundation and was escorted by Lillian Bennell through the breathtaking foyer to the front door. It was almost one o'clock. Novo must have checked in by now, he thought. He started his car, turned out of the drive and headed downtown.

Halfway to the Belvedere Inn he swerved off the boulevard into the lot of a fast-food restaurant and ordered a roast beef and melted cheddar sandwich and coffee. When the food arrived he took his tray to an outdoor table on the tiny paved terrace and chewed on what he had learned this morning. He was convinced of several propositions. First, any one or any combination of the people who worked on the Bennell trust in that magnificent house might have offered Ben Richmond a bribe to decide the case so as to keep the trust in being. But then a bribe might also have been offered by any one or any combination of the several Bennells who had fought the suit to break the trust. And if those political columnists were right, and Benneco's Latin-American interests were closely tied with the dirty-tricks department of the American intelligence agencies, the CIA itself could have offered the bribe if it, like Lillian Bennell, felt its operations threatened by the termination of the trust. Loren made a mental note to call Frank Bolish within the next few days and learn more about the CIA connection. With his network of informants within the government, Frank might be able to tell him whether it was CIA men who had tried to keep Loren out of the case by crippling him.

Loren sat on the terrace facing the stream of boulevard traffic, the sunlight beating on his shoulders. He felt a slow wet crawling down his spine—not sweat but an icy-cool sensation, the same feeling he had experienced in the sub-basement of the law library before the hit men had appeared. The feeling of eyes watching him. From somewhere. Everywhere.

He had shrugged off that feeling the last time and the watchers had been there. He couldn't shrug it off again. He restrained the impulse to let out a yelp and bolt for the car. Very slowly he finished the sandwich and coffee, savoring the last bites as if he might never eat again. He tossed the wrappings into a garbage can and crossed the terrace to the double row of cars in the parking lot and slipped behind the wheel of the VW and watched the restaurant and the terrace through the windshield. People were moving about in all directions, from the lot into the building, from the building to the terrace, from the terrace back to the building or to the lot. Cars going in and out of the lot formed a perpetual traffic jam at the entranceway. There was no way of telling if any of the hundred or more people in his sight had a special interest in him.

He waited for a break in the traffic, gunned the VW out of the lot, took the boulevard east to a side street and made a right, then another right and some lefts, driving haphazardly until he was lost, and satisfied that he must also have lost any followers.

That was when he realized that a professional who wanted to track him would simply have planted a homing device in or on the VW. The thought made him feel naked and vulnerable and more than a little frightened. He stopped at a service station for a fill-up and directions and then wove circuitously toward downtown, turning in the VW at the rental agency and hailing a cab back to the Belvedere.

The electric clock behind the registration desk read 1:55 when he entered the lobby and asked the clerk if a Mr. Novo had checked in. The sandy-haired clerk flipped through his card index with ink-stained fingers and looked up. "Yessir. Couple hours ago. Room 978."

Loren took the elevator to the fourteenth floor and the fire stairs down five flights, feeling like a secret agent in a bad movie, and tapped on 978. The door opened instantly as if at an electronic signal and a short powerful-looking man with tangled coal-black hair and a glowing pipe in his hand stood facing him warily.

"Tommy Novo?"

"I'm Novo," the other grunted.

"I'm Mensing," Loren said. "Hooft sent you with a package for me."

"Let's see some ID," the short man said. Loren handed him the driver's license and the law faculty card from his wallet, "Describe what's in the envelope," the short man demanded.

"Marc said a key and some writing. And it's not an envelope, just a sheet of scratch paper folded over and taped around the edges."

"The duck flies down with the prize in his beak." The short man motioned Loren into the room, shut the door, reached inside the pillow slip on the bed and handed him a sheet of paper. "Wish I knew what this charade was about."

"You and me both," Loren said. "Okay, now you let me see some ID." The other flashed a driver's license and a private investigator's license in the name of Thomas J. Novo and sat down on the edge of the bed, watching Loren with sentry's eyes.

"Anything happen to you after the blowouts?" Loren asked. "Did you have a feeling you were being trailed?"

Novo shook his shaggy head. "Someone bird-dogs me, I know it in five minutes. Anything else before I head for home?"

Loren thought quickly. "One more job. I want you to keep an eye on me for a while and see if I'm being watched. If you spot anyone, get a description and let me know. It should take you till evening."

"Shit," Novo said. "And my daughter's playing first base in the Little League game tonight....Oh, hell, a job's a job. What's your room number and your schedule for the rest of the day?"

"1419. I'm going there now. When I leave, you'll see me." They shook hands inside the doorway and Loren darted for the fire stairs and climbed five flights, his hand in his pocket pressed tightly against the paper.

He chain-locked the door and sat in the chair, rested the sheet of paper on the Formica-topped table and gently lifted the strapping tape from one sealed edge. A small steel key clattered to the tabletop. Loren inspected it carefully. It did not look like a room key but it could have been the key to anything else—a locker, a deed box, a desk drawer. He turned the key over. There was a number etched in the tiny barrel: A536. He stripped the tape from the other edges of the paper and spread it on the table, written side up.

FIRST CAPITAL CITY TRUST CO SAFE DEPOSIT BOX YOUR NAME

That was the sum total of the message.

The handwriting was Ben Richmond's. Loren had seen it too often not to recognize it now.

He snatched the directory and the phone, found the number of First Capital City, spun the dial and asked the answering voice how late the bank was open. A magnolia-kissed female voice informed him that the bank opened its doors every weekday morning at 8:30 and shut them every afternoon at 2:00.

Loren checked his watch. The hands pointed to 2:14. He hung up the phone gently and bellowed unseemly words.

He lowered himself into the plastic armchair and buried his chin in his hands. At least until Val Tremaine reported back to him, there wasn't much more he could do, but he was damned if he'd waste the rest of the afternoon watching TV game shows. He stalked to the phone and dialed and listened to Dunphy's private line ring twelve times without answer. He checked the directory, dialed the court administrator's office and was told that all seven justices were in conference and would remain so for several hours. He broke the connection, dialed 978 and heard Novo's soft grunt on the other end.

"Me again," Loren said. "I've got an idea how you might get home in time for your daughter's game. Come on up."

Loren sat in the bathroom with the phone directory and a blank page of his pocket notebook balanced on his knees, working out a schedule while Tommy Novo systematically searched the rest of the suite for bugging devices. After Novo gave the all-clear sign, Loren straightened the chaos in the main room while Novo checked out the bath. By three o'clock he was satisfied. "No bugs. Of course, you don't need a device planted in a room or a car to bug someone, just the right equipment and a listening post hundreds of yards away. There's no way you can be sure someone isn't spying on you these days. You either learn to live with it or you go fruitsy. What's our next play?"

Loren motioned him into the bathroom and turned on the shower full blast. Behind the roar of water and a continuous flushing of the toilet Loren told him the rest of the plan. "I'm going out and be conspicuous for a while. You watch me and see if anyone else is. Be back in your room at 4:30." He shut off the water and they left the room, boarding separate elevators to the lobby.

For the next hour Loren wandered the streets, dropping into a bookstore on one block, browsing in a record shop around the corner, peering into furniture-store windows, stopping at a cocktail lounge for a quick scotch. Heavy gray clouds massed overhead, threatening a sudden storm. The temperature fell fifteen degrees in sixty minutes. Loren kept his eyes front, careful not to look around for a glimpse of Novo, not to act like someone who knew he was being shadowed. That casual hour of sauntering the city streets was one of the longest and most difficult of his life.

At 4:30 he reentered the Belvedere and took the elevator to 14 and the fire stairs to 9. Novo flung the door open at the first light tap. "You wore a tail the whole trip," he announced as Loren slipped in. "Nice piece of tail too. Did you spot her?"

"I didn't even spot you," Loren said. "Give me a description."

"Woman in her middle twenties, taller than average, dark-brown hair in a pixie cut, curled under at the neck. High cheekbones. Sort of cute face but not really beautiful. Built like a fashion model—small tits, not much ass. Wore a tan blouse and slacks and carried a brown purse. I'm amazed you didn't spot her. She's not a pro; did too many things a pro wouldn't."

The description sounded like no one Loren knew, and he wondered how many more unknown quantities might be mixed into this devilish case. And when had this woman begun to shadow him?

"When you started drifting back this way she split," Novo went on. "I trailed her down Kingsley for a couple of blocks, then she grabbed a cab and I lost her. Got the cab's number though."

"Let me have it," Loren said. "Then you can go home. I've got a local operative who can take it from here."

Novo checked his watch. "If I skip supper and don't hit any radar traps on the Interstate I can just about make it. Thanks for the break, Mr. Mensing." They shook hands and Novo locked the door behind the two of them and trotted toward the elevators while Loren used the fire stairs up to 14.

In his own room Loren tried the number Val had given him. It rang twelve times and no one picked it up. Nothing to do now but wait. When she called or dropped by he would put her on the trail of the shadow with the fashion model's body. He adjusted the deadbolt and chain lock, stripped off his outer clothing and dropped into a sorely needed nap. From somewhere beyond the mists of sleep, thunder rolled and rumbled violently.

The phone's harsh ringing jerked him awake. He rubbed his eyes, groped for the handset and muttered into the mouthpiece.

"Hi, Loren. Want an earful?"

He stared blearily at his watch on the night table: two minutes past six. He'd been out more than an hour. Rain beat harshly against the windows. "Come on up, Val," he said, and sprang to his feet and splashed icy water on his face and threw his clothes on with the speed of a fireman. She rapped; he unbolted and opened and smiled. Her hair was drawn back in the ponytail and she wore a pale print blouse and corn-colored slacks and Hush Puppies and she was drenched to the skin, her clothes clinging to her. "I scored," she said brightly. She tapped the dripping vinyl portfolio that she carried under her arm; it was fat with unseen contents. "Bennell's disease, Benneco Industries, the foundation—the works. You just woke up, didn't you? Your shoes aren't laced."

Loren looked down at his feet and began to laugh raucously. "It's been a rough day," he said when he was able to speak. "And from the looks of that portfolio I'm going to be up half the night reading. Sit down, dry off and tell me what you found."

"Hey, could I grab a hot shower first? The temperature's gone crazy and my teeth are chattering so hard I'm afraid they're going to chip if I don't get warm and dry. And then a bite to eat. I got caught up in this stuff and skipped lunch."

Loren remembered that she'd had no breakfast either. The poor soaked kid must be starving, he thought. In his unlaced shoes he staggered to the phone and dialed room service and ordered two brandies and a jumbo shrimp cocktail. Behind him he heard the closing of the bathroom door, the plop of wet clothing against the tile floor. Thoughts that had very little connection with the Richmond bribe and the Bennell family held his mind in a distinctly pleasant grip. He heard the muffled rush of shower water, visualized her under the soft warm spray, and tied his shoes and went to the closet to get his robe and toss it in to her.

And then almost as soon as it had started the roar of water died.

He heard the swish of the shower curtain being swept back, the pad of feet. The door flew open and she stood on the threshold of the bathroom. Tanned and naked. Water dripping from her body onto the tiles. Her face corpse-white under the tan, her eyes stunned and vacant. A small cake of hotel soap in her hand.

And tiny streams of blood mingling with the dripping water, crawling down her arms and breasts and belly.

"May I bor—borrow your styptic pencil, Loren?" she asked in a tight quivering voice.

SEVEN

THE NEXT hour was a blur of fear and frenzied movement. Val sat naked on the rim of the tub and cleansed the cuts with soap and warm water and dabbed at herself with the styptic pencil from Loren's shaving kit until the bleeding stopped. Loren studied the soap she had been using to lather herself. The glistening edge of a razor blade winked in the center of the off-white cake.

Someone had entered the room while he was at the foundation and substituted a razor-bladed cake of soap for the used piece already in the shower dish. And the sight of a used cake of soap in the shower was so commonplace that neither he nor Novo had thought to check it when the two of them searched the room. It was the easiest thing in the world to insert a razor blade into a piece of soap. Somebody had wanted Loren to cut himself to ribbons the next time he showered, maybe to sever an artery. His stomach churned with guilt that Val had taken the punishment meant for him, and with an unreasoning panicky sense that enemies were spying on him from every corner. He felt an urge to rip the room apart. He thought of the satisfaction Moraga and Rojas had seemed to feel at the prospect of maiming him and clenched his hands in fury and fright. This incident bore their hallmark, that same quiet pleasure in terror.

When the cuts had closed, Val gulped down both of the brandies and washed off the clinging fragments of antiseptic pencil with warm water and a freshly unwrapped and carefully inspected cake of soap while Loren mopped the blood with a sopping bath towel. "The airport hotel's a good place to move to," Val suggested. "My car's in the lot across the street, I'll drive you. We'll stop on the way at a doctor friend of mine. I want some shots in case there were germs on that blade. You sure you don't want to call in the cops?"

"What good would it do? First of all I'd have to explain why it happened, and second, even if I did that, which I can't, they'd probably write it off as a nasty practical joke." And if he told them he thought CIA agents were responsible, they would likely try to put him into the mental hospital for observation. "No, the thing to do is to change locations and lie low." He sat on the toilet-seat cover and took her hand in his own. "Val, I'm sorry this happened to you. I feel as if I'd cut you up myself. Maybe you should bug out of this and let me handle it."

She gave him a wry little smile and squeezed his hand. "I don't think I'm scarred for life or anything. But God, I almost fell over when I looked down at myself and saw all the blood. Loren, you're going to tell me what the hell is going on here. And whatever the game is, I'm staying in it till I meet the son of a bitch who did this."

"You're sure? These guys aren't sexists, they'd take out a woman as fast as they would a man."

"I'm not giving you a choice," Val said calmly. "All right, get your things together while I dress, then check out. I'll meet you across the boulevard with the car."

Loren packed his two-suiter with an excess of care, like someone trapped in a snakes' nest, running his hands through his clothing with infinite gentleness. No more surprises awaited him. The last thing he did before zipping the suitcase shut was to shroud the bladed soap bar in the discarded wrapper from a fresh cake and stow it by itself in one of the two-suiter's center pockets.

They drove through the empty downtown canyons, through cool evening darkness and the dregs of the storm. Val turned the five-year-old Pontiac onto the ramp for the expressway, sped west to the outlying suburbs, exited after a few miles and wound through residential streets. In front of a low ranch-type house with a signpost on the immaculate front lawn that read PAUL W. SIEGEL, M.D., she braked to a stop. Loren waited in the car while Val ran in. She was out ten minutes later, rubbing her upper arm. "No problem with germs," she said as she slipped behind the wheel. "Paul says they can't live in soap anyway but he gave me some shots just to be certain." She swung into a K-turn and headed back for the Interstate. "That was an incredibly vicious thing to do to anyone," she said, her profile pale in the dimness of the car. "Like those bastards who put razor blades in apples and give them to kids on Halloween. I was hired on a case like that last year. Caught the guy in half a day's work."

"What happened to him?"

She swerved onto the ramp for Interstate West. "The court gave him a suspended sentence. God, I hate lawyers! But not you, Loren."

The Pontiac left the highway at the airport exit. In the broad plain downhill to their right Loren could see the expanse of airport grounds, the parking lot east of the runways, the hundreds of tiny squares of light in the steel-and-glass tower of the new hotel half a mile west of the air terminal. He would have given years of his life if he and Val could take the next Transstate flight home and never think of the goddamned case again. He felt the outline of the tape cassette and the note and safe-deposit-box key in his pocket and knew that Val was right. He wasn't given a choice. Val snatched a ticket from the machine at the entrance gate of the parking lot and they drove down row after row until she found and maneuvered into a slot. They locked the car and strode hand in hand to the kiosk where the escalator took them below ground to the tunnel train station.

Loren had read about the construction of the new multimillion-dollar airport facilities but all of his trips to the capital since the project's completion had been by auto. Beneath the parking lot the engineers had built a brightly lighted tunnel through which an unmanned "people mover" click-clacked along an oval track on a perpetual circuit that connected the parking area, the terminal building and the airport hotel. A train slid silently into the station and Loren and Val stepped into one of the tiny two-person cubicles. They sat side by side on the orange plastic seat as the train clicked through the long garishly lighted tunnel. "If anyone followed us they'll think you're flying somewhere," Val remarked over the robotlike sounds.

The lobby of the airport hotel, an escalator flight up from the point where they left the tunnel train, was a bright oval twenty stories high, carpeted in flame red, with low couches upholstered in rose velvet and glass-and-chrome tables beside giant plants in scarlet pots. Val registered them as Mr. and Mrs. V. J. Tremaine and they rode with the bellgirl on an external elevator with sheet glass on all four sides, bordered with bright bulbs. As the cage rose to the sixteenth floor, the view of the airport with planes lifting into the evening sky grew more magnificent every second. Within the soundproofed hotel the thunder of jet engines was a muted rumble.

Loren didn't bother to unpack. As soon as the bellgirl had pocketed her dollar and left, they went back to the elevators and rode to the revolving restaurant on the roof. They took a table on the slowly rotating outer rim and ordered Chateaubriand and a bottle of Burgundy and savored the view of the moving horizon and the purple-gray mountains in the distance. Unwinding. Trying to

banish the horrors and perplexities for an hour. Talking of little
things—music, movies, likes and dislikes. By the time they had
finished their coffee and liqueur it was deep black dusk, studded
with airfield lights like diamonds. They went down to the room
and sat in matching soft blue armchairs, with a tiny maple table
between them on which Val set her portfolio.

"Thanks for not rushing me," she said. "I needed time."

"You don't have to summarize the material for me, I can read
through it tonight."

"I want to," she insisted. "When I'm finished you'll tell me
what it's about. I've been wretched all day, imagining how I'd feel
if I'd been born a Bennell. I want to talk it out."

"I'm listening," he said simply.

"There was a man named Jabez Bennell who was a sailor," she
began. "He jumped ship in Boston Harbor in 1832 and settled in
Massachusetts. He was the first Bennell to live in America. He
married and had a houseful of kids and ever since then his family
has been subject to this disease. There's an unpronounceable
medical name for it. Wait a minute, I wrote it down." She fished
among the papers in the portfolio until she found her notes. "Here
it is: autosomal dominant striatonigral degeneration. Bennell's
disease for short. A professor of neurology at the University of
California Medical School identified it about five years ago. He
got in touch with the Bennell Foundation and the foundation got
court permission to use income from the trust to finance a gathering of all known members of the family out at the medical center
in Los Angeles."

"I know about the meeting," Loren said. "I visited the foundation this morning and picked up a lot of details. Tell me, what are
the chances of any given Bennell getting the disease?"

"There was a medical journal article I photocopied that's in
there somewhere with those papers. It said that only someone who
actually has the disease can pass it on to children, and each child
of a diseased parent has a fifty-fifty chance of inheriting it himself.
So if you know your parents escaped you know you're safe, but if
your parent had it you've got an even chance of getting it too. It's
transmitted genetically and can't be detected till it's too late and it
isn't medically treatable once it is detected. The longest anyone's
been known to live after developing symptoms is twenty months.
Of utter hell."

Loren felt the trapped hopelessness he had felt at the Belvedere
when he had stared at that razor blade gleaming through the cake

of soap. But this time there was no enemy to hate, not even an unseen one. Just the common human fate of pain and death. He wanted to drive all that out of his head. He fought a perverse urge to tell her to shut up.

"Tell me about Benneco Industries and the CIA," he made himself say.

Val reached into the portfolio for a handful of photocopied newspaper pages held together by a paper clip. "There's very little in print on that delicate subject but here are a few Frank Bolish columns and one or two by Jack Anderson. They're all pretty much on the same theme—that Benneco is sort of a two-way conduit for dirty tricks. Spies from the South American dictatorships where the company's established come to the states as Benneco employees and harass dissident students from the home countries, sometimes beating them up or framing them on criminal charges so they can be deported and tortured back home. CIA agents go down to those countries as Benneco employees, act as advisers to the local intelligence people, help the juntas stay in power and sabotage unfriendly neighboring countries."

"Do you believe it?"

Her shrug was a gesture of helplessness and disgust. "Anybody with power is going to use it to hurt people without it. That's why I love plants so much and most people so little."

Loren recognized the echo of his own cynicism in her answer and wanted to embrace her like a newly discovered sister. Instead he settled deeper into the soft blue chair and thought of Moraga and Rojas. Was it possible that they were not CIA men but members of counterpart agencies from one of those dictatorships, using forged credentials either with or without CIA's approval? He lost himself in labyrinths of thought. Could Moraga and Rojas, using those same credentials, have approached Ben Richmond, demanded in the name of national security that the Bennell trust be kept intact as long as possible, and offered him the money that unknown to them he so desperately wanted for his mistress if he would swing the case their way? Knowing the judge as well as he had, Loren still could not decide how Ben would have reacted in such a situation. But if that were the answer, it would explain much: the shoebox full of money, the attempts to maim Loren.... Much but not everything. There was still the mystery of the woman with the pixie hair who had shadowed him downtown, and the matter of how Moraga and Rojas had learned almost instantly that Dunphy had called Loren into the case. He would have to mull over those items later.

"You're dreaming again, Loren." Val's voice jerked him back to reality. "I said now it's your turn to explain things to me. That was our deal, remember?"

"I remember," Loren said, and reluctantly dug into his pocket for the Richmond cassette. He set it on the maple table beside Val's portfolio and drew a long ragged breath. "This is going to hurt me," he said, "but here goes, from the top."

He talked for almost half an hour, describing his own clerkship under Richmond, the multiple debts of gratitude he owed the judge, Ben's death, the call from the court to investigate the shoe-box, the incident in the underground garage that almost cost him his legs, the tape that had been slipped into his suitcase—every development before he had followed Hooft's advice and retained Val to help and the later developments like the safe-deposit-box key in the lawbook. The only thing he refused to do was to play the tape for her. He had to stop three times and gulp down glass-fuls of water from the bathroom sink. When the story was over, his voice was hoarse and raspy and his throat felt arid and cracked.

"So even though you started out refusing to believe the judge could have taken the money, you're convinced now that he did, and you hate yourself for not still having blind faith that he didn't sell out, and now you have to find out who bribed him and tell the whole story to the court."

"That's it," he said. "Still want to stay in the game?"

"More than ever. I owe a debt now too." Tenderly she felt her ribs beneath the print blouse, then she raised her arms high over-head and stretched catlike in her chair and gasped at the stab of pain. "God, I'm worn out," she yawned. "Okay, what's the menu for tomorrow?"

Loren drew from his wallet the scrap of paper on which he'd jotted down the number of the taxi Novo had seen taking the shadow woman away this afternoon. "Find the driver of that cab," he told her. "Between four and four-thirty this afternoon he picked up the woman I described, a couple of blocks from the Belvedere. I want to know where he took her. And another thing, send one of your people over here about nine in the morning with an agency car. I'm borrowing my wheels from you for the duration."

"You got it." She eased to her feet and Loren stood in turn and she kissed him softly on the mouth. "I'm glad we're together," she whispered.

He put his arms around her very gently, remembering the razor cuts, and nuzzled her lovely neck. "Sure you don't want to stay?" he said softly into her ear.

"Wouldn't be fair," she said. "I'm feeling sore as hell already and it's going to be agony tonight. We have time."

They kissed again at the door and Loren watched her walk down the red-carpeted corridor, holding herself a little stiffly. When the elevator door cut off her tiny figure at the end of the hall, he locked himself in and sat down again in the silken depths of the blue chair and sifted through the pile of photocopies she had left. He tried to read but his mind refused to make connections between one sentence and the next. His body seemed to be charged with tension and his nerves quivered as if a part of him that had been paralyzed had come alive again. He wanted her back so badly. Just to look into her eyes, to talk with her about life and people and what counted and what didn't count in the long painful crawl from womb to grave. He wanted to hold her naked against him and water plants with her and show her the book he was writing on the Third Reich and forge something real with her.

And she had narrowly escaped being murdered today and carried on her own body the scars that were meant for him.

He threw off his clothes and stood under the roaring shower, first scalding hot then biting cold, until his mind was together again and he could think objectively. He lay in bed in his pajamas, pillows propped under his neck, and spread the papers around him and began to read.

Until at 11:27 by the digital clock on the night table the phone rang.

The only person in the world who knew he was in this room tonight was Val. He scooped the receiver up in the middle of the second ring.

"Mr. Mensing?" It was a woman's voice but not Val's. A voice he didn't recognize. A ball of cold fear formed in his stomach. He tried not even to breathe into the phone, groped desperately for what he should say. After what seemed hours but was actually no more than five seconds he cleared his throat.

"I...I'm afraid you have the wrong number," he said. "This is Mr. Tremaine."

"Mr. Mensing, it's vital that I see you tonight," the woman insisted. "I know it's you, I followed you and the blonde woman from the Belvedere. I'm downstairs in the lobby. Please let me come up."

Loren banged his fist against the night table in fury and self-disgust. With the haste and panic of their escape from downtown they hadn't bothered to look for the woman shadow again when he had checked out, but she had been there and stuck with them and had not been fooled by their maneuver with the tunnel train.

"Oh, please, Mr. Mensing," she begged, and he thought the desperation in her voice was real.

"Are you a tall slender brunette," he asked, "about twenty-five, and do you wear your hair curled under at the neck?"

"Yes," she said.

"What's your name?" he growled.

"Marisa. Marisa Bennell."

Bennell. A voice in his head predicted that the last wisps of doubt about the connection between the Bennell case and the shoebox would soon dissolve. "Give me five minutes," he said, and dropped the phone in its cradle and made a dash for the clothes closet. Half dressed, he stuffed the photocopies back into Val's portfolio, which he then stowed inside his two-suiter. He slipped the Richmond cassette within the folds of an unused towel on the bathroom shelf and was just fitting the safe-deposit-box key onto his ring when the knock sounded on the door. "Just a second," he called, and fumbled with his shirt buttons and belt buckle. Standing to one side of the door, he unhooked the chain and twisted the knob slowly.

The young woman in the entranceway fitted Novo's description precisely except that she had changed to a blue-denim jumpsuit. She darted into the room and Loren slammed the door behind her. She turned to face him, holding out her hand. "Thank you for seeing me," she said. Her voice was soft, subdued but intense, her hand moist and almost clammy. Something about her reminded him of a frightened fawn.

"Sit down," he said, "and tell me how long you've been following me and why, and what brings you out of the shadows." As they crossed the room to the blue armchairs he studied her face. Her eyes seemed feverishly bright and there was a touch of unnatural color to her high cheekbones. She sat on the edge of the soft deep chair as if afraid of relaxing. Loren wondered when she had slept last.

"I've been following you the last two days," she said. "Yesterday I couldn't make too much sense out of where you went except that the blonde you had lunch with at the Midwood Mall is the same woman who visited you at the Belvedere this morning and drove you here a couple of hours ago. You spent most of yesterday afternoon at the law school and most of this morning at the Bennell Foundation. I lost you after you gunned out of the roast beef place but picked you up again at the hotel."

"It's always nice to know when your privacy's been invaded," Loren said. "Mind telling me why?"

"Because the man I work with asked me to. That's why I'm here now. He wants to see you tonight. You probably know his name if Lil gave you the usual pitch at the foundation today."

"Let me guess," Loren said. "John Philip Wood? The Communist hippie who's trying to tear down the South American juntas?"

She gave him a forlorn little smile. "Lil would be funny if she weren't so pathetic. She handed me that same version of the lawsuit over the trust when I went to work at the foundation."

Loren fought to absorb what she was saying and its implications. "You work at the foundation? But you certainly weren't there today or you couldn't have followed me....Ah. You must be the graduate student who's doing the thesis on Stanford Ives Bennell. Lil said you were sick with flu."

"That's right," she said. "I've been playing dedicated grad student since February while being Woody's spy in the enemy camp."

Loren surrendered to the cushiony embrace of the chair, leaned back and closed his eyes and concentrated. "But your friend Woody is working to terminate the trust? I take it that at least that much of Lillian's account was true. Which means that you must be working for the same end, and since you're a Bennell you must be one of those who were on the losing side of the suit."

"I wasn't a named party but you can certainly say I lost by the court's decision, yes. When that trust is broken up I am entitled to one-eighth of the proceeds, probably something like twenty million dollars, and Woody is entitled to the same amount. We want our shares now, Mr. Mensing. We believe we were cheated out of them. We won that suit all the way until the supreme court ruled against us by one vote. I don't think that just happened."

Loren said silent thanks that he'd hid the cassette before she had knocked on the door. He wondered how much the woman really knew. Very cautiously, keeping his voice neutral, he ventured a question. "How do you account for the court's decision?"

"Someone was paid off," she said. "Maybe more than one. You're a law professor and a sort of unofficial detective. I believe you know or suspect that what I'm saying is true and that's why you're in Capital City. Woody and I can help. We don't know who took the bribe but we do know who paid it."

"Tell me," he said, his heart racing.

"Woody has to tell you himself. It's a long story. Won't you please let me take you to him?"

"Why can't this Woody come here?" Loren demanded.

"He could be killed if he comes out of hiding," Marisa answered calmly. "There have been three attempts on his life and one on mine in the last few months. I can't force you to come with me, Mr. Mensing. In fact I can't even phone Woody from here and have you talk with him because there's no phone where he is." She held out both hands to him in a desperate pleading gesture. "Please trust me a little?"

Loren felt the cool moisture of her hands again, studied the dark smudges under her too-bright eyes. "Are you sure you're all right? Maybe a doctor's office is where I should take you."

"No doctor can help me," she said simply. "My father died of Bennell's disease when I was a child."

Loren gripped her hands tighter, searching for the right words to say and knowing there were none.

"It's all right," she said. "It's like being in a war, you get used to it after a while. If I die tomorrow, I've lived and loved and been loved and wanted things more intensely this last year than in all the rest of my life. I guess that's why being in danger doesn't mean so much to me. I have Woody, who's been in worse danger longer, and every day I may develop the symptoms of Bennell's disease and die anyway." Almost involuntarily she smiled. "Funny, most kids in their twenties hate the thought of that thirtieth birthday. I've got five more years, but if I make it to that day I'm going to run through the woods and sing and dance and just go out of my skull with joy and Woody and I are going to celebrate like no one's ever celebrated anything before."

"Save me a ticket to the gala event," Loren said, and released her hands and took a long breath and a chance. "Okay, I'll go with you to see Woody. I hope you have wheels because I'm fresh out."

"My car's in the airport lot. Easier to bury it in the crowd of cars there. We can take the tunnel train. It's a bit of a drive."

An escalator took them from the lobby to the subbasement that housed the train tunnel. It was near midnight and the station area was deserted. They sat on a bench in the garish light and waited for the distant clacking of the train to come closer. "It's never more than an eight-minute wait," Marisa said. "The trains run all night even when there's no one riding them. Like ghost trains."

They rode the half mile to the parking lot in a tiny white cubicle and took the escalator to ground level. Several hundred cars stood neatly parked in their slots, rows of steel hoods gleaming in the moonlight. They wove through the serried ranks, Marisa darting careful glances about as if searching for watchers in the deep shadows. She unlocked the passenger door of a Volvo and slid into the driver's seat, and when Loren had followed her in and slammed the door, she turned the ignition key and the car sped out of its slot.

She took the expressway east, toward the city, turning off at the Lord Avenue ramp that hung precariously on reinforced pillars between blocks of brick tenements and dilapidated brownstones. At the first major intersection she made a right into an ill-lighted street scarred with potholes, lined with ramshackle storefronts, bars, soul-music shops and fast-food joints. Loren read a sign on the wall of a brick building: SUNDRIES-BAR-B-QUE-BAIL-BONDS. The sidewalks were crowded with black men and women and children, running, walking, strutting, playing, delighting in the cool night breezes. Marisa swung off the main drag into another long block of abandoned houses with knots of black teenagers playing in the garbage-littered yards.

"Woody taught me this trick," she said. "Drive through the ghetto for ten minutes and you can lose any whites if you know what you're doing....Watch out!" She hit the brake pedal, then fed gas and shot forward. Loren threw out his hands to keep from slamming into the windshield. Out of the corner of his eye, through the side window, he saw a black youth heft a rock in his hand, then hurl it at the Volvo full force. It smashed against the wing window six inches from Loren's head with a thunderclap explosion. Cracks radiated through the shatterproof glass. The Volvo roared past the suddenly emptied lot. The rock thrower had dematerialized.

Marisa made a quick left and then a right, turned into another main street of the ghetto. Loren was all but choked with rage. The Volvo swerved onto the next access road to the expressway. "They know the route I've been taking," she said quietly. "I can't go that way anymore."

Loren fought down the last of his anger, tried to think again. "What are you saying? That the black punk with the rock knew who you were, that he was trying to kill you specifically?"

"They've probably paid other kids to watch for the car and do the same thing if they spot it. I'm sorry it happened while you were with me, Mr. Mensing, but it gives you some idea of what Woody and I are fighting."

Loren lapsed into silent puzzlement while Marisa turned off the expressway and drove down a dark narrow street dotted with warehouses and concrete loading bays. Beyond the warehouses the lots fronting the street were empty, the earth leveled and sterile. Waiting for something that wasn't going to come. "Urban renewal?" Loren asked.

"They tore down everything in the area," she nodded, "and then the money ran out. Here we are." She braked a block beyond the devastation, next to an empty storefront, the glass in its show windows long since smashed. Across the street was a massive brick and stone structure with its front doors boarded up. Loren could barely read the letters cut into the stonework above the doors: HUMBER. The only sound was the ticking of the Volvo's motor. "Quick now," Marisa said, and darted out of the car and across the street. Loren followed her into the doorway of the old building. With swift deft movements she unboarded the door, inserted a key into a padlock and, when the door was open a few inches, reset the lock and readjusted the boards.

They stood in a high-ceilinged lobby, ghostly dim, smelling of long disuse. A stone fountain loomed in the center of the cracked tile floor. At the far end of the lobby Loren saw two steel doors.

"This is the old Humber Hotel," Marisa said. "It's been deserted for years. Even the derelicts won't camp here, there's a rumor it's haunted. We've got twelve flights of fire stairs to climb. Want to take the east stairs or the west?"

"West," Loren said.

She tugged open the steel fire door in the west wall and they climbed, the slap of their shoes on the stairs eerie in the thick semidarkness. Loren was panting by the sixth flight. They rested for a minute and resumed at a slower pace. Finally, when it seemed he had been climbing stairs half his life, she held out a hand to halt him and they went through another fire door into a long narrow corridor with moonlight filtering through a window at one end. He heard a chittering scurrying sound that made him think of rats in the walls and shuddered. They followed the corridor in the other direction, away from the window, stopped at a solid-looking door with 1208 in grimy brass figures on the topmost panel. Marisa knocked loudly, four quick raps. No sound came from the other side of the door. Then Loren heard a low padding noise like someone approaching in felt slippers. Marisa whispered her name. A key scratched and the door opened. On the threshold stood a thickset man in T-shirt and jeans and moccasins. He held a gun pointed at Loren's middle.

"It's all right, Woody," Marisa said. "This is Loren Mensing. Mr. Mensing, John Philip Wood. Woody, someone tried to smash Mr. Mensing with a rock as we were going through the ghetto. Three blocks south of Bender, on Conners Street. We have to work out a new route."

"Jesus," Woody muttered. "Anyone hurt?" His voice was deep but curiously gentle and compassionate. It reminded Loren of the voice of a priest he once knew.

"Just the wing window in the Volvo," she said. "Let's go in, shall we?"

It was one of the strangest rooms Loren had ever entered. Thick blackout curtains muffled the tall windows. Coleman lanterns on the floor and hanging from wall hooks threw grotesque shadows. Two sleeping bags lay side by side on a threadbare Oriental rug. A stack of cardboard cartons on each side of the sleeping bags served as night tables. Rows of canned foods stood in neat military order on improvised shelving, flanked by two thermos jugs. Twin canvas chairs faced each other against the corridor wall near a sterno unit on which a coffeepot bubbled merrily. An M-16 rifle rested on an old olive-drab file cabinet within easy reach.

"Mr. Wood, is this your full-time residence?" Loren asked in amazement.

"Woody to friends," he replied. "No, it's one of three holes I have but this is the safest. It's not bad when you get used to it. Hell of a long walk to the john though. What are you drinking? I've got some scotch you can have straight or with water from the thermos or coffee."

"Just tell me why you wanted to see me," Loren said. "It's late, I'm tired and it's been a rotten day." They sat in the canvas chairs while Marisa knelt over the spirit lamp and poured Woody a cup of coffee. He fondled the thick china mug in his powerful hands and drank greedily.

"You've been in the city two days now," Woody began, "so I assume you have a working knowledge of the Bennell trust, Benneco Industries, the lawsuit and Bennell's disease."

"Enough to get by. Marisa said you and she will each take a one-eighth share when the trust terminates. Another distant relative of yours explained why you were so concerned to claim your share now."

"Dear old Lil," Woody said. "Long-haired radical freak wants all the Benneco stock so he can infiltrate the management and blow the patriotic activities of our gallant CIA. And you know, she's absolutely right."

"I've heard her side," Loren said. "I'm willing to listen to yours."

"Have you ever been in Argentina, Professor? Or Brazil, Uruguay, Chile since our government murdered Allende? Any of the other fascist dictatorships down there? The Philippines?"

"I've never felt an urge to leave any tourist dollars there after the books and Amnesty International reports I've read." In fact he had long ago reached the decision that not only could he not in conscience spend his money in such places but he couldn't spend it in America either, a decision that for practical reasons he had never implemented.

"I've been in all of those countries," Woody said softly. His eyes seemed to burn in the shadowed gloom. "Underground most of the time. Working with the people, doing journalism for the movement. I've seen the secret police arrest and hold friends of mine indefinitely just for speaking against some stinking dictator. Men, women, children. No rights, no due process, no nothing. Members of the opposition political party, former congressmen, workers, students, journalists, clergy, poets, trade unionists. They're taken to secret interrogation centers, beaten, burned, flogged, flayed, given electric shocks, mutilated for life. Your tax money supports these horrors, Professor, and every time you pull into a Benneco station and tell the guy at the pump to fill her up, you're putting a few more bucks into the operation."

"I'm not going to argue with you, Woody," Loren said.

"I knew a woman in Uruguay," he said, his voice low, hypnotic, falling upon the darkness like rain. "She was living with a poet who opposed the regime. She was four months pregnant when the local Gestapo arrested her on suspicion. They stripped her naked in one of those prison cells and made her hold a forty-pound block of ice against her stomach until the baby died. I knew a pastor in Manila. Marcos' secret police grabbed him three years ago. For six weeks they wouldn't give him a drop of water, made him drink his own urine. He's either still in the slam or dead. Dead, I hope. I've seen teenage boys with their mouths and penises barbecued by cigarette lighters. There was a girl in Argentina named Dolores whom I cared for very much. She was eighteen years old, Professor. They grabbed her, gang-raped her, shaved her head, knocked out all her teeth, and cut off her nipples with an electric saw. This is as common in those countries as buying a newspaper to read on the way to work, and the fucking pigs that do it go to Mass and Communion every day. Do we want to use the leverage of all that Benneco stock in the trust, and all the cash that's coming to Marisa and me, to rub the world's nose in that shit until somehow they make them clean it up and put away the people that have made torture of the helpless a patriotic act? You bet your ass we do, Professor."

The intensity of his voice was almost a physical presence, and Loren remembered what Lillian Bennell had said—that Wood could hypnotize the gullible as a snake hypnotizes a bird. Listening to his words, watching his thick powerful hands clench and unclench in the wavering light, seeing his eyes burn with something like tears at their corners, Loren wanted Woody to win, wanted him to take the money and use it to blow all that filth and horror into atoms, whatever it took to do it. And he wondered if he too was being hypnotized. He knew that Woody would not have hesitated to offer Ben Richmond a substantial cash bribe if it would gain him and Marisa the money and stock for their fight. But then he remembered that it was Woody's side of the case that had lost the suit.

"Who do you think is trying to stop you?" Loren asked. "CIA?"

Marisa, sitting Indian fashion at Woody's feet, answered for him. "Not directly," she said. "They know what's happening but in case things go wrong and we come out on top they need to preserve their deniability."

Woody reached down to stroke her hair lightly. "It's a team of hit men from these dictatorships. A joint effort of three or four countries down there with Benneco connections. I don't know how many are in the group. They were let into this country for the express purpose of doing whatever has to be done to keep Benneco's status the way it is. CIA turns its back, like they do when the Korean spooks corrupt our congressmen or the Iranians carve up a few dissident students. If the hit men get caught, why, no one ever heard of them, they were just your ordinary nonpolitical killers. If they put Marisa and me out of the way they're heroes, probably get some medals."

"Do you have any of their names?" Loren thought of Moraga and Rojas, with their CIA credentials and their casual approach to crippling another human being.

"Just one," Woody said. Something cold and deadly crept into his voice as he spoke. "But he's the one that counts. The head honcho. The boss of the team. Did you ever hear of Bruno Ernesto Schreyach?"

Loren rummaged through accumulated memories of his reading over the years, books and articles and reports about abuses of human rights in various countries. Somehow that name seemed dimly familiar, so that he was half certain he had encountered it before, but try as he might he couldn't remember where. "Better fill me in," he said when he had given up, and tried to get more comfortable in the canvas chair.

"Schreyach is a specialist in intelligence and security." Woody kept his voice under tight control. "He's one of the best in the field. He ran the secret interrogation centers in Uruguay and then later in Argentina and he also handled personal security for a couple of military dictators. We'd call him the chief of the secret service. He's been underground for the last couple of years, they say. I know where. Right here in this city, somewhere within a few square miles of us. He's the one who found a way to get the supreme court to rule against breaking the trust. He's hunting me right now just as I'm hunting him."

"Why would you want to hunt him?" Loren asked.

Woody's voice cracked. His answer was almost a sob. "Because he's the filthy son of a bitch that tortured Dolores!" He lowered his head, turned away from Loren and Marisa. Loren heard the muffled sounds of his grief. Marisa crossed the room, filled another mug with scotch, set the mug in Woody's hands. He rocked back and forth in the canvas chair in a silent rhythm of mourning. "They let her go after they were through with her," he muttered. "I saw her the day they released her, in a filthy little hut in the poorest section of the city. I threw up all over when I saw the repulsive horror they'd turned her into. Somewhere she'd found a knife. She cried and begged me over and over to kill her and I couldn't do it, I was just too sick and torn up to do it. She gasped out some kind of prayer and plunged that knife into her own heart in front of my eyes. I made her and myself a promise while she died there. I swore that some day, ten, twenty, thirty years if it had to be that long, I would take Doctor Schreyach alone with me to some place miles from anywhere, and I would break his arms and legs and cut his eyes out with a knife and skin him alive strip by strip. I'd keep him alive as long as I could and piss in his face while he was dying." He began to laugh as if he already had Schreyach in his hands. Sharp wild frenzied laughter. Loren had heard that kind of hysterical laughter before, in the violent ward of a mental hospital. But he remembered his own rage and grief over Lucy and thought that he almost understood. He tried to shut out the frenzied sounds by burrowing into his memory, straining to recall exactly where he had read that torturers in various countries insisted on being addressed as Doctor, as if they were practitioners of an old established profession.

Woody gulped the rest of the scotch, choking the laughter off. "Sorry," he said. "You fantasize things like that when you see the pieces of someone you loved. I know the difference between dreaming and the real world. When I see Doctor Schreyach, it's going to be me against him, *mano a mano*, very quick and bloody. Luck has been good to me, it's brought him within reach. I'll do the rest."

The intensity of Woody's hate was like a flaming torch and Loren recoiled from its heat. With the remnants of his rational faculties he rejected the whole story as an impossible mad fantasy. Two mortal enemies fighting a primitive silent war to the death in an American metropolis was a concept that refused to mesh with the elements of the familiar universe. But it generated a sense of its own reality that Loren could feel, and that turned his stomach to ice. He had to get away from it for a few minutes. Change the subject. More data, that was what he needed. Nice clean objective data that would chase the blood and nightmare away.

"Tell me more about yourself, Woody. Lillian said that your mother was one of the eight remaindermen—er, remainderpersons—named in Stanford Ives Bennell's trust. Did she—forgive me for asking personal questions—but did she die of Bennell's disease?"

"Yeah," he said. "When I was a kid. Marisa's father did too. The doctors didn't know what it was then of course. But I had the same fifty-fifty chance of dying from it as Marisa. I guess that's why I took a lot of risks when I was younger. I knew I might begin a long painful dying any minute."

"You were in college when you turned twenty, I guess," Loren prodded him. He had a compulsion to know about those years of Woody's life, with each day lived in the shadow of death. He wondered if there was something sick about his wanting to know.

"Twelve years ago," Woody said, remembering, "I was a junior at the University of Connecticut. My parents were dead. I had no close family and no friends. No one wanted a potential corpse for a buddy. It was like in combat, where people don't dare care about the other guys in the unit too much because anyone can die any minute. I was a loner at Connecticut. I did a lot of reading about the conditions of life, how the wretched of the earth lived, how the people in power stepped on everyone else. Somehow I made up my mind that I should do something to change that. Maybe I was afraid that if I made it to thirty I'd have a hell of a lot of money and power someday too, and needed to train myself not to use them to hurt. It was a very quiet lonely kind of training, like becoming a priest or learning karate but different. When the Vietnam war got hot, the more I read about it the more I knew that was part of what I was fighting. I led peace marches. Broke into draft boards. Some spooks photographed me at a rally and a couple of weeks later my own board appraised me that I'd just been reclassified 1-A. Maybe I could have fought it out in court on medical grounds or conscientious objection—I don't know. I didn't. I split. I wound up down in South America and saw close up the same kind of rotten sadistic dictatorships we were supporting with blood and money in South Vietnam. I got into some urban guerrilla action. My Spanish was good enough and I learned how to use a gun and a knife and a Molotov cocktail. There's still a price on my head in three or four of those countries, under different names I assumed. After the amnesty I came back to the States. I did a little checking into Benneco and the estate and discovered that if old S. Gordon Bennell died or signed away his rights in the trust the foundation would have to break up and we could all take our shares in the trust property. I wanted that block of Benneco stock in the trust so I could use it to expose how the company and the CIA have been playing footsie with those military dictators. I paid old S. Gordon triple his annuity to assign his rights and then organized some of the other Bennell relatives and they started the suit. Along the way I met Marisa. We've been a team for a year and eight months now, right, kid?" He tousled her hair with a playful hand and she held it to her mouth and kissed it.

"All the way, darling," she said. "Till death." And she gazed up at Woody with such a depth of love in her eyes that Loren felt a pang of utter loneliness. He needed to retreat from the radiance of her love as he had needed to back away from the flame of Woody's hate. More questions—that was it, more questions.

"Did you two, ah, meet at the family conference where the doctors told everyone the facts about the disease?"

"Hell, no. I was wanted by the FBI when they held that but I heard about it later. Marisa was there. We met much later than that."

"But wait a minute." Loren looked down at Marisa, the lamp-light glowing on one side of her face. "You must have met and talked with Lillian Bennell at that meeting, right?"

"I suppose so," she said. "There were so many people and we were all too frightened to do much socializing."

"But four months ago you were able to present yourself at the foundation under a false name and persuade her to let you do this phony graduate thesis with the Bennell family papers! Didn't she remember you from the meeting?"

"It's not phony!" Her voice rose in a spasm of anger. "It may have started out as a cover story but I've really gotten interested in the whole family. I guess reading *Roots* had something to do with it, but I've been taking a lot of notes, and if I can stay another year or two I'll have enough for a history of the Bennells."

"You'll make another mint on top of the mint you'll get from the trust," Loren grinned. "You still haven't answered my first question."

"Next time you look into Lil's eyes you'll see the answer," Marisa told him. "She's got about twenty-eighty vision and refuses to wear glasses. Besides, I look more respectable now than I did when I was twenty."

Uncomfortable as the canvas chair was, Loren felt himself drifting into sleep in it. He had been through more than enough for one day and night. And when he remembered that he had to get up early in the morning and visit the safe-deposit vault at First Capital City Trust, he knew it was time to make a move. He struggled out of the chair and stretched his cramped muscles and yawned prodigiously. "Let's call it a night," he said. "I'm dragged out."

"Me too," Woody confessed, and stood up and offered his hand. "Keep pulling in the same direction, buddy. Between us we'll nail the bastards to the wall." His grip was like that of a steel vise. "Honey, before you take the professor back to his hotel you maybe ought to show him where your place is just in case he has to get hold of you in a hurry."

"Good idea." She held out her hands and Loren lifted her to her feet. In the flickering shadows of the oil lamps she seemed extraordinarily lovely. Woody unlocked the door and walked them down the musty corridor to the fire exit. "Stay in touch," he said, and the steel door creaked shut behind them as they began the long trudge down twelve flights in the dark.

EIGHT

THEY wove through empty streets in the empty night. Downtown was a ghost city with phantom lights blazing in its towers. Loren twisted in his seat and tried to watch through the rear window for signs of any following cars but he could barely keep his eyes focused. His head drooped and the buzzing in his ears refused to go away. Twice he shook himself out of a waking doze.

Marisa turned into a street dominated by high-rise apartment buildings, then down a narrow driveway at the side of one brick structure, with a low attached garage at its end. She pressed a button on the Volvo's dashboard and an electric eye raised the overhead door. She maneuvered into a numbered slot and tugged at Loren's arm. "We're here," she said gently.

"Ah, but where are we?" he muttered through a mammoth yawn.

"My place. Come on, let's go upstairs. I'll fix you a drink and a map of how to get here from the airport."

A double brandy, he thought, would push him over the edge of sleep. He stumbled out of the Volvo and their footsteps clattered hollowly on the concrete floor. A self-service elevator stood open at the far end of the garage. Marisa pressed 4 and the cage hummed as it lifted them. She inserted a key from her purse in the door directly across the hall from the elevator, eased the door open with one hand and with the other snapped on an overhead light from the switch just inside the foyer.

And screamed.

A long beige snake with dark brown markings lay coiled lazily on the area rug a foot from the doorway, its head lifted, forked tongue probing the air.

Loren thrust her out into the corridor and slammed the door just as the snake darted to strike. Marisa stumbled against him, gagging, eyes wide with horror, making little whistling moans as she clung to him. He fought back a shudder and held her tight, muffled her cries against him. Through the haze of his own panic he thought, *Schreyach has found her place and left a calling card, like the razor when he found mine.*

"Come on," he whispered in her ear. "Back to the car. It's all right, it's all right...." His mind raced. Fear shot adrenalin through his body. He stabbed the elevator button and the humming cage lowered them to the garage. He led her through the silent steel jungle of parked cars, keeping her close against him, his own nerves screaming, straining for every sound. *What was that ticking?* Then he realized that it had to be coming from the Volvo, cooling down. He took the key ring from her stiff hands, helped her into the passenger seat, let himself in and gunned the motor. The electric eye released them into the driveway. He sped through the graveyard streets, not knowing where he was, searching for signs that would point him to the expressway. Marisa hunched in the corner of the seat, a wad of tissue against her mouth, her eyes still haunted. Loren held her with one hand and drove with the other.

Ten blundering minutes later he found the signs, turned left, then right into a boulevard with an access ramp to the highway. He tore west on the expressway, got off at the airport exit, parked in the lot as Val had parked earlier, led Marisa across to the escalator. Below the earth they waited for the next tunnel train to the hotel. Loren kept his arm around her shoulders, could feel the shuddering of her body. The train clicked to a stop, all but empty, and they sat silently in a cubicle as the gleaming white walls slid by. The escalator lifted them to the bright lobby, warm with red furniture and soft music, and they crossed to the glass elevator. Loren had to look at the key in his pocket to remember the number of his room. In the sixteenth-floor corridor he lowered her into a plush settee while he unlocked his door and cut his hand up to the light switch. His stomach churned with fear. If they had found Marisa's hole they could have found his too. He flew through the room, opening drawers, lifting pillows, inspecting the bathroom. What he was looking for he didn't know: another snake, tarantulas, scorpions— it could be anything. He made himself complete the search and found nothing. Not even his shaving kit was out of place. He led Marisa in from the corridor and locked and chained the heavy door behind them. "You're safe now," he told her.

"Oh, Loren, that was hideous. I've been frightened to death of snakes ever since I was a child....Loren, I have to tell Woody."

"You have to get some rest," he said. "And so do I. And Woody can't help us now. There's not a square foot of space outside this room we can be sure is safe. So you're staying here with me."

He had to soothe her another ten minutes before she regained any semblance of control. Then he went into the bathroom and ran a tub of water almost too hot to touch and gingerly unwrapped a fresh cake of soap, making very certain it had not been tampered with before setting it in the porcelain recess in the wall. When the tub was ready he handed Marisa his robe and told her to lock herself in, soak and try to relax. As soon as he heard the squeak of the bathroom lock he undressed, struggled into pajamas, took some blankets and a pillow from the king-sized bed, collapsed into one blue armchair and lifted his feet to the other. Within two minutes he was dead to the world.

He had no recollection of changing beds during the night. There was a blur of dream motion at the back of his mind, a rustling whisper of garments, a sensation as of falling onto a soft fleecy cloud that magically supported his weight, but nothing he identified as happening to him. It was only when he stirred awake for a moment and saw the luminous figures 5:46 on the digital clock on the night table and felt the mattress beneath him and the sheets covering him that he knew. Thick window drapes held back the sunrise, kept the room in semidarkness, but he could feel Marisa curled snugly against him, warm and lovely and breathing softly in her sleep, with her hair spread on the pillow, caressing his cheek. *Oh Christ, I couldn't have!* Then he realized that he was still wearing his pajamas, and that Marisa was still wrapped tight in his robe, and he knew that he hadn't.

The muffled roar of a jet making altitude penetrated the room. He felt Marisa stir, saw her eyes come slowly open beside him. "Morning," he whispered.

"Hi," she said. "I was afraid to sleep without someone next to me. Did you mind?"

"My pleasure," he said, still groggy and not thinking clearly, and brushed his lips against her cheek.

"Thanks for, well, for nothing," she went on. "I didn't think you were the kind that would take advantage of the situation."

"We were both too pooped," he said. "No, that wasn't it. I guess it was the way I saw you looking at Woody last night. Come on, let's go back to sleep."

"My brain's awake now. I've had it. Loren, how can I ever get back into my apartment?"

Loren considered for a minute, then he knew the answer. "That blonde I was with yesterday is a private detective. When it's a decent hour, I'll call her and have her send an operative who knows how to handle snakes. He can check the place out for other gifts. I think you'd better find a new apartment but I'll get you a private room on this floor till you're settled."

"Let me stay here," she said. "Please, Loren? I'm—I'm frightened so much I'm clammy all over. I was so careful renting that place! And there's 24-hour security-guard service and you can't get into the garage without a device they give you for your car that gets you past that electric eye but they found the place anyway and left that awful snake and I have to go for my tests in three weeks....Loren, I just don't have any defenses left."

"Tests?" For an errant moment he thought she was making some reference to her cover as a graduate student. Then he remembered. Lillian Bennell had mentioned that the trust paid all the expenses of a special medical checkup each year for each Bennell descendant subject to the disease. "Oh, in California you mean."

"It's like an early-warning system. They have machines they put you under that can tell if you're likely to show the symptoms over the next twelve months. It's not infallible but if you pass the tests you can at least plan a little ahead. If you flunk...." Without warning the tears flooded out of her, and she shook and clung to Loren tightly enough to scare him a little. "Oh, God, why do I have this thing inside me? Why?" She sobbed against him and he held her close and stroked her hair and tried to comfort her as if she were a child afraid of the dark, saying words that meant nothing but let her know that he was with her.

It was almost seven before she fell asleep again. Loren set his internal alarm for eight and lay down himself. When he woke again, he noted that it was six past eight and inched out of bed as stealthily as possible so as not to disturb her. He picked up the phone and carried it into the bathroom, easing the door shut behind him, and set the receiver on the toilet-seat cover and himself on the rim of the tub and made a call.

"Hi, Val. Sleep okay last night?"

"Awful," she told him. "And I'm sore all over today. What's up?"

"Couple of changes in your schedule. Forget about tracing the cab driver who picked up that woman. I've already found her, and when she wakes up I'm sending her to your office. Give her protection. Meanwhile, contact every place within a hundred miles that keeps snakes and find out if any of them sold or lost a pet recently. When you locate the one that did, tell them to send someone that knows how to handle snakes to 6472 Murray Drive. The girl who's coming to your office lives there. Both of you go out to her place and let the handler into apartment 4-G. After the snake's gone, search the place for any other surprises. When she's packed and left, see what you can learn about the snake. I'll call you later and explain. Another thing I want you to do is to get me as much background as you can on a man named John Philip Wood." Quickly he summarized all that Lillian Bennell and Woody himself had revealed about the young rebel's life. "And don't forget that car for me this morning."

"I hope you know what kind of a bill you're running up," she said. "What are you going to be doing today?"

"Bank business," Loren replied, and fingered the deposit-box key on his ring. "Good luck."

He shaved and dressed noiselessly and waited till 8:45 to wake Marisa and explain what she was to do. While she was dressing the phone shrilled. It was the desk clerk, reporting that the man with the car was waiting at the curb. "I'm off," Loren called into the bathroom. "You stick with Miss Tremaine till you hear from me." He took the elevator to the lobby and pushed through revolving doors into the harsh sunlight.

A blue Ford compact waited with its motor running in the semicircular loading zone in front of the hotel. A young black man with a Clark Gable mustache was sitting behind the wheel. Loren almost fell over with surprise when he opened the passenger door and heard the overture to Tchaikovsky's *The Tempest* on the car radio. "Did Miss Tremaine send you to pick me up?" he asked, recovering.

"Sure did, man. I'm Bob Jackson."

Loren offered his hand to the young man. "How did Val find out I was a classical music nut?"

"Shit, man, this is for me! My mama was a cleaning woman at Carnegie Hall, she snuck me into concerts when I was little and I got to dig 'em. Want me to drive us downtown and then I'll grab a cab back to the shop?" He didn't wait for Loren to answer but gunned the Ford out of the parking area and made a screaming left into the road that led to the expressway. They were silent for a few minutes, both exulting in the wild splendor of Tchaikovsky's storm music. Jackson hung a sharp right onto the downtown exit ramp.

"Working for Miss Tremaine long?" Loren asked.

"Three years now," he said, and merged into the thick com-

muter traffic on Terhune Boulevard. "She took me out of the juvenile offenders' home and gave me a job. Another year or so and
I'll go to work as an investigator for the public defender. She's the
baddest white chick I ever met but she don't pay enough for me to
keep up my record collection. Hey, I see some cabs in front of that
hotel, you take the wheel and I'll split." He tore across the intervening traffic lanes into a no-parking zone, threw Loren a mock
salute and slammed the driver's door, leaving Loren to slide across
and start the Ford again and rejoin the stream of autos before a cop
came by.

Twelve minutes of bumper-to-bumper driving later, Loren
swung into an overpriced parking lot between two steel-and-glass
business towers a block from his destination. First Capital City
Trust was a tan stone fortress with slits of windows recessed into
its front wall. He strode into the welcome chill of air conditioning
and bent over a Formica writing surface in the center of the high-
ceilinged chamber, pretending to fill out a deposit slip while he
oriented himself. Tellers' cages lined the north wall, loan officers'
cubicles the south. Above the line of cages a long strip of surreal-
istic mural had been painted on the wall, illustrating the history of
money. A half door with a counter at waist level cut off part of the
west side of the floor space. Loren detached the key from his ring
and crossed the carpeted floor to the stern gray woman behind the
counter. "Mr. Mensing," he said. "Box A-536."

The woman thrust a ledgerlike volume across to him. "Would
you sign in, please," she said.

Loren hesitated a moment. From the estates he had handled for
his father's firm he knew the standard procedure. A person who
rents a safe-deposit box must make out a signature card and must
sign again whenever he wants to enter the vault where the boxes
are located, with an attendant checking the signature against the
original each time. Most banks have an employee who reads the
obituary notices in each day's local papers and checks the names
against the master lists of depositors. Once the bank learns that a
customer is dead, his account is frozen and any safe-deposit box
he may have rented is sealed, not to be opened except in the presence of someone from the inheritance-tax bureau. As a lawyer
Richmond would have known all that. He wouldn't have dared
take out this box under his own name in his home city. That was
why he had used Loren's name. But how could he have worked
things so that Loren could pass the signature scrutiny and be allowed access to the box after Richmond's death?

Then Loren knew what the answer had to be. He smiled, and signed his name as he had thousands of times before, and the gray woman compared the signatures and pressed the buzzer that released the door lock.

He'd been right. Wily Ben had simply taught himself to forge Loren's signature, no doubt using as models the hundreds of genuine signatures on the memoranda Loren had written when he'd been the judge's clerk. Richmond had used not just Loren's name but his handwriting. Loren marched down the black marble staircase to the lower level and showed his key to the vault attendant, who escorted him to the wall of boxes and inserted his own key into one of the holes for box A-356 while Loren placed his in the second. The box in his hand, Loren followed the attendant to an alcove hidden behind a gold-trimmed black curtain. The attendant parted the drape and Loren was alone in the tiny cubicle with the box. The box he dreaded to open. He threw back the gray steel lid.

The box was packed tight with money, twenties and fifties and some hundreds. Loren forced himself not to think about what the money might mean, and riffled through the bills, counting....Nine thousand two, nine thousand three, a total of ninety-four hundred dollars. And beneath all the money, at the bottom of the box, he found a long white envelope, blank except for "Loren Mensing" in Richmond's handwriting across the front. He tore the flap open with a fingernail and a sheet of plain white bond fluttered to the table. Loren used an ornamental paperweight on the table top to anchor the sheet without leaving his own prints on its surface. Carefully he read the handwritten letter.

Dear Loren:

Your reading this means several things. First, I am now worm food. Second, you've received the cassette I arranged to be sent to you after my death. Third, you've found the key to this box and the second message which I left for you in the spine of Volume 2 of Story. I was confident that you'd read these words one day.

I want you to take what you find in this box and give it to the woman I described on the tape. It isn't much money but it was all I could raise without having embarrassing questions asked. I hope she'll understand that this is my way of saying how thankful beyond words I am that we had each other.

I realize that under the law of wills this transaction is il-

legal, since this letter lacks the proper testamentary formalities, and also that no estate taxes will be paid on the
money you transfer. I beg you nevertheless to do this for
me, Loren; to remember what I did at various times for
you, and do this for me, and then to destroy this letter.

The money is to be given to Corinne Kirk, who at this
writing is employed as an investment analyst by the Bennell Foundation in this city. Please tell her how grateful I
am for the times of peace and happiness she gave me.

Thanks from the bottom of my heart, Loren, and good-
bye.

Fondly,

BEN

Loren felt as if a bomb had gone off inside his head. Suddenly
everything he thought he had known about the origin of the shoebox money and all the other aspects of this nightmare had been
shattered into atoms and a hornet's nest of fresh puzzles let loose.
Had Corinne Kirk seduced Ben, either on her own initiative or on
behalf of the foundation, in order to influence his decision in the
Bennell case? Was there a connection between Ben's affair with
Ms. Kirk and the activities of Bruno Ernesto Schreyach and his
goons? If the money Ben wanted the Kirk woman to have was the
money in the safe-deposit vault, then where in the name of common sense had the much larger sum of money in the shoebox
come from? And what was Loren's ethical responsibility in the
matter of Ben's posthumously received request?

He remembered the list of the serial numbers on the shoebox
bills, the list that Abelson had compiled and given him Tuesday
evening, and dug the folded sheets out of his hip pocket. Then he
spread the deposit-box money on the table in front of him and
scrutinized the serial number of each bill, hunting for patterns,
consecutive numbers, connections between the numbers on the
shoebox bills and the numbers on the money before him. He found
nothing but three brief consecutive runs of twenties and one of
fifties. None of the numbers even came close to the figures on the
long runs of consecutively numbered shoebox bills. One more fi-
asco.

The first question that confronted him was what to do with the
money. That was an easy one. The safest place in the world to

keep the ninety-four hundred dollars was, for now, in the deposit box. He returned the bills to the steel container, stowed Richmond's letter in his breast pocket and rang for the vault attendant. Together they relocked the box in its wall niche.

Loren took the marble staircase to ground level and strode out of the bank into the noise and pollution of a business day. He needed to consult with someone on how to handle the money, and Dunphy was the only logical person to see. Besides, it was about time he visited Conor on another matter.

The ancient elevators in the lobby of the State House boasted sculptured arches over each cage entrance, doors polished to the gleam of a Marine recruit's belt buckle, and elderly operators who manipulated buttons and levers from the comfort of padded secretarial chairs and called out the floor number whenever the cage came to a stop. Loren stepped out at the fifth floor, where the justices had their chambers. A security guard took his name and pressed touchtone buttons on an interoffice phone. While the guard was still on the line a paneled door at the end of the hallway slowly opened. Loren glanced down the corridor. Conor Dunphy was pushing his way through, his shillelagh in one hand and a briefcase in the other. Loren half ran to meet him.

"I thought ye'd dropped through the earth!" Dunphy's eyes were alight behind his thick spectacles as he stuffed the briefcase under his arm and held out a powerful hand. "They said at the Belvedere you'd checked out about dinnertime yesterday and no one knew where you'd gone. What's been happening?"

"More than I like to think about," Loren answered. "I'll need at least an hour to fill you in. Are you free?"

The chief justice's broad Irish face shadowed over with disappointment. "Loren, you couldn't have picked a more godawful time. A limousine's coming in two or three minutes to take me to the governor's mansion. There are problems with the budget appropriation for the court and I'm hopelessly hog-tied the rest of the day."

"Well, the report can wait," Loren said, "but there's something I have to ask you that can't." He lowered his voice so that Dunphy could barely hear him. "It's about Ben."

Dunphy nodded slowly, and something in his eyes told Loren that he already knew what the question would be. He gestured to a door set in the wall, with EXIT in black letters painted on a red glass box over the lintel. "Walk me down the fire stairs to the street," he suggested. "That will give us some privacy." Loren held the door wide, let Dunphy lead the way and set the pace. The chief justice made the descent with extreme caution, planting his shillelagh carefully at each step before leaning his weight on the stick and going down another stair. A thump of wood against metal punctuated every step of the way. "Ready when you are, young sleuth," he said brightly.

"Conor," Loren said, "I know you put that cassette in my suitcase."

Dunphy stood motionless. His fingers gripped the stick more tightly, then loosened again, and he took another hobbling step. "Caught with my pants down," he said, not unhappily. "I had a feeling you'd not be puzzled by my little mystery for long."

"Ben wouldn't have entrusted that tape to anyone but a very close friend, and among the people in the house Tuesday night the closest friend he had was you," Loren explained. "Want to tell me about it?"

When they reached the third-floor landing, Dunphy paused to catch his breath, then continued his slow descent with a step-step-*thwack* step-step-*thwack*. "I did what Ben asked me to do," he said. "Three weeks ago yesterday I happened to be rummaging through a file cabinet in my chambers for some damn thing or other when I noticed a funny-looking envelope wedged against the far corner of the drawer. Well, I knew I hadn't put it there; I'd never seen it before in my life. My name was on the front in Ben's handwriting. So I opened it and inside there was a tape cassette and a note."

"Do you have that note?"

"Upstairs, hidden away. Ben reminded me of how long we'd been friends, of all the favors we'd done each other over the years." *Just as he had in his note in the deposit box*, Loren thought. "Then he begged me to do him one final favor, something he described as the biggest he'd ever asked of anyone. He asked me to keep the tape hidden till eight months after his death and then I was to mail it anonymously to you. I was not to play the tape myself under any circumstances or let anyone else have it."

"I had a hunch it might have been like that," Loren said. "At the time you found the tape, what was your reaction?"

"I tried not to think about it at all. I suppose if I had had to make a guess I'd have said there was a woman involved in it but that would have been pure speculation. Then when this other mess came up involving Ben, the shoebox and all that, I decided that you should be called in because I had a kind of sick intuition that the tape and the shoebox might be connected. That's why I jumped the gun by a month and slipped the tape into your suitcase Tuesday."

"Then you still have no idea what's on the cassette?"

"Do you think I'd violate my best friend's dying confidence?" Dunphy burst out. Then, more calmly: "But I take it you have played the tape, so I have to ask you something I dread to hear you answer." He halted again, cane planted firmly, and gazed with savage intensity into Loren's eyes. "Does Ben confess that he took a bribe?"

"No," Loren said. "Until I played it I thought just what you did, but there's nothing Ben says that seems to connect with the shoebox."

The chief justice expelled a rush of air. "Thank God," he murmured. "I've had nightmares about having to make Iris and Jeanette listen to Ben admitting his own corruption. I'll sleep sounder tonight for what you've just told me. I...I guess it's none of my business what he did say on the tape."

"I can't be sure yet," Loren said. "But I do need to tell you at least part of the story because Ben has thrown a hell of an ethics problem at me from his grave and I need some advice." He held open the ground-floor fire door and stood aside as Dunphy hobbled through into the ornate foyer. "When are you free? Sometime this weekend?"

"Try me tonight," Dunphy told him. "You've got my home number. There's the limo for me. Thanks ever so much for relieving my mind, Loren." They shook hands at the State House entrance and the governor's chauffeur held the rear door open as the chief justice maneuvered painfully into the limousine.

The clock in Soldiers' Memorial Tower sounded eleven mellow booms and the first wave of lunchgoing government personnel streamed out of the State House. Loren merged himself with the human tide that moved in the direction of his parking lot. It was time to arrange a confrontation with Ben Richmond's woman.

He drove aimlessly about the city, the car radio turned just low enough to hear as he worked out a plan. Halfway to his destination he remembered Val and Marisa and the snake, and hunted for a place to park that would be reasonably near a building with a pay phone, and couldn't find one. He headed out of the business district to the area of elegant residences off Duke Boulevard. Five blocks from the intersection of Duke and the private street that housed the foundation headquarters he pulled up to the curb, fed a meter and entered the cool dim artificial twilight of a palatable-looking restaurant with COGBURN'S in neat blue script above the recessed entranceway. He closed the phone-booth door behind him and dialed the number of the Tremaine Agency. After the fifteenth ring he hung up and tried the foundation's number.

Luck was with him. Corinne Kirk was still at her desk.

"Ms. Kirk, my name is Mensing. I'm an attorney and I've been asked to handle certain...aspects of the estate of the late Justice Ben Richmond. You knew the judge, I believe?"

The silence at the other end seemed endless. Finally her voice came over the line, sounding dim and far away, not at all like Japanese wind chimes. "I knew him," she said.

"The judge left something for you," Loren said smoothly, hating himself. "Something I don't think he would have wanted Mrs. Richmond to know about." He paused but she said nothing, and for a moment he was afraid she had left the phone. "It would help if we could talk about it," he said.

"Would you like me to come to your office, Mr....Mensing was it?" Her voice was poised and calm now, the voice of a woman in control.

"Well, actually I'm just a few blocks from you right now, and if you can make it I'd appreciate it very much if you'd join me at Cogburn's for lunch." Again there was hesitation from the other end. "It's extremely important, for everyone's sake."

"Give me half an hour," she said, and hung up.

Loren looked up the number of the *Democrat* in the directory anchored to the wall between the phones, then sealed himself into his booth again and fed coins into the slot. A bored and raspy voice answered on the fourth ring.

"Frank Bolish around?" Loren asked.

"Who wants to know?" the rasp demanded.

"The name's Loren Mensing. Frank knows me." And indeed he did. Bolish had built a national reputation as a hard-hitting muckraking political journalist, exposing lies, cover-ups, corruption and dirty dealing on every level from a small-town magistrate's court to the Pentagon and the White House. It was rumored that three out of every four government officials who knew him offered regular prayers that he be struck by a bolt of lightning. During the nightmare years of Vietnam and Watergate, Loren had given Bolish a few tips that had led to major exposés in the journalist's syndicated column. Now it was time to ask a favor in return.

"Loren, you stupid bastard!" The same old Bolish voice, deep, raucous and blustering. "What shithouse did you pop out of? Where you calling from?"

"Right in town, Frank. I see by the papers you're still tearing the clothes off the emperors three times a week?"

"World without end, baby," Bolish roared. "In fact I've got a hot column in the Olympia and a 2:00 deadline so I can't shoot the shit with you right now."

"This is a business call. Frank, remember those columns you did a while back about the CIA using Benneco Industries operations in South America as a cover for sabotaging local governments that were too far left?"

"What about them?"

"I have reason to believe," Loren said carefully, "that it's still happening. And furthermore, I believe there's an extremely nasty person from below the border who's up here with CIA's silent backing to help keep those activities from being blown. Ever hear of Bruno Ernesto Schreyach?"

"Jesus!" Bolish bellowed. "When I was in Uruguay for Amnesty International about five years ago I saw some of the son of a bitch's handiwork. Group of teenage students who'd been locked up without a trial for belonging to the wrong organization. God, they were like butchered meat....What makes you think he's in the States?"

"Not just in the States but right in this city. I have my reasons, Frank. The main one is that he's tried to cripple me twice since Tuesday. Want to help me nail him?"

"You're on, brother," Bolish said solemnly. "What do you need?"

"Mucho information. Check all your contacts in Washington, comb through your files, put together everything you can on Schreyach. Description, background, likes and dislikes—the works. Shoot for some kind of verification from your whistle-blowing pals in D.C. that the CIA knows about Schreyach's mission. This may net you a month of red hot columns if you get the breaks. How soon will you have some facts for me?"

"Hell, on a story this big I'll stay on the phone all day. Where can we meet for dinner tonight?"

"The Steerhorn Lounge, out at the airport hotel. I'll see you in the bar, say about eight?"

"Deal," Bolish said. "You're buying. And you better know what you're talking about, baby. Ciao."

At 12:19 by Loren's watch she entered the restaurant, standing in the entranceway, peering into the dimly lighted room as if searching for someone. Loren decided that the situation called for him to take a risk. He rose from his booth in the rear, stood conspicuously in the aisle and beckoned her over. She wove through the irregularly spaced tables and approached him, looking cool and enticing in a lime-green pantsuit, her reddish-blonde hair falling loosely to her shoulders. When she was close enough to recognize him, he saw a puzzled expression steal across her face. "Why, Mr. Mackenzie!" she said. "Haven't you gone back to New York yet?"

That was the reaction Loren had hoped for. If she were tied in with the other side, she would have known by now not only what Loren Mensing looked like but also that there was no such person as Jack Mackenzie from *Businessways* magazine. Loren did not think she could have faked the proper response on a split second's warning; if she had, she was the premiere actress in the city.

"Sit down, please," Loren said. "I'm Mensing, the man who called you. Mackenzie doesn't exist."

Her confusion was replaced by anger. Her face seemed to grow taut with it and her eyes blazed.

"I'm sorry I had to deceive you the other day," Loren went on. "But what I told you on the phone just now was the exact truth. Ben did ask me to give you something."

With her head tilted birdlike to one side she scrutinized him through caution-hooded eyes. "Is your first name Loren?" she asked.

"That's right."

She lowered herself into the booth opposite him with a graceful fluid motion. "Ben talked about you several times," she said. "In some ways I think he thought of you as a son. I can believe that if he left something for me he'd leave it with you."

They ordered cocktails and Loren began to tell her of the cassette and the safe-deposit box and the money, keeping his voice soft, trying to suppress all emotion from his tone. She listened intently, her Bacardi untouched on the snowy white tablecloth, her eyes glistening with tears she refused to shed until Loren told her what Ben had said on the tape about her abortion. Then her head lowered and she groped for her napkin and pressed it against her face. Loren could hear the low passionate sobs.

"I think he felt guilty and grateful to you at the same time, if that makes any sense," he said. "But he was never very good at showing feelings. He was raised the old way, which dictated that a man never displayed feelings, and the legal training and his being a judge reinforced that repression. But I know he was a very tender and sensitive man."

"He was the most sensitive man I'd ever met," she told him. "I think that was why we cared for each other so much, because I'm the same way. You can't play a man's game like investment counseling without turning yourself into a male stereotype, or maybe I should say the stereotype of the pushy bitch businesswoman. But with Ben I didn't have to play that role, I could be me, and he could talk about his feelings....Do you know how many times I prayed that his wife would leave him, or crawl into a hole and die and let us have a few good years together? And then that awful night Ben came to me and told me he had cancer. That was the night I learned what hell was all about."

Loren left her in the darkness of her silence, alone and reliving pain. Around them cutlery chinked against plates, drinks and meals were ordered, waiters scurried, two dozen conversations buzzed. Loren wished he knew how to ease her grief. He had learned most of what he had come here for, learned it by tearing open Corinne Kirk's emotional wounds. He despised himself but he had become convinced that she was not one of the enemy. Whatever doubts he had had about her feeling for Ben had dissolved in the sounds of her weeping. There was only one thing left to ask, and he waited until a semblance of self-possession came back to her.

"Ben said on the tape that you and he first met about eight months after he came on the court. That was quite a while before the lawsuit to break the trust was filed."

"I suppose so," she said, and wiped her eyes again and drank deeply from her water tumbler.

"What was Ben's reaction when the case was appealed to the supreme court?"

Fury possessed her face and voice again. "Do you mean did I take advantage of our love to brainwash him about how important it was to keep the trust going?"

"No, not that way," Loren said. "Before this talk I guess I suspected something like that. But not now. I'm just trying to see the situation as Ben must have seen it. He couldn't give you up; he couldn't let you influence his vote; he didn't dare do what he should have done and disqualify himself from the case because he was afraid someone would ask why and that would be the end of the world for him. A conflict like that would have torn him apart but he'd never show it. He'd take it like the Spartan boy in the story who let the fox tear his guts out without making a whimper."

"He showed it to me," she said quietly. "He tried to stop seeing me once he knew the case would come before the court. It didn't work. We just couldn't keep away from each other. But we had to be twice as careful as ever before that no one saw us, and we never never talked about the case. I swear it, not even once."

"But he knew how you felt about it? He must have."

"No one in this world can say if he did, or if it had any effect on his decision. He never talked about it. After it was over and done with we broke our necks arranging our schedules so we could sneak away for a weekend together, and I've never in my life seen anyone looking as relieved as he was those two days. It was as if a mountain had been taken off his back. We laughed again and loved again."

Loren felt a sharp pang of loneliness gnawing in his own belly. "And it was only a few months later that he learned about the cancer," he said.

Her eyes filled with tears again. "Oh, please, Mr. Mensing, don't ask me anything more. I didn't want him to leave me the damn money, I didn't know he'd do anything so foolish. I don't want a penny from him. Keep the money, give it to charity— anything—just let me alone." She looked at him through her haunted eyes. "Please."

"It was Ben's way of saying thank you for all the happiness you brought him," Loren said. "Not a good way but all he could do. I'll see that the money gets into Ben's estate."

"Does that mean it will go to—?" She did not finish the question, and Loren wondered whether she had made a decision never to pronounce Iris Richmond's name.

"Some of it," he said. "I think I could persuade her to donate her share to the American Cancer Society if that would make you feel better about it."

"Ben would have liked that," she said. "Would you please go now, Mr. Mensing? I have to be by myself for a while."

Loren tossed down some money on the table, rose and stood over her. "I wish there were some way I could have avoided hurting you like this," he said, and touched her shoulder tentatively in a gesture of farewell.

The urge to get away from Corinne Kirk's silent agony overpowered him and he drove toward the expressway without thought of the speed limit. Just short of the entrance ramp he swerved sharply into a gas station where he ordered a fill-up and asked where the pay phone was. In the open enclosure he dialed the Tremaine Agency and caught Val in the office.

"Feeling any better?" he asked.

"Not as sore as this morning," she said. "I'll survive. I like Marisa a lot, Loren. Thanks for sending her."

"Where is she now?"

"She's moved out of that apartment and for the time being she'll stay at that house I'm building out in the sticks. I'm having a phone put in today and I'll be sleeping out there myself till this mess is over."

"What about the snake?"

"I found where it came from with three phone calls. It's a trans-Pecos rat snake, a very ugly and vicious-looking brute but not venomous. It's found in the Big Bend region of Texas, along a stretch of the Rio Grande. The one in her apartment was stolen from an animal-supply house in the city after closing yesterday. With the right equipment it's easy enough to drive past that electric-eye device into her garage, and you can beat her apartment lock with a credit card."

"Not a poisonous snake," Loren repeated. "Whoever planted it didn't mean to kill Marisa, just terrorize her."

"Unless they didn't know it wasn't poisonous," Val said. "At any rate a handler came from the supply house and took it out of there with no trouble and I searched the place and didn't find any more booby traps and Marisa couldn't find anything missing so she packed some things and moved out."

"I don't suppose there are any clues to the person that did it?"

"The police have been to the supply house. I doubt they've come up with anything. No one called them to report what happened last night, so now that the snake's recovered they'll probably drop the investigation. The supply house people don't want the publicity and would just as soon forget it."

"So would I," Loren said. "In case I need to see Marisa, would you give me directions to your house?" He found a scrap of paper in his wallet and scrawled notes as Val dictated the route. "Okay, I think I can find it. Right now, except for digging up some poop on John Philip Wood, your part of the case seems to be at a dead end, so relax for a bit."

"Surely you jest!" she exclaimed. "If you knew how much you've disrupted my routine business....Well, I work better under pressure so what the hell. See you later, Loren."

Loren paid the attendant for the gas and steered the Ford onto the expressway ramp without paying attention to the road. He drove downtown all but unconsciously while his mind raced. He had to be sure there was rational basis for his conviction that whatever the explanation for that shoebox full of money, Ben Richmond had not sold out. On that cassette and in those posthumous letters Ben had stripped himself naked to Loren, baring the secrets of his life as he had never done before. If one of those secrets was that he had taken a bribe in the Bennell case, Loren was positive he would have confessed that too. His torment over having to reach a decision in the case while remaining the lover of a woman involved indirectly in the litigation had been genuine; Corinne's description of Ben's agonies was too real to have been faked. Now that Loren had talked to Corinne, all the extraneous elements that had seemed to condemn the judge—the fund-juggling, the renting of the safety box in Loren's name, the convoluted series of communications designed to reach Loren after Ben's death—now made sense.

The only thing that didn't fit was the shoebox. That and the Schreyach gang's role.

It was time to check out an angle Loren had had no chance to consider until now. The odds were against him but it was the only lead to the shoebox money he had left. He felt in his pocket to make sure he still had Abelson's list of serial numbers from those bills and turned off the beltway at the ramp that fed into the downtown business district.

NINE

THE senior vice-president of the Federal Reserve branch in Capital City was a rotund and red-faced gentleman named Sanford J. Bissonette. Behind his gleaming walnut desk in the corner office on the third floor of the bank building he sat like a genial Napoleon, exulting in the quiet efficiency of the operation he commanded. Loren had spent forty minutes convincing the little banker that he was a well-known mystery writer who had come to research a novel about a murder in the Fed's money vault. Spontaneous and totally imaginary as the plot and all its ramifications were, the idea seemed to have a huge appeal for Bissonette, whose head bounced gleefully up and down during Loren's recital like the head of a boy at a Fourth of July picnic bobbing for apples.

"Marvelous," he repeated nasally, rubbing his palms together in a frenzy of delight. "Simply marvelous, Mr. Hoch! I swear, where in the world you writers get your ideas is beyond my comprehension."

"Then you don't mind giving me some technical assistance?"

"Well, I certainly wouldn't want any errors to creep into your little fable. Exactly what would you like to know?"

"Well," Loren said, crossing his legs and balancing his notebook on one knee, "let's begin with the body in your vault. The police find a big bundle of currency stuffed in the dead man's pocket. Naturally they want to learn all they can about the history of this money. So they come to you. Now, just from looking at those bills, could you tell them anything about when they originated, whose hands they'd gone through—anything along those lines?"

Bissonette deposited his spectacles on the leather desk blotter and began to polish them with a tissue. "What I could tell your investigators," he replied precisely, "would be of very limited help. Given the serial number of any Federal Reserve note, we could check back with the Bureau of Printing and Engraving and find out from their records when the bill had been printed and when it had been shipped from the Bureau to the appropriate Federal Reserve agent, and then check with the regional bank and find out when the F.R. agent had released the bill."

Loren halted his furious scrawling of notes and raised a hand in bafflement. "I'm afraid you lost me somewhere. Could we backtrack a bit and go through it more slowly?"

The banker beamed, obviously pleased to be a part of the creative process. "Too much information too fast, eh? You see, Mr. Hoch, when the Bureau of Printing and Engraving in Washington sends out a shipment of new money, it goes by truck to whichever of the Federal Reserve's twelve regional banks the money is intended for. Do you have a dollar bill?"

Loren dug a single from his wallet and handed it to Bissonette. "The serial number of this bill," the banker announced, "is D35641643A. The D in the serial number means the same thing as the D in the seal in the center of the bill's left half and the same thing as the printed figure four you see in several places on the face of the bill, namely that this piece of currency was originally shipped by the Bureau to the regional bank in Cleveland. As I said a moment ago, the Bureau's records would indicate when this bill was shipped to the Cleveland F.R. agent."

"What," Loren asked politely, "is an F.R. agent?"

Bissonette gazed at Loren with a slight smile of superior knowledge. "The Federal Reserve Board has an agent in each of the twelve regional banks who is also the chairman of the board of directors of that bank. The bills are shipped to the appropriate agent and he in turn holds them in escrow, so to speak, until they are collateralized—that is to say, until they're actually released to the bank itself. The regional bank's records will show the date the F.R. agent has released a given bill. In due course the money will go to a commercial bank and from there into public circulation, but beyond the point where the F.R. agent releases a bill there are no reliable records of its history. You can't search the title to a piece of currency as you can to a piece of land." The banker allowed a tinge of sadness to darken his shining smile. "I do hope I haven't just ruined your plot for you...."

Loren sat bolt upright in his green leather chair, his eyes blazing as the implication of Bissonette's lecture suddenly struck a spark. The bills in the shoebox looked new enough. The brainstorm just might work. He groped for Abelson's list of numbers taken from the shoebox money. "Let me make sure I understand. If I gave you the serial number of a recently printed bill, you could check with the regional bank, tell me the date that bill was released by the F.R. agent into the system, and be absolutely certain that no one could have gotten hold of the bill before then?"

Sanford J. Bissonette bobbed up and down affirmatively.

"Then you have just given me a whale of an idea," Loren almost shouted. "Would you mind if I put it to a test? Suppose I give you a few sequences of serial numbers I happen to have jotted down recently and you tell me when the bills were released. All right?"

The banker allowed a moment of doubt to settle upon his roundly glowing features. Then his face brightened again and he beamed like an indulgent uncle. "Well, it's a Friday afternoon and I've never helped write a mystery before. All right, let me have your numbers."

Slowly Loren read off the first and last numbers in each of the consecutive runs of bills Abelson had written down on the sheet. Bissonette copied the numbers carefully on a crested notepad, then excused himself and left the office. Loren sat and drummed his fingers against the chair arm. Waiting, waiting. Wondering if this could be the break in the case. Five minutes. Ten minutes. He crossed the room to a low walnut table, neatly decorated with copies of several banking journals, and tried to find something in their pages that would occupy him until Bissonette returned. Nothing worked. He paced to the window, studied the patterns of street traffic, tried to read the marquee of the movie house four blocks down the boulevard, paced some more, sat some more. Twenty minutes after he had stepped out of the room, Bissonette bounced back into his office. In his hand he carried a sheet from the same notepad, its surface filled with neatly penciled numbers. He settled into his brown leather executive swivel chair and leaned back expansively.

"The bills whose numbers you gave me were issued over a period of several years," he announced. "The earliest sequence was printed in October of 1970. Then we have a sequence that—"

"Pardon me," Loren said, "could we jump ahead to the latest sequence, please? That's the one that's most relevant to the...ah... the story idea I had. When were the bills released that are the newest of those I read out to you?"

"Well, there are two sequences that I could best characterize as neck and neck." He read out the first and last serial numbers of two of the runs of bills Loren had dictated to him. "The first sequence was released to the Fed in Chicago last December. The second was released to the St. Louis Fed in January of this year."

January of this year. *At least two weeks after Ben Richmond's death.* Then someone had paid forty-nine thousand dollars to a judge who not only had long ago rendered his vote in the Bennell case but was dead to boot. It was all a scam, a posthumous frame-up, part of someone's elaborate scheme to discredit the court's four-to-three ruling in the Bennell case. And Loren could prove it.

"Ah, Mr. Hoch? Still with us? Have I demonstrated what you need to know?"

"You most certainly have," Loren said abstractedly. "I'm more grateful than I can tell you." He thanked the beaming vice-president with a profusion of heartfelt superlatives and made his departure. In the corridor outside Bissonette's office he pressed the button for an elevator, and when a cage sighed open for him he hit the button for the fifth floor, where according to the downstairs directory the bank's law library was located. He needed a quiet place where he could think, where he could try to reassemble the once again shattered fragments of the case.

He found the small vacant room where the bank's research collection was housed, took a chair in the obscurest corner and sat with his elbows on the library table and his chin cupped in his fists. His ecstasy at finding irrefutable proof that Ben Richmond had not compromised his integrity was matched only by his hopeless confusion at what that proof implied. For if Ben had been the victim of a posthumous frame-up, the only conceivable purpose of the persons responsible must have been to let the shoebox be discovered in the expectation that it would lead to the reopening of the Bennell lawsuit. And if that were true, then the forces Loren had come to think of collectively as the enemy—the foundation, Benneco Industries, the CIA, Bruno Schreyach and his terror specialists—couldn't be behind the frame, since the side they favored had won the suit and they had no reason in the world to want the judgment questioned. No, it had to be someone on the other side— the side that had fought to end the trust, the losing side—who was the engineer of the frame. The side of Marisa and Woody.

Loren recoiled from that conclusion as he had from the snake in Marisa's hallway. It was too wild, too chancy, a strategy of desperation. But he could not shake the conviction that both Marisa and Woody believed so religiously in the rightness of their cause that they might not have scruples about destroying a dead man's reputation if it served their high purpose. There was only one thing wrong with Loren's theory: it did nothing to explain why the Schreyach forces had tried first to cripple him and then to have him cut himself to shreds in the shower when logically they should be on his side.

Loren decided to verify one matter without further delay. As-suming that the frame had worked, and that Loren had eventually reported to the court that Ben had almost certainly sold his vote in the Bennell litigation, would the court have the legal power to re-open a matter that had been *res judicata* for more than a year? He scanned the shelves and pulled down several volumes of the state statutes, the supreme court rules of practice and procedure, and Fleming's five-volume treatise on the law of trusts and estates. He read furiously, scrawled notes, cross-checked, skimmed relevant cases, made more notes. By 4:00 he had established the existence of at least three theories the court could use effectively to reopen the litigation and reexamine the propriety of terminating the trust within the lifetime of the healthy octogenarian S. Gordon Bennell.

He still wasn't satisfied. A part of his mind that refused to work on strict reasoning rebelled at accepting the notion that Woody and Marisa were the adversary. He needed more data, more tangible elements to work with. He had to find out exactly how that shoe-box had wound up in Ben's closet. He buried his head in his arms and concentrated fiercely.

And after a while he saw the answer.

At first he couldn't accept it. Despite the basic simplicity of his solution it was too baroque, too complicated. But this time he could perform the crucial test of his theory at once.

He swung out of the chair, hunted through the room for a tele-phone directory, thumbed through the Yellow Pages under E, ran his eyes down a particular alphabetical listing. APACHE, ARCO, BILLY'S....That was it! All the proof he needed. He tore out of the tiny library, stabbed the elevator button, raced through the de-serted ground floor corridor of the bank to the lot where he'd left the Ford, crawled through the nightmare congestion of downtown traffic and the even worse nightmare of the homebound bumper-to-bumper brigade going west on the expressway to the residential suburbs. Three times in four miles a single stalled car forced an entire lane of traffic to a grinding standstill. Loren shifted lanes like a madman, pounded his horn raucously and cursed. An eter-nity later the traffic began to thin and Loren turned off the high-way and wove among the two-lane blacktops, stopping twice at gas stations for directions, and finally he saw it. Cut into the hill on his left was the steeply rising private lane, flanked by twin rows of whitewashed stones like the borders of a rock garden. As he crested the hill the huge stone house lay dead ahead. He braked in the macadam driveway, between a gleaming Fleetwood that he hadn't seen before and a blue Toyota he recognized as Jeanette's. He hit the bell and heard the hollow echo of chimes within the house and the sharp rapping of footsteps on the parquet floor. Iris Richmond stood in the doorway, tall, wrinkled, patrician, wearing a long black dress and a look compounded of curiosity and mild anger, a glass of frothy green liquid in one hand.

"Why, Loren, how nice to see you again. Please come in and join us. Jeanette and Norm have stopped by for cocktails."

"Excellent!" Loren said and, marveling at that stroke of luck, he followed her down the hall to the spacious front room of his Tuesday-night conference with the justices. He hoped he had not looked strangely at Iris when she had answered the bell. He knew so much more now about her private life and Ben's than he had known three days ago, so much that he wished he had never had to know and that he would never let her know that he had learned. He felt as he imagined a child might feel after happening upon its parents making love.

Jeanette and Abelson sat in twin velvet chairs with a pitcher of the foamy green drink on the low table between them. "Hi, Loren," Jeanette called. "Just in time for a grasshopper." Abelson grunted a greeting and wrung Loren's hand in his strangler grip while Iris poured Loren some of the thick syrupy beverage.

"I have good news for all of you." Loren leaned back in the barrel chair he had sat in Tuesday evening. "Ben did not take a bribe and I can prove he didn't. The money was put in his closet after he was dead."

He studied the rush of emotion to the women's faces. Iris' features came alight with an almost unbelieving excitement and joy; Jeanette's dark eyes gleamed with silent gratitude. Abelson kept his poker face but Loren thought he detected a hint of cool satisfaction and he felt very good indeed. Instantly they bombarded him with demands that he explain his statement in full detail and, settling back and sipping his drink, he described his visit to the Federal Reserve and what he had discovered there, being careful to drop not even a hint about all the other aspects of the case that had plagued him.

"My God," Abelson muttered solemnly at the end of the recital. "I never knew you could tell so much from serial numbers."

"Neither did whoever planted the money," Loren pointed out. "So now we come to the question of who that somebody was, and I think I know the answer to that one too. Iris, remember all those questions I asked you Tuesday about visitors to the house and people who had access to Ben's suite?"

"Of course," she answered carefully, like a witness on the stand. "You were extremely thorough, but I thought we had reached a dead end as far as trying to establish that someone could have slipped the shoebox into Ben's closet."

"We did," Loren said, "and I've thought it over again and I'm now more convinced than ever that no one had the means and opportunity to smuggle the box in and upstairs."

Jeanette Richmond leaned forward, her knees almost touching Loren's, her eyes intense. "But, Loren, that doesn't make sense! You say Father was innocent and then you say no one else could have—"

"No *one* else could have," Loren interrupted, "but two people could, and did."

A buzz of exclamation rose from the three listeners. Loren sat back and let them absorb what he had said, and when the room was quiet again he went on. "Let's take the second step first. How did the box get upstairs? Well, as I remarked Tuesday night, there is an obvious suspect. The maid, Angella Carmer, who cleaned that suite regularly and without supervision after Ben's death. Sometime before she quit last month, supposedly to get married, she put that shoebox in the closet."

Iris Richmond's face turned as chalky white as if she herself had been the person accused. "Loren, that's impossible," she insisted. "I specifically told you Tuesday that Angella never once brought anything into this house that was large enough to hold a shoebox."

"Exactly," Loren said. "Knowing your memory for details, I took your word for that and ruled the maid out on that basis. But I didn't consider the possibility that she had an accomplice. Someone else who actually smuggled the box into the house to a place where she could pick it up and hide it behind Ben's suitcases."

He paused again and finished his drink. There was not a sound in the room until he set down his empty glass.

"Once again there's an obvious suspect for the first step of the job. Remember that exterminator who came here in March with a story about Ben's having ordered an inspection for termites before his death? Iris, you told me Tuesday that that man carried a tool kit or equipment bag of some kind around with him on his inspection. Remember? Now tell me, was that tool kit large enough to hold a shoebox?"

She sat motionless in her chair, fingers clutched together, eyes far away in concentration. It was as if she were willing herself back in time to the day three months ago when the exterminator had come to her door. Then, very slowly and deliberately, she raised her head until her eyes were level with Loren's and staring intently into his. "I believe it was," she said. "Yes! I'm sure of it now. It was a big monster of a bag with a flap over the front so you couldn't see what was in it. I recall thinking it was large enough to contain a vacuum cleaner, and wondering if that was how they got rid of termites."

"Now, you told me Tuesday that this man did not go upstairs at all but that he did take his kit down to the basement with him. Right?"

"That's right," she said.

"Did you go down to the basement with him?" he demanded.

"I did not," she answered firmly.

"*Voila!* That was where he hid the shoebox. Angella simply picked it up later and sneaked it upstairs into Ben's closet when the chance came along. A neat little two-step. It's the only theory that covers all the facts."

Norman Abelson sprang from his chair and paced across the rug in front of Loren like an attorney addressing a jury. "Mensing, that's insane," he shouted. "Why in the hell would an exterminator do any such thing?"

"The answer's implied in the question," Loren said. "He wasn't an exterminator. And I can prove it. Someone get me the Yellow Pages." Jeanette half ran across the room to the ornately carved shelf on which the directory and the telephone itself rested. "Iris," Loren continued, "tell me again—what was the name of the exterminating company the man said he worked for?"

The widow retreated into dazed reflection for a moment as her daughter came back with the phone book in her hand. "Why, it was Ajax, I think. That's right, Ajax Exterminators. It was on the side of his van and on the back of his overalls. And it was on the business card he gave me and the bill his company sent, the one I showed you Tuesday evening."

"Anybody can get a business card printed." Loren declined to mention that he had done so himself within the past seventy-two hours. "Anybody can get a name painted on a truck van or stitched on overalls or printed on a phony bill form. Jeanette, open the Yellow Pages to the E's and start reading the alphabetical list under Exterminators and Fumigators. Aloud, please."

Jeanette dropped into her chair, balanced the thick directory on her knees, bent her head to read the fine print. "ABC Pest Control," she recited. "Aardvark Exterminators. Allied. Antimite, Apache, Arco, Billy's Bugsaway...."

"That's far enough," Loren said. "There is no Ajax Exterminators. Ever since you mentioned that name, Iris, I've had the nagging feeling that it sounded a bit too much like the names of all the fictitious businesses in all the B movies I've ever seen. There's your proof that the termite inspector was a fake. When we check the company's address, we'll find a vacant lot."

Norman Abelson sank back into his chair and sat uncomfortably on its foremost three inches. "You've convinced me," he said. "It's not mathematical proof but it sounds plausible enough to be worth pursuing with everything you've got. What's the next step?"

"One I should have taken a couple of days ago but never had the time for." Loren crossed to the phone, opened his pocket notepad to the city address and phone number of Angella Carmer as Iris had dictated them Tuesday evening. He spun the dial and listened to a muffled ringing before an operator's recorded voice broke into the line.

"I'm sorry, the number you have dialed has been disconnected...."

Loren slammed the phone down, dialed directory assistance and asked for the current number of Angella Carmer, spelling both names precisely. The operator advised him that no number existed under such a name, which was exactly what Loren had expected to hear. He replaced the receiver and turned to face the room.

"There's no phone in her name anymore. Of course, it's possible that she got married and moved, as she said she would, and that her new number is in her husband's name, whatever that may be. I'm going to find out." He dialed the Tremaine Agency and waited for fifteen rings before he hung up and checked his watch. Nine past six. She must be on her way to that house of hers in the sticks. At first he was tempted to follow the directions she had given him over the phone at lunchtime, drive to the house, set her on the missing maid's trail and have another talk with Marisa. Then he saw that the timing was all wrong. He needed rest, Val needed rest, he had to make his report to Dunphy before his eight-o'clock dinner date with Frank Bolish, and he was reluctant to talk to Marisa as long as he suspected her of complicity in framing Ben. Let the two women spend the night undisturbed, he decided.

Later he could tap Val's impressions, find out if she thought Marisa might be hiding anything. He would have given much if he could be certain she wasn't involved. He couldn't reconcile the way she had clung to him last night, her trembling desperation to live unshadowed by the threat of physical degeneration and death in her twenties, with the suspicion that she had coldly schemed to destroy a dead man's integrity.

He declined Iris' invitation that he stay for dinner, accepted the heartfelt thanks of the Richmonds and Abelson and drove back to the expressway, where he turned east, exiting at the airport ramp. He set the chain lock on his door, stripped off jacket and tie and enfolded himself in the blue armchair, organizing his thoughts. Then he hunted through his much-thumbed notepad for Conor Dunphy's home number.

Luck seemed to be in his corner for once. Not only was Conor at home but from the sound of his voice he seemed reasonably sober. The phone cradled against his shoulder, Loren gave the chief justice a complete if concise report on one carefully isolated subject, the only aspect of the case he was ready to reveal to Dunphy or any other outsider at this stage of the game. The Bennell connection, the silent war between John Philip Wood and Bruno Schreyach, the private emotional torment in which Ben Richmond had lived—these Loren kept strictly to himself.

At the end of his explanation of how he had established Ben's innocence in the matter of the shoebox money, Loren waited for Dunphy to react. He heard nothing, not even Dunphy's loud ragged breathing. The silence seemed to drag on for hours. Then an ear-shattering roar of joy exploded over the wire. "Glory hallelujah!" Dunphy burst out rapturously. "You pulled it off again! God, that is the best single item of news I've heard since I came on the court....So what happens now, if I may be so bold?"

"Now," Loren told him, "we go on the offensive." He went on to summarize the case he had constructed against the mysterious termite inspector and Angella Carmer as the grass-roots agents who had planted the shoebox and the steps he planned to take to have the maid located and questioned. "Once we get a statement from her, find out who hired her, we simply pull on the chain till the last link's in our hands."

"Gorgeous! Gorgeous!" Dunphy exulted. "Well, you go ahead then, young sleuth, and yank that chain for all you're worth. I'll be pacing like an expectant papa till I hear from you again."

"It may take a few days before there's anything to tell. Sleep tight, Conor."

The digital clock on the night table read 7:48. Twelve minutes to grab a shower and change for dinner. Loren spun the phone dial again. No one answered at Val's house. After twenty rings he slammed the receiver down. Mild curiosity about the absence of both Val and Marisa was giving way to a subtly gnawing fear.

He showered, changed to a pullover and slacks, and just before leaving the room he tried Val again. Same result. Nothing. He cursed, banged the receiver into place and told himself very firmly that Val was a capable, feisty woman who could take ample care of herself and did not need the male equivalent of a mother hen fretting about her. The thought did nothing to decrease his anxiety. He locked the door carefully behind him and made for the glass-walled elevator.

Scanning the long oval bar from the entranceway to the Steerhorn Lounge, he spotted his man instantly. With his six-three height, huge shoulders and chest and thick gut, Frank Bolish was a hard man to miss even in a mob. He sat hunched forward on a high stool at the far end of the dimly lit room, a gigantic stein of dark Bavarian beer half empty on the bar in front of him. Anyone who didn't know him would have taken him for a longshoreman or a truck driver and would have conjured up the mental picture of a bruiser whose every other word was what used to be called unprintable, who cherished his union card and drank like a fish and had never read anything more complex than an Executioner paperback. This was precisely the impression that Bolish worked like a dockhand to convey, allowing no hint of the realities—that he was fluent in both the cultivated dialect and the gutter slang of four languages, that he had two master's degrees under his belt and had read widely in Marx and Nietzsche and Freud and Sartre without benefit of translators—to penetrate the macho persona through which he glared balefully at the world.

Loren edged through the congregation of drinkers, peanut munchers and ripe-breasted barmaids, and as he came into view Bolish set down his stein and thrust out a damp hand at him. "Hey, man, you look good," the journalist rumbled. "What are you guzzling?"

"Make it a Southern Comfort on the rocks." Loren snatched a just then vacated stool three drinkers down the bar and squeezed it into the space between Bolish and the wall, and for fifteen minutes that went by like fifteen seconds they drank and swapped yarns and ogled the waitresses. Then they ordered fresh rounds and took their drinks with them through the bead-hung archway that led into the restaurant area. A red-jacketed attendant led them to a table in the far corner and they ordered prime rib with baked potato and a bottle of Chateau La Pelleterie 1970 and made a pilgrimage to the well-stocked salad buffet in the center of the room, where they piled their plates high.

"Okay, Frank," Loren said as they attacked their salads. "Time for you to pay your share of this feast. What have you got on Bruno Schreyach?"

Bolish popped an overloaded forkful into his mouth. "There's not a whole lot known about the guy's life. He's about forty, Argentinian by birth but he's lived and operated in eight or nine countries. The first time anyone heard of him was about 1962 when he went to work as a sort of high-class bodyguard for some old Nazis who were hiding in Uruguay and got scared shitless by the Eichmann kidnapping. There are rumors he took out a couple of Israeli agents around that time but no one ever found the bodies. In the middle sixties he turns up as a unit leader in one of those death squads the juntas keep handy in fascist dictatorships. You know, to kill dissidents for the government. That job led him into interrogating prisoners, and he did that for five or six years. You've seen the reports, I've seen some of the people he cut and burned, and believe me, you don't want details while you're eating."

Loren remembered the quiet fury in Woody's voice as he described the butcheries Schreyach had presided over. "What does he look like? Any photographs floating around you could snag for me?"

"Nothing less than fifteen years old. He's sort of medium build, Latin in appearance, soft-spoken so I'm told. Doesn't slobber at the mouth when he's at work like a sadist in a comic book, just does his job quietly and efficiently like a good cop." The waiter served their main course and they put the salad plates to one side. "I can tell you how you'll know him if you ever see him, though," Bolish continued.

"Let's hear it," Loren said.

"By 1974 Schreyach was involved in handling security arrangements for some of the top honchos in the Uruguayan government. In June of that year two carloads of urban guerrillas went out to get the minister of internal affairs, who I'm told was a sadistic bastard even worse than Schreyach. The minister and Schreyach were in the back seat of a chauffeured limo when they made the hit, right on one of the main boulevards of the capital. The limo was peppered with machine gun fire and the driver and the minister were riddled in three seconds. Schreyach leaped over into the front seat and kicked the driver's body out of the way and gunned that limo out of the area at ninety kilometers per hour. A block away he smacked into the back of a freight truck and his head sailed right through the windshield. The impact literally sliced the nose off his face, and blood just gushed down out of those empty holes into his mouth. He didn't let it stop him. Somehow he got the limo started again and tore out of there till he'd lost the guerrillas."

"You sound as if you were there," Loren said.

"I interviewed the truck driver and two of the hit men," Bolish said. "For a while everyone hoped Schreyach was dead too but he got to a hospital in time—carrying his severed nose in his hand, they say—and the doctors sewed it back on. But that's how you can recognize him if you ever see him close up. There's a fine network of little white lines around the edges of the nostrils and they stand out against the tan of the rest of his face unless he's taken to darkening them with greasepaint."

Loren squinted his eyes almost shut, trying to reconstruct the face of the man in the law library basement who had called himself Moraga, and who was of medium build and Latin appearance and soft-spoken, and who had set about his job of crushing Loren's legs with the quiet efficiency of a good cop. Had there been tiny white lines around the nostrils? Loren sealed himself into a vacuum of thought for several minutes while his food grew cold on his plate, and for the life of him he simply couldn't be sure. The splash of coffee into his cup as the waiter poured him a refill brought him back to his surroundings.

"Hello again," Bolish said. "It's a good thing I know your moods or I might have called for a doctor. Anyway, Schreyach's kept a very low profile since that shoot-out. Actually he hasn't been seen once in public after that as far as I can learn. The word is he's been transferred into secret intelligence work—liaison with CIA and that sort of game—but I can't get verification of that."

"I take it then that your contacts in Washington haven't been able to confirm that he's here in the States."

"Not so far," Bolish said, "but I've still got lines out. Of course, if he is here as you claim, and if he's on some covert operation CIA knows about, the facts are going to be buried pretty deep. But you give me two more days and I'll have the answer one way or the other....Now when are you going to let loose with what this shit is all about?"

"When I find out myself," Loren said. "What are you having for dessert?" And over deep-dish apple pie and another several cups of coffee they lit the lamp of memory, rekindling the embers of old friends and enemies, old wars and loves, until an apologetic waiter hovered over their table and politely pointed out that it was after midnight and that the restaurant had closed ten minutes ago. Loren apologized and left an especially large tip under his napkin and exchanged final handshakes and goodnights with Bolish in the dim deserted lobby. As soon as he had chained himself inside his room again, he snatched up the phone and tried Val's number.

And once more the phone rang twenty times at the other end without being picked up.

TEN

HE COULDN'T sleep. His mind kept rearranging everything that had happened into crazyquilt patterns and refused to let itself be shut off for the night. The five cups of coffee he had drunk while reliving old crusades with Bolish jangled his nerves to a state of almost painful alertness, like that of a safecracker's sandpapered fingertips. He tried lying perfectly still in bed and imagining he had no body. It didn't put him out. He tried focusing his concentration intensely on the gentle hum of the air conditioner and letting the monotone lull him to rest. It didn't put him out. The tiny click of the digital clock as one minute number gave way to another was like a bomb going off every sixty seconds. The luminous figures blazed at him like the eyes of a predator. And the crazy patterns kept forming in his mind, so that finally when the clock read 3:26 he gave up, lurched from the bed to the blue armchair and, dead tired as he was, analyzed the thoughts that were keeping him awake.

The train of ideas began with a supposition: Suppose one of the people at the Bennell Foundation—Lillian; Harlow Emmet; Roy Taylor; even, arguably, Corinne Kirk—had been siphoning funds from the trust over a long period of time? If so, the suit to terminate the trust, instigated by Woody, would have been a frightening prospect indeed, because if the action should be successful there would have to be a final and meticulous outside audit of all the trust accounts prior to the distribution of the property, and the embezzler's dippings would almost certainly be exposed. If the hypothetical embezzler had happened to discover Corinne Kirk's affair with Justice Richmond, or if the embezzler was Corinne herself, would it not have been an irresistible temptation to use that knowledge to force Richmond to rule in favor of maintaining the trust? A double-edged offer perhaps—cash payoff if Ben cooperated, public disgrace if he didn't.

There was just one thing wrong with that lovely theory: A substantial chunk of the hypothetical payoff money hadn't been put into circulation until after Richmond's death.

But suppose the shoebox cash wasn't the payoff money? Suppose the explanation behind that money was still unknown, and that the real bribe money had been the cash Richmond had put in the safe-deposit box? Again Loren found a hole in that theory. Having admitted so many other damning things in his posthumous communications to Loren, wouldn't Ben have admitted having been blackmailed or bribed if either event had in fact happened?

Loren tortured his brain, paced and slumped in the armchair and agonized in the cool dark silence of the room, but he could not devise a plausible alternative to his earlier suspicion. It must have been Woody and Marisa who had planted the shoebox money as a step in seeking the reopening of the Bennell litigation.

And then as if in a burst of light he saw that it didn't have to be that way at all. He saw another possibility. Wild, yes; untested, yes. But conceivable. Suppose the hypothetical embezzler was Lillian Bennell. After all, as the only resident director, she would be in the best position to manipulate money, and, more important, she was the only one of the four Loren had interviewed at the foundation who had given vent to an unquenchable fear and loathing of John Philip Wood and all his works. With the outcome of the lawsuit she had been lucky: the court had defeated Woody's move to end the trust by a four-three vote, rendered lawfully and impartially. But Lillian would never assume that Woody would tuck his tail between his legs and abandon his quest just because of one serious setback. She would expect him to try again by other means, and again, and again. Aggressive infighter that she was, she would hardly be averse to a single bold stroke that could blunt in advance the threat of any future moves Woody might make. What bold stroke? Why, bribing the Richmonds' maid and paying a phony termite inspector to plant the shoebox full of money in Ben's house after Ben's death. Money whose serial numbers would demonstrate conclusively that it was not a bribe Richmond had taken in his lifetime! Money which would therefore be readily accepted as having been planted by Woody after Richmond's death in a desperate attempt to discredit the court's ruling and have the case reopened. In other words, the purpose of planting the shoebox was to frame Woody on a charge of having framed Ben!

The theory accounted for every element in the case Loren could think of except that it didn't explain the role of the Schreyach goons in the matter. Loren could surmise only that they did not know the real story behind the shoebox money and were fighting tooth and nail to keep the foundation intact for their own reasons. In the lonely darkness the theory did not seem totally insane.

Of course the jolly octogenarian, S. Gordon Bennell, might die of natural causes any day, and his death would automatically end the trust. Loren asked himself what he would do about that if he were the putative embezzler. And the obvious answer struck him squarely in the face. If he had it in his power, he would arrange for the old man to disappear in such a way that his body would not be found and his death could not be legally established, so that the seven-year waiting period mandated by the law would have to run out before S. Gordon would be presumed dead and the trust property distributed. Seven years was much longer than the probable remainder of the last annuitant's life and, more important, it was a fixed length of time. The embezzler would have bought that time in which to skim off as much additional trust property as possible and then make tracks for parts unknown.

When he remembered how well S. Gordon Bennell was being guarded by private detectives hired by the foundation, he began to wonder whether an official of the foundation might still be able to spirit the old man away and dispose of him in a quiet place. He decided that when he finally reestablished contact with Val he would have her check with those operatives in St. Louis and find out if any unusual incidents had taken place around S. Gordon's home. On impulse, and hoping that she was not the type to get angry if awakened in the middle of the night, he picked up the phone and tried Val's number again.

And once again got no answer.

He stumbled back to bed and tried to smother the nagging sensation that all his neat hypotheses had hopelessly missed the mark and that somewhere buried in his experiences of the last ninety hours was the key that would magically unlock the door. As the first wisps of light filtered under the bottom edge of the drapes and touched the corners of the room with pale gray, he drifted into a sluggish and unrestful sleep.

A droning wheeze in the corridor woke him a little after nine: the maids vacuuming outside, damn them. His body felt drained and bone-weary. His mind rebelled against further thought. And when he was more fully awake he realized with a start that it was Saturday morning and he had nothing to do. The case had become a waiting game. He must wait for Val to call so he could put her on Angella Carmer's trail and find out why she hadn't been home all night. He fumbled for the receiver, tried Val's house again and for the sixth time in a little more than twelve hours was greeted with no answer.

After a shower and shave he decided to take advantage of the lull in the action. He slipped on a light pullover and the swimsuit he had had the foresight to pack, rode the glass-walled external elevator to the mezzanine level, which opened on the Olympic-size hotel pool. He spread a towel over a white plastic lounge and lay stretched flat on his back under the already broiling sun, closing his eyes, letting the sweat roll off him, savoring the lethargy in which the only realities were the splash of divers and the squeals of children and the roar of planes overhead. He drifted to the edge of sleep but never quite lasted for more than a few minutes' nap at a time. He hauled himself to his feet and jumped into the cool bracing water and swam furiously and went back to his lounge, where he lay on his stomach and squinted out of one eye at the three goddesses in string bikinis who had appropriated the lounges next to his own.

He slipped in and out of sleep again and was beginning to wonder what time it was when he felt a cool shadow fall over him from behind. He turned and there was Val, perched on the edge of the lounge, looking down at him with a kind of friendly mockery in her gray-blue eyes. "So this is how the great detectives work," she whispered.

"I've been trying to call you all night," Loren told her peevishly. "Where have you been and what's been going on?"

"Tell you upstairs. Your shoulders look barbecued. It's time you got out of the sun anyway." She looked up at the moving bubble that glided down the hotel's outer wall from the top floors. "Come on, we can grab that one."

They had the cage to themselves and Loren studied her as they ascended. She leaned against a wall as if desperately tired, and her eyes were drawn and her mouth taut. Something told him she had been up all night. "How did you know I'd be out at the pool?"

"You forget they gave me a key to the room too when we checked in, Mr. Tremaine," she said. "I came by, saw the agency car in the lot and all the spare towels gone from the bathroom. It figured. Loren, I had to see you in a hurry. All hell's broken loose again."

Loren let them into the room and chained the door. "Tell me," he said.

"I got to meet Woody last night. Those hit men had half killed him. They pulled him into an alley and nearly strangled him with a piece of piano wire."

"Is he all right?"

"He's got a vicious cut all around his neck and he talks like a frog but otherwise I think he's okay. He'll tell you the story in a few minutes. I told him and Marisa to park in the airport lot and take the train over. They were supposed to come half an hour after me and take the elevator up here if I wasn't waiting in the lobby. What's been happening at your end?"

"I found out who planted the shoebox." Rapidly Loren summarized the developments since his post-lunch phone conversation with her yesterday, and when he had brought her up to the present, Val scooped up the phone and dialed. "I'm putting Bob Jackson on it," she said as she waited for an answer. "He can canvass the maid's neighborhood and pick up the—Oh, hi, Bob. Got a job for you, starting like an hour ago." As she was giving Jackson the details a sharp staccato tattoo sounded on the door. Loren put his mouth against the paneling. "Marisa?"

"Let us in, Loren!" Her voice was high and tight with fear. He unfastened the chain lock and opened the door and they slipped in, Woody chain-locking them in with a swift blur of motion. He looked gaunt and haggard, his clothes were hopelessly disheveled, and there was a wild look in his eyes that Loren had not seen in them before. It was the look of one who has tasted death. He collapsed into one of the armchairs and Marisa, white-faced and trembling, rushed to the bathroom and ran tap water into the drinking glass and handed it to Woody. He held the glass between his bruised and shaking hands, gulped the water gratefully. As he threw his head back to swallow, Loren saw the deep red gash that ran across his neck like a bloody ornament. He sat on the bed's edge, waiting for Woody to regain control. When Woody had set the empty glass on the bureau, Loren decided that it was time to ask questions. "Can you talk about it?"

"Not much." His voice came out cracked and hoarse, almost with a note of hysteria. "Last night, maybe eight o'clock, I got hungry. Took a chance on walking to a bus stop and hitting a cafeteria downtown. They got me on the way back. I was trying to catch a return bus and like a damn fool I took a shortcut through an alley. Two men must have been following me all along. They raced up behind me and threw piano wire around my neck. Show him, honey." Reluctantly Marisa opened her purse and handed Loren a long thin noose of fine wire, its bright surface smeared reddish brown. She touched it with abhorrence as if it were another snake. "Go on," Loren said.

"I got lucky. Didn't have much wind left but I kicked the front man in the balls and then got to work on the bastard who was tightening the wire behind me. Broke some ribs for him. They got away but they'll feel pain for a while. I beat it fast before a prowl car came by. Then I phoned the place where Marisa calls to leave messages for me and got word I should give her a ring at Miss Tremaine's house. I told her what happened to me and she told me about the snake Thursday night."

"Val and I had been out to dinner and stayed talking till around eight-thirty," Marisa continued. "We'd been home only a few minutes when Woody called. We drove to the Humber right away. The wire was so deep in his neck we had to cut it out with pliers. He refused to see a doctor or call the police. We stayed there all night, taking care of him and telling Val the whole story."

"At least you know they haven't found the Humber yet," Loren pointed out.

"They're panicking," Woody croaked triumphantly. "They've never come out in the open like this before. We've got 'em on the run, honey! Three more days and I'll have Schreyach's hide in my paws."

Val hung up the phone and slid along the bed to sit beside Loren. "Bob's on his way," she said. "All right, now you know what happened last night and why we couldn't get hold of each other. Frankly, Loren, I don't think I can hold out on the cops any longer. They can check out all the medical facilities and find those thugs a lot faster than my people can."

"Don't you touch it!" Woody shouted painfully. "For God's sake, this is my hunt. Give me till Monday anyway. I have contacts of my own. I'll have him by then, I swear to God I will."

"Mr. Wood, you want me to just buzz off and let you and this creep Schreyach have a private duel. I can't oblige you. I've got a license and legal obligations."

Marisa Bennell sprang out of the armchair and clutched Val's hands in supplication. "Oh, listen to him, Val. Give us just till Monday morning. Please?"

Val patted the other woman's hands, thought the request over, her eyes narrowed. "Tell you what," she said. "This is not the kind of story I want to explain to some cop who's a stranger to me. I've got a close friend in the detective bureau. He was our best man when Chris and I got married. He's out of town now but he's due back on the job first thing Monday morning. I give you till then. That's when Loren and I open the bag and let it all spill out."

Marisa threw her arms around Val and hugged her fiercely.

"Oh, you're a doll, Val."

"A damn fool you mean. Now there's one condition: Marisa, I don't want you to be near Woody over this weekend. You can go back to your place or stay with me but I will not let you get caught in any crossfire between him and Schreyach."

"I don't want her around," Woody said. "Honey, this is the last act. You drop me off a half mile or so from the Humber and leave the rest to me. Go stay with Val." He bent over and kissed Marisa's forehead. "I know what I'm doing, kid."

"I'll go." Marisa's eyes glistened with a combination of gratefulness and anxiety. She embraced Val again, and hand in hand she and Woody crossed to the door and let themselves out. "I'll phone the house later to make sure you got back safely," Val called down the corridor after her. Loren fastened the chain lock again behind them. Now that they were alone, Val seemed unable to stand up anymore, and Loren was afraid she might keel over from exhaustion. "God, what kind of impossible nightmare have we all stumbled into?" she demanded.

"One that's almost over," Loren whispered. "I think. Look, why don't you grab some sleep? Nothing's going to happen for a while and we've both had some rough sledding lately."

Val crossed the room to the far wall, moving slowly and dreamily as if walking through water. She tugged at one of the thick drapes, let a wedge of bright hazy sunlight into the room. The light shone gold around her. Then she drew the drapes tight shut, plunging the room into sudden half-darkness, her back still turned. Loren wondered what she thought she was doing, and felt a stirring deep inside him, and he knew. She swept her hands behind her neck and unfastened the band around her ponytail, letting the hair fall freely below her shoulder blades. The next moment her shoulders were shaking and she was wriggling out of her bright print blouse, which fluttered slowly to the carpet at her feet. Loren gazed at her naked back. He was almost afraid to breathe. He took a few hesitant steps across the room and she stood perfectly motionless in the dimness. When he was next to her he bent to kiss her shoulders and neck and her hair and his arms encircled her waist, caressing her belly with feather-light strokes, feeling the little puckers of flesh where the razor blade had cut her. The muscles of her stomach writhed and pulsated under his hands, and with a thrill of delight he knew that she was performing a sort of belly dance for him and pressed his lips against her neck. His hands rose along her midriff, fondling tenderly, until they cupped her adorable breasts and she swayed back against him and moaned with urgency and she tore at the fastening of her slacks and wriggled them down her legs and kicked them away and squirmed in his arms until she was facing him and her body was molded fiercely against him and her lips parted to receive his kiss. And, still clinging together, they glided across to the bed and reached for each other in a slow peaceful rhythm of offering.

He had no idea how long it lasted. The digital clock on the night table didn't exist anymore. They coupled and slept awhile, nestled together and coupled again and slept some more. Restoring each other. In the dimness he couldn't see the razor marks but felt the tiny scars against his lips when he kissed her breasts and belly. She lay in his arms, relaxed and totally at peace and unbearably lovely in her nakedness. The brushing of her thighs against him made him want her again fiercely, but when he remembered the horror she had seen and that she'd had no sleep last night he couldn't find it in him to kiss her awake. He closed his eyes and disengaged himself from her and yawned. When he blinked himself back to awareness, he noticed for the first time in hours the luminous figures on the clock: 8:22. They'd spent almost eight hours sleeping and making love, and beneath her aggressive shell she was so lovely and sensitive and giving that he wished they could stay here eight days, or even eight months. And in a strangely detached way he began to wonder if he had stumbled into love.

Then, shelving that thought as if afraid of it, and having nothing else to do and nowhere to go, he began to think about the case again. He propped pillows under his shoulders and closed himself off in his private mental space, rooting around in all the events and all the words that had been said since Tuesday afternoon, just about one hundred hours ago, when the gunmen who called themselves Moraga and Rojas had led him out of the law library. He let the train of events run through his mind—the nightmare in the underground garage, the summons from Dunphy, the meeting with the justices at the Richmond house, the tape Dunphy had slipped into his suitcase, all the way to the attack on Woody last night in a downtown alley. There was something buried in that pile of events. Something that kept nagging him, as if taunting him to find it. Something too small to see, or perhaps too large. He squeezed his eyes shut so tightly he saw white rockets and pinwheels blazing behind his eyelids but the more he strained to capture that elusive something the farther it seemed to recede.

There was a rustling of sheets and he felt the shift of weight on the mattress, opened his eyes and focused blearily in the dimness. He could make out Val, sitting up now and watching him, and he could imagine what he must look like to her. "Was I that lousy?" she asked him playfully. "You look like you just swallowed a quart of castor oil."

He slid over against her, kissed her mouth softly. "You were too good," he whispered. "Just out of this world. I can't put it into words. You make me want to keep you next to me forever."

"My big gentle loving bear," she smiled. "Oh, you'll never know how good inside I feel with you." She held his hand between her own and drew it to her breasts. "You were thinking about the case again, weren't you?"

"A little," he admitted, and made tiny love bites on her rounded shoulder. "There's something I've seen or heard that's gotten to me like a splinter under a fingernail. I can feel it but I can't find it, it's just too tiny for me to see." He rubbed his mouth against her breasts. "Ah, this is so much better. So much."

"Have you thought about giving yourself an incentive to find whatever it is?"

"What kind of incentive?" he mumbled absently.

"Something I read in the newspaper once, or maybe it was a self-help book." She ran her nails lightly down his back as he fondled her. "The trick is, you deny yourself something you want very badly till you remember whatever it was you've forgotten. Say it's booze if you're a heavy drinker or a cigarette if you smoke a lot."

"Suppose you're a sex maniac?" Loren asked, and stroked her thighs with long smooth caresses.

"We won't discuss that," she said, laughing. "Anyway, when you remember whatever it is, you treat yourself to a heaping helping of whatever you denied yourself—like a prize."

Like a prize. A prize. A prize.

"That's it!" he roared, pulling away and leaping to his feet. In the dimness outside the cone of golden light from the bedlamp he fumbled on the floor for his hastily discarded swim trunks, then started pacing back and forth past the bed, feverishly, enfolded again in a private universe. Systematically he ran the sequence through his memory again, in fast motion, with the events of a day compressed into seconds of concentrated analysis. It fit. Everything in the monumental pile of circumstances fell magically into place. It was bizarre—some of it was almost impossible to accept—but it formed a coherent whole, firm and clear and horrible. He paced faster and faster, fitting each piece of the puzzle into the next, connecting one sequence with another until he perceived the shape of the picture.

Suddenly he stopped in his tracks and with a shock he saw that Val had jumped out of bed and was standing in his path, naked, her fingers digging frantically into his shoulders. He smiled at her inanely and laid his hands on top of her own, disengaging her. "I get sort of caught up like this now and then," he said. "Don't worry—it's not a fit or anything. You know those 'I Found It' bumper stickers? Well, I could use one. I got what I was after, and you gave me the key. Do I get you as the prize?"

"Whoa, boy! I'm not so sure I want a whirling dervish for a lover. Maybe you'd better calm down and explain what set you off."

The phone screamed then and Loren rushed for it, barking hello into the mouthpiece. He listened for a few seconds and beckoned to Val. "It's for you. Bob Jackson."

She perched on the edge of the bed and took the phone from him. "Yes, Bob.... You did?....She was *what*? Oh, dear God. Hang on a minute." She dropped the phone on the pillow, and in the lamp glow Loren saw that her face had gone white. "Loren, Angella Carmer's been murdered. Strangled with piano wire."

Loren reached past her, snatched up the handset. "Bob, this is Mensing, the guy you picked up here yesterday morning. Give me the whole story, quick. When and where did it happen? Who found her?"

"Ain't much to tell," the youthful voice reported. "I went out to the chick's old neighborhood and asked around, found a gal friend she'd stayed in touch with. Angella had told this gal she was calling herself Samantha Bradley now and was living in this big highrise over on Wyndmoor Avenue. I found this building but didn't get no farther than the lobby when a cop stopped me and asked me what I wanted. I shucked him and then I commenced to asking myself a few casual questions, like why was there a cop in the lobby? The doorman was a black dude so I bought him a few beers when he got off and picked up a fair amount of poop from him. He told me there was a chick got herself strangled with piano wire in 19-D."

"When was the body found?" Loren demanded.

"This morning. The window washers were doing the outside of the building today. One of them was in his harness rig outside the front-room window of 19-D and he happened to look across the room and saw this chick lying all twisted on the floor and he climbed in the nearest window he could open and called the fuzz. From what the doorman told me they ain't got clues nor suspects nor nothing."

"You didn't tell the officer that stopped you that the dead girl used to call herself Angella Carmer?"

"Didn't tell him a thing, man. But the cops know their onions in this town. They'll be onto that other name tomorrow, no later. So what's my next move?"

Loren returned the phone to Val, resumed his pacing while she listened to Jackson's story. "Good job," she said finally. "Now go home and forget it, we'll carry the ball for a while." When she had hung up she slid across the bed and rummaged in the darkness for her clothes.

"Did you catch the time of death?" Loren asked. "I forgot to ask Jackson."

"The doorman told Bob that the police think it was between seven and nine last night," Val answered. "Same general time as the attack on Woody with the same method. Looks like Schreyach's trying to take out anybody who can tie him into this." She froze in her tracks, her blouse half buttoned. "Oh, God, and Woody's all but disabled and alone in that empty hotel! Loren, we have to warn him."

"Relax," Loren said. "He's in no danger, believe me. Sit down. Listen to me. I've got a horror story to tell. Wait a minute, I have a call to make before I begin." He lifted the receiver and dialed the number of Val's house, counting the rings, hoping that Marisa would be there and pick up the phone. Seven, eight, nine—then he heard the sound of the receiver being raised on the other end and let out a long breath. "Marisa?"

"Yes?" Her voice was hesitant, still fearful.

"Loren. Listen, I want you to drive back here to the hotel. It's important....No, nothing's happened, no one else has been hurt. Val and I are still here and we'll be waiting for you. Lock the house tight and leave now, okay? We'll expect you in forty-five minutes or so." He hung up, crossed the room to Val, who sat in one of the blue chairs, watching him anxiously as if uncertain he still had his wits. Loren dropped into the twin chair and looked at her intently, wondering how to begin. "Have you ever met one of these word nuts?" he asked finally. "Someone who insists you speak precisely and gets mortally offended if you use may for can or infer for imply?"

"I know a few professors like that," Val said carefully. "And I hope I haven't met another this week."

"You haven't," he grinned. "But what just struck me a few minutes ago, and what I realized was the tiny thing I couldn't get my hands on before, is precisely that. A verbal blunder. *The same blunder twice.* The first was on paper, the second I heard. Put 'em together and the case is solved."

"I'm waiting," she said, and leaned forward tensely, a frown of concentration on her forehead.

"When a corporation or institution is considering hiring your outfit for an investigation, have you ever been told that you'd be apprised of the board of directors' decision in due course, or words to that effect?"

"I suppose everyone in business has. What's wrong with that?"

"Not a thing. But have you ever been told that you'd be *appraised* of the decision?"

Val closed her eyes and seemed to be thinking into her past professional life. Loren didn't wait for her to answer his question. "Apprise means to inform and appraise means to evaluate. The words are just close enough in meaning so that a careless speaker might mix them up. And some careless speakers habitually confuse them."

Val sprang to her feet with the tawny grace of a lioness. "This sounds like it's going to be a long story and I'm thirsty, not to mention that I haven't eaten all day." She walked to the mirrored bureau and stretched out a hand for the used water glass on its polished surface.

"Freeze!" Loren yelled. "Don't touch that!"

Val whirled, her face ablaze with anger. Loren rose and put an arm around her waist, led her back to the chair. "I didn't mean to shout, partner, but that glass is important. Use the clean one in the john, okay?" He waited until she had returned from the bathroom with a full tumbler of water in her hand.

"As I was saying, that particular verbal confusion is one I've encountered twice since I came to this city. The second time was Thursday night at the Humber Hotel. Woody made some remark about the draft board reclassifying him after they were *appraised* of his antiwar activities. I don't embarrass people by correcting their language so I didn't say anything and just barely registered it in my memory. Then just now I realized that I'd seen that mistake before. Literally seen it. It was on the cancelled bill that the mysterious termite inspector had sent to Ben Richmond's widow. 'If you see any more signs of termites, please appraise me.' "

Val phrased her question with exaggerated care. "Are you trying to tell me that the fake termite inspector was Woody himself?"

"None other," Loren said. "What do you think?"

"I think it stinks! That is one of the flimsiest arguments I've heard a grown person put forward in my life. Why, any number of people might confuse appraise and apprise. I might myself!"

"I don't like it any more than you do, and for the same reason I gather you don't. We both have a weakness for people with a rage for decency. That's the way Woody struck you, wasn't it?"

"He's almost a fanatically compassionate person," she said. "That isn't just my own impression, Loren. Marisa and I had a long woman-to-woman talk yesterday before Woody called. She loves him so much it hurts. She'd die for him. I will not believe she could be wrong about something like that."

"I think I can show you how she could be," Loren said. "Just how much do we know—really objectively know—about John Philip Wood?"

Val drummed silently on the chair's upholstered arm.

"When you asked me to check on him yesterday, you mentioned that Lillian had said she'd had the Kurtz agency investigate Woody. I was able to sneak a peek at their report. There's no doubt that Woody was a leader of the student-protest movement at the University of Connecticut, that the draft board reclassified him 1-A in retaliation and that he went underground and lived in various parts of South America before the amnesty."

"How do we know the man who went into exile is the same man that came back?" Loren interrupted her.

Amazement widened Val's eyes until Loren was almost afraid they might explode. "An impostor," she whispered.

"Why not? There's enough money at stake so a really clever con man who was about the same size and age as the real Woody might take a long chance. It's quite possible that the guy we know as Woody killed the real Wood in South America a few years ago and came back when it was safe, hoping that as Wood he could collect Wood's one-eighth interest in the Bennell trust fund. I wouldn't be surprised if he made a trip to St. Louis to see if he could speed the transfer a bit by killing S. Gordon Bennell. We know how well the foundation keeps the old boy guarded, so it's safe to assume Woody gave up and settled back to wait for him to die naturally."

"You've got no proof, Loren," Val told him fervently. "None!"

"If he has a record anywhere, the fingerprints on that water glass he drank out of will give us the proof. But I'm not finished yet. Somewhere along the line, our man—whether he's the real Woody or a fake—met Marisa."

"Loren, if you try to tell me she's mixed up in this...." Val cut in.

"Only as a victim," Loren said. "He met Marisa, found out that she would inherit her own one-eighth share when the trust folded, and saw a way to double his take. He used all his charm to get into her confidence and then he pulled one of the most fantastically ambitious long-range con schemes in human history. He created a completely imaginary spy-thriller universe and made her believe in it. He played on her loneliness, her sense of death being always with her, her social sympathies. My God, he played her the way Casals played the cello! He made her his partner in a one-hundred-percent fictitious crusade against political filth. The scenario had all the tried and true ingredients: sadistic torturers from fascist dictatorships, CIA dirty tricks, love, danger, vengeance—the whole ball of wax. Months of buildup spiced with a few carefully rigged pseudo-attempts on each of their lives and she bought the whole farm, right down to the bit about the silent *mano a mano* between Woody and Schreyach. She was so completely a part of this imaginary web of intrigue that she could take a totally extraneous incident, like that black kid's throwing the rock at her car while she was driving through the ghetto, and assimilate it into Woody's scenario. And damn it, I believed it too for a while. He knows how to make people believe."

A look of detached objectivity had replaced the emotions on Val's face and she seemed to shrink in her chair. "Loren, don't you think maybe it's you who is dreaming up a fantastic universe? There are just no facts that support this elaborate structure you're building!"

"Let me finish building it," Loren insisted. "We'll get the facts later. All right, somewhere along the line he has to get Marisa to marry him. That's the linchpin of the whole scheme. For all we know, they've been secretly married a long time. The idea is that after the trust is finally terminated and they each collect one-eighth, there's going to be one last attack by Schreyach and company, and that one will be a success."

"Loren, you can't believe what you're saying," Val cried.

"But then Woody becomes impatient," Loren went on as if he

hadn't heard her. "S. Gordon Bennell refuses to get sick and die and Woody knows he can't kill the old man. So he devises another fantastic scheme. He offers the old boy triple his annuity for the rest of his life if he'll relinquish his mini-interest in the trust. Then he organizes the Bennell relatives who benefit by termination and they band together and bring their lawsuit. Of course, he has to tie this in for Marisa's benefit with his crusade against fascism, so he explains that his real purpose is to get his hands on the Benneco stock in the trust and use the leverage that will give him to expose the company's links with the CIA and the corrupt juntas. He makes her feel even more like a character in a spy movie by arranging a cover identity for her and getting her into the Bennell Foundation. Everything goes like clockwork. They win on the trial level. They win on the intermediate appellate level. And then the whole magnificent scheme goes boom because of a four-three reversal in the supreme court! Imagine how Woody must have felt about Ben Richmond when that decision came down."

"Loren," Val said quietly, "you're almost getting me to believe in this nightmare."

"And now we flash forward six months," Loren said. "Ben Richmond dies and Woody hits on a last desperate gamble to reopen the litigation. He works out a scheme to plant a shoebox full of money in Ben's house, wait for it to be discovered, and then lay a false trail to show that the winning side in the case, the foundation or Benneco or whoever, bribed Ben to vote the way he did. He played the part of the Ajax exterminator himself—the appraise-apprise slip shows that—and he paid Angella Carmer to do the rest. And notice that he shelled out big money on this last gamble. Forty-nine thousand in the shoebox, enough to Angella so that she was able to move into a fancy highrise in the Wyndmoor section, plus incidentals like renting a truck. But if the gamble paid off, he'd have made thousands of times his investment. Are you still with me?"

"It's a rough ride but I'm hanging on," she said.

"Once the box was discovered and the court brought me in, Woody and his goons, Moraga and Rojas, went into high gear. First he sends them downstate to throw a scare into me. Now, observe one interesting thing about the apparent attempt to cripple me in the underground garage. Remember how those women students of mine got me out of that? Gael Irwin told me that the two men acted so sinister when they asked for directions that she immediately concluded something fishy was up. And, Val, that was precisely the impression those men wanted to leave. They didn't want to cripple me. They wanted to be stopped before they ran me over, and if the girls hadn't come along they would have pretended they'd heard people approaching and buzzed off without leaving a mark on me. The idea of that little exercise was simply to plant some seeds in my mind, to get me thinking about Latin-American dictatorships and CIA conspiracies and spies and torture, so that later on, when I began looking into which of the court's decisions might have been involved in the bribe, I'd have a huge shock of recognition when I encountered all those elements again in the Bennell case! This was how they programmed me to identify the Bennell decision as the one in which Ben had been supposedly bribed. Am I still making sense?"

"I'm afraid to answer that," she said.

"Woody knew I was investigating early in the game. Remember, he had Marisa tailing me as early as Wednesday, and he wanted me to get suspicious that I was being watched. Then he started softening me up, like with the razor blade in the soap. Just to scare me, cut me a little, build up an atmosphere so that when he made the big pitch I'd be primed for it. The big pitch of course was Thursday night when he had Marisa bring me to meet him at the Humber. He had to sell me on the reality of his war with Bruno Schreyach and all the rest of his imaginary universe. He had to make me a believer. You must have seen him at work when you met him last night. He is frighteningly good at it."

"I know," she said. "There was something bugging me all the while I was listening to that intense hypnotic voice of his and watching those weird shadows from the Coleman lamps. You just put your finger on it, Loren. It was like being at a faith-healing rally, or in a revival tent."

"That's exactly it. We were both being subtly manipulated to believe in something that in the cold light of reason we'd reject in half a minute. As was Marisa. All right, let's talk about snakes for a while. Marisa and I finding that snake right inside the door of her apartment was the *coup de grâce*. We couldn't help but accept Woody's crazy scenario after that. But look at the facts: A, it was a nonpoisonous snake; B, Marisa is deathly afraid of snakes; C, Woody specifically suggested that Marisa should stop off with me at her apartment that night before she drove me back here. The idea was not to kill or maim either of us, just to scare us both, and to demonstrate to me that there were terrorists out there who didn't want me or Marisa or Woody to win.

"But he made one huge mistake, and I caught it yesterday. The money he put in that shoebox included one run of consecutively numbered bills that were so new they hadn't been issued at the time Ben Richmond died! So much for the hypothesis that Ben had been paid off by the foundation or by Schreyach or whatever. That discovery of mine explains why the other side has hit the panic button. Woody and his goons killed Angella Carmer last night, and then he had them literally strangle him half to death with piano wire right afterward, which gave him the best possible alibi and threw off any suspicion I might have been developing about him. And that, partner, is how we come to be here today. And when Marisa knocks on that door in ten minutes or so, I'm going to have to destroy her whole world, her faith in Woody, her love, her reason for living. It's going to be just about the cruelest thing I've done. I hope you can soften the blow for her. Excuse me, I've got to make another call." He picked up the phone again and dialed the Richmond home and was momentarily disconcerted when a young woman's voice answered.

"Jeanette? Loren. How are things with you?"

"Maddening," she said. "I've been waiting to hear that you've located Angella Carmer and that she's talked."

"We located her," Loren said, "but she isn't talking. But I think we're in the homestretch anyway. Let me talk to your mother, please." There was a silence followed by some whispers and rustling noises and then he heard Iris Richmond's high thin quaver.

"Loren, did you just tell Jeanette that the investigation is almost complete?"

"Something like that. Things have been happening fast since yesterday. Look, Iris, I want you to come down right away to the airport hotel, room 1604. Please take the station wagon."

"Why is this necessary, Loren?" Ben Richmond's widow demanded. "The weather report predicts severe thunderstorms all evening and I really don't like to drive at night even in perfect weather."

"Jeanette can drive you then." Loren tried to conceal the edge of impatience in his voice. "It's very important, believe me. I want you to go downtown with us and see if you can identify someone I'm going to point out to you."

"Identify whom?" He could detect the irritation in her tone.

"Iris, I just can't tell you now, but please leave as soon as possible. And remember the station wagon. We'll be waiting for you."

"Well," she hesitated, "if you absolutely insist...."

"Thanks a million, Iris. I'll see you in an hour." He hung up the phone and motioned across the room to Val, who still sat in the blue chair as if stunned by Loren's arguments. "Your turn on the horn," he said. "Have Bob Jackson meet us here an hour from now. Don't take no for an answer."

"My God," Val murmured, bounding to her feet, "you're forming a war party. I take it we're going to storm the Humber Hotel and see if Mrs. Richmond can identify Woody as the exterminator?"

"You hit it. And if she says he's the man, Jackson can hold him while you call the police, or vice versa if you want to play it that way. There may be some action."

"If Woody's the son of a bitch that had that razor blade put in the soap, I'll show him some action." She sat beside him on the bed, snatched up the receiver, but her finger spun the dial only once. "Room service....Yes, this is Mrs. Tremaine in 1604. Please send up two complete steak dinners as soon as you can. Medium rare." Loren whispered a correction into her ear. "No, make that one medium rare and one medium. Two bowls of French onion soup." Loren nodded. "Baked potatoes with plenty of butter and sour cream." He nodded even more enthusiastically and grinned with delight at how she had divined his tastes after only one quick luncheon. "How soon can we be served, please?....Fifteen minutes? Dandy." She depressed the disconnect button and turned to Loren.

"Now that the important business is out of the way, I'll give Bob a buzz. Even the Marines get to eat before they go into combat, lover."

ELEVEN

MARISA arrived with the first thunderclaps of the storm as Loren
and Val were finishing their meal. She and Val sat in the matching
armchairs and Loren perched on the bed. Thunder exploded savagely outside while Loren repeated the substance of the case
against Woody. Marisa fought like a fury against his indictment.
When he accused Woody of having been responsible for the
snake, she screamed and flew at him and tore at his eyes with her
nails, and it took him and Val together to subdue her, the three of
them writhing on the bed, Val holding her arms in a vise and
stroking her soothingly at the same time. When Loren returned
from dabbing iodine on the scratches on his cheeks, Marisa lay
collapsed on the bed like a heap of dead rags, sobbing softly
against Val's breast. He waited in the short corridor that led to the
bathroom, staying out of Marisa's sight while she cried her soul
out, waiting for Val to come and signal him that she was ready for
another assault. After a few more minutes he stopped hearing the
sounds of crying and ventured around the corner. She sat erect
now but motionless, as if catatonic. In the lightning flashes that
burst in the dim room he could see the tears welled in her eyes. It
was as if she had withdrawn into a private place where she could
not be hurt anymore, and Loren knew it was useless to continue
talking to her. He could not have despised himself more if he had
just raped her and slashed her to bloody ribbons. He stepped into
the front room again and patted her shoulder and said stupid things
that were meant to comfort her.

A timid rapping broke into his mood and he stalked to the door
and flung it open. Jeanette and Iris Richmond stood at the threshold, sopping wet in glistening raingear. Without explanation Loren
motioned them into the short interior hallway, out of sight of the
other women. He couldn't endure to go through the recital a third
time in one night, and fortunately it wasn't necessary to tell the
Richmonds anything at this juncture. "Just wait here a few minutes," he said. "Once the last person in the group joins us, we'll be
off. You came in the station wagon, I hope?"

Jeanette shook her rain hat against her knee and stared at him curiously. "Just as you asked. Does that mean it's going to be a large group that's riding downtown?"

"Six of us," Loren said. "We three, the two women in the front room and a young man who should be here any minute."

Iris Richmond looked full into Loren's eyes, her own glistening wetly. "And just who are those young women?" she wanted to know.

"One's a private investigator who's been working with me. Let's forget the second girl for the moment." Another knock on the door relieved him of having to explain further and he opened it to admit a drenched and miserable-looking young black man whose slicker was alive with falling water and whose wide-brimmed hat was sodden from the downpour. "Hey, man, the whole damn city's just one big duck pond tonight. I surely wish I was in my pad with Shostakovich and a six-pack."

"When the gig's over I'll buy you the new recording of his Tenth Symphony and all the Michelob you can drink," Loren promised. "This job may be a lot nastier than the weather."

Jackson's eyes searched the room and widened a bit as he took in the abundance of women. "Hey, do I count *four* chicks in this party?"

"Four it is," Loren said, "and they're all coming with us. We have a date with a remarkable man."

Rain pounded on the station-wagon roof, spattered the windshield in thick heavy drops so that they couldn't see more than a foot or two ahead as the wagon slithered downtown. Jackson drove, keeping the car at a steady cautious thirty-five with the rain shimmering under the high beams of the headlights. The streets had turned into man-made creek beds. Loren and Val sat in the rear, Marisa between them, the Richmond women in the front with Jackson. Thunder exploded, deafening as artillery, and Loren felt a sick tightness in his stomach. They made a detour to the Midwood Mall where Val ran into her office for two high-power flashlights and a Colt Combat Commander. Then they swung north to the blighted area of downtown, their faces tense. No one spoke. The big station wagon rocked under the whistling wind, shuddered with the assault of the storm.

Jackson turned left into a long narrow street, dark and ghostly, the thick bulk of warehouses looming on both sides. "We're close," Loren said. "Another four or five blocks." They passed the leveled area Loren remembered from Thurs- day night and he saw

the lone dark finger of the Humber Hotel, stark against the surrounding emptiness in the glare of a lightning flash. "Take the next
right," Loren directed. Jackson spun the wheel and they skidded
into a dead-end street and parked at the curb. Loren studied Marisa's face, white and numb in the clammy darkness. "It's time,"
he said softly, taking her hand. They locked the car and huddled
under umbrellas and trudged quickly across the street through the
murk and emptiness and fiercely falling rain.

"Suppose he spots us from up there?" Val whispered as they
came within fifty feet of the hotel. "I saw at least one army rifle in
his room last night."

"He's got nowhere to go," Loren said, "and no help anymore.
My guess is he paid off his goons last night and they're thousands
of miles away by now. And he's hurt badly enough so he should
probably be in the hospital. You and I and Bob and your gun
should be enough to handle him." They took shelter in the hotel
doorway from the wall of falling water and Loren pulled down the
boards across the front door as he had seen Marisa do Thursday
night. He was about to ask Marisa for her key when he pushed
lightly against the door and it gave under his weight. "Unlocked,"
he said. "Woody's getting careless."

"Or else he done flown the coop," Jackson added. They tiptoed
into the musty lobby, Val spearing a path along the filthy tiled
floor to the west fire stairs with her flashlight beam. Loren tugged
the steel door open and they crowded into the area at the foot of
the stairs, trembling with cold and something more than cold.

"It's too rough a climb for Iris." Loren glanced up the high
stairwell uneasily. "Let's make him come down. Iris, you and
Jeanette wait here with Bob. Don't move, don't talk, just wait.
Val, you and I will roust him."

"I'm coming," Marisa said.

Her voice was a flat determined monotone, her head oddly
tilted, and Loren wondered if she was still in shock. He wrestled
with the thought for a moment, then decided she had a right to be
there. "Okay," he said. "Forward, march." And the three of them
began the long exhausting climb.

They took the stairs slowly, in total silence except for the
soggy slap of their shoes on the concrete, pausing every other
flight to breathe and rest for a minute. Thunder echoed through the
hollow tower as if resonating through a drumhead. Marisa shuddered at every clap and Loren held her tightly about the waist. Six
to eight, and a rest. Eight to ten, and a rest. Two more to go. They

climbed the last two flights in a headlong rush as if frantic to get to the top and break the silent tension. Loren eased the door open and squinted down the long bare corridor. When Val tried to slip past him, he held her by the shoulder. "Wait," he whispered. "No flash now. Wait till the lightning comes again."

There was a bang of thunder and at almost the same second a sheet of lightning tore through the window at the end of the hall, etching the corridor in acid white. Loren blinked unbelievingly. Then the flash was gone and the corridor was plunged in eerie darkness. "Did you see it?" he whispered to Val.

"See what?"

"Woody's door. It was wide open. Something's wrong here, Val. Give me your light and stay back." He slid silently down the corridor behind the cone of wavering light from the flash. When he reached the open door he hugged the wall to one side, waiting for something to happen, to hear something. Total silence. He threw the beam into the room, crouched low in the doorway.

And saw Woody lying twisted in agony on the floor.

Eyes open, mouth gaping. Head thrown back so that the ugly gash on his throat stood out black in the flash beam. Bubbles of blood still trickling down his chin from a corner of his mouth. Hands clutched to his belly, stained dark and wet.

Loren raced past a neat row of suitcases and dropped to one knee beside him, feeling for a pulse. None. He rose, ran to the doorway, his eyes questing up and down the corridor.

"What's happened?" Val's voice came loud and tight from out of the dimness.

Loren jogged up the corridor to her side. "He's dead. Shot in the stomach. It couldn't have happened more than a couple of minutes ago. The killer must be making a getaway down the other fire stairs."

Marisa shrieked, a high piercing unbearable scream, again and again. With her head thrown back and saliva dribbling from the corner of her mouth she rocked and shuddered helplessly, and Loren and Val grabbed for her to keep her from falling. She screamed and her fingers tore at the empty darkness and Val and Loren took the brunt of her helpless fury and held her tightly until the spasms subsided and she swayed against them, moaning and sobbing low.

"Come on, Val, he's getting away!" Loren roared.

"I'm not going to leave Marisa. Let him go, Loren. Let the police find out who killed him."

"I can't," Loren said, and took Val's pistol and flashlight from the filthy floor where he had dropped them to hold Marisa and raced back down the hallway, the beam darting ahead along the walls almost at ceiling height until he picked up the dirt-choked EXIT sign on the east wall and made for the other fire door. He threw back the door, stood on the landing with ears straining for a sound other than the thunder and the rain. It took him half a minute for his hearing to adjust. Then he heard it. Somewhere on the stairs below, several flights beneath him—how many he couldn't guess. The quick wet slap of retreating footsteps. Slupslup*tump* slupslup*tump*. Not racing but moving quickly, as if afraid of losing footing and stumbling in the darkness. Loren grabbed the rotting banister rail and leaned far out over the staircase, aiming his flash beam down the long well between the flights of stairs. He saw only what might have been the edge of a moving shadow, five or six flights below.

Pistol held ahead of him, safety off, he began to run down the steps, racing, breathing raggedly, taking them two and three at a time in the semidarkness, risking a turned ankle or worse at every step. He had to see who it was. He had to know if the rest of his suspicions, the suspicions he had not divulged even to Val, were right. Hit a landing, turn, leap down another flight, hit a landing, turn. God, God, if only he had a walkie-talkie or some way to communicate with Jackson, get him to block the other end so the killer would be trapped! Then he knew he couldn't do that; the killer had a gun and Jackson didn't. The slap of the other's steps was louder now, Loren was gaining—slupslup*tump* slupslup*tump*.

He leaned precariously over the banister, shouted down the stairwell. "This is the police! The building is surrounded. You can't get out." No answer but more footsteps. Loren sped down the staircase, lurching in the blackness, counting the landings as he raced down—six, five....

And suddenly his feet weren't under him anymore and he felt himself falling through empty space. He cried out, dropped the flash and the gun, threw his hands out to break his fall. His palms slammed against the wall and he fell in a heap, picked himself up, groped for the light, felt something wet and sticky on his hands. There was the boom of a steel door closing below and Loren cursed and knew the other had made it to the lobby. He raced through the fifth-floor corridor, the light beam darting ahead, showing him the rotten floorboards, the spiderwebbed doorways. Above his footsteps he heard the scurrying of rats in the walls, the chitter of little furry rodents. He tore the west fire door open, cupped his bloody hands to his mouth. "Jackson!" he roared. "You and the women get up here. Now!" He panted hoarsely, rubbing his mangled palms against his wet raincoat, gulping deep grateful breaths of the fetid air as the clatter of several sets of footsteps rose along the stairwell. "Hurry, damn it, hurry!" he wheezed. Jackson left the women behind, ran the last two flights three steps at a time. "Val's upstairs with Marisa. Marisa's in shock. There's a dead man on the twelfth floor. Shot a couple minutes ago. Killer just got out. Down the other fire stairs. Through the lobby. See anyone? Hear anything?"

"Nothing," Jackson said, panting, as Jeanette and Iris stumbled up the last flight.

"All right. You two stay here. Don't move. Bob, go up to twelve and help Val. Give me the car keys. I'm calling the cops and an ambulance." He spun around and raced the questing flash beam down the last five flights to the dim lobby and the street door. The door was open to the raging night, the protective boards cluttered in the entrance as if thrust out of the way by the escaping murderer. Loren wasted no time examining the scene. The killer must have had a car nearby, parked on one of the other side streets. He ran through the torrent of rain to the station wagon, fumbled with the front-door key, finally got in. He slid into the driver's seat, started the car, gunned it into a U-turn and skidded into the empty main street he had come from. There had to be a phone somewhere. He rocketed down the street at fifty, straining to see the lights ahead that would mean people, a bar, a restaurant, a gas station. A phone. The leveled blocks, the blocks of dark abandoned building hulks, stretched on without end. At each intersection he scanned the cross street right and left for lights.

It seemed hours later when he found them. Snakelike blue and red neon tubing in the window of a low brick structure. Corner bar. He spun the wheel, braked at the curb, splashed through the curtain of rain to the doorway. The long narrow bar was all but empty: bored barman mopping the counter with a rag, a couple of seedy-looking men nursing beers, an ax-faced old crone in a corner booth hunched over a bloody mary. Loren half ran across the debris-strewn floor of the bar to the scarred wooden phone booth in the far corner, next to the washroom door. He pushed into the narrow cubicle, dug coins from his pocket, fumbled them into the slot and asked directory assistance for the city police. He dialed the number he was given and asked the desk sergeant for the homicide detail. There was a series of clickings that sounded like tiny explosions, then a low disinterested growl. "Homicide."

"There's a dead man in the old Humber Hotel," Loren said. "Shot twice in the stomach. Up on the twelfth floor....That's right, the old Humber, on Weston just north of Hunt....I know it's deserted. Besides the dead man there's a woman in shock so send an ambulance fast....My name? Jon Smyth, no h in the Jon, no i in the Smyth." He banged the receiver into its cradle, studied his palms. The blood had dried into a red crust. He turned up his raincoat collar and returned to the street and the filthy night. He gunned the station wagon into the empty center lane. Going south. Away from the Humber. Into the residential district across town.

He slid into a vacant space across the street and half a block from the stucco highrise and turned off the motor and waited. Rain drummed on the roof in a fierce tattoo. From the driver's seat he peered up through the streaming windshield at the windows of the northwest corner suites, counting balconies as his gaze lifted. Three showed lights. So did four and five. Six was dark.

Loren knew the darkness proved nothing. The man could be asleep or out on an innocent errand, or Loren might have beaten him back to home base. He hunched down in his seat, wet and miserable inside and out. The smell of sodden clothing filled the confined space.

He thought of the women he had left at the Humber. The prowl car would be there by now; the beat cops would be taking their stories. The ambulance for Marisa should have arrived. He thought of how in a few short hours she had lost everything that had been holding her precarious life together and he ached for her. He knew they'd be hunting for him soon, that they'd put out a bulletin with the station wagon's number, and after that any cruising black-and-white might spot it. The only thing that gave him time was the ferocity of the storm. Accidents, lines down, other emergencies would keep a lot of the cars off routine patrol. He needed at least a couple of hours. He had to do this alone. No Val, no cops—just he and the other, until the last shred of doubt was gone.

The glare of headlights in the rearview mirror almost blinded him. He sprawled across the front seat, below the level of the windows, waiting for the car to pass. It slithered by and its taillights glowed like match flares as it slowed and turned into the basement garage of the highrise. A late model Chrysler with a license number he couldn't make out in the rain. That had to be him. Loren trained his eyes on the windows at the northwest corner of the sixth floor and counted the seconds.

Two and a half minutes from the time the Chrysler had disappeared into the bowels of the building, the sixth-floor darkness blossomed into pale gold light. A tiny shadow flitted along the windowpanes. Back and forth and away, back and forth and away. Flitting like a black moth against the light. Loren waited. He thought he knew what the other was up to. If his hunch was right, the man would come down again soon, with suitcases, and drive away again. He decided to wait twenty minutes.

He kept his eyes on the light and the darting shadow six floors up, holding his wristwatch up to his eyes at intervals. Ten minutes swept by on its luminous hands, then four more.

Headlights stabbed the mirror and Loren crouched again. Another car swayed and hissed through the rain-soaked street. When it had passed, he raised his eyes to follow its retreat. A blue and white dome light whirled lazily on its roof. Cops. The car made a right two intersections down the street, vanished.

Loren stared up at six northwest. The lights were dead. The man must be on the way down. Loren began to count the seconds again. Give him three minutes. He straightened in his seat, fingered the key in the ignition switch. Three minutes crawled by. Nothing. Was the elevator slow getting up to him this time? Could he just have turned out the lights and gone to sleep? Loren cursed when he thought of the possibility that there might be a rear exit from the basement garage.

He had his hand on the door handle, ready to cross the street and go up to six and force the issue, when he heard the muffled roar of a motor and the Chrysler shot to the top of the ramp from the basement and made a sharp right into the street, heading away from Loren as the police car had. Loren gave him two blocks' start, then twisted the key and spun the wheel.

The car ahead made another right, then a left onto a six-lane boulevard, taking the broader avenue at a steady thirty-five, making no attempt to shed a tail. The beat of the rain seemed to diminish; Loren could see clearly through the windshield now, between the blurs of the wipers. The signs along the boulevard gave him the answer to where the Chrysler was headed. The car ahead lurched onto the sharply curving ramp that connected with the westbound lanes of the expressway. Loren gave him time to build up speed again, then made his own turn onto the ramp. On the expressway he fed gas, cruised at fifty until he spotted the Chrysler again, then slowed to thirty-five, keeping several city blocks back of the other car's taillights. Four miles from where it had picked up the highway the Chrysler's right-turn signal light winked in the darkness like a ruby. Airport turnoff. Above the clouds Loren heard the drone of a plane. He gave the Chrysler a bigger lead, made his own exit, followed the access road to the entrance to the huge parking lot. Cut his lights.

Beyond the entrance gate he saw the lights of the Chrysler as it passed twin rows of dark drenched parked cars. He turned into the lot, opened the window to snatch a square of pasteboard from the automatic ticket dispenser, coasted along the same lane the Chrysler had used. He eyed an empty slot and swerved into it, locked up, jogged on a diagonal line through the lot, sloshing through puddles in the gravel. Veering toward the bright mouth of the tunnel into the earth.

He caught sight of the other, approaching the kiosk from a different angle. Lurching through the rain and wind. Loren crouched behind a parked car until the figure had vanished down the escalator. He ran to the top of the moving stairway, waited till the other had stepped off at the bottom. Then he began his own descent. He felt naked and vulnerable, alone in the fierce glare of the incandescents set in the roof of the white-painted boarding area, as the escalator lowered him gently.

The benches bolted into the floor of the station area were empty. But Loren saw the man, leaning against a tall pillar, looking down the track, back turned to Loren. As Loren reached the foot of the escalator he heard a sudden *click-clack* as the tunnel train slid into the station. The dark figure hefted the suitcase at its feet. The long white line of train doors gently whispered open and the man stepped into one of the compartments.

Loren bounded across the platform, caught the edge of the closing door against his palm and entered the same cubicle. The door shut behind him. The man seated on the white plastic bench stared up through a thicket of reddish-gray brows. Behind his misted glasses his eyes seemed vacant and unfocused. Loren looked down at him miserably.

"Evening," the other grunted. "Pity the poor brutes who have no place to lay their heads on a night like this."

"Pity," Loren said quietly.

The train clicked through the long white tunnel. The men in the tiny cubicle were silent, motionless. The quiet stretched taut between them. They were like two frozen statues in the steady glare of the underground light.

"You know," the other said. His voice was detached, emotionless.

"All of it," Loren said. "It's over, Conor."

The chief justice of the state supreme court squeezed his eyes shut, and Loren could not be sure if the moisture that trickled down the sides of Conor's nose came from the rain or tears. "I knew it was over as soon as I did it," he said. "I don't know where I was going, I swear before God I don't. The gun's in the suitcase. When I got somewhere I think I would have used it on myself."

"It's too late for that," Loren said.

The train slid into the airport station and the doors whispered open. No one stepped in, no one stepped out. The doors swung shut and the train clicked away down the long tunnel.

"Christ, I'm tired," Dunphy said, his head bent. "I wish I could sleep. Pretend none of it ever happened, never wake up."

"Too late for that too," Loren told him.

"I know," Dunphy said.

"Want to tell me about it?" Loren said.

"Sit down."

Loren dropped onto the bench beside the chief justice and they sat and stared at the empty white wall of the cubicle. The train slid into the hotel station and the doors whispered open. No one stepped in, no one stepped out. The two men might have been the last people alive in the world. The doors shut and the train swung around the bend in the track and clicked away up the long tunnel.

"How long have you known?" Dunphy's voice was low, toneless. He might have been talking about an abstract problem in epistemology.

Loren tried to remember when he had felt the first faint pricklings of suspicion but couldn't pin it down. "I guess I suspected that something was fishy a couple of days ago when I analyzed that extremely realistic attempt to crush my legs in the law-school garage. What struck me was that whoever sent those goons after me must have known about the court's sending for me to investigate the shoebox almost as soon as the decision had been made. Who were the first ones to know I'd been sent for? Iris and Jeanette Richmond, Abelson, and the justices themselves. Then Tuesday night after our conference I checked into the Belvedere Inn, and by Wednesday morning Woody had already instructed Marisa to pick me up at the Belvedere and shadow me until further notice. Same deduction, same suspects. By Thursday afternoon the other side had not only found me but had been able to slip a razor blade into my shower soap. Further confirmation."

"The razor blade wasn't my doing," Dunphy muttered. "I... don't want you to think I'd have you hurt."

Loren thought of Val stumbling naked and bloody out of the shower. "You didn't care who you hurt," he said coldly. "There were a lot more pointers you left behind. One of them was the similarity between the bogus attempt to cripple me downstate and the real accident that crippled you. Another was that lawsuit Woody supposedly instigated to terminate the Bennell trust prematurely. I couldn't buy that. The strategy of the suit was just too sophisticated for a nonlawyer like Woody to have thought up all by himself. It pointed to someone in the background with legal training. Then there was a third clue. Tuesday night, when I was questioning Iris about the exterminator's visit—which at that time looked perfectly innocent and aboveboard—I asked if she had been present when Ben called the extermination company. She said she hadn't personally heard any such call but that she hadn't been the least suspicious when the exterminator came because one night at a restaurant before he went into the hospital he'd expressed concern about the possibility of termites in the house. Who was present at that dinner? Just the Richmonds themselves, Abelson and his wife, and you.

"Around 8:00 last night I really began putting it all together and seeing how Woody must be a fake and how there had to be someone behind him—a lawyer, and one who was intimately acquainted with the court and the Richmond family. Frankly, I thought it was Abelson. I didn't want to believe it was you. I should have known that those goons who went after me at school knew a hell of a lot about the building layout, the connection with the underground garage and all of that. Abelson had never been connected with the law school. He couldn't have briefed them on where to go and what to do for that charade. You're the former dean, Conor—the only one of the inner circle who could have done that.

"My reason kept prodding me that it had to be you and I kept fighting it. I told myself it wasn't airtight, that I couldn't be morally certain, that I might be hopelessly wrong. I kept my suspicions completely to myself. Until tonight when I chased you down those fire stairs. Then I was morally certain. That peculiar noise you made racing down those stairs as fast as you could with one foot. Two squishy footstep sounds and a thump, two squishes and a thump. That was your shillelagh, Conor, and that triple sound was almost exactly the same sound I heard Friday lunchtime when you and I walked down the fire stairs of the State House from the fifth floor down to the street.

"And right when I knew it was you, I tripped over my own feet and took a tumble, and that gave you the chance to get away. I'll never know if that was pure accident or if subconsciously I didn't want to catch you there and willed myself to slip."

The train clicked to a stop and the doors flew open and no one stepped in or out. Loren had no idea how many times it had traversed its endless circuit while he was speaking or even what stop it was making now. They might have been alone in that dank stuffy compartment for years. The doors slid shut and the train clicked into the long hollow tunnel.

"Conor, what in God's name happened to you?" Loren's voice was broken with anguish. He couldn't look Dunphy in the eye but stared vacantly at the blank wall of the cubicle. "You gave me my start in teaching. You fought like a tiger to get me tenure, you've been a better father to me than my real father ever was, and here you've murdered one man and been an accessory in the murder of a woman and you've planned and schemed to destroy your best friend's reputation and leave his widow on the brink of a nervous breakdown. And for what? What could you do with the Bennell money that you couldn't do with your salary as chief justice?"

"It wasn't for the money," Dunphy growled feebly, and tapped his knobbed cane against the toe of his right shoe. "The money was secondary. You'll never know the pain I live with every day and every night, physical pain and mental pain. My foot that isn't there throbs all the time as if every little bone in it were being crushed over and over again. I have to drink a bottle a night to get any relief." He sunk his chin into the depths of his sodden raincoat. "That police car did it to me. Roared out of nowhere like a demon from hell, crushed my foot and left me so that I couldn't stand like a man, couldn't walk like a man, looked like a deformed freak and lived with the memory of those crumbling bones day after day after day. And could I get a judgment against the state to repay me for the loss of my self? I could like hell. We have the noble old doctrine of governmental immunity in tort in this jurisdiction. The king can do no wrong. When the realization of the injustice of it all seeped into my bones, Loren, I remembered how you had argued with me back in law school about the infinite capacity of the law to be the enemy of fairness and decency. And I knew then that you were right, and I cursed and shook my fist and howled at the night until my voice was choked with my own tears.

"I wanted my own back, Loren. Not just from the society but from the uncontrollable powers of chance or fate or whatever you want to call it. I raged to be made whole. Day after day I hobbled to court and judged, and maybe the pain made me a better judge and maybe it didn't—I leave that to the scholars—but I bided my time. Silence and exile and cunning. Waiting for the occasion to come. And one day I began to consider the two hundred or so million dollars sitting in the Bennell trust fund and I began to read all I could get my hands on about the family and the disease and the whole background. And I saw how I could carve a piece of that stupendous fortune for myself and give the back of my hand to the powers that be at the same time. I had to know that I was not a pawn in the hand of chance but a mover of events!" His voice climbed to a pitch of frenzy in the tiny cubicle and Loren squinted to hold back his tears.

"The plan grew slowly," Dunphy went on. "It all turned on young John Philip Wood, the draft evader who'd gone underground, the ultimate taker of one-eighth of that trust. He'd been out of sight and sound for years. I needed a ringer, someone who could take Wood's place, bide his time in patience and wait for S. Gordon Bennell to pass away from this disgusting planet and then collect his share, half of which would be my share. There was a young man I defended the year before I gave up criminal practice and went to work for the law school. His name was Charles Eades and he was the most hypnotically persuasive young con man I'd ever had the ill luck to be retained by. He could make you believe the law of gravity was a hoax. He could spin you the most fantastic yarn in the world and you'd believe every word."

Loren thought back to all of the grandly complex contrivances in the labyrinth maker's scheme, like the two-step device for smuggling the shoebox into Ben's house and the printed exterminator's bill, signed with an anagram of Eades' real name and sent to Iris after the phony inspection. "I know," he said.

"I put out a very discreet feeler," Dunphy continued, "and reeled him in, and without incriminating or committing myself in any way I put the proposal to him. It seemed to intoxicate him. He lived to ensnare people in his own fantasy worlds. I really think he was half mad. He began learning everything there was to know about the Bennells and all their works and pomps. He was a quick study; it took him only a few months.

"And then he slipped his leash. I swear to you, Loren, I never planned any violence, never. But after it was all over I learned what Eades did. He went down to South America, spent months dogging the trail of the real John Philip Wood, who of course had gone through eight or nine false names by then. But Eades was a bloodhound. He hunted day and night and finally found him, working with the poor in one of the stinking suburbs outside Buenos Aires. He strangled Wood and buried the body so deep it hasn't been found yet. And then he came back to the States and quietly took up the identity of John Philip Wood in the confidence that the real Wood would never come back to call him a liar, and he sat back and spent my money and waited for S. Gordon Bennell to die."

"That's not all he did," Loren cut in. "He met Marisa Bennell and slipped his leash again. Learned all he could about politics in the Latin American dictatorships and snared her in another one of those webs of his, planning to take over all of her share in the trust by simply marrying her after distribution time and then arranging a fatal accident."

"I didn't find out about all that till it was too late to stop him," Dunphy said. "I swear on my word of honor, Loren, I didn't want anyone to be hurt. Do you believe me?"

"I don't know and I don't care. What you did intend was disgusting enough. All right, you had your plan and Eades embellished it with his own, but S. Gordon Bennell gave the laugh to both of you by staying in the pink of health well up into his eighties, and he was too well guarded for Eades to try to kill him. So you worked out a legal gimmick. Pay the old man triple his annuity to sign away his rights, then bring a lawsuit to terminate the trust. And it worked like a charm all the way to the supreme court until Ben Richmond cast the swing vote that dropped your plan dead in its tracks. Throwing you and Eades back to square one."

"I saved Ben's life, you know." Dunphy's voice quavered and he looked at Loren like a dying man begging for a sip of cool water. "Eades wanted to kill him when the decision came down. I talked him out of it, told him I'd find another way. I did care about Ben."

"Sure you did. And right after he died you set out to frame him as a corrupt judge. You and Eades dreamed up the plan to sneak the shoebox into the house. If Iris didn't find it soon enough on her own, you'd have seen to it that she did. And then there'd be an investigation and you'd make sure enough clues were dropped so that the investigator would conclude it was the Bennell case that had led to the bribe and you could persuade your colleagues that in the interests of justice the case should be reopened.

"You picked me to be the investigator and Eades began drawing me into the imaginary world he'd created for Marisa. You even used that cassette tape Ben hid in your file cabinet. You broke his confidence by playing it and you saw how it could be interpreted as giving him a need for quick money and a motive to sell out. That's why you slipped the tape to me Tuesday night—so I'd reach that same conclusion." Loren broke off before he said any more. Since the tape had not named Ben's paramour, Dunphy couldn't know that she had been Corinne Kirk. If he had known, and leaked the affair to the media, the court might well have reopened the Bennell case on that ground alone, obviating the need for the elaborate shoebox frame. Loren made up his mind that Dunphy would never learn how simply he could have accomplished his purpose if only he had known the woman's identity.

"And then everything fell apart again," Loren continued, "when I proved from the serial numbers on that one run of shoebox bills that the money must have been planted after Ben's death. It was early Friday evening, Conor, when I explained to you how I'd cleared Ben. As soon as I hung up the phone, you got word to Eades. And he hit the panic button then, didn't he? He decided the only way to insure his safety was to destroy all the people who could tell the truth about the whole scam. He strangled Angella Carmer Friday evening and had his men half kill him just to throw suspicion off himself and give him an alibi and to keep the illusion of his imaginary world running awhile longer. He paid off his goons and sent them packing. Those suitcases I saw in the Humber Hotel tell me he was getting ready to pull out himself. The only link he had to sever yet was you."

"And I had to destroy him," Dunphy said. "When he told me about killing that black maid I'd seen so often at Ben's house, that was the last straw. I knew I'd created a monster, like the sorcerer's apprentice. I had to take control of events again and undo what I'd done as far as I could. He sent for me and I brought my gun. He would have killed me if he'd been faster. He was still weak from having himself garroted the night before. He went for me and I caught him in the pit of the stomach with Seamus here." He banged his shillelagh into the linoleum floor of the cubicle. "Then I waited for the next thunderclap, just in case there was a patrol car passing by outside, and I shot the dirty dog where he lay and made my exit. Just before you came on the scene."

Loren shook his head sadly, thinking of the long involuted story, the webs within webs, the snares and corruptions that had festered for years before this night. The train clicked into a station again and Loren swiveled to read the sign in the boarding area: AIRPORT PARKING LOT. He grasped Dunphy by the elbow as the compartment door opened. "Come on," he said. "We have to go to the police station. I'll carry your bag. Jeanette and Iris will be there waiting for us."

"Oh, my dear God," Dunphy whispered. "Ah, Loren, don't make me face them. If you've ever cared a damn for me please for God's sake don't make me face them."

Loren said nothing, stood with his shoulder wedged against the door frame, holding it open. Very slowly, his eyes misted with tears, Dunphy hoisted himself to his feet, head bent, and stumbled out of the cubicle and limped to the escalator and rode silently side by side with Loren. Up into the weeping night.

TWELVE

LOREN was run ragged for the better part of a week, working with various officials to untangle the threads of the case. There were daily conferences with police and prosecutors, an anguished meeting with the other justices of the court, a session with the governor and the attorney general of the state on the propriety of indicting a sitting chief justice for murder. There were grueling interviews with the media, in which Loren kept as low a profile as possible. In the few free moments he could snatch he went to the hospital to see how Marisa was doing. She lay white and still and shrunken in the hospital bed, seeing nothing, hearing nothing, and Loren sat and held her hand for an hour. He called the Richmond home to see if Iris was all right and Jeanette told him that Norm Abelson and his wife were looking after her. He called Val Tremaine's office several times but never seemed to catch her at her desk.

It was on the Thursday morning after he had brought a haggard Conor Dunphy to the police station that the phone in the midtown hotel room where he had hidden himself shrilled fiercely, jarring him out of uneasy sleep. He groped for the receiver in the darkness and muttered gibberish into the mouthpiece.

"If that's supposed to mean it's five A.M. I can tell time for myself." It was the deep rumble of Frank Bolish. "My God but you've been elusive lately! Nice headlines you've been making."

"Frank, I'm not giving interviews." Loren tried to check his anger. "It's been a wretched week and I'm half dead so—"

"I didn't call to interview you, dummy. I wanted to pass on some news about a mutual friend of ours." The journalist paused, cleared his throat importantly. "Bruno Ernesto Schreyach."

Loren jerked upright in bed, feeling as if someone had thrown lye in his face. "Schreyach!" he repeated. "What about him?"

"He's dead," Bolish grunted, and Loren detected a quiet satisfied pleasure in his voice. "Been dead more than two years now in fact. And he died screaming in pain, which maybe proves there's still a little justice left in this miserable world. Want details?"

"What do you think?"

"Remember I told you about his nose being sliced off, and how the doctors sewed it back on, and about the little white scars at the base of his nose?"

"I couldn't forget a story like that," Loren said.

"Well, I had a long confidential phone conversation yesterday with the surgeon who performed the operation. He's in exile now but he wasn't talking for publication. The junta back home would send someone to take him out in two minutes if this ever leaked. But the doctor had had some good friends mutilated in Schreyach's prison and saw his chance to even the score. During the operation to graft Schreyach's nose back on he infected the bastard with a slow-acting poison that would spread through his body like cancer and give him three or four weeks of the tortures of the damned before it killed him. It worked beautifully. His bosses had him buried secretly and clamped the lid on the story so no one else would get any bright ideas about knocking off secret-police officials. Outrageous violation of the Hippocratic oath. Makes you want to go whoopdedoo, doesn't it?"

"No comment," Loren said mechanically, but he felt a spasm of elation almost like sexual release and wondered whether he shouldn't be ashamed of his delight. "Thanks for the tip, Frank. I appreciate knowing," he said finally.

"Give me a buzz when the heat's off," Bolish told him, and hung up.

For the few remaining hours of the night, Loren slept more serenely than he had all week.

One more long day and evening of meetings and conferences and, at least for a while, it was over. Dunphy had voluntarily resigned from the court, the governor had appointed Meyer Goldner as acting chief justice, and the grand jury would convene in two weeks to determine whether to indict Conor for murder and on other charges. The San Francisco police had picked up Moraga and Rojas, who turned out to be CIA-trained former members of an anti-Castro terrorist group turned private hit men. Loren snatched three hours of sleep, lurched awake at eight and showered and shaved and packed his two-suiter and checked out. While he was settling his bill, Val walked into the lobby. He waved to her, hefted his suitcase and followed her outside where her Pontiac was parked in a taxi zone. He tossed the bag into the rear and settled in the passenger seat beside her.

"It's been a bad week," he said. "I missed you."

"A rough one for me too. You look beat."

He studied the circles under her eyes and the tautness around her mouth. "Likewise," he said. They drove in peaceful silence to the expressway and west along the superhighway to a county road at the edge of the inhabited area around the capital. Then she wound through a maze of back roads until the last houses were miles behind them and they were deep in wooded country. She turned onto a dirt track that curved around a lovely unspoiled hill and ended in front of a trim redwood-and-glass split-level tucked into the hillside out of sight of the world.

"So this is the famous house," he said. "How long did it take you to build?"

"Almost four years. Bit by bit. That was my therapy after Chris died. Come on, I'll give you the grand tour."

He followed her through long cool rooms furnished for total comfort, the floors glistening with wax, the scent of freshly planed wood everywhere, mingling with the odor of the plants. Dozens and dozens of plants, potted and hanging from slings and from hooks on brass chains. She named each plant as they passed from room to room—sea grape and sweet olive and temple bells and baby tears, flamingo flowers and honey bells and jade plants and lantana. "My private paradise," she said. "Not many people get to see it."

"It's you all over," Loren said. "I wish I didn't have that noon plane home to catch."

She gestured toward the phone on a low mahogany table in front of the couch. "Cancel," she said. "Change your flight to Monday morning. Another two days of piled-up paperwork at the law school won't kill you."

He grinned slowly at her and felt a warmth spreading through him that did not come from the heat of the morning. "Will your agency run itself over the weekend?"

"It damn well better. I need a rest as badly as you."

"You twisted my arm," he said, and they shared a long eager kiss before he reached for the phone. When the change of reservation was completed, Val yanked the cord from the wall, her eyes bright, and began to unbutton her blouse.

That weekend was like nothing Loren had known before. They drove to a delicatessen in the tiny village six miles away and bought a whole pineapple and platters of cold roast beef and turkey and macaroni salad and slaw, loaves of fresh fragrant pumpernickel bread and half a dozen bottles of iced Sangria. Then they returned to the house and stowed the smorgasbord in the refrigerator. There would be no cooking over these holidays. Val threw open the sliding glass doors to the redwood deck that hung canti-levered over the hillside and they dragged mattress pads out to the scorching center of the deck and toasted themselves, fingers inter-twined, until the flower-patterned sun pads were drenched with their sweat and the heat had baked the accumulated anguish of the last ten days out of their bodies. Val screwed a garden hose into a wall nozzle and they stood in the shivery cold spray, squealing like children and splashing and clinging naked under the icy delight of the water. They patted each other dry and ran breathlessly to the cool dim bedroom and made long slow lazy love and slept and ate pineapple and loved again. Living by their own clocks, in their own universe. They lay together in the scented dark and talked of their wants and needs and dreads and woke before dawn to draw back the drapes over the eastern window and watch the unearthly beauty of the sun rising over the distant mountains. They opened to each other like flowers and renewed each other.

And in the blue hour before Monday dawn he caught himself looking at his watch for the first time since Friday and knew that the spell was breaking. He lay on his side and gazed at her with a sadness rising in his throat that almost choked him and bent to run his lips over her breasts one last time until she stirred awake and sighed sleepily and smiled at him and they shared a final lovemak-ing in an infinitely slow sweet rhythm that Loren wished would go on till the end of the world.

Afterward they held each other close and listened to the dawn music of the birds. "You're a miracle," he told her softly. "You've made me remember something I came close to forgetting."

"What's that?" she asked him.

"How good life can be." He hesitated, groping for the right words, until she began to look questioningly at him. "I wish," he began, "I wish I could ask you to chuck the agency and everything else and come stay with me." It was one of the hardest things he had ever made himself say.

"Thanks for not asking," she said gravely, and smiled at him in a way that told him she knew how much he wanted her, and was grateful.

"You have your own life and your own world that you made for yourself. I don't see you giving all that up just for a man." In his thoughts he begged and pleaded with her to do just that.

"I need to keep my world," she said. "This house, my plants, my work, my freedom. We couldn't survive as a twosome. We'd be at each other's throats in a month if we lived together full time. Because you need your world too. The way we'll do it will be so much better—believe me. Every time we're together will be special. I want us always to be special for each other."

"If only our worlds were the same," he whispered.

The alarm clock hidden behind a nest of plants on the dresser top buzzed wasplike in the pale dawn and they rose with a leaden reluctance and made their quiet preparations to leave. As they left the house Loren saw a brown cottontail staring at them for a moment from the dewy grass before it wheeled and bounded into the woods. Val spun the Pontiac into the dirt track that girded the hill and they began the all too brief drive to the airport. Loren flicked on the radio, adjusted the dial to the frequency of the state university's all-night FM station. The music was filled with a shivering loveliness, and he turned up the volume so it filled the car.

"It's so sad and beautiful," Val said. "Do you know what it is?"

"Schoenberg," he answered. "*Transfigured Night.*" He knew he would never hear it again without thinking of her, and they listened to its haunting strains in silence. Val turned off the two-lane blacktop onto the eastbound expressway. The last leg of the trip. Their last few minutes. *You'll never see her again*, a voice inside him whispered.

"You'll watch out for Marisa?" he asked.

"I'm stopping at the hospital right after I drop you off. She'll start to live again, and I'll help all I can. You know, I've sort of adopted her as my kid sister ever since that night we almost spent at the house."

"I hate myself for what I had to do to her," he said. "Will you ask her please not to hate me?"

"I will. I'm going to fly out to California with her when she goes for those annual tests."

"Will you call and let me know the results as soon as they're in?"

"Of course." She swerved onto the access road to the airport, and when she had negotiated the sharp curve she took her right hand from the wheel and held it out to him. "We'll pull her through," she smiled.

"And each other?" he asked.

The Pontiac braked in the traveler-discharge zone, outside the entrance to the Transstate ticket counters. Loren hauled his suitcase out of the backseat, set it on the curb and leaned into the car. She inclined her head and their lips touched in a good-bye kiss.

"Take care of yourself," she murmured.

"See you soon," he said, and wondered if he would.

He slammed the door and watched her car merge into the stream of city-bound traffic until it was an indistinguishable steel dot among a thousand others. He felt drained and pensive and half convinced that the weekend had been nothing but the dream of a very lonely man. He turned out of the dazzling sunlight and trudged through the high-ceilinged emptiness of the airport to the plane that would lift him home.

PUBLISH AND PERISH/
CORRUPT AND ENSNARE:
A DOUBLE AFTERWORD

There's nothing so finely calculated to make you feel ancient as being asked to revisit the books you wrote, and the life you lived, almost forty years ago.

In 1971, at age 28, I was invited to uproot myself from the East Coast to the Midwest and become a professor of law at St. Louis University. Around the time of my move I sold my first short story to the legendary Fred Dannay and *Ellery Queen's Mystery Magazine*. After a few years of academic life, and of selling more stories, I began to wonder if I should try my hand at something longer. The result was *Publish and Perish*. I wrote the first draft in microscopic hand-printing on a yellow legal pad, making the story up as I went along. It felt like having all my teeth pulled without novocaine. I don't know how I made myself face that legal pad every day and grind out a thousand words more or less, but somehow I got through the ordeal and eventually sat down at the typewriter to prepare a version that could be read without a magnifying glass. My agent at that time was an elderly gentleman named Oliver Swan, who several decades earlier had represented Margery Allingham, Sax Rohmer and other luminaries. It was Ollie who sold the novel to G.P. Putnam's Sons and mystery editor Marcia Magill. The contract between the publisher and me is dated January 15, 1975. Does anyone need to be told to whom I dedicated the book? Fred Dannay, without whose guidance I would never have written a word of fiction worth reading.

Recently I reread the long letter I wrote Magill almost forty years ago, replying to all her requests for changes, most of which improved the book vastly. One of the problems that stumped us for quite a while was what its title should be. I had originally submitted it as *The Masked Furies*, which she didn't like. Thinking of the novel as possibly the first of a series, I next suggested a legalese sort of title whose key words, like Erle Stanley Gardner's *The*

Case of, could be used again and again. How about *In the Matter of the Blazing Men*? She didn't like that one either. Finally one afternoon I came home to find that the Putnam folks had sent me a telegram—the first I had ever received, and I believe the last. That telegram, on yellow paper with perforations along both edges, is still in my file. "MAY WE USE AS TITLE PUBLISH AND PERISH? EVERYONE HERE APPROVES. MAGILL PUTNAM'S." Well, frankly I wasn't happy: to my mind that title misleadingly suggested an academic whodunit with satirically described faculty meetings, classroom crimes, professorial suspects and the like. On the other hand, the Putnam editors were professionals and I was a newbie. With a certain amount of hesitation I signed off on the title.

Of all the reviews *Publish and Perish* received, good, bad and indifferent, the one I remember most fondly was written by John Dickson Carr for his monthly *EQMM* Jury Box column. With my usual modesty I shall limit myself to quoting one paragraph. "Don't think you have solved everything until it's all over; Mr. Nevins, a newcomer already master of his craft, has set traps for the overconfident as well as the unwary. This very sophisticated performance, told with absolute fair play and much charm of style, offers the most attractive mystery in months." Wow! I couldn't resist writing John Carr, telling him how much I admired his dozens of novels and thanking him for his much too kind words.

Which in fact they were. But I suspect it was thanks to comments like these that my maiden effort as a novelist was chosen as a main selection of the Mystery Guild book club. In that format it stayed in print for five or six years, earning royalties that nicely supplemented the salary of an underpaid young professor. It was also translated into some other languages. I particularly like the title of the Italian version, *Il Sorriso dell' Assassino*, but can't explain why without giving away something important in the plot.

How well the book stands up decades later I'm incompetent to judge. Over those decades the genre has moved irrevocably, in the words of Julian Symons, "from the detective story to the crime novel." Fair-play plotting in the tradition of Carr, Queen and Christie was becoming rare even in the Seventies and is all but extinct today. But I still love that tradition and have tried to keep it breathing as best I can.

In the contemporary whodunit evocation of time and place weighs far more than convoluted plot. How does *Publish and Perish* fare on those counts? The events take place in the summer of

1974, when war still raged in Vietnam and the war against that war raged in America's streets. Its law schools shared that atmosphere and I was part of one of those law schools, ideally situated to make use of it in a novel. Whether I made *good* use of it is for others to judge.

Any reader who's determined to know exactly where the events of *Publish and Perish* take place is doomed, I'm afraid, to frustration. I was living in St. Louis when I wrote the book but made a deliberate decision to set it not there or in any other particular city or state but instead in what I like to call the undifferentiated Midwest. Why? Because it gave me the power to make up laws, geographic details, whatever, just the way I wanted them, unbound by mere facts. Some specific details come from St. Louis, some from elsewhere. The high-rise where the Dillaways live is much like the building I lived in myself at the time, right down to the door-locking arrangement which figures prominently in the final chapters, but again I exercised my divine right to reconfigure anything that needed to be changed for the story's sake.

One thing I didn't change was the federal law on which some of the plot hangs. The Copyright Act then in force was bifurcated in nature. On publishing a work with the proper copyright notice, the author received 28 years of protection. If the copyright wasn't renewed in Year 28, the work fell into the public domain at the end of that year. If the copyright was renewed, the work was protected for a second 28-year term. But who owned the renewal rights in a particular copyright? As a general rule, the answer was what common sense would expect: The author. But what if the author died before renewal time? Common sense would expect that in that event succession to renewal rights would be governed by the author's will. On this point common sense got stymied. If the author died too soon to renew, the renewal copyright passed to a successor class consisting of the author's surviving spouse and children. Only if there were no members of that class did the author's will determine ownership of the renewal copyright.

What this meant can best be explained with a hypothetical. Suppose my will leaves all my copyrights to the Home for Homeless Cats. At the time of my death, my earlier works have already been renewed and are in their second term but my more recent works are still in their initial term. I die survived by a wife and one child. Result? It's only the earlier works that the kitties get to own for the rest of their copyright lives. (The works' lives, not the kitties'.) They (the kitties, not the works) also own the stuff I didn't live to renew, but only until each such work comes up for renewal. To that extent my will is nullified, or we might say bumped, and ownership of the work during its renewal term passes to my widow and child, the statutory successor class. Sorry, cats. That in a nutshell was the renewal structure of the Copyright Act at the time of *Publish and Perish*. That is why Graham Dillaway's widow couldn't cut Graham's son by his first marriage out of his succession to the renewal copyrights in the novels his father didn't live to renew. As a law professor I became something of an authority on this and other collisions between copyright law and authors' wills, and the subject crops up in other novels and stories of mine. Copyright law today has a different and saner approach but I won't burden this memoir with more legalese.

How about the characters? Well, Loren Mensing is a special case. Whenever I'm asked whether he's my alter ego, my reply—the one to which lawyers are regularly doomed and which never fails to infuriate nonlawyers—is usually Yes and No. Clearly we share a few similarities besides our day jobs and love of classical music. But the biography I created for Loren has very little to do with the life I've led. I have never solved a crime or had people try to kill me. My days and nights are quite boring next to Loren's, at least those that have made it into novels or stories.

Of the other characters in *Publish and Perish* there are three I find particularly vivid but I can't take credit for them because they were drawn from life. One of these—James Foxworth, the author of countless paperback novels written at white heat and peppered with eyeball-popping locutions—was an anorexically disguised version of Michael Avallone (1924-1999), the Ed Wood of the written word, who was a neighbor of mine in New Jersey before I moved to St. Louis. Foxworth's private-eye character Steve Dusk is my take on Avallone's best-known creation, PI Ed Noon. After *Publish and Perish* came out, Avallone told me that while I had been working on the book he'd been trying (without success) to sell a paperback historical adventure series about an Errol Flynnesque pirate by the name of, you guessed it, James Foxworth. Strange are the ways of fate! More than any other author I've ever met, Avallone measures up to Casper Gutman's words to Sam Spade in *The Maltese Falcon*: "By Gad, sir, you're a character, that you are!"

The other two characters drawn from life are the doomed Lucy and the ebullient Gael, both of them dead now too. Gael was the younger but she died first. The day we met is commemorated, distorted, whatever, in the first scene of *Publish and Perish* where she and Loren Mensing join a box brigade taking legal materials down several flights of stairs from the law library. The real Gael and I were on that staircase one day in the late summer of 1971. A day or two later I discovered that she was in a class I was teaching. It was a huge class but she would have stood out in a group much larger. Within a few years after she'd graduated and moved to San Francisco, she told me she had gotten jobs by truthfully telling potential employers: "I am a fictional character." That character reappeared in short stories and other novels of mine, making her last bow in *Into the Same River Twice* (1996): older, less mercurial, practicing law in an old established firm and about to marry a wealthy WASP in front of an Episcopal bishop. Nothing like that happened to the Gael of the real world, where she was rear-ended by a drunk driver and spent years in constant pain, needing special ergonomic office furniture to be able to work at all. Then she was invaded by something infinitely worse which on March 7, 2004, took her life. Thank you, Lou Gehrig. Not.

Lucy was older but outlived Gael by almost four years. She was the first love of my life. I met her when JFK was in the White House and we were in college. We were separated for almost thirty years—my fault, I fear—and during that endless hiatus I wrote *Publish and Perish*, describing her as I remembered her although I made her much more downbeat than she ever was in real life. How we reunited is a story too complex and personal to be told here or anywhere else, but it happened in December 1990. The second phase of our relationship lasted a little over seventeen years, the final ones marked by one health problem after another. For the last six months of her life she was in medical facilities near her home on the Jersey shore. Even after a tracheotomy she could never get back to breathing normally. She couldn't speak and had to be tube-fed for months. Then she improved and was moved from the ICU to a rehab center but at best she could say only a few words. I went east early in January 2008 and arranged to see her but she suffered a relapse and we had to cancel. She improved again. I made another date to see her. She had another relapse and died three days later. What hideous timing: I never got to say goodbye to her. Reading *Publish and Perish* today, I am shaken by how many passages written almost forty years ago capture how I thought and felt about her. Perhaps the last line says it best: "He knew that she would come to life as a sudden stab of loss within him, whenever he saw the gleam of starlight on dark water."

~ ~ ~ ~ ~

My second novel, *Corrupt and Ensnare*, is perhaps the only mystery to have been directly inspired by a justice of the U.S. Supreme Court. To the best of my recollection it happened in 1973, my second year as a professor at St. Louis University and a regular contributor to *EQMM*. Justice William O. Douglas came to our campus to give a lecture and the law faculty took him to dinner before his speech. The rain came down furiously that evening. I was a newbie on the faculty but somehow wound up sitting only a few places away from Douglas. After dinner he told us about his recent visit to China, where he had become interested in a case currently before that country's highest court. The appellant had been convicted of raping a woman in Village A despite his claim that at the time of the crime he had been in Village B some distance away. Douglas sketched the situation and then challenged us to figure out what the high court did about it. No one could. After pausing for effect, he told us: the court sent its investigator to Village B, where he confirmed the defendant's alibi. The anecdote astonished us because in the Anglo-American legal system there's a razor-sharp distinction between questions of law and questions of fact. Appellate tribunals deal only with the former, never the latter. The idea of a detective attached to a high court was mind-boggling but eventually it took root and I began asking myself: What kind of situation might plausibly lead Loren Mensing to be asked to serve as unofficial detective for such a court?

Life answered that question for me in the form of a recent political scandal in a nearby jurisdiction where such scandals are never in short supply. The Illinois Secretary of State had died suddenly, and a shoebox in one of his closets was found to be bulging with cash. Voila! What if just such a shoebox were to be found in the house of a recently deceased state supreme court justice?

At this early stage in my writing life I hadn't yet begun my first novel and hadn't even dreamed of trying to write one. My exclusive domain was short stories. The first fruit of what Douglas had planted in my mind was "The Possibility of Termites" (*EQMM*, May 1974; collected in *Night Forms*, 2010). Revisiting that story today, I find it too cerebral by half, but it could hardly have turned out otherwise within the magazine's word limits.

By the time that tale appeared in print I had started writing *Publish and Perish*, which came out a year later and did so well that I soon began thinking about a second Loren Mensing novel.

Would it be possible to expand that over-cerebral termite story to book length? I soon realized that the easiest way to add relationships to the puzzle plot was to set the novel in Loren's home state, not the faraway jurisdiction of the *EQMM* version. Being a law professor, he'd surely be acquainted with some of the members of his home state's highest court. Upon the discovery of the shoebox, the other justices would certainly want to know the truth before the scandal went public. What if the court's chief justice had been on the law faculty with Loren before being appointed to the bench? (During my time at St. Louis University three of my colleagues have served on the Missouri Supreme Court.) So far I had done nothing to make the relationships between Loren and the other characters as intense as I wanted them. But what if the deceased judge had been a mentor and father figure to Loren, so that investigating the older man's apparent corruption would be bound to tear the younger one apart emotionally? I had still done nothing to generate the kind of action and suspense that the *EQMM* version lacked, but in principle at least that was a no-brainer: soon after Loren reluctantly commits himself to act as detective for the court, someone makes the first of several attempts to remove him from the picture. At some point in this thinking process I caught on that I had the elements for what, if I handled them right, might turn into one whale of a book, combining a complex plot and virtuoso reasoning as in Ellery Queen, legal gimmickry as in Erle Stanley Gardner, and the dark suspense and emotional anguish that has long been identified with Cornell Woolrich.

Since Loren in this novel is still a professor at the same law school as in *Publish and Perish*, its events had to take place in the same unidentified state somewhere in the Midwest. Some descriptive details come from St. Louis, notably the Richardsonian Romanesque mansion where the Bennell Foundation is headquartered, which in the real world is Cupples House, an art museum on the grounds of St. Louis University. Others I borrowed from elsewhere or, like the garish Humber Hotel, made up out of whole cloth. The disquisition on what one can learn from the letters and numbers on any piece of paper money I owe to the late Professor Gerald T. Dunne, former vice president and general counsel of the St. Louis Federal Reserve Bank and one of my colleagues and faithful readers. The appraise-apprise business I owe to another law professor, now long dead, who used the former word for the latter almost on a daily basis. Some of the characters who appear onstage briefly or not at all are named after law faculty colleagues or fellow mystery writers. (Is there anyone reading these words who can't identify the real-world original of The Honorable Jon Lutz?) That vigorous octogenarian S. Gordon Bennell was based on an old friend of mine, Hollywood action director Spencer Gordon Bennet (1893-1987), who really was playing golf, squash and handball well into his eighties.

I've been asked more than once about what may be the most powerful scene in the book, the one in the hotel room with the razor blade embedded in the cake of soap. I was well along with drafting the novel when I literally dreamed that scene—the only time it's ever happened to me—and scurried out of bed and to my typewriter, knowing I had to fit it in somehow. Before submitting the manuscript I confirmed that a blade could indeed be embedded in moist soap, cutting a couple of fingers in the process.

Publish and Perish for obvious reasons was dedicated to Fred Dannay, the closest to a grandfather I've ever known and the editor who made a mystery writer out of me. But who, you may be wondering, was the man to whom I dedicated *Corrupt and Ensnare*? William Witney (1915-2002) was the greatest pure action director that ever lived, the Spielberg of his generation, my closest Hollywood friend. I've loved his films since childhood, written about him for decades, based a character on him now and then. If you're into old movies and haven't discovered Bill Witney, stop reading this book and google his name *now*. Check out the website his son has devoted to him.

www.williamwitney.com

Read director Quentin Tarantino's all but idolatrous tribute to him. Hunt down a copy of Bill's book of reminiscences (*In a Door, Into a Fight, Out a Door, Into a Chase*). Above all, watch some of the movies he directed, like *Zorro's Fighting Legion, Spy Smasher, Stranger at My Door*.

Corrupt and Ensnare came out in the fall of 1978. Reviews were by and large flattering. A newsmagazine for attorneys asked the rhetorical question: Why was I still teaching if I could write such an excellent novel? One dissenter, however, sent me a near-illegible letter beginning "Your book stinks!" and then told me what he *really* thought of it. Personally I think it's stronger than *Publish and Perish* but commercially it didn't do nearly as well as the earlier book. Perhaps it will fare better this time around the track.

RAMBLE HOUSE's

HARRY STEPHEN KEELER WEBWORK MYSTERIES
(RH) indicates the title is available ONLY in the RAMBLE HOUSE edition

The Ace of Spades Murder
The Affair of the Bottled Deuce (RH)
The Amazing Web
The Barking Clock
Behind That Mask
The Book with the Orange Leaves
The Bottle with the Green Wax Seal
The Box from Japan
The Case of the Canny Killer
The Case of the Crazy Corpse (RH)
The Case of the Flying Hands (RH)
The Case of the Ivory Arrow
The Case of the Jeweled Ragpicker
The Case of the Lavender Gripsack
The Case of the Mysterious Moll
The Case of the 16 Beans
The Case of the Transparent Nude (RH)
The Case of the Transposed Legs
The Case of the Two-Headed Idiot (RH)
The Case of the Two Strange Ladies
The Circus Stealers (RH)
Cleopatra's Tears
A Copy of Beowulf (RH)
The Crimson Cube (RH)
The Face of the Man From Saturn
Find the Clock
The Five Silver Buddhas
The 4th King
The Gallows Waits, My Lord! (RH)
The Green Jade Hand
Finger! Finger!
Hangman's Nights (RH)
I, Chameleon (RH)
I Killed Lincoln at 10:13! (RH)
The Iron Ring
The Man Who Changed His Skin (RH)
The Man with the Crimson Box
The Man with the Magic Eardrums
The Man with the Wooden Spectacles
The Marceau Case
The Matilda Hunter Murder

The Monocled Monster
The Murder of London Lew
The Murdered Mathematician
The Mysterious Card (RH)
The Mysterious Ivory Ball of Wong Shing Li (RH)
The Mystery of the Fiddling Cracksman
The Peacock Fan
The Photo of Lady X (RH)
The Portrait of Jirjohn Cobb
Report on Vanessa Hewstone (RH)
Riddle of the Travelling Skull
Riddle of the Wooden Parrakeet (RH)
The Scarlet Mummy (RH)
The Search for X-Y-Z
The Sharkskin Book
Sing Sing Nights
The Six From Nowhere (RH)
The Skull of the Waltzing Clown
The Spectacles of Mr. Cagliostro
Stand By—London Calling!
The Steeltown Strangler
The Stolen Gravestone (RH)
Strange Journey (RH)
The Strange Will
The Straw Hat Murders (RH)
The Street of 1000 Eyes (RH)
Thieves' Nights
Three Novellos (RH)
The Tiger Snake
The Trap (RH)
Vagabond Nights (Defrauded Yeggman)
Vagabond Nights 2 (10 Hours)
The Vanishing Gold Truck
The Voice of the Seven Sparrows
The Washington Square Enigma
When Thief Meets Thief
The White Circle (RH)
The Wonderful Scheme of Mr. Christopher Thorne
X. Jones—of Scotland Yard
Y. Cheung, Business Detective

Keeler Related Works

A To Izzard: A Harry Stephen Keeler Companion by Fender Tucker — Articles and stories about Harry, by Harry, and in his style. Included is a compleat bibliography.

Wild About Harry: Reviews of Keeler Novels — Edited by Richard Polt & Fender Tucker — 22 reviews of works by Harry Stephen Keeler from *Keeler News*. A perfect introduction to the author.

The Keeler Keyhole Collection: Annotated newsletter rants from Harry Stephen Keeler, edited by Francis M. Nevins. Over 400 pages of incredibly personal Keeleriana.

Fakealoo — Pastiches of the style of Harry Stephen Keeler by selected demented members of the HSK Society. Updated every year with the new winner.

Strands of the Web: Short Stories of Harry Stephen Keeler — 29 stories, just about all that Keeler wrote, are edited and introduced by Fred Cleaver.

RAMBLE HOUSE's LOON SANCTUARY

A Clear Path to Cross — Sharon Knowles short mystery stories by Ed Lynskey.

A Jimmy Starr Omnibus — Three 40s novels by Jimmy Starr.

A Niche in Time and Other Stories — Classic SF by William F. Temple

A Roland Daniel Double: The Signal and The Return of Wu Fang — Classic thrillers from the 30s.

A Shot Rang Out — Three decades of reviews and articles by today's Anthony Boucher, Jon Breen. An essential book for any mystery lover's library.

A Smell of Smoke — A 1951 English countryside thriller by Miles Burton.

A Snark Selection — Lewis Carroll's *The Hunting of the Snark* with two Snarkian chapters by Harry Stephen Keeler — Illustrated by Gavin L. O'Keefe.

A Young Man's Heart — A forgotten early classic by Cornell Woolrich.

Alexander Laing Novels — *The Motives of Nicholas Holtz* and *Dr. Scarlett*, stories of medical mayhem and intrigue from the 30s.

An Angel in the Street — Modern hardboiled noir by Peter Genovese.

Automaton — Brilliant treatise on robotics: 1928-style! By H. Stafford Hatfield.

Away From the Here and Now — Clare Winger Harris stories, collected by Richard A. Lupoff

Beast or Man? — A 1930 novel of racism and horror by Sean M'Guire. Introduced by John Pelan.

Black Hogan Strikes Again — Australia's Peter Renwick pens a tale of the 30s outback.

Black River Falls — Suspense from the master, Ed Gorman.

Blondy's Boy Friend — A snappy 1930 story by Philip Wylie, writing as Leatrice Homesley.

Blood in a Snap — The *Finnegan's Wake* of the 21st century, by Jim Weiler.

Blood Moon — The first of the Robert Payne series by Ed Gorman.

Bogart '48 — Hollywood action with Bogie by John Stanley and Kenn Davis.

Calling Lou Largo! — Two Lou Largo novels by William Ard.

Cornucopia of Crime — Francis M. Nevins assembled this huge collection of his writings about crime literature and the people who write it. Essential for any serious mystery library.

Corpse Without Flesh — Strange novel of forensics by George Bruce

Crimson Clown Novels — By Johnston McCulley, author of the Zorro novels, *The Crimson Clown* and *The Crimson Clown Again.*

Dago Red — 22 tales of dark suspense by Bill Pronzini.

Dark Sanctuary — Weird Menace story by H. B. Gregory

David Hume Novels — *Corpses Never Argue, Cemetery First Stop, Make Way for the Mourners, Eternity Here I Come*. 1930s British hardboiled fiction with an attitude.

Dead Man Talks Too Much — Hollywood boozer by Weed Dickenson.

Death Leaves No Card — One of the most unusual murdered-in-the-tub mysteries you'll ever read. By Miles Burton.

Death March of the Dancing Dolls and Other Stories — Volume Three in the Day Keene in the Detective Pulps series. Introduced by Bill Crider.

Deep Space and other Stories — A collection of SF gems by Richard A. Lupoff.

Detective Duff Unravels It — Episodic mysteries by Harvey O'Higgins.

Diabolic Candelabra — Classic 30s mystery by E.R. Punshon.

Dime Novels: Ramble House's 10-Cent Books — *Knife in the Dark* by Robert Leslie Bellem, *Hot Lead* and *Song of Death* by Ed Earl Repp, *A Hashish House in New York* by H.H. Kane, and five more.

Don Diablo: Book of a Lost Film — Two-volume treatment of a western by Paul Landres, with diagrams. Intro by Francis M. Nevins.

Dope and Swastikas — Two strange novels from 1922 by Edmund Snell

Dope Tales #1 — Two dope-riddled classics; *Dope Runners* by Gerald Grantham and *Death Takes the Joystick* by Phillip Condé.

Dope Tales #2 — Two more narco-classics; *The Invisible Hand* by Rex Dark and *The Smokers of Hashish* by Norman Berrow.

Dope Tales #3 — Two enchanting novels of opium by the master, Sax Rohmer. *Dope* and *The Yellow Claw.*

Double Hot — Two 60s softcore sex novels by Morris Hershman.

Dr. Odin — Douglas Newton's 1933 racial potboiler comes back to life.

Evangelical Cockroach — Jack Woodford writes about writing.

Evidence in Blue — 1938 mystery by E. Charles Vivian.

Fatal Accident — Murder by automobile, a 1936 mystery by Cecil M. Wills.

Fighting Mad — Todd Robbins' 1922 novel about boxing and life

Finger-prints Never Lie — A 1939 classic detective novel by John G. Brandon.

Freaks and Fantasies — Eerie tales by Tod Robbins, collaborator of Tod Browning on the film FREAKS.

Gadsby — A lipogram (a novel without the letter E). Ernest Vincent Wright's last work, published in 1939 right before his death.

Gelett Burgess Novels — *The Master of Mysteries, The White Cat, Two O'Clock Courage, Ladies in Boxes, Find the Woman, The Heart Line, The Picaroons* and *Lady Mechante*. Recently added is A Gelett Burgess Sampler, edited by Alfred Jan. All are introduced by Richard A. Lupoff.

Geronimo — S. M. Barrett's 1905 autobiography of a noble American.

Hake Talbot Novels — *Rim of the Pit, The Hangman's Handyman*. Classic locked room mysteries, with mapback covers by Gavin O'Keefe.

Hands Out of Hell and Other Stories — John H. Knox's eerie hallucinations

Hell is a City — William Ard's masterpiece.

Hollywood Dreams — A novel of Tinsel Town and the Depression by Richard O'Brien.

Hostesses in Hell and Other Stories — Russell Gray's most graphic stories

House of the Restless Dead — Strange and ominous tales by Hugh B. Cave

I Stole $16,000,000 — A true story by cracksman Herbert E. Wilson.

Inclination to Murder — 1966 thriller by New Zealand's Harriet Hunter.

Invaders from the Dark — Classic werewolf tale from Greye La Spina.

J. Poindexter, Colored — Classic satirical black novel by Irvin S. Cobb.

Jack Mann Novels — Strange murder in the English countryside. *Gees' First Case, Nightmare Farm, Grey Shapes, The Ninth Life, The Glass Too Many, Her Ways Are Death, The Kleinert Case* and *Maker of Shadows*.

Jake Hardy — A lusty western tale from Wesley Tallant.

Jim Harmon Double Novels — *Vixen Hollow/Celluloid Scandal, The Man Who Made Maniacs/Silent Siren, Ape Rape/Wanton Witch, Sex Burns Like Fire/Twist Session, Sudden Lust/Passion Strip, Sin Unlimited/Harlot Master, Twilight Girls/Sex Institution*. Written in the early 60s and never reprinted until now.

Joel Townsley Rogers Novels and Short Stories — By the author of *The Red Right Hand: Once In a Red Moon, Lady With the Dice, The Stopped Clock, Never Leave My Bed*. Also two short story collections: *Night of Horror* and *Killing Time*.

John Carstairs, Space Detective — Arboreal Sci-fi by Frank Belknap Long

Joseph Shallit Novels — *The Case of the Billion Dollar Body, Lady Don't Die on My Doorstep, Kiss the Killer, Yell Bloody Murder, Take Your Last Look*. One of America's best 50's authors and a favorite of author Bill Pronzini.

Keller Memento — 45 short stories of the amazing and weird by Dr. David Keller.

Killer's Caress — Cary Moran's 1936 hardboiled thriller.

Lady of the Yellow Death and Other Stories — More stories by Wyatt Blassingame.

League of the Grateful Dead and Other Stories — Volume One in the Day Keene in the Detective Pulps series.

Library of Death — Ghastly tale by Ronald S. L. Harding, introduced by John Pelan

Malcolm Jameson Novels and Short Stories — *Astonishing! Astounding!, Tarnished Bomb, The Alien Envoy and Other Stories* and *The Chariots of San Fernando and Other Stories*. All introduced and edited by John Pelan or Richard A. Lupoff.

Man Out of Hell and Other Stories — Volume II of the John H. Knox weird pulps collection.

Marblehead: A Novel of H.P. Lovecraft — A long-lost masterpiece from Richard A. Lupoff. This is the "director's cut", the long version that has never been published before.

Master of Souls — Mark Hansom's 1937 shocker is introduced by weirdologist John Pelan.

Max Afford Novels — *Owl of Darkness, Death's Mannikins, Blood on His Hands, The Dead Are Blind, The Sheep and the Wolves, Sinners in Paradise* and *Two Locked Room Mysteries and a Ripping Yarn* by one of Australia's finest mystery novelists.

Money Brawl — Two books about the writing business by Jack Woodford and H. Bedford-Jones. Introduced by Richard A. Lupoff.

More Secret Adventures of Sherlock Holmes — Gary Lovisi's second collection of tales about the unknown sides of the great detective.

Muddled Mind: Complete Works of Ed Wood, Jr. — David Hayes and Hayden Davis deconstruct the life and works of the mad, but canny, genius.

Murder among the Nudists — A mystery from 1934 by Peter Hunt, featuring a naked Detective-Inspector going undercover in a nudist colony.

Murder in Black and White — 1931 classic tennis whodunit by Evelyn Elder.

Murder in Shawnee — Two novels of the Alleghenies by John Douglas: *Shawnee Alley Fire* and *Haunts.*

Murder in Silk — A 1937 Yellow Peril novel of the silk trade by Ralph Trevor.

My Deadly Angel — 1955 Cold War drama by John Chelton.

My First Time: The One Experience You Never Forget — Michael Birchwood — 64 true first-person narratives of how they lost it.

Mysterious Martin, the Master of Murder — Two versions of a strange 1912 novel by Tod Robbins about a man who writes books that can kill.

Norman Berrow Novels — *The Bishop's Sword, Ghost House, Don't Go Out After Dark, Claws of the Cougar, The Smokers of Hashish, The Secret Dancer, Don't Jump Mr. Boland!, The Footprints of Satan, Fingers for Ransom, The Three Tiers of Fantasy, The Spaniard's Thumb, The Eleventh Plague, Words Have Wings, One Thrilling Night, The Lady's in Danger, It Howls at Night, The Terror in the Fog, Oil Under the Window, Murder in the Melody, The Singing Room.* This is the complete Norman Berrow library of locked-room mysteries, several of which are masterpieces.

Old Faithful and Other Stories — SF classic tales by Raymond Z. Gallun

Old Times' Sake — Short stories by James Reasoner from Mike Shayne Magazine.

One Dreadful Night — A classic mystery by Ronald S. L. Harding

Pair O' Jacks — A mystery novel and a diatribe about publishing by Jack Woodford

Perfect .38 — Two early Timothy Dane novels by William Ard. More to come.

Prince Pax — Devilish intrigue by George Sylvester Viereck and Philip Eldridge

Prose Bowl — Futuristic satire of a world where hack writing has replaced football as our national obsession, by Bill Pronzini and Barry N. Malzberg.

Red Light — The history of legal prostitution in Shreveport Louisiana by Eric Brock. Includes wonderful photos of the houses and the ladies.

Researching American-Made Toy Soldiers — A 276-page collection of a lifetime of articles by toy soldier expert Richard O'Brien.

Reunion in Hell — Volume One of the John H. Knox series of weird stories from the pulps. Introduced by horror expert John Pelan.

Ripped from the Headlines! — The Jack the Ripper story as told in the newspaper articles in the *New York* and *London Times.*

Robert Randisi Novels — *No Exit to Brooklyn* and *The Dead of Brooklyn.* The first two Nick Delvecchio novels.

Rough Cut & New, Improved Murder — Ed Gorman's first two novels.

R.R. Ryan Novels — Freak Museum and The Subjugated Beast, two horror classics.

Ruled By Radio — 1925 futuristic novel by Robert L. Hadfield & Frank E. Farncombe.

Rupert Penny Novels — *Policeman's Holiday, Policeman's Evidence, Lucky Policeman, Policeman in Armour, Sealed Room Murder, Sweet Poison, The Talkative Policeman, She had to Have Gas* and *Cut and Run* (by Martin Tanner.) Rupert Penny is the pseudonym of Australian Charles Thornett, a master of the locked room, impossible crime plot.

Sacred Locomotive Flies — Richard A. Lupoff's psychedelic SF story.

Sam — Early gay novel by Lonnie Coleman.

Sand's Game — Spectacular hard-boiled noir from Ennis Willie, edited by Lynn Myers and Stephen Mertz, with contributions from Max Allan Collins, Bill Crider, Wayne Dundee, Bill Pronzini, Gary Lovisi and James Reasoner.

Sand's War — More violent fiction from the typewriter of Ennis Willie

Satan's Den Exposed — True crime in Truth or Consequences New Mexico — Award-winning journalism by the *Desert Journal.*

Satans of Saturn — Novellas from the pulps by Otis Adelbert Kline and E. H. Price

Satan's Sin House and Other Stories — Horrific gore by Wayne Rogers

Secrets of a Teenage Superhero — Graphic lit by Jonathan Sweet

Sex Slave — Potboiler of lust in the days of Cleopatra by Dion Leclerq, 1966.

Shadows' Edge — Two early novels by Wade Wright: *Shadows Don't Bleed* and *The Sharp Edge.*

Sideslip — 1968 SF masterpiece by Ted White and Dave Van Arnam.

Slammer Days — Two full-length prison memoirs: *Men into Beasts* (1952) by George Sylvester Viereck and *Home Away From Home* (1962) by Jack Woodford.

Slippery Staircase — 1930s whodunit from E.C.R. Lorac

Sorcerer's Chessmen — John Pelan introduces this 1939 classic by Mark Hansom.

Star Griffin — Michael Kurland's 1987 masterpiece of SF drollery is back.

Stakeout on Millennium Drive — Award-winning Indianapolis Noir by Ian Woollen.

The House of the Vampire — 1907 poetic thriller by George S. Viereck.

The Illustrious Corpse — Murder hijinx from Tiffany Thayer

The Incredible Adventures of Rowland Hern — Intriguing 1928 impossible crimes by Nicholas Olde.

The Julius Caesar Murder Case — A classic 1935 re-telling of the assassination by Wallace Irwin that's much more fun than the Shakespeare version.

The Koky Comics — A collection of all of the 1978-1981 Sunday and daily comic strips by Richard O'Brien and Mort Gerberg, in two volumes.

The Lady of the Terraces — 1925 missing race adventure by E. Charles Vivian.

The Lord of Terror — 1925 mystery with master-criminal, Fantômas.

The Melamare Mystery — A classic 1929 Arsene Lupin mystery by Maurice Leblanc

The Man Who Was Secrett — Epic SF stories from John Brunner

The Man Without a Planet — Science fiction tales by Richard Wilson

The N. R. De Mexico Novels — Robert Bragg, the real N.R. de Mexico, presents *Marijuana Girl, Madman on a Drum, Private Chauffeur* in one volume.

The Night Remembers — A 1991 Jack Walsh mystery from Ed Gorman.

The One After Snelling — Kickass modern noir from Richard O'Brien.

The Organ Reader — A huge compilation of just about everything published in the 1971-1972 radical bay-area newspaper, *THE ORGAN*. A coffee table book that points out the shallowness of the coffee table mindset.

The Poker Club — Three in one! Ed Gorman's ground-breaking novel, the short story it was based upon, and the screenplay of the film made from it.

The Private Journal & Diary of John H. Surratt — The memoirs of the man who conspired to assassinate President Lincoln.

The Secret Adventures of Sherlock Holmes — Three Sherlockian pastiches by the Brooklyn author/publisher, Gary Lovisi.

The Shadow on the House — Mark Hansom's 1934 masterpiece of horror is introduced by John Pelan.

The Sign of the Scorpion — A 1935 Edmund Snell tale of oriental evil.

The Singular Problem of the Stygian House-Boat — Two classic tales by John Kendrick Bangs about the denizens of Hades.

The Smiling Corpse — Philip Wylie and Bernard Bergman's odd 1935 novel.

The Spider: Satan's Murder Machines — A thesis about Iron Man

The Stench of Death: An Odoriferous Omnibus by Jack Moskovitz — Two complete novels and two novellas from 60's sleaze author, Jack Moskovitz.

The Story Writer and Other Stories — Classic SF from Richard Wilson

The Strange Case of the Antlered Man — 1935 dementia from Edwy Searles Brooks

The Strange Thirteen — Richard B. Gamon's odd stories about Raj India.

The Technique of the Mystery Story — Carolyn Wells' tips about writing.

The Threat of Nostalgia — A collection of his most obscure stories by Jon Breen

The Time Armada — Fox B. Holden's 1953 SF gem.

The Tongueless Horror and Other Stories — Volume One of the series of short stories from the weird pulps by Wyatt Blassingame.

The Tracer of Lost Persons — From 1906, an episodic novel that became a hit radio series in the 30s. Introduced by Richard A. Lupoff.

The Trail of the Cloven Hoof — Diabolical horror from 1935 by Arlton Eadie. Introduced by John Pelan.

The Triune Man — Mindscrambling science fiction from Richard A. Lupoff.

The Unholy Goddess and Other Stories — Wyatt Blassingame's first DTP compilation

The Universal Holmes — Richard A. Lupoff's 2007 collection of five Holmesian pastiches and a recipe for giant rat stew.

The Werewolf vs the Vampire Woman — Hard to believe ultraviolence by either Arthur M. Scarm or Arthur M. Scram.

The Whistling Ancestors — A 1936 classic of weirdness by Richard E. Goddard and introduced by John Pelan.

The White Owl — A vintage thriller from Edmund Snell

The White Peril in the Far East — Sidney Lewis Gulick's 1905 indictment of the West and assurance that Japan would never attack the U.S.

The Wizard of Berner's Abbey — A 1935 horror gem written by Mark Hansom and introduced by John Pelan.

The Wonderful Wizard of Oz — by L. Frank Baum and illustrated by Gavin L. O'Keefe

Through the Looking Glass — Lewis Carroll wrote it; Gavin L. O'Keefe illustrated it.

Time Line — Ramble House artist Gavin O'Keefe selects his most evocative art inspired by the twisted literature he reads and designs.

Tiresias — Psychotic modern horror novel by Jonathan M. Sweet.

Totah Six-Pack — Fender Tucker's six tales about Farmington in one sleek volume.

Trail of the Spirit Warrior — Roger Haley's historical saga of life in the Indian Territories.

Two Kinds of Bad — Two 50s novels by William Ard about Danny Fontaine

Two Suns of Morcali and Other Stories — Evelyn E. Smith's SF tour-de-force

Ultra-Boiled — 23 gut-wrenching tales by our Man in Brooklyn, Gary Lovisi.

Up Front From Behind — A 2011 satire of Wall Street by James B. Kobak.

Victims & Villains — Intriguing Sherlockiana from Derham Groves.

Wade Wright Novels — *Echo of Fear, Death At Nostalgia Street, It Leads to Murder* and *Shadows' Edge*, a double book featuring *Shadows Don't Bleed* and *The Sharp Edge*.

Walter S. Masterman Novels — *The Green Toad, The Flying Beast, The Yellow Mistletoe, The Wrong Verdict, The Perjured Alibi, The Border Line, The Bloodhounds Bay* and *The Curse of Cantire.* Masterman wrote horror and mystery, some introduced by John Pelan.

We Are the Dead and Other Stories — Volume Two in the Day Keene in the Detective Pulps series, introduced by Ed Gorman. When done, there may be as many as 11 in the series.

Welsh Rarebit Tales — Charming stories from 1902 by Harle Oren Cummins

West Texas War and Other Western Stories — by Gary Lovisi.

Whip Dodge: Man Hunter — Wesley Tallant's saga of a bounty hunter of the old West.

Win, Place and Die! — The first new mystery by Milt Ozaki in decades. The ultimate novel of 70s Reno.

You'll Die Laughing — Bruce Elliott's 1945 novel of murder at a practical joker's English countryside manor.

RAMBLE HOUSE
Fender Tucker, Prop.   Gavin L. O'Keefe, Graphics
www.ramblehouse.com   fender@ramblehouse.com
228-826-1783   10329 Sheephead Drive, Vancleave MS 39565